UNDER PRESSURE

Water seeped into Angie's mouth. She needed to take a breath. She closed her eyes and forced herself to picture oxygen filtering through her gills, sliding effortlessly into her bloodstream, slowly refilling her lungs. She needed to *breathe*!

Angie panicked and gasped for air . . .

Her nose and mouth had filled with water. Frigid liquid sang in her ears. *I'm drowning!* The darkness would come next. Then the suffocating tightness of her body closing down from the inside out.

But nothing more happened. Trembling, Angie forced herself to remain sitting at the bottom of the pool. They work! she thought. The gills work! The realization brought her more horror than the touch of the water had.

REEFSONG

Carol Severance

A Del Rey Book
BALLANTINE BOOKS • NEW YORK

A Del Rey Book
Published by Ballantine Books

Library of Congress Catalog Card Number: 91-91969

ISBN 0-345- 37231-X

Manufactured in the United States of America

First Edition: September 1991

Cover Art by Richard Hescox

This story is dedicated to *the* grand old man of American Samoa, John A. Kneubuhl, who really did teach Angie to fly

. . . and, of course, to Puluai Craig, who held the net.

Acknowledgments

I would like to thank the following people for their assistance during the creation of this story: University of Hawaii at Hilo faculty members Dr. Daniel E. Brown, who helped Zed design the TC enzyme; Dr. Donald E. Hemmes, who explained the biology of the Lesaat sea; Dr. William D. Heacox, who provided my first glimpse of Pukui's night sky; and, of course, Dr. Craig J. Severance, who did his very best to keep this tale anthropologically honest. I would also like to say *mahalo nui loa* to Kahikāhealani Wight and Kauanoe Kamanā for their assistance with the Hawaiian language. Vonda N. McIntyre, Rhea Rose, and Dr. Thomas J. Griffin offered invaluable comments and encouragement, and on two separate occasions computer specialist Annie Yu Brown rescued the entire manuscript from the ether. Most especially, I would like to thank John A. Kneubuhl (Sione Nupo) for sharing his time, his extraordinary storytelling skill, and his cultural insights. His was the gift of Le Fe'e. Any errors to be found in this story are entirely my own.

Chapter 1

Angie blinked as she stepped from the lift into the observation tower—first to assure herself she was fully awake, then again, rapidly, to activate the distance grid in her telescopic implants. The eastern sky was much too dark for this early morning hour.

"Spit on the lines," she muttered. The darkness wasn't part of any night sky. It was smoke! There was a fire in Sector Five.

She strode to the control console at the center of the tower and keyed a system-wide alarm sequence.

"Fire Control," she said into the opened mike, "this is Central Forest Preserve. We have a primary alert in Sector Five. Repeat. Serious burn in Sector Five. Please order a full fire crew to the site stat. Put secondary lines on standby. I'm transmitting fire coordinates now."

She keyed in her visual estimates of the fire's location and dimensions, then focused the lookout tower's cameras on the site and activated a continual-update order. Her own estimates remained a steady orange glow at the top of the monitoring screen, showing that the computer-assisted camera system had verified them as accurate.

"Central Forest," the control watchman's voice drawled through the tower speaker; he sounded irritated, as if he'd rather not be disturbed. "Double-check your sighting and coordinates."

"They've been double-checked and more, Central," she said, a little sharply; she paused to steady her voice. "Please enter an immediate scramble order before this gets out of hand." The smoke had become a billowing silhouette against the rising sun.

"Scrambling a full crew's pretty costly, lady," the watchman said. "I'll need an okay from Warden Dinsman before I can proceed." She could almost hear his slow grin. He would be up for a bonus if he could talk her out of the full crew. The forest preserve ranked low on the Company's list of priority expenditures. The only reason they supported it at all was because of pressure from the U.N., and even that was waning with the continued food shortage. The watchman probably had orders to stall or even deny all but the most serious fire calls from the preserve.

Well, two could play the bonus-and-deduction game. "Log your name and your credit number, Watchman," Angie said. "You're talking to Warden Dinsman."

There was a pause—to pull his feet off the desk, no doubt—then, rather hesitantly, a name and number appeared on her recording monitor.

"You got my crew ordered yet, Mr. Hansen?" she asked.

"Order confirmed," came the instant reply.

"Good. Tell 'em to pack their shovels. This ain't no picnic I'm invitin' 'em to." It was an old fire-liner's joke. The watchman wouldn't understand it, but it served to take the edge off Angie's anger and her growing concern.

There was way too much smoke out there. It was spread over too great an area to have been started by a lightning strike during the night. And it was directly east of Tower Five. Even with the satellite alert system off-line, it should have been noticed and called in an hour before.

Angie's right shoulder tingled as the sector lookout crews began checking in. As usual, Tower Two, far to the west, was first to make contact. Then Tower Four. Then Three, with a triple buzz, to remind her that Gates and Abada had a trainee on-site. She pressed the individual locator implants along her upper arm to acknowledge each call. The tingling stopped.

Come on, Five, she urged silently. Where the hell are you? Wake up, Chandler!

Chandler was alone at his station. His partner had been flown out with a broken ankle two days before, after stepping into a fireloving gopher hole. Angie pressed a finger over the Tower-Five implant, activating a search signal. A faint itch brushed her shoulder, telling her that Chandler was out there, just not responding. She keyed the alarm inside Tower Five again.

Finally, reluctantly, she tapped the alert that would wake her own partner. She and Nori had been up most of the night repairing the grav plates on their flitter. When the jury-rigged job was complete, Nori had insisted they stay awake awhile longer to celebrate. Angie smiled slightly as she recalled the direction the celebration had quickly taken. Nori wasn't much of a mountain man, but he knew how to show a lady a good time. It hadn't been easy to leave his warm bunk when the time had come for her dawn watch.

Angie turned away from the black smudge of burning forest and stood to walk a routine watch around the tower's perimeter. This wasn't the day to risk a trash fire in the backyard.

A seemingly endless blanket of evergreens stretched in all directions from the tower. Acre upon acre of forest land. The trees grew too slowly for the preserve to be classified as an active CO_2 farm. But the Company-owned property fell under the U.N.'s Earth Preservation Service guidelines nevertheless, simply because it was one of the very few stretches of indigenous forest left in the Northern Hemisphere. All other arable land, most of it owned or controlled by World Life, and regardless how marginal, was used for food production.

The importation of a partial protein-conversion enzyme from the newly discovered waterplanet, Lesaat, had eased the problem somewhat. But the supply of the life-saving digestive enzyme was limited. Widespread famine still plagued Earth's ever-expanding population.

A wisp of smoke in Sector Three caught Angie's attention. That would be the Company-run rest lodge on Lake Wendell, filled to capacity, she was sure, with well-fed World Life Company executives on holiday.

"If they spent as much effort feeding the rest of the world as they do themselves," she muttered, "I could retire and spend enough time up here to see that days like this never happen." She glanced back across the tower at the rising smoke. This unexplained fire in what she considered her home territory made her angry. When she was here, she was supposed to be able to relax.

As an environmental anthropologist Angie spent most of her time troubleshooting under a U.N. mandate to protect the planet's ever-diminishing food supply. During her twelve years of active duty, she had helped to solve everything from tree blight on the great South American tree farms to creeping forest fires in East Africa, from workers' disputes in Canadian canneries to relocating rebellious New Guinea tribesmen.

In the last case, much to the Company's dismay, she had used laws more than a half-century old to provide a way for the indigenous tribesmen to retain at least a portion of their own land. Her rate of success in preserving natural resources and thus assuring Company profits elsewhere, however, was such that even the most conservative administrators were willing to pay her deliberately exorbitant fees.

In between jobs, though, she always came back to these high, dry mountains. She much preferred the patient, whispering pines to the explosive growth of the tropics where most of her troubleshooting work was done. Her parents had once owned a small ranch adjoining this preserve, and she had spent most of her youth hiking and camping in the nearby mountains.

Her decision to become a troubleshooter had been based primarily on the knowledge that there were so few such wilderness areas left on Earth; she wanted to do what she could to save them. She had realized early on in her work that saving natural *human* resources, despite Company opposition, was equally satisfying.

Still, Angie treasured the scattered days and weeks of isolation from human conflict that her interim fire warden's job provided. Her current two-month stay at Tower One was as long a continuous stretch as she had ever managed. She would have liked to believe that the long break in the need for her crisis-intervention services indicated some small improvement in the world situation, but she suspected it was just a fluke.

The lift door hissed open as Angie finished her circuit of the lookout tower. Nori fumbled with the Velcro fasteners on his shirt as he stepped from the lift. His ordinarily well-groomed hair stood on end, and his eyes, for once without their fine shadow of makeup, were red rimmed from lack of sleep.

"What's going—" He stopped when he saw the smoke. His already pale face turned paler.

"Sorry, Watchman," she said as she returned to the console. "Looks like we should have made it a shorter night."

He laid a warm hand on her shoulder. "A difficult thing to do with a woman of your talents, Warden. I'd been warned about troubleshooters' stamina, but—" He blinked rapidly, then keyed a set of visual coordinates.

Angie's original estimates maintained their steady glow at the top of the screen. Nori's flickered near the center, just below those of the computer-assisted cameras. They were close, but not exact.

"You called it right," he said. "As always."

She smiled. "I told you that last visual implant would make a difference."

"Humph! A lien on half your lifetime's savings and a ten-year mountain service indenture, all for a few meters' accuracy. What's it good for?''

It was an argument they had had before, and one that she was weary of. The reminder that he had accessed her personal financial records irritated Angie as it always did, but because she had deliberately structured those records to be misleading, she addressed only the second part of his complaint.

''It's a simple contract extension,'' she said. ''To make sure this mountain post stays open for me.''

''Your talents are wasted out here in this wilderness,'' he said. ''With your genotype and your training, you'd qualify to work anywhere in the Company system—on Earth or off. You could have any administration job you wanted.''

''Work in admin? I'd rather shovel dung on Mensat,'' she replied. ''Meaning no offense to your own ambitions, of course.''

''Of course,'' he said dryly.

Mensat's primary industry was the mining of giant guano deposits; assignment on the odoriferous planet was considered the most degrading of all forms of employment. World Life had purchased immediate use-rights to Mensat when it was first discovered, and had learned too late that while humans could survive there, they could do so only in very small numbers and in very great discomfort. The only financially viable product Mensat offered was its natural fertilizer, and it would be centuries before the Company recouped its original use-rights investment. Dedicated Company men like Nori did not like to be reminded of that crowning example of Company greed.

Still, he persisted. ''I've heard they're about to start producing a new total-conversion enzyme on Lesaat; the algae farms are bound to need new recruits. You could—''

''Oh, Nori,'' she said. ''The Company's been trying to pass off that rumor for as long as I can remember. You know better than to try it on me.''

Nori watched her for a moment, then smiled slightly and shrugged.

''I'm not interested in going off-planet,'' she told him. ''Not even to a place that's being touted as 'Earth's new South Pacific paradise.' '' Nori had shown her Lesaat's most recent recruitment brochures just the afternoon before. ''Nobody's going to turn *me* into a squid just to—''

''The job I'm talking about is different,'' he said quickly. ''They need a ranking troubleshooter to—''

"I'm not interested." Angie suspected that the Company had already approached the other ranking shooters about this job, and been turned down. She had made it clear for years that she was not open to such requests.

"But this is only a temporary—"

"Give it a rest, Nori. We've been over this a hundred times. I do not want to leave Earth."

"Well, I wish you would at least consider—"

"What are you trying to do?" she snapped. "Get yourself a recruitment bonus at my expense?"

His touch disappeared from her shoulder. "You're a stubborn woman, Angie."

Angie sighed. She had heard that before, too. She indicated a flickering digital gauge. "Wind's up a bit."

"Towers check in yet?" he asked.

"All but Five."

They both lifted their gazes to the fire.

"Must have been multiple lightning strikes," Nori said. "Burn's too big for just one."

"You hear any thunder last night?" Angie asked.

He shook his head.

"Neither did I."

She stood. "Take the deck. I'm going to go see what's going on out there." Crossing to the lift, she kicked off her moccasins and stepped into one of the readied fire suits.

Nori slid into the control seat. He touched in the change-of-deck command and activated the tower recorder—a Company man's move. "Fire Rescue is already on its way," Nori said. "There's no reason for you to go out there."

"I can reach the tower at least ten minutes sooner than the rescue bus," she replied. She sealed the heat-resistant coverall across the tops of her thighs and in a slightly off-center line down her chest. "If Chandler's in trouble, it might make a difference." She bent to pull on double-soled boots.

"The leading edge is damn close to the tower already, if these readings are right," Nori said. "Let Rescue do its job, Warden."

Sure, she thought, by the book, regardless of the possible consequences to the guy in trouble. Nori was a Company man down to his socks. She paused just long enough to meet his gaze. "Let me do mine," she said.

He frowned and turned back to the console. She snapped on the fire suit's hood, a little surprised that he had given up so easily.

"Nori," she said as she stepped into the lift. He was still for a moment. Finally, he turned.

"Wish me luck?"

"You're a damn fool, Angie, why can't you just . . ."

She sighed again and punched the lift doors closed. "Never let 'em get too close," she muttered. Nori was a competent enough lineman when it counted, and he had been good company during his stay at Tower One, but his Company line and his constant attempts to recruit her for off-planet work, not to mention his veiled overprotectiveness, were becoming irritating. Despite her fondness for him, Angie was looking forward to the time when his field rotation ended.

Never get too close, yourself, she mused.

Angie pushed the flitter to full power as soon as she was aloft. As she drew closer, the smoke in Sector Five appeared darker, angrier than before. It blocked the rising sun's direct rays. She activated the cabin radio.

"Tower One, this is Tower One Flitter," she said. "I'm about to cross the sector line."

"Are the grav plates holding level?" Nori responded.

"Plates are okay, but the hatch is still sticking. I damned near broke my wrist getting it closed."

"It's the pneumatic springs," he replied. "There's nothing we can do without replacements. Supply says they can't get new springs from the manufacturer until the air cargo strike is settled."

Angie sighed. Unlike the total cooperation she received while on troubleshooting assignments, supply problems were a way of life here on the preserve.

About ten years before, World Life Company had agreed to maintain the area as an ecological preserve in return for full title to it and the adjoining downslope farm and industrial lands. Aside from their own rest lodge, however, they did little to keep the preserve's support facilities in good repair.

It was rumored that the multinational World Life Company had been created by former members of the South American drug cartels around the turn of the century. As their illicit drug markets shrank and the danger of being killed or prosecuted rose, they dropped out of sight and began quietly investing in legitimate industrial and agricultural enterprises.

The resultant, highly profit-oriented World Life Company soon became recognized as a growing force in the international money market. Other businesses, particularly large insurance companies and banks, scrambled to include themselves within its ranks.

It was widely believed that the Company had, in those early years, encouraged the fundamentalist fervor of the times, particularly as it related to outlawing abortion and artificial birth control in many parts of the world. By doing so, they created a desperate, demanding, and entirely legal market for the carefully controlled food resources the Company was soon able to provide.

After nearly seventy years of maneuvering, World Life controlled almost all of Earth's resources, including this high mountain forest preserve, and it was Angie's opinion that the morals of the Company founders had been passed on directly to their successors.

Angie focused and refocused, searching for the touch of fluorescent yellow that would pinpoint Tower Five. She had paid for the paint herself, after becoming disgusted with the administrative hassle of getting the Company to do it. They'd be just as happy to see the whole forest burn, she thought. Then they could turn their terraformers loose and turn it into a fireloving farm.

"Idiots," she muttered. She had told Company Admin that many times, to their faces, but it never made a difference. They just paid her ever more exorbitant fees and continued to lease her services from the United Nations. She keyed an update of her position and the fire's movement.

"Okay, I see the tower," she said finally. "Twelve degrees left of the main smoke column. Looks like the front edge is very close to it. There's too much smoke to see clearly. There's a lot of deadfall in this sector. The fire's going to be burning hot. Warn the crews, and enter an order for clearing crews to move through the rest of the sector as soon as the fire's out."

"Bookkeepers'll squawk about the cost," Nori replied.

"Bugger the bookkeepers," she said. "I'll send them a bucket of ash."

The flitter bucked slightly. "I'm hitting heat drafts now." She kept her voice steady despite her rising adrenaline.

"Fire-rescue flitter is ten minutes off the Tower Five bearing." Nori's voice, thick as it was with underlying tension, was an irritant in the flitter's small cabin. "They request you hold your position until their arrival."

"Bugger them, too," Angie muttered. The flitter bumped hard again. She fought the controls and adjusted the pressurized grav plates until the flitter steadied.

"The flit's fireloving jumpy," she said. "Grav plates seem to be holding, though. That makeshift intake valve is letting smoke into the cabin, so I'm shifting to suit transmission." She flipped her faceplate closed and tongued on the oxygen intake and radio switch. She activated the auto-exhaust, and the pall of smoke cleared quickly from inside the flitter.

"I have the tower in sight again," she said. She pressed the implant on her shoulder. A strong itch responded. "My locator spots Chandler right at the site. Why the hell doesn't he get out?"

Nori said. "From here, it looks like the front edge is about to run right over the tower."

Angie blinked twice. "It's about a hundred meters off. I'll circle—"

Suddenly a klaxon blared. Angie jumped and swore. She slapped the keyboard to turn off the siren.

"Tower One Flitter, this is Fire Rescue." The rescue pilot's voice was almost as loud as the klaxon. Angie winced.

"Pull back from the fire zone, Flitter One. Repeat. Pull back from the fire zone."

"Turn down your fireloving volume, Rescue," Angie snapped. "We're on a radio line. You don't have to scream to be heard."

"Oh . . ." A pause. Then, some decibels lower, "Sorry." The pilot's voice was young, excited, inexperienced. Angie groaned quietly. Trouble always came in bunches. She could still taste the smoke on the back of her tongue.

"That's better," she said. "Now, why the hell did you trigger my alarm?"

"You've passed inside the fire safety zone, Flitter One."

"I'm aware of that, Rescue."

"You're too close to the leading edge. Pull back from the zone immediately."

"I have crew in the tower, Rescue," Angie said, trying to maintain patience. "He's not responding to the alerts."

"Move back, Flitter One. We'll get your man out. That's what we're trained for."

"What's your ETA?"

"Seven minutes thirty seconds."

"Not good enough."

"Damn it, Flitter One! Move back. That's an order."

"Suck ash," Angie replied. She fought the bucking flitter closer to the tower.

"Angela, love." A new voice, calm, controlled—blessedly familiar—interrupted the pilot's unintelligible response. "Get your pretty ass away from that fire."

Angie grinned. The knot in her stomach began to loosen. "Sally Goberlan," she called. "What are you doing back on the line? I thought you got kicked upstairs." She had partnered with Goberlan many times on troubleshooting assignments. There was no question of inexperience here.

"Just passing through on a routine inspection when your fire call came in," Goberlan said. "Rescue was short on supervisors, so I accepted their request to come along. Seemed like a good way to see you in action on your own turf. I see what you mean about Company support up here. The equipment on this bus is archaic. I've had access to better in the New Guinea Highlands."

Angie laughed. They had been caught in a collapsed highland cave once with only a flint knife between them. It had taken them seven days to dig and scrape their way out. They had become good friends along the way.

"You're dealing with a training crew, by the way," Sally added.

"Spit," Angie muttered. "Well, tell 'em from me that this is not, repeat, *not* a training run."

"Heard and understood," Goberlan said, "but let's play it by the book if we can. Give the kids a proper lesson and all that. You know the procedure. If your man's still in the tower when leading edge hits sixty meters, we'll let him ride it out. It'll be hot, but if he's suited up, he can survive."

"Yes, Mother," Angie said. She swung the flitter in a careful curve around the tower, then caught her breath as the external ladder came into view. "Forget the book, Sal."

She began a fast descent. "Chandler's not in the tower. He's on the outside ladder, not moving."

"Our ETA is five minutes." Rescue's pilot was back on the line. "Please pull back."

"Leading edge is closing fast," Angie replied. "You'll never make it in time."

"We get no life readings but your own from the tower area, Flitter One."

Angie brought the flitter as close as she dared to the tower. She blinked rapidly, trying to establish extreme close focus on Chandler's still form. Black smoke billowed across her field of vision before she could tell if he was breathing.

"There's no point risking your life for a dead man." The rescue pilot was pleading now.

"I'm foaming the ladder." Angie leaned forward as far as her helmet and the flitter's viewscreen allowed and counted softly as a cloud of white, anti-incendiary foam sprayed from the flitter's port nozzles. It pushed through the smoke and settled. For an instant, Angie had a clear view of Chandler's body, frosted white against the brilliant yellow of the tower ladder. She blinked, and blinked again, before the smoke poured back.

"He's alive, Rescue. But just barely. I'm going down."

"There's no way you can tell—"

"I can see his chest moving, damn it! I'm setting down at the base of the ladder and will climb directly—"

"Negative! Negative! Do not attempt ground landing!" The pilot was shouting again, her voice shrill and frightened.

Angie forced her own voice to stay calm. "Five's flitter is aflame on the tower roof, Rescue. There's no other way to reach him."

"The flames are gonna hit that tower any—"

"Goberlan?" Angie said as she fought the flitter to the ground.

"I'm with you," Goberlan replied instantly. Her voice was as calm and measured as before. The pilot protested in the background.

"I'm going to need a foam dump as fast as you can get it here," Angie said. "I'll only have one shot at him."

"Roger. We have the tower in sight."

"Angie, be careful—"

"Nori, get off the fireloving line!" Angie shouted.

"How far up the ladder is he?" Goberlan's smooth voice pulled her back to calm.

"Just below halfway. His right arm and leg have slipped through the rungs. That must be what's holding him up there."

"Are you on the ground yet?"

"I'm opening the hatch now. *Damn* these fireloving springs! Nori, I want a complete overhaul on this crate the instant this is over. I don't care how many admin heads you have to bash to get it done. *That's* an *order!*"

The hatch slammed open, clanging against the flitter's side. Instantly, the cabin was filled with smoke—and the roar of the fire. Angie tongued her suit's auditory dampers to muffle the din.

"Leave the hatch open if it's giving you trouble," Goberlan said. "Keep the auto-exhaust on full. It'll clear as soon as you're back inside. How's the foam on Chandler? Holding?"

"Too much smoke to tell. I'm on the ladder and climbing. It's bloody hot out here, Sal."

"Suit coolants on full?"

"On overdrive. The ladder rungs are warm even through my gloves. Why the hell is this fire so hot?"

"See your man yet?"

"I can't see a damn—" Angie's hand met an obstruction. "Wait . . . Okay, I've got him. Spit, his suit is as hot as the ladder."

"Can you get him down?"

Angie attached two lifelines to the ladder. She hooked one to her own chest harness, then moved carefully up the ladder until she could feel the utility belt around Chandler's waist. Fumbling in the smoky darkness, she attached the second line to the rapid-descent loop at the back of Chandler's belt.

"Talk to me, Angie," Goberlan said. "What's happening?"

Angie climbed another rung to where she could see the faint outline of Chandler's helmet. "Lifeline's attached. I'm trying to free his arm . . . Oh, damn . . . How close are you, Sally?"

"ETA, two minutes."

"I need foam right now. His faceplate is open. Jammed. I can't move it. He must have been climbing up when he passed out, because he's been in the flames."

"I hear you. We'll alert the burn center in Denver and foam on arrival. Can you get him off the ladder?"

Angie yanked an emergency oxygen canister from her belt and pressed it over Chandler's mouth and nose. "Stay alive," she whispered.

Aloud, she said, "I'm freeing his leg now." She leaned her shoulder into Chandler's waist and climbed another rung. The man's full weight sank into her shoulder. His leg caught, then released suddenly from where it had slipped through the rung. Angie clung to the ladder with one arm while she grasped Chandler tightly with the other.

"Okay! I've got him!" She was startled at the intensity of her own relief. "I'm sending him down on the lifeline." She checked to be sure Chandler's line was clear, then slid him off her shoulder. Suspended by the lifeline harness, he hung facedown, bent at the shoulders and waist.

"I need foam, Rescue. He's burning up, and I have no way to cool him." She glanced down. "The grass is aflame at the edge of the tower platform. It looks like the platform is burning, too. Note that, Rescue. Something smells real bad down here, and it's not just the smoke." Bracing Chandler's line away from the ladder, she activated a rapid release. His limp form slid swiftly toward the ground.

"ETA, forty-five seconds, One. Front line is at twenty meters. Flitter on tower roof is fully engaged. We'll only have time to foam you once and get out. There's no way we can make a lift."

"We can't go in—" The pilot's voice was silenced abruptly.

Angie stopped Chandler's descent when the line count showed him to be within two meters of the ground. "We'll ride it out in the flitter," she said. "I'm descending now." She activated her own line, pushed away from the ladder, and slid in a blur to Chandler's side. When the line bounced her to a stop, her feet were centimeters from the ground. She had the line disconnected and was reaching for Chandler before her boots hit the deck.

"Foaming, Flitter One."

Angie ducked instinctively as a white cloud suddenly engulfed her. The temperature dropped instantly. She yanked away Chandler's lifeline, slung his limp form over her shoulder, and sprinted through the snowy foam toward the flitter.

"Front edge is on you, Flitter One." Goberlan's voice continued, as cool as the foam. "We're moving back. We'll cool you down and lift you out as soon as the line passes. Good luck, Angie."

Angie stuffed Chandler headfirst through the flitter's open hatch, then swung herself inside. She reached back to swing the hatch door closed. "If you've made it this far, Chandler, you're going to make it all the way," she called out.

The hatch door didn't move.

"Damn!"

She yanked again on the hatch handle. Flames licked across the opening; the brilliant orange startled her after so long in the smoky darkness. She could feel the heat intensifying, even through the insulating layer of foam. Chandler could never survive the heat of the fire in his open suit. She wasn't even sure she could. She had to get the hatch closed.

She leaned out into the flames, grabbed the door's edge with both hands—and pulled. "Move, damn you!" she yelled. The door shifted.

"Move!" The hatch swung half the distance before sticking again. Flame, jagged streaks of yellow and orange, sliced across her vision. Her hands and arms felt as if they were scorching.

She braced both feet against the cabin wall and yanked with all her strength.

"Move!"

There was another instant's hesitation, then the hatch slammed shut. The flames disappeared abruptly, and the roar of the fire changed to the sudden scream of the auto-exhaust. The smoke was so thick that Angie could barely see past her faceplate.

"Angie! Our life monitor shows you back in the flitter. Are you all right? How's Chandler?"

Angie tried to blink away the smoke. There must be something wrong with the auto-exhaust. It was supposed to be silent. The darkness had grown opaque.

"Talk to me, Angie."

Why was it so hard to breathe?

"Flitter one . . ."

"Smoke," Angie forced out. "The smoke won't clear." Her legs felt like rubber.

"Did you get Chandler into the flitter, Angie?"

Sally Goberlan's voice.

What was *she* doing here? Suddenly, Angie felt very cold.

"Goberlan?"

"Did you get Chandler inside the flitter?" Goberlan insisted. "Answer me, Angie."

The smoke was condensing inside her helmet. Angie shook her head to clear it, then blinked to snap her nictitating membranes into place. "I can't . . ."

Her vision cleared. "Oh, mother of mountain," she breathed.

"Angie, what's going on down there?"

Her hands, both of them, had been caught across the palms by the slamming hatch door.

"Talk to me, Angie." Goberlan's voice had taken on the dead-calm tone of one who knows her listener is in serious trouble. Angie had used the tone herself often enough to know. She tried, but was unable to disengage her close-up focus.

"We estimate seven minutes to lift out, Angie. We'll try to get close enough to foam you in five."

How long does it take for a person my size to bleed to death? Angie wondered. Her mind kept sliding away from the problem.

"Hold on, Angie."

"Holding," she whispered.

It was a long time before she was able to close her eyes.

Chapter 2

~~~~~~
~~~~~~

Le Fe'e's song was faint inside the burial cave. Fatu suspected that was more a result of the human presence in the cavernous chamber than of the cave's distance from the sea. He heard melancholy in the faint rumble of surf pounding the outer reef. He tasted loneliness on the still, damp air.

I miss her, too, he replied silently. Le Fe'e only existed in his niece's imagination, but in her absence, Fatu drew comfort from the sounds and smells she had claimed were the god's own. He wished for a return to freer, more joyous days.

Despite her late parents' recorded wishes, Fatu's attempts to bring Pua back to Lesaat had consistently failed. The Company inspectors had claimed they were not closely enough related. They insisted Pua was safe with her mother's family on Earth. It was an unsatisfactory compromise, even if it was true, which Fatu doubted.

He pulled his attention back to the cave. It's a place to fit my mood today, he thought. Moisture shimmered deep in moss-lined crevices and dripped, dripped, dripped like perpetual tears onto wet stone. Slime molds shimmered in bioluminescent rainbows where they were not faded to slick gray by the Earther's harsh, artificial lights. The damp air, cooler by far than that outside the cave, smelled of spilled candleberry oil, mildew, and human sweat.

A nightcrawler, confused by the unnatural glare of fluorescent lamps, crawled into the light, flipped onto its side, and punctured its dye sack. Fatu glanced toward the small sound and sighed, saddened yet further by the creature's mistake. Only during the phosphorescence of true night did the nightcrawlers' procreative spores become viable. This one had given its life for nothing.

"I will mourn for your lost children," Fatu chanted quietly in Samoan. "As I must mourn for my own." It was a song he had sung all too often of late.

Toma glanced back to meet his look for a moment. The planetary super looked tired, but Fatu did not doubt that he was fully alert. The bastard Klooney and the visiting Company inspector either did not hear or chose not to react. Fatu sighed, and retreated to silence again as Klooney ripped open the final basket of human burial remains.

A fine cloud of gray dust lifted. Klooney snuffed and sneezed. "Damn mildew," he muttered. He scratched at his forearms, not a wise thing to do with nails as sharp as his. His arms were covered with thick, dark hair, matted with sweat and the dust from previously disturbed burial packets. The gray talc clung to the hair in damp wads. The Earther stepped back to avoid the settling dust. Klooney glowered at him.

"I oughta get hazard pay for workin' in here, Yoshida," he said. "Look at this. I'm gettin' a rash already. Reef-rotted air in here tastes like the inside of a coffin."

It is the inside of a coffin, Fatu reminded him silently. Klooney was a fool of a man, bright enough to do the Company's dirty work, but too stupid to realize that his present status as the Company's chief waterworld thug would end the instant his services were no longer needed. Instead of the land leases he expected, his ultimate reward would most likely be a late evening swim with the suckersharks. An event to which Fatu, quite frankly, looked forward.

Fatu folded his arms across his broad chest and leaned against the wall. The moist stone was cool against his bare back. His lavalava clung in damp folds to his hips and thighs, and his oiled hair hung heavy over his shoulders. It was streaked with gray. I'll be as white as the snow trees soon, he mused. I'm getting old before my time.

"Just get on with it," Yoshida said. He was wearing a Company dress uniform, which, despite the several hours they had been inside the damp cave, was still spotless. Inspector's insignia glimmered on his sleeve cuffs. He removed a folded handkerchief from his chest pocket and patted it against his perspiring forehead.

Klooney wiped a sweat-dampened sleeve across his own face and sneezed again. He scattered a handful of charred bone fragments across the stone ledge. "There's nothing in this one either," he said. "I told you there wouldn't be." A bone shard slipped through his long fingers and tumbled to the ground.

Fatu straightened, but Toma motioned him back and bent to retrieve the relic. He picked it up carefully with the tips of his fingernails and placed it back among the others.

"What's the matter, Toma?" Klooney asked. "You afraid of disturbin' Fatu's ghosts?"

"I prefer not putting them to the test," Toma said. He dropped his gaze to Klooney's left hand, where the upper third of his index finger was missing. Klooney had lost it to an unexpectedly bold scissors worm in this very cave just a few weeks before. The reddened stump was just beginning to regenerate.

Klooney glanced back at Fatu, narrowed his eyes, then growled and spat. Not, Fatu noted with some satisfaction, anywhere near the burial remains. His warnings about ghostly retributions had not stopped the man from following Company orders, but they had not been entirely without effect. Klooney scratched his arm again.

"Enough," Yoshida said. "I'm not interested in hearing about your stupid superstitions." He frowned at his stained handkerchief, folded the cloth over on itself, and returned it to his pocket. "Continue the search."

"Where am I supposed to look?" Klooney asked. He snuffed and sneezed again. "This is the last of the burials. We've been over this cave a dozen times in the last five months, and I've opened these reef-sucking baskets of refuse every time. Your damn research records ain't in here."

"I've searched the cave as many times myself, Inspector," Toma said, "both before and after your security teams went through it. Klooney's right. We're wasting our time in here. We should be out on the reef deciding what to do about the harvest."

"There is nothing to decide," Yoshida said. "When the Company's ready to harvest the algae, you'll be informed."

Toma settled his hands on his hips. He, too, was wearing Company dress, but the uniform was faded and worn thin with use. The legs and sleeves had been cut short, revealing heavily muscled thighs and shoulders. Yoshida's cold look followed the motion of Toma's long-fingered hands, then lifted quickly to his face.

"If the Earth-based algae isn't cleared from Pukui before the typhoon season starts," Toma said, speaking with the calm reason that made him so effective in his job as liaison between the waterworlders and Earth, "we're going to lose the entire reef, and probably three or four others directly downcurrent."

Yoshida said, as if quoting from World Life's policy manual, "The preservation of the current algae crop and the recovery of the total-conversion research records have priority over all other aspects of Pukui management. The orders stand."

"This is the year of alignment, Inspector," Toma said. "A month from now, our two moons will cross paths directly over Pukui. The tides will be at their peak, and that's just when the storms are due. The algae nets are full to straining right now; they're barely holding during ordinary squalls. If they get hit by typhoon winds and swells at extreme high tide, they're going to rip right open."

"I've heard this before, Doctor."

"Well, listen to it again," Fatu said, stepping forward at last. "Try to *comprehend* it this time, and for god's sake repeat it to your idiot supervisors back on Earth. Pukui's Earth algae has already been allowed to grow too thick. Neither light nor nutrients are reaching the inner algal masses. They're full of rot. The coral beds underneath aren't getting enough oxygen, so the reef itself is beginning to die."

Fatu lifted a hand to stop Yoshida from interrupting. He saw Toma make the sign for caution, but he ignored it.

"So far, the damage is restricted to the reef flats directly under the active algae pens," he said. "But if that algae breaks loose, we won't stand a chance of saving this lagoon. It'll bloom over both the inner and outer reefs long before the storm season ends. You know what that means. You've seen what loose Earth algae can do to Lesaat's reefs."

Yoshida turned his skeptical look toward Klooney.

Klooney shrugged and nodded. "It's true. There ain't enough squids on the planet to clean a major storm spill out of Pukui. Hell, the size of the inner reef alone is twice what we could handle. The barrier reef is three times that. Let that 410 Standard loose out there, Inspector, and it ain't gonna stop growin' till the whole place is dead. You're pushin' your luck already, holding the harvest off this long."

The Earther remained silent for a time. Think about it, Fatu urged. Think about who's going to take the fall if the most valuable reef on Lesaat is lost, whether the missing records are found or not.

Pukui had been providing the Company with consistently high profits for twenty years, ever since Zed and Lehua Pukui began controlled farm operations there. Earlier settlers had misjudged the potential of Lesaat's nutrient-rich waters and allowed Earth-based algae to grow wild over unprotected reefs. It had bloomed and spread so rapidly that harvesting wasn't possible in time to save the underlying coral. Three prime atolls were fully destroyed before the Company halted operations and began seeking experts to do the job right.

Zed was a phycologist and oceanographer, Lehua a geneticist. Both were eager to accept the land titles that came with offers of permanent resettlement on Lesaat. Within a year at Pukui, they had devised a safe containment system for the algae and designed the physical changes humans needed for efficient, long-term work on the waterfarms.

Pukui continued as a key research center for the study and processing of the desperately needed protein-conversion enzyme. The atoll's loss would be catastrophic to more than just the waterworlders who lived and worked there.

Inspector Yoshida rubbed his stubby fingers across his chin. He looked down at his hand and frowned, just as he had at the handkerchief earlier. He started to wipe his fingers on his trouser leg, but caught himself before they touched the clean gray fabric. He used the already soiled handkerchief to clean them instead.

Klooney sneezed. He hacked and spat, then rubbed his eyes with the backs of his dust-laden hands, cursing when it made him cough and sneeze again.

Time to get them out of here, Fatu decided, before Klooney starts wondering why today's "mildew" is so much more irritating than it's ever been before. He took another step forward. "You people have done enough damage for today. I want you to leave."

"We'll leave when we're ready," Yoshida said.

Toma stepped quickly between them. "Sorry, Inspector, but this *is* private property. We can only stay for as long as Fatu gives his consent."

"But I'm not—"

"Both U.N. and Lesaat law give him the right to ask us to leave," Toma said.

"This is an official Company investigation," Yoshida insisted.

Toma nodded. "And I am the ranking Company official on Lesaat. If anyone could grant you the right to disregard Fatu's request, the planetary supervisor could. But without a U.N.-

authorized search warrant I am unable to assist you. I am, in fact, required to enforce the law which states that you—'' He glanced at Fatu. ''—that *we* must leave.'' He motioned toward the entrance.

Yoshida glared at Fatu. "You won't get away with this much longer, Fatu."

"Bring my niece back," Fatu said, "and I'll give the Company free access to the entire atoll."

"She's not your niece," Yoshida said. "Not by any civilized legal definition. She stays where she is."

Fatu folded his arms again. He arranged his long fingers in a gesture that caused Yoshida's eyes to darken. The Earther's thin lips tightened, and his shoulders tensed. Do it! Fatu urged. Give me the excuse I need to crush your tide-pissing skull right here in this cave.

"Pump him full of penta," Klooney said, unwittingly breaking the moment of tension, "and he'll tell us right now." He lifted a quick hand toward Toma. "Yeah, yeah. I know. Free citizens can't be truth-drugged without their consent. How much longer you think it'll be before the Company finds a way around *that* law, Doc?"

"I have no idea," Toma replied coolly. "But for as long as Lesaat remains a U.N. protectorate under Company control, I have no choice but to see that the laws as they stand are obeyed. That's what World Life pays me for, Klooney—and they pay me very well—to keep the Company in strict compliance with the law. Now, leave that stuff as it is and get out."

Klooney's hands rolled into fists, but a sneeze erased any menace from his stance. "Reef-suckin' moldhole," he muttered. He eyed Fatu darkly as he picked up one of the lamps and crossed to the entrance. He dropped to his knees and crawled outside.

Toma motioned for Fatu to follow.

"I have work to do here," Fatu said. He gestured toward the scattered burial remains.

"You come with us," Yoshida snapped.

Fatu dropped his cool glance down the front of the Earther's clean gray suit, then brought it back to his face. He said nothing.

Yoshida began, "I'll order an Earth waterguard unit out here if I have—"

"If the inspector is going to take an accurate report on Pukui's current condition back to Earth," Toma said with his perpetual, damnable reasonableness, "he needs to see the farm from below the surface. You know the reef better than I do, Fatu. I'd like you to pilot the sub."

"Is that an order, Doctor Haili?" Fatu asked softly.

"Yes," Yoshida said.

Toma held Fatu's look for a moment. "A request," he said finally. Yoshida cursed in frustration.

Fatu smiled slightly. As he crouched to exit the cave, he trailed the tips of his long fingers along the cool, damp wall. The soft pop and hiss of another ill-fated nightcrawler followed him from the shadows.

Chapter 3

Angie woke to cool wetness. Viscous fluid slid slowly across her bare skin, crept over her chin, and covered her cheeks. She heard it bubbling in her ears. No! It slipped into her mouth and nose, and abruptly she was back in the mountain river, freezing cold, trapped in the speeding, dark current. She was suffocating! No! *No!*

Something hot touched her veins. *Fire!* Angie thought, and the panic would have been total if all sensation had not abruptly ceased.

Rhythmic chanting drew her back. The words were meaningless, but the cadence of the song was comforting. Angie fought her way back to consciousness. Something soft and dry caressed her forehead. A hand? The thought formed slowly. No. The touch was too delicate, the stroking tendrils too long. She thought about opening her eyes.

I must be immersed in an EM field, she thought. The realization brought her tremendous relief. It meant that the great darkness she had just left had been a result of sensory deprivation, not a sign of her own insanity. The dep tank's electromagnetic stasis field must still be holding her immobile. She shivered mentally as she remembered the fire, the hatch—the reason why she was here.

Cautiously she moved her eyelids. They lifted after a brief struggle. Not a full immersion, then. At least her facial muscles were under her own control. Staring straight up at the olive-drab ceiling, she was startled to see a spray of mildew. That has to be in my mind, she mused. Denver's too dry for mildew to grow on the walls.

Something moved just at the edge of her vision.

"Who's there?" she whispered. Her voice was low and hoarse. "Come closer, so I can see you."

"Turn your head." It sounded like a child's voice, a girl.

Angie started to comply, then stopped as a sliver of fear brushed her consciousness. "I—I can't." Angie didn't understand the intensity of her aversion to moving. She wanted to move. Wanted it desperately, but she knew she must not.

"You have to do it sometime."·

Angie tried to mask her fear with anger. "I'll move when I'm fireloving ready. Who are you, anyway?" She blinked twice, and stared hard at the ceiling. It *was* mildew!

"I'm Pualeiokekai noun Zedediah me Kalehuaokalae."

Angie shifted her gaze to the right.

"It's okay to just call me Pua," the girl said. She had moved to just within Angie's range of vision. Angie blinked back to standard focus. The child was older than Angie had guessed. Twelve, Angie thought, or maybe thirteen. Her golden brown skin had the silken smoothness of prepubescence. A faded yellow ribbon banded the girl's forehead, holding back long, thick, very black hair. Her equally dark eyes radiated challenge.

"Let's see if you're as tough as everyone says you are," Pua said. She lifted one dark brow and stepped back out of sight.

Without thinking, Angie turned to follow.

And was dropped into chaos—mental, visual. Her heart pounded, and the blood roared in her ears. The ceiling spun while the air slid without control from her lungs. She squeezed her eyes closed and gasped for a return breath that wouldn't come. Her mind screamed. She fell, tumbling, spinning . . .

The girl laughed.

. . . and Angie caught herself in midfall. She clung to the laughter. It remained the only stable thing within her consciousness. A ragged breath finally brought oxygen back to her lungs. Cautiously she sucked in another breath. Then another. The laughter faded, and the spinning slowed.

"What happened?" Angie forced out. "What did you do?"

"Nothing. You just moved your head."

Angie counted methodically to slow her heartbeat. Tentatively, she opened her eyes. The room spun for a moment more, then settled. The girl was standing about two meters away. She was short, with broad shoulders. She wore a white turtleneck with the words Think Wet! painted sloppily in yellow across the front. The sleeves and the lower edge of the shirt had been shredded and braided into intricately patterned fringe. At least it looked intricate—Angie's focus was still unsteady.

The girl's mouth twitched as if she was restraining a smile. Angie took a slow, careful breath. "What happened?" she asked again.

Pua came a step closer. "It's called hysterical paralysis. The drugs that make you sleep so long mess up your balance center, and that mixes up your stress system. You know, that fight-or-run-away thing? Anyway, you can't do either the whole time you're in the tank, so when you wake up, your mind kind of freezes. Some fish do it, and some animals, I think, but not because they've been in a deprivation tank."

The image of a mule deer frozen in her flitter's headlights crossed Angie's mind. Is that how the deer felt? She moved her head cautiously to the side again, and back. It left her slightly dizzy, but the intense dread it had generated earlier was gone.

"Some people can't ever move on their own," the girl went on. "The admin people hate it when that happens, 'cause the drugs that make 'em move turn them into drones like my Auntie Kate."

Angie frowned.

"Katie's nice, though," Pua said quickly. "She just can't think very fast, and she talks kind of funny."

Angie wasn't frowning about anybody's Auntie Kate. She had never heard of such a reaction to simple healing tanks. The girl didn't appear to be deliberately lying, but . . . Angie moved her head again; there was still no response from the rest of her body.

"Pacific Islanders usually come out of the paralysis easiest," Pua said. "Do you have Polynesian ancestors?"

"Not that I know of," Angie replied.

The girl's gaze slid across Angie's body again. "You're big enough, but your skin got awful white before they gave you that last melanin treatment. Usually the darker skin colors are dominant when there's a mix."

Angie stared at her. "Are you a genetics expert, too?" she asked. She wondered why anyone would bother with her skin tone while she was still in recovery. She wondered who this strangely adult-sounding child was.

Pua shrugged. "My mom was."

"Are *you* Polynesian?" Angie asked. Now that she was looking for it, she recognized the slight upward turn to Pua's eyes, the fullness of her face—and her skin tone.

Pua nodded. "I'm Micronesian, too. My mom was Hawaiian,

and my dad came from Truk.'' Angie noted the past tense, but decided not to remark on it. The girl's chin had lifted as she spoke, a movement that stated conscious pride in her ancestry, but pain had touched her eyes for just an instant.

Who are you? Angie wanted to ask. What are you doing wandering around in a critical-care unit?

"Can you see my hands?" she asked instead.

Pua glanced down. "They're still inside the recon gel baths. Dr. Waight took out the regrowth nets this morning.''

A tremendous pressure lifted from Angie's mind. If they had used regrowth nets, it meant her hands had not been totally destroyed. They had been repairable. Or at least regrowable.

"How do they look?''

Pua brought her gaze back to Angie's face. Her expression was entirely neutral. "They look fine to me.''

"Can you turn off the EM field?''

Pua shook her head. "I'd get in too much trouble.''

Angie sighed, and closed her eyes. She felt a feather touch on her brow. "What are you doing?'' she asked.

Instantly the touch disappeared.

"Don't stop. My face is the only place I have any feeling.''

Tentatively, the touch returned to her forehead.

"You were here before, weren't you? While I was still asleep?'' Angie relaxed under the stroking tendrils. "I remember someone singing . . .'' A feather, she thought, and the thought made her want to laugh. Angie, the tough-assed troubleshooter, stroked to wellness by a bird. Sally would enjoy that one.

She wondered what her favorite troubleshooting partner had learned about the source of that mountain fire. She knew Sally would run a full investigation of the event, regardless of any official Company report. Troubleshooters kept a closer eye on Company activities, and on each other, than most admin execs realized.

"You talked in your sleep,'' Pua said.

Angie realized the comment was meant as an answer to her question.

"Mostly about trees and mountains and stuff. That was kind of boring, but sometimes you talked about a guy named Nori.''

Angie opened her eyes.

"You talked about stuff you used to do together up in that tower.'' Pua lifted a questioning brow. "Weren't you supposed to be *working* up there?''

Angie blinked, wondering if it was possible to blush in an EM field.

Pua giggled suddenly. "I liked it better when you talked about Sally Goberlan. Sally was the best."

That made Angie laugh, too. "Sally is definitely the best," she agreed. "But what—"

A pneumatic doorlock hissed. Pua backed quickly away.

"Damn it, girl! I told you to stay out of here!" It was a man's voice. Loud and angry. Angie could just make him out at the edge of her vision. Very dark skin, tall. His features remained indistinct because of the angle.

"I wasn't hurting—"

"I warned you, Pua . . ."

"Leave her alone," Angie said.

"What?" The man moved closer quickly, obviously startled to hear her speak. As he stared down at her, his anger turned quickly to concern. He called over his shoulder, "Waight, get in here! She's awake! Pua, you get out."

His eyes were too pale for the color of his skin to be natural. A scar, a true scar, ran from his right temple to his chin. A doctor? Angie thought. Somehow, she didn't think so. He acted more like admin. What would a Company man be doing in a reconstruction hospital?

"What's going on, Crawley?"

A woman appeared at Angie's side. An old woman, with eyes even paler than the man's. She blinked, and Angie caught the telltale glint of gridded lenses. Visual implants, she thought. Good ones. The woman leaned over her.

"You *are* awake!" She sounded genuinely surprised.

"Is there some reason I shouldn't be?" Angie asked.

"No, I . . ." A lie. Angie saw it clearly in the woman's expression. "Of course not, Warden. You're just a little ahead of schedule, that's all. How do you feel?"

"I don't feel anything," Angie said.

"Can you . . . "

"Move my head?" Angie said when the woman hesitated. "Yes. The girl helped me break through the paralysis. Why was I—"

The almost colorless eyes shifted abruptly. "Pua, what are you doing here? What did you do to her? Tell me exactly what happened when she woke."

"I didn't do anything, Doctor Waight, I just—" Pua paused.

When she spoke again, her voice had grown tight, calculating. "I'll tell you everything, if you let me go home."

The woman cursed softly, and shifted her look back to Angie. "My name is Doctor Ruby Waight, Warden. I did the surgery on your hands. You do remember what happened to your hands, don't you?"

"Yes," Angie said softly. And thank you very much, Doctor, for your compassionate concern.

"Good." Waight motioned toward the man. "This is Walter Crawley, our administrative liaison. You'll have to pardon our momentary confusion. The drugs normally hold people under a day or two longer than this. It must have been your trouble-shooter's conditioning that made the difference. I should have taken that into account." She flashed a light in Angie's eyes and touched a flickering monitor that Angie could just barely see.

"Now, this is important, Warden," Waight said. "I want you to tell me everything you remember about waking up. All the details."

Angie disliked the woman immensely. She was tempted to repeat Pua's conditions for speaking, but decided she had better deal with her own needs first. She said, "I could remember better with the EM field turned off."

Waight's curse was the same one she had offered the girl.

"I'd like to get up," Angie said.

That brought a quick, hard laugh. "You'd fall flat on your face if you tried to get up now, Warden. Give the drugs time to clear your system. You'll be out of here soon enough." She did something below Angie's field of vision, and abruptly Angie felt sensation in her legs, her arms, her hands—her hands didn't feel right.

"It would be best to keep your hands in the gel for a few more days," Waight said. "Until you get used to the feel of them. The EM stimulation has kept the rest of your body in reasonably good shape. You should be fully recovered and functional in a few weeks."

Angie blew out a slow breath. She hated lying still. "How is Chandler?"

"Who?"

"The lineman she rescued," the admin man said.

The doctor's eyes darkened for an instant. "He's alive. He's been moved to rehab."

"In Houston?"

Waight glanced at Crawley.

"Hawaii," he said.

"Hawaii! Why isn't he at a burn center? How long have I been here?"

The look that passed between Waight and Crawley left Angie feeling suddenly cold.

"Five months."

"Why was Chandler sent to Hawaii?" Angie demanded.

Again the quick exchange of dark looks. "His lungs were too badly damaged to be restored without full reconstruction," Crawley said. "He was re-formed in the waterfarm tanks."

"The waterfarm— You replaced his lungs with gills!"

"Total regrowth of full body parts is very expensive, Warden," Crawley said. "Not to mention time-consuming. It's only done when the Company can be reasonably assured that the worker's future earning potential warrants the cost. Chandler was only a lineman. He had no special skills."

"He was only eighteen years old! How could he possibly have developed special skills?"

"He had signed the standard Company contract, Warden," Crawley said. "We were entirely within our rights to invoke the alternate-employment clause when he couldn't make the decision for himself."

"He would never have selected water work as an alternate. He was a mountain man."

"He's been fitted with high-grade gills and webs," Waight broke in. "He'll be trained for midlevel management, so his salary will go up. And he's received a substantial disability bonus, of course."

"A disability bonus!" Angie cried. "You turn a man into a fireloving *squid*, and then offer him a disability bonus?"

"Don't say that!"

Angie turned her head at Pua's sharp command. She blinked away the dizziness, then blinked again to bring the girl's image closer. Pua's smooth skin had gone pale; her dark eyes flashed.

"Pua," Waight said. "Go outside."

"Don't say what?" Angie said.

"Damn it—"

"Don't call that man a squid!" Pua's cold stare no longer resembled that of a child.

"What—"

"Shut up, Pua. Crawley, get her out of here!"

"Only a *real* waterworlder has the right to call a man a squid," Pua said. Crawley reached for her, but the girl hissed and lifted a hand toward his face. He jerked back as a fistful of writhing tentacles snaked forward. They coiled back one by one until only the central one remained extended. It was a gesture as old as time. Presented by the sweet-faced girl, it was as obscene a thing as Angie had ever witnessed.

"Suck reef, Admin," Pua said. She backed toward the door, the fringes on her shirt swinging in time to her smooth steps. She met Angie's look again, for just an instant, before she disappeared.

Crawley went after her.

"Who is that?" Angie cried as the door hissed shut behind them. "What have you done to her!"

"Don't try to lift your head, Warden," Waight said.

"She's only a kid! It's against the law to change—"

"Lay back, Warden, or I'll turn the EM field back on." A barely perceptible tingle spread across Angie's back.

"No!" She dropped her head back onto the softly yielding surface of the EM platform. "Who is she?" she asked.

What is she? she asked silently. What is going on here? A shiver slid along Angie's arms. She tried to make herself believe it had been caused by a fluctuation in the fading electromagnetic field.

"Pua is a waterworlder," Waight said.

"I could see that!" The girl's waterworld alterations were more than obvious. But her hands were unlike any waterworlder's Angie had ever seen. Her fingers had been so long, so . . . Angie thought suddenly of a holo she had once seen of an octopus in open water, its graceful, twisting tentacles outspread. She pushed the image away.

"Pua's waterworld alterations were done while she was still *in utero*," Waight said. "Her parents ran a research farm on Lesaat. Pua was the one success they had in trying to create a second generation not dependent on Earth's reconstruction labs. We didn't even know she existed until a year ago, when a Company crewman discovered her tying up holes in one of the algae nets."

Angie remembered Pua's proud acknowledgment of her ancestry. Pacific Islanders were the most sought after recruits for the Lesaat waterfarms, Angie knew, because both their physiological and psychological makeup had proved to make them the most adaptable immigrants. They were also, as a group, among the poorest of Earth's residents, and were thus the most easily conscripted.

Angie tensed her back and shoulder muscles, then her legs and her arms. Only her hands did not respond. Or she didn't feel them if they did. She forced herself to relax.

"Pua's parents are dead," Waight went on. "Pua mistakenly fed them a poisonous variety of sea cucumber about six months ago. We transferred all three of them back here immediately after they were stricken, but only the girl lived."

Waight removed something from the side of Angie's neck.

"That makes my shoulder itch," Angie said.

"It's just your locator implants," Waight replied. "One of them was probably triggered by the EM field." She touched one of the line of monitors behind her and the itch faded.

"Children aren't allowed on Lesaat unless they're with immediate family," she said, "so we've been forced to keep Pua here. She's a dreadful child. She's full of superstitious nonsense about ghosts and sea creatures. She thinks it was her spells that kept you alive in the dep tank. And she has absolutely no respect for property or privacy. Even keeping her decently dressed has proved impossible."

Angie shifted her gaze back to the ceiling. The woman's face and voice were so full of lies she could no longer bear to watch.

"Still, her presence here is providing me with an invaluable research opportunity. Until now, waterworld reconstruction work has been restricted to the growth of webs between the recruit's existing fingers, and a minimal extension of the fingers themselves. But if I can find a way to reproduce Pua's—"

"This is Hawaii, isn't it?" Angie said. "That's why there's mildew on the ceiling." She felt, more than saw, Waight's startled upward glance.

A scream trembled at the back of her throat. Hawaii! World Life Company's corporate headquarters. Site of its primary waterworld reconstruction station. The image of Pua's grotesque fingers writhed sinuously against the backdrop of the mildewed ceiling. At the back of Angie's mind, a child's voice asked, *Do you have Polynesian ancestors?*

"What did you do to my hands?"

There was a long pause. "Your injuries were such that standard reconstruction wasn't possible," Waight said finally. "Your hands were crushed beyond surgical repair. They had to be removed. We considered attempting full regrowth, but that would have taken at least three years, even being pushed."

Another pause. "Bionic prostheses would have been simpler

and faster, but we judged that, being a troubleshooter, you wouldn't be satisfied with those."

Angie squeezed her eyelids tight.

"We tried something new," Waight said. "A cloned transplant."

"From *her*?"

"We also took the opportunity to augment your oxygen intake capacity."

Gills! The thought of the distant mountains was like a knife sliding through Angie's soul.

There was a sound from the direction of the door. Waight looked up as Crawley walked to Angie's side. He met her look and smiled. "I see you've heard the good news, Warden."

"You won't get away with this," Angie said. To her relief, her voice remained dead steady. The more serious the problem, the calmer the tone. She could still hear Sally's entirely toneless monologue carrying her through the eternity of that fire.

One of Crawley's thin brows lifted. "We're not 'getting away' with anything, Warden. Everything we've done fits within the legalities of your contract."

"I work for the U.N.," Angie said. "Not World Life."

He shrugged. "Under the circumstances, the U.N. was only too happy to lease us your services in return for providing you with our expert medical care."

"It's not uncommon for new recruits to wish they could change their minds at this point," Waight said. "But remember, this is a tremendous opportunity for you. If you injure these hands, they'll regenerate on their own, very quickly. You'll have exceptional grip strength and flexibility—"

Angie's manufactured calm fled. "I don't give a firefly's damn about flexibility! I am not a recruit! I had nothing to do with this decision!"

"Mr. Yoshida assured us this is the course you would prefer," Waight said.

"Who the hell is—" She stopped. "Nori?"

Waight nodded. "Nori Yoshida. Your second-in-command at the forest preserve and," she added with a slight frown, "personal companion. Ordinarily, I disapprove of sexual alliances at the work site, but in this case it proved advantageous, since he was privy to your personal desires."

Angie stared at her. "Nori did this?"

"Mr. Yoshida came here immediately after you arrived," Crawley said. "When we showed him the extent of your injuries, he insisted you would be grateful for the opportunity to work on Lesaat. He explained how eager you were to find a field position off-planet."

"That's a lie!"

Again, Angie tested the muscles of her lower body. Without actually moving, she couldn't be certain if they were actually reacting, or if the response was only in her mind. She found it difficult to breathe.

"I won't go to Lesaat," she said.

"According to our records, you owe the Company a lot of credit," Crawley said. He waved a loose-wristed hand toward Waight and the shelf of monitors beyond the EM platform. "Completely aside from all this, I mean."

"I owe half the cost of my last visual implants," Angie said. "Call the debt, Admin. I have more than enough to cover it. And don't think you can charge me for the rest of this sham. I'm not a fireline grunt like Chandler. I'm fully insured."

"Of course you are," Crawley said. "By World Life itself. For all medical treatment made necessary by injuries incurred while performing your standard duties."

"Which include the rescue of endangered crewmen," she said.

"Not when there's an official rescue team on-site," he said. "You flew into the danger zone over the stated and recorded objections of your own tower partner, and you repeatedly refused to leave the area, even after being ordered to do so by a U.N. troubleshooter equal to your own rank."

Angie remembered Nori's smooth, white fingers touching on the tower recorder—just before he recommended not going to the fire, just *after* their discussion concerning off-planet work. And Sally . . . They had used her, too, but without her knowledge. Angie knew Sally would never have been a conscious part of this.

"Your actions put an entire rescue crew in jeopardy, Warden. You could face criminal charges for that," Crawley said. "But you're fortunate. In exchange for taking part in Dr. Waight's transplant experiment, the Company has agreed not to press charges and to waive the cost of your treatment and rehabilitation, contingent on your cooperation—"

Angie sat up. Her vision spun, but to her immense relief, her body responded.

"Stop her!" Waight called.

Her right shoulder smacked Crawley squarely in the chest.

There was a quick, sharp pain in her right arm, and others at her side. EM patches, she thought. And other things? She hoped she had done herself no permanent damage, then almost laughed at the absurdity of the thought. Metal and plastic clattered to the ground.

"Don't let her fall!" Waight cried.

Angie kicked toward the voice. Her foot struck something soft, and there was a grunt of pain. Waight's hand slipped from her left arm. Angie continued her forward movement. Her hands moved along with her, startling her because she had expected them to be restrained. The sudden return of sensation below her wrists confused her momentarily.

Crawley grabbed her right shoulder, and she used him as a lever to help her roll from the platform. The floor had the resilience of concrete. The room went dark, then brilliantly bright again.

"Be careful of the hands," Waight called breathlessly.

"I'll show you my hands!"

Angie swung at the advancing Crawley as hard as she could, trying to form her hand into a fist. The blur of flesh-colored tendrils that registered on her already spinning vision proved that the mental command had not reached her new fingers. The strength of her swing was powerful, however. The thin strands of her newly grown fingers snapped across Crawley's face like a whip.

His scream was sharp and shrill. He threw himself bodily atop her to stop her from hitting him again. At any other time, she would have been able to escape him easily, but now her drug-laden system failed her. She flailed at Crawley with limp, useless hands.

"You idiot!" Waight snapped. "I told you to be careful of her hands. Hold her still while I . . ." Angie felt the hot sting of a tranquilizer dart. She continued to struggle, but her muscles stopped responding. She lay helpless in Crawley's grasp.

Blood ran freely from four deep gouges along his right cheek; they crossed the existing scar almost at right angles. His blood, hot and sticky, dripped onto her forehead.

"I'll make you sorry for this, Warden." His eyes were wild with fury.

"Suck ash, Admin," she forced out.

"Get up!" Waight demanded. "Get off of her!" She pushed Crawley aside. "Damn it! She's bruised three tips. Look, they're starting to swell already." Angie felt the doctor's probing fingers on her own, but was unable to move in response. She pictured again the wild swing at Crawley and felt the last of her control slip away.

"Take her into rehab," Waight said. "She obviously doesn't need any more muscle stimulation."

Crawley lifted her, and for a brief time she was conscious only of blurred walls and doors. Finally she was dumped onto a chaise in a small pale yellow room.

"Strap her in," Waight said as Angie tried to steady her vision. "That muscle relaxant will wear off fast." Crawley wrapped Velcro restraints around Angie's upper arms and across her thighs and ankles. Waight secured her wrists, then submerged her hands in separate troughs of transparent gel.

As her muscular control began to return, Angie fought the restraints. Her struggle resulted only in a grunt of satisfaction from Crawley. She stopped.

"I won't do it," she said. It came out in a rasping whisper.

Crawley wiped a hand across his cheek and looked down at the blood.

"Come on," Waight said, motioning toward the door. "She'll be safe enough here. The longer we wait to treat those cuts, the worse they'll scar. You found that out the last time."

Crawley's pale eyes darkened further, but he turned to the door without objection.

"I won't do it, Crawley!" Angie called after him. She counted slowly and very methodically to slow her heartbeat.

Finally, she looked down at her hands.

Chapter 4

~~~~~~~~~~~~~~~~~~~~~~~~~~~~~~~~
~~~~~~~~~~~~~~~~~~~~~~~~~~~~~~~~

"Oh, mother of mountains!" she moaned.

Angie had seen many holos of waterworlders, and she had even shaken hands once with a visiting Lesaat delegate. But nothing had prepared her to accept the snaking tendrils that now extended from her own wrists. Only the vague shape of true hands remained—flat central palms, each edged with five webbed tentacles. The tentacles were longer than the fingers they had replaced, and thinner by far. They writhed in slow, random movements through the viscous healing gel.

Each thin tendril ended in a tiny, needle-point nail, which explained the damage her wild swing had done to Crawley's face. As she watched, the tendril that should have been her left thumb curled upward. It twisted to display an underside lined with shallow, round depressions.

Angie gagged and turned away. By activating her telescopic vision, she could make out a fine web of cracks in the paint on one wall. They revealed an underlayer of dark green. The color of evergreens in deep shade, she thought. Even if it was just a layer of mildew, she wished they had left the wall green.

Lesaat, she thought. Earth's new South Pacific paradise.

She had only been ten years old when the waterplanet was discovered, but she could still remember the excitement in the news announcer's voice. "It has two great continents at the poles," he had crowed, "and a scattering of tropical coral atolls circling the equator. There's enough room for at least a third of Earth's population."

"Well, *I'm* not leaving these mountains," Angie had promptly declared.

Her father had laughed, and promised, "Nothing will ever get this family out of these mountains, Angie girl."

But something had. Prohibitive taxes had eventually forced Angie's mother into an office job in Denver. She had been killed in a commuter crash two years later, and within another two, Angie's father had been forced to sell their land, the last of the privately held ranches in the state, to the Company and move downslope. Shortly after, Angie had been accepted into the U.N. troubleshooter's school in Wyoming.

The widely exalted promise of Lesaat had not been realized either. The pole continents had turned out to be ice-covered year-round, and the atolls provided too small a land base to support great numbers of immigrants. Only a very few had relocated there to farm Earth-based algae in the nutrient-rich seas.

Algae! Angie thought. They've turned me into a fireloving algae farmer! Mother of mountains, Nori! How could you do this to me? She caught her breath in a sob, then angrily stopped. She forced her breathing to slow. In through the nose. Out, slowly, through the mouth. She tried to center her feelings, tried to reestablish enough calm to think.

My hands!

The dark green cracks swam out of focus.

Damn you, Nori!

Angie clutched at the anger, holding it tight in her mind. It was much easier to deal with than the pain of Nori's betrayal. Never get too close, she remembered thinking just moments before this horror had begun. She exhaled slowly through clenched teeth.

The hiss of the lock brought Angie's attention back to the door. It was Pua, wearing the same Think Wet! T-shirt hanging loose over faded shorts. Her hips were narrow, but her thighs were heavily muscled. A swimmer, Angie thought. This time, Pua kept her hands in plain sight. Her fingertips reached almost to her knees.

A fringe of white and yellow cloth was tied around one ankle; a braid of what looked like hair circled the other. Her long, wide—too wide—feet were encased in cloth slippers.

"What do you want?" Angie asked.

Pua lifted a hand to brush her long hair away from her face. The golden brown tendrils slid smoothly through the ebony mass. She crossed to Angie's side and looked down at the gel baths, then moved around her to draw aside a curtain of the same drab color as the room. Angie had not even noticed the curtain.

Behind a wall of windows, the Pacific shimmered brilliant blue under a midday sun.

Pua pressed her hands against the glass and stared out. The webs between her fingers were translucent, the thin flesh turned almost incandescent with the daylight glowing through. Her long, tapered fingers slid in graceful curves over the window's smooth surface. Angie forced herself to watch.

Pua's hands were smaller than her own—they looked a little small for the girl's body size—but otherwise they appeared identical to those extending from Angie's own wrists.

"They won't let me swim here," Pua said. "Outside in the open ocean, I mean. They say it's too dangerous."

The fingers of one hand slid inward until the hand became a fist, still pressed against the glass. "They're afraid I'll leave and never come back."

"Would you?" Angie didn't know what to say to her. It wasn't the girl's fault the Company had done this thing.

"Yes." Pua paused. Her fist opened, and she tapped a quick tattoo against the windowpane with her nails. "No. There's no place to go. There are too many people. This ocean doesn't taste right, and it's the wrong color. It doesn't sing . . ." She dropped her hands to her sides. "I hate it here. Earth is a stupid place."

"The whole Earth isn't like this recon station," Angie said. "Not all Earthers are like Waight and Crawley."

"Some of them are worse," Pua replied. "Doctor Waight took me to a swimming beach once, a place for station employees and their families." She pointed. "Down there. They had a big screen up over the whole beach, so people could lie outside without worrying about the sun. Hardly anybody was swimming. When some dolphins came near the shore, somebody started screaming, 'Sharks! Sharks!' and everybody ran up on the beach. It was really dumb."

Angie smiled in spite of herself. "I'd get out of the water in a hurry, too, if I thought there were sharks in there with me."

Pua snorted. "How can anybody mistake dolphins for a shark pack? They don't sound or feel anything alike."

Angie thought for a moment, then said, "We get sharks up in the mountains sometimes. Inspectors from admin—long on teeth and short on brains. Mostly, I ignore them."

The side of Pua's mouth lifted into a small smile. "We have that kind on Lesaat, too."

"So what happened down on the beach?" Angie asked. "Did you go in the water?"

Pua sighed. "Before I could convince Dr. Waight it was safe, somebody noticed my hands. He started pointing and saying things, and complaining about how squids shouldn't be allowed on public beaches. I told him to suck air, and he got mad and started kicking sand at me. Some other people started to say things then, so Dr. Waight made me leave."

She turned to face Angie. "Those were people who see waterworlders all the time here in the station. They work with them every day. Do you think people outside would act any different?" She cocked her head. "Would you, if you had met me before?"

She glanced down at Angie's hands, her look as much of a challenge as her words. She stepped forward and reached into one of the recon gel baths.

"Don't!" Angie said as rippling pressure ran the length of her fingers. She tried to pull away.

Pua giggled. "You're curling them backwards."

"Don't touch me, damn it!"

Abruptly, the grip around Angie's palm turned hard. Angie caught her breath in surprise, then winced as the pressure increased. She was helpless to return or even resist the girl's grip. "Enough!" she gasped finally. Instantly, the pressure released.

"If your hands still had bones, I could crack them," Pua said. She met Angie's look for a moment. "Just so you know."

Then, to Angie's surprise, she began stripping open the Velcro restraints. Angie considered her unexpected freedom for an instant, then swung her legs from the chaise and tried to stand. She stumbled forward, nearly falling, on limbs that felt like rubber. Her hands proved useless when she tried to use them to balance herself against the wall. She cursed, and sank to the floor in disgust.

Pua sighed. "This is going to be harder than I thought."

"What's that supposed to mean?" Angie demanded.

Pua lifted a small circular weight from the tray and brought it to Angie's side. She squatted and slipped it over the tip of Angie's left thumb. "Roll that up," she said. "Pull it into your palm."

"I'm not interested," Angie said. The weight dropped from her limp thumb. Pua snagged it with the tip of a finger before it reached the floor.

"You have to learn sometime," she said.

"What I have to do," Angie said, "is get out of here."

"I've been trying to get out for six months," Pua said. "And

I know how to trip just about any lock they can make. You'd
never have a chance. Anyway, where would you go? What could
you do? With those, I mean, when you can't even use them?"
She gestured toward Angie's hands.

Angie stared down at her trembling fingers. Work with what
you have, she thought. The troubleshooters' unofficial motto
mocked her. She tried to fold her hands into fists. The webbed
lower sections responded well enough, but her thin fingers
twisted and tangled, totally beyond her control.

Pua fitted the weight back onto Angie's thumb. "Hold it
there," she said.

Angie held her breath and tried. What choice do I have? she
thought. There was only one medical facility on Earth that could
fully restore her hands, and it was owned and operated by World
Life. If she was ever to find a way out of this, she was going to
have to do *something*.

"No, no. Not that way," Pua said. "Here, watch me."

Angie watched, then tried again. Unsuccessfully. "There
aren't any bones to use as leverage. How do you control which
way the muscles move?"

"Pretend it's your tongue."

"What?"

"Your tongue doesn't have any bones, and you move it well
enough," Pua said.

Angie became suddenly conscious of her tongue. It felt huge
in her mouth. She curled it, first up, then down against the backs
of her teeth.

Pua rolled the weighted thumb inward toward Angie's palm.
"Hold it there," she said. "No, don't try to move it. Just think
about your tongue and hold your hand steady." She tightened
the curl of Angie's thumb.

Angie frowned, and focused her attention on her thumb and
her tongue.

"That's good!" Pua cried, and the weight promptly slipped
off Angie's unintentionally relaxed thumb. Pua sighed. "Well,
pretty good."

Angie stared at her hand. She focused on the thumb again,
trying to curl it in toward her palm. It wavered for a moment, but then began to turn inward. She pressed her tongue
against the roof of her mouth and curled the thumb tighter.
Pua looked up at her and grinned.

"See?" she said. "It's easy. Dr. Waight will hook you up to
the biofeedback machines soon. They have a standard set of

training exercises they put all the regular tankers through. But doing it with your tongue is better—it takes less time.''

"How do *you* know how much time it takes?" Angie asked.

Pua looked quickly down at her hands. "I—I don't really." She glanced up. "I'm just guessing."

Angie shook her head and smiled. She found herself actually liking this strange girl. "I'll tell you what, Waterbaby. If you'll teach me how to use these hands without Waight and Crawley monitoring my every move, I'll teach you how to tell a proper lie. You'll never survive here otherwise."

The challenge returned to Pua's eyes. "Nobody else around here knows when I'm lying. So, how come you think *you* can? Here, hold that steady. Good. Now try it with the other hand. Don't move it. Just hold it still."

"Reading people's voices and body language is a big part of how I make my living," Angie said. "It lets me know when I can trust someone." Watching the delicate precision of Pua's fingers as she adjusted the tiny weights, Angie found it hard to believe these were the same hands that had caused her such crushing pain earlier.

"My dad said you should always find out what a person wants most before you trust them," Pua said. Suddenly, she laughed. "Look at your hand."

Angie looked down. The long slender fingers of her left hand had wrapped neatly around one of the narrow legs of the tray. She was gripping the plastic post loosely, but securely. In her surprise, Angie almost let go. More by relaxing than by concentrating, she retained the hold. She tried to move one finger, and watched in amazement as it uncurled and rose in slow, uneven increments. She laughed and relaxed, and it wrapped around the tray leg again.

Pua was beaming, genuinely pleased.

Angie watched her for a moment before asking, "What is it *you* want most, Pua?"

Pua's smile disappeared. She straightened. "I want you to take me to Pukui."

"Pukui?"

"That's my reef on Lesaat."

Angie's hand slipped from the tray. She pulled her feet under her and stood. "I'm *not going* to Lesaat!"

Pua didn't move. Only her eyes shifted as Angie took a step forward. "Dr. Waight wants to keep me for her experiments, but if you promise to do what Mr. Crawley wants, he'll fix it so you can take me with you. I know he can do it. He's the one who's really in charge.''

"I won't do what Crawley wants," Angie said. "And even if he does find a way to force me off-planet, I'm sure as hell not going to take—"

"I could help you."

"I don't need any help. Spit!" Angie cursed as she stumbled on her weakened legs.

"What are you going to do when they put you in the water?" Pua asked.

Angie stiffened. She lifted a slow hand to the side of her neck.

"I was there when they tested your gills," Pua said.

Angie had forgotten all about the gills. The velvety touch of her new fingers ran down a sensitive line which she knew from holos must be the outer edge of a gill flap.

"Dr. Waight thought your panic was just a reaction to being taken from the dep tank so suddenly," Pua said, "but I could tell you were really scared. I could taste it. You were afraid to go under the water."

Angie remembered. During her dark sleep in the dep tank, she had relived the nightmare of that stupid boating accident she'd had the year before. She shuddered as she recalled the horror of icy suffocation she had experienced while being sucked through an underground river channel. I thought I had dealt with that fear, she thought. Then she admitted reluctantly that her way of dealing with it had been just to stay away from the water.

She swallowed hard and leaned against the side of the chaise, wishing she could hurl it across the room instead. Her hands refused to fold into fists.

"They won't care," Pua said. "When they find out, they'll just push you under water and hold you there."

"I'll let them drown me," Angie replied.

Pua snorted. "You can't drown! Your lungs seal off as soon as your face is submerged, and your gills start feeding oxygen right into your bloodstream. If you take me with you, and we go right away, I can go into the water with you. In the beginning, I mean, until it doesn't scare you so much. Then after you do the job they want, you can look for a way to get your other hands back. That's what *you* want most. I can tell."

Work with what you have, Angie thought.

"You need me, Mountainlady," Pua said.

Spit!

"What do they want me to do out there, anyway?"

Pua blinked. Trying to decide whether to lie or not, Angie thought. She's settled on me as her best bet for getting home, but she's smart enough not to trust me.

"I think they want you to find the TC records," Pua said. It was at least a partial truth. "Or maybe the algae's broken out of the holding pens. There might have been a big storm or something."

Or something, was Angie's guess.

Pua pushed away from the wall and crossed to the chaise. She leaned across it, resting her chin on her crossed hands. Her fingers dangled for a moment, then wrapped neatly around her wrists. "Do you know much about algae farming?"

Angie shook her head. "The only waterfarms I've ever seen were on news holos. I once saw a pirated training tape on algae-farming techniques, but that's about it. I don't know anything about how they process the protein-conversion enzymes." Only land-owning waterworlders and high-ranking Company scientists were privy to that information.

Pua frowned.

"Tell me about these records they're looking for," Angie said. "How did they get lost?"

Pua hesitated again, then again apparently settled on the truth. "My mom hid them, before . . ." She looked down, then quickly back up. Her unblinking stare was defiant.

"What are the records about?" Angie asked.

"They tell how to process the new total-conversion enzyme my mom and dad made," Pua said. "The Company wants to claim the rights to making it, so they can—"

"A total *protein*-conversion enzyme?" Angie suddenly remembered Nori talking about a new total-conversion enzyme on Lesaat. Could he have been telling the truth? The Company had been promising such an advance for so long that very few took the claims seriously anymore.

Pua was nodding. "It makes it so people can get all the protein they need from just eating grains. It makes all those amino acid things, or something. I tried it once, but I didn't like only eating cereal. There are too many good things to eat on the reef."

Angie frowned. "Pua, are you sure you know what you're talking about?"

Pua straightened. "Ask Mr. Crawley, if you don't believe me. He keeps asking *me* about it."

"Mother of mountains," Angie muttered. If a way had been

found to allow humans to synthesize *all* the essential amino acids from just cereal grains, there could truly be an end to world hunger. This could provide a real chance for eventual large-scale human expansion through the wormhole nexus as well, since feeding large groups on extended journeys had so far proved to be a critically limiting factor.

Angie shook her head. She wondered if she was experiencing a relapse into the hallucinations of her long sleep. Still, the existence of such a valuable commodity would explain why the Company was willing to take the chance of turning a ranking troubleshooter into a waterworlder against her will. The potential profits, not to mention the probable payoffs within the U.N. itself, would be enormous.

"Uncle Fatu told me we could make enough TC just at Pukui to feed half the Earthers," Pua said.

"If this stuff is real, why did your folks hide it?" Angie asked. "I should think they'd have been eager to get it on the market. They could easily have convinced the Company to pay them a hefty percentage of the profits."

Again Pua hesitated. "I don't know," she said finally. It was a very definite lie. Angie lifted a brow.

Pua glared. "My dad refused to give the processing records to the Company because he was afraid if he gave up control, they would restrict production just to keep the price real high."

"Pua, not even World Life could afford to be that greedy. There are too many starving people here on Earth."

"They already restrict the *partial*-conversion enzyme. They have a big stockpile they never even use," Pua said. "And that's the *truth*!"

It was. At least the girl believed it to be. Angie tried again to fold her hands into fists. Even if she had a way to get her own hands back right now, she knew she couldn't use it. There was no way she could walk away from *this*. The troubleshooters had been trying to catch World Life in a major, *provable* criminal activity for as long as she had been in the service. It was the only hope the U.N. and the rest of the world governments had of ever breaking the Company's hold over the Earth.

Slowly, awkwardly, Angie's fingers coiled inward toward her palms.

"Total regrowth is expensive," Crawley said later, when Angie made her demands.

"So is my cooperation," she replied. "I want guaranteed

regrowth of my own hands as soon as the job on Lesaat is finished.''

"What else?'' His smile was smug. He hadn't even asked her
why she had changed her mind.

"While I'm in the field, I want twice the top-rank troubleshooters' pay and full privileges—that means total cooperation
from the Company and its local reps, Crawley.''

"I'm familiar with troubleshooters' field rules,'' he said.

"I also want all off-world bonuses, I want to take Pua with
me, and I want to leave immediately.''

The last brought a momentary frown. They want me out there,
but not quite yet, she thought. I wonder why. She remembered
that Waight had shown concern at her earlier-than-expected
awakening.

"You'll need at least two weeks of training with those hands
before you go,'' Crawley said.

"Two weeks as Waight's guinea pig, you mean,'' Angie said.
"I'm not interested. Pua can teach me what I need to know. I
don't plan to keep these things long. Also, Pua knows Lesaat.
She *cares* about it. I want someone with me I can trust.''

"You would trust Pua?'' He laughed. "Warden, you disap-
point me.''

"I also want full title to the Central Forest Preserve.''

Crawley's breath caught. "That's impossible! The Company
never gives away ownership of Earth properties.''

Angie relaxed against the back of the chaise. He stared at her.

"I might be able to arrange a lease,'' he said slowly.

"Clear title,'' she said.

To her surprise, he remained silent. He actually seemed to be
considering her demand. World Life *never* gave up land titles.
She had only asked for the preserve to take a measure of how
seriously they needed her on Lesaat.

"All right,'' he said. "I'll arrange it. But you get the title
transfer and medical payoff *after* the job is finished, and *only* if
it's finished.''

"Post the contract on the public net,'' she said quickly, to
disguise her amazement. There was little doubt now that at least
part of what Pua had told her was true.

Crawley frowned again. "High-security channels only.''

"Good enough.'' Angie knew enough people with security
access to be certain the contract would be noticed and remembered. The details would remain private to all but a very few,
but numerous copies would be placed in protected storage. There

would be no way for the terms to be changed after she had left Earth. Crawley's expression made it clear that he understood her reasoning.

"Tell me something, Crawley," she said. "Why did you choose me for this particular assignment?"

He glanced down at her hands, then returned his cool look to her face. "You were the only ranking shooter we could find who was interested in going off-planet."

Slowly, Angie reminded herself. Breathe very slowly.

"Just what is it you want me to do?" she asked in a dead-calm voice. "I'm sure you know my troubleshooting experience has been primarily land-based."

His smile was slow, but telling. It made it clear that he knew about her river accident, and was pleased to be sending her to a place where she would have to face her fear of the water. This had become a very personal contest between them. He picked at the sealant bandage on his cheek, realized what he was doing, and pulled his hand away.

"You've already heard about the TC enzyme," he said. "Your job is to find the missing records and save Pukui Reef. We want you to salvage the samples that are hidden somewhere in the growing pens before the winter storms spill the overgrown Earth algae into the open lagoon. If that happens, the algae will grow wild and eventually kill the reef."

It disgusted but did not surprise Angie that Crawley had been monitoring her talk with Pua. She had already guessed that the girl hadn't reached her so easily by accident. It had occurred to her that Pua might be part of the deception, but somehow that didn't feel right.

"Is what Pua said about the Company restricting the partial-conversion enzyme true?" she asked. "That would be highly illegal if I'm not mistaken."

"Of course it's not true," he said. His lie was as clear to her as the bandage that covered his scarred cheek.

Oh, Sally, she thought, I hope you have your investigator's nose to the ground out there, because I am caught in this one deep and dirty. There's no way in hell they're going to let me come back to Earth to expose all this. And there's no way at all that I can refuse to go. Not with the entire human future at stake.

"I'll need access to waterfarm production techniques and information on local politics and lifestyle," she told Crawley. "I presume you have tapes on both."

"You can study the farm-management holos during transit,"

he said. "As for the other, you'll be going in as temporary farm boss. Your authority, as long as you stay within the law, will be absolute as far as the waterworlders are concerned. There's no reason for you to be concerned with local customs."

Angie lifted her brows, but he didn't seem to notice.

"I'll give you a list of people we want you to locate and question," he said. "Your troubleshooter's rank, and the U.N.'s Statement of Urgent Need we've acquired, will empower you to truth-probe as many waterworlders as you need to get the information we want."

Angie felt a cold chill of anger go down her back. So *that* was it. Only a fully ranked troubleshooter could administer truth drugs against an individual's will, and then only under specific and very critical circumstances. She wasn't being sent out to solve a humanitarian problem, or even an ecological one. She was being sent out to secure the Company's future profits.

She remembered that Nori had said something about the Company needing a ranking troubleshooter on Lesaat. She wondered what would have happened if she had fallen for his recruitment pitch earlier? Would he have stopped her from going out to that fire? Would there have been a fire?

"There are already Company security guards at Pukui to assist you," Crawley said. "We've been authorized to send Earth waterguards out if that becomes necessary."

"Why would I need Company marines?" she asked. World Life's gilled police force was only called on for the most violent of Earth's conflicts. To her knowledge, they had never been sent off-planet. "I should think everyone involved would be eager for the missing records to be found. As both farm boss and an official U.N. rep, I should be receiving full cooperation."

"There are . . . factions on Lesaat," he said, "that would rather see Pukui Reef lost than give up control of the TC's potential profits. It's not the *Company* that wants to restrict processing, Warden. It's the damn waterworlders who think they can take the law into their own hands and get away with it."

It became dirtier and dirtier.

"What about Pua?" Angie said. Now that her decision was made, Angie found herself eager to go. Crawley was clearly not going to give her any further useful information. Remaining in his presence would only fuel her anger, and she already had a surfeit of that.

"We want you to find out as much as you can about Pua, too," Crawley said.

Angie laughed. "I'm sure you do, Admin, but that's not what I meant, and it's not part of the contract. Whoever—whatever—Pua is, is her own business. I just want to know the legalities of taking her with me."

Crawley stared at her for a moment. "You'll be certified as Pua's legal guardian for the length of your stay on Lesaat. When you return to Earth, you'll have to bring her back here. Minors can't stay on Lesaat without family." His smile was entirely without humor. "She won't be pleased when she learns her little trick to get back home didn't work."

Angie smiled back. "You might be interested to know that Pua wasn't the first one to tell me about the total-conversion enzyme."

"What?" Crawley's dark skin paled. His eyes turned hard. "Who told you?"

"Your 'recruitment' officer," she said. "Back at the forest preserve, before the fire."

"Yoshida?" Crawley's voice had turned to ice.

Welcome to hell, Nori love, Angie mused.

Angie stared at the great mound of Mauna Loa as she and Pua were ferried from the recon station in South Kona to the Ka'a spaceport on the southeast shore of Hawaii Island. Mauna Loa, like her sister mountain, Mauna Kea, rose to almost fourteen thousand feet above sea level. Measured from the sea floor, they were the two tallest mountains on earth.

Their peaks each bore a layer of snow, incongruously white against the fierce azure sky. Observatory domes, once used by Earth's best astronomers, stood stark and empty. They housed museums now, the pilot explained, but few people cared to brave the altitude to visit them.

Great swaths of hardened lava streaked Mauna Loa's smooth slopes. Some stretched all the way to the sea, particularly near the southern tip of the island. On the flatlands, near the shore, the ground was dry and barren. There was a tropical rain forest to the northeast, Angie knew, but it was hard to believe any such lushness could exist so near this windswept lava desert.

Somewhat to Angie's surprise, Pua remained silent throughout the long ride. She sat slumped against the back of her seat. The only time she glanced up was when the pilot pointed out the Hawaiian settlement at South Point.

"Government gave the Point to the Hawaiians back at the turn of the century," the pilot said. "Officially, it was part of the

Native Reparations Act, repayment for the U.S. overthrow of the monarchy a century before that. It was really just a payoff, to get the locals to stop opposing the spaceport."

"My mom was born at South Point," Pua said so softly Angie almost didn't hear. "That's where they were supposed to take me after she and Daddy died." She slumped back in her seat again, head bent forward so that her hair blocked Angie's view of her face. Moisture splashed onto the back of the bulky gloves Crawley had insisted they both wear while they were still on Earth. She quickly rubbed it away.

"Good riddance to bad real estate, if you ask me," the pilot said.

Angie watched Pua for a time, then looked down again. It disturbed her to think that this flat, desolate stretch of land might be her last view of Earth. She turned her look back to the mountain, but gathering clouds had obscured its distant peak.

Chapter 5

~~~~~~~~~~~~~~~~~~~~~~~~~~~~
~~~~~~~~~~~~~~~~~~~~~~~~~~~~

At the ship captain's order, Angie and Pua were billeted separately from the other Lesaat immigrants.

"New tankers and management personnel don't mix," the captain explained. "I don't like trouble on my ship, so I want you and the girl to stay out of sight up here in crew quarters. The girl especially. Some of the squids were forced to leave kids of their own behind. They won't take well to her at all."

Angie was pleased to note that she could now consciously form her hands into fists. Forcing them to relax after the captain left proved considerably more difficult.

As soon as they were under way, Pua established a regimen of exercises that Angie followed assiduously during the ten-day passage. She rolled weighted fingers and squeezed tension bars even while eating or studying holotapes of Lessat's algae-production techniques.

There was frustratingly little information about the latter. There was no mention of the new TC enzyme in the tapes, of course, but Angie had expected at least a comprehensive explanation of the everyday algae-farm operations—not to mention better quality holos.

"What're you doing?" Pua asked as she attempted to adjust one of the tapes for proper viewing.

"Trying to change the damn color."

"Why?"

Angie shifted her gaze from the holo's shimmering sea to Pua's curious look. "Are you telling me it's *supposed* to be yellow?"

"I told you that Earth ocean was the wrong color," Pua replied.

Angie frowned and turned back to the holo. She asked the computer for a water-content analysis.

Like Earth's oceans, the Lesaat seas were alive with micro-organisms. To a depth of about twelve meters, single-celled di-noflagellates created a rich layer of plankton. On Lesaat, this microscopic algae reflected light in the yellow and orange wave-lengths rather than in the blue as on Earth, and thus turned the sea gold. The waterworld plankton was bioluminescent as well, the computer went on, so that the seas were lit at night from below the surface.

"The coral and trees and stuff light up at night, too," Pua said. "It never gets real dark like on Earth, only a little when Shadow's high. And not even then if either of the moons is up."

"Shadow?" Angie asked.

"The shadow the planet makes when the sun is on the other side," Pua replied. "It's called an eclipse."

Angie took a deep breath and returned her attention to the production tape.

"What's all this about pumping cold water up from the deep ocean?" she asked later, while viewing a particularly vague tape. "I understand the need for the energy-conversion cham-ber, but I thought Lesaat was supposed to provide the perfect environment for growing Earth-based algae."

"It does," Pua replied. "There's lots of natural inflows of deep ocean water—that's what keeps the lagoons clean. But we need the pipes and pumps to control how fast the algae grows."

She pointed into the holo to a large pipe that ran along the center of the inner reef under the algae pens. "Water from down deep has lots of nutrients. So, when we want the algae to grow faster, we open the valves along this main feeder pipe. The ocean water mixes with the lagoon water and feeds the algae."

She shifted her pointing fingers to two smaller pipes running parallel, one to each side of the larger, central tube. "When we want the algae to stop growing so fast, we make the water go through these secondary pipes. They don't have outlets, and they're not insulated, so the lagoon water around them gets real cold. I guess algae doesn't like to be cold. I don't either, but sometimes I have to do it when I want to swim deep, especially outside the lagoon."

Pua pulled her hand back and separated out a single, long strand of her ebony hair. "Pukui's lucky," she said. "There's an almost straight channel, an old lava tube, that leads right through the outer barrier reef. That's where the main deep-water pipe is laid. One end hangs down into the deep ocean where it's really cold, and the other leads into the lagoon. At other farms, they have to run the main pipe through natural passes, or sometimes even over the top of the barrier reefs. They're kind of ugly.'' She squinted as she examined the single hair closely.

''Why don't they cut underwater passages?'' Angie asked. ''The coral can't be that dense.''

''They've tried that, but there's one kind of really sharp coral that grows fast in places where the reef's been damaged,'' Pua said. ''It grows around the pipe and punches holes in it. Besides, blasting on the reef can make the fish and stuff get cigarettes. Then you can't eat 'em 'cause they'll make you sick.''

''I believe the technical term for that is ciguatera,'' Angie said with a smile.

Pua shrugged. She lifted the hair very precisely with the thin, sharp tips of her fingernails.

''Pua, *what* are you doing?''

Pua glanced up at her. ''Trying to decide whether you're ready to try picking this up without your nails snipping it off. You're still awful clumsy when it comes to precision movements.''

Angie gave a quick demonstration of how precisely she could now mimic Pua's favorite rude hand signal, then turned back to the tape. Pua laughed, smoothed the hair back into place, and joined her. She leaned across Angie's shoulder to poke a long finger into the shimmering holo.

''This isn't really what a harvest barge looks like,'' she said. ''They're a lot smaller and dirtier. They're flatter, too, and don't have that thing they call a drying cage on top. The drying is done inside. It's part of the processing.''

''Crawley told me these tapes were up-to-date,'' Angie said.

''Well, he was wrong. See how they show the machine sucking the algae from the center of the net? It's never done that way unless the algae is already dead and is just going to be destroyed.''

She motioned again with her thin finger. ''The prime algae is along the inside edges of the net where it gets plenty of light and nutrients. The swimmers have to get inside the net and vacuum it onto the barge by hand, otherwise the net tears and the algae spills out. That's why standard Earthers can't work on Lesaat. Their fingers are too short and stubby to untangle the net and pick the little bits of algae out. Their nails aren't sharp enough either.'' She clicked her own sharp nails together in a short, staccato beat. She did that often, as if testing her own dexterity.

''When the middle part gets too old and rotten, they blow up the methane that's in it and let it burn. That kills all the algae so they can clean it out safely and start a fresh batch.''

She motioned again toward the holo. ''If they did it this way, too much of the live algae would escape. It's a lot harder to clean up a spill than to just contain it right in the first place.''

Angie nodded. That part she understood. The first, and most impressive, of the holotapes had been a history of algae farming on Lesaat. It described how the first settlers had destroyed entire reefs in their eagerness to exploit the planet's potential.

The 410 partial-conversion enzyme had been discovered decades before at the Company-run aquaculture labs in Hawaii, but had proved of little practical value. Not enough of the particular blue-green algae from which the enzyme was processed could be grown in Earth's polluted seas to make it profitable. No economical way to synthesize the enzyme was ever found, so neither the Company nor the world's poor benefited from the discovery.

When the wormhole nexus was opened at midcentury and water-rich but land-poor Lesaat was discovered, the 410 PC suddenly become important news again. The disappointment over Lesaat's inability to provide a physical outlet for Earth's excess population was tempered by the discovery that its warm tropical seas provided an ideal growing environment for 410's Earth-algae base.

The first settlers turned the Earth algae loose to grow wild across several prime lagoons. The aquatic environment proved so perfectly suited for its rapid growth, however, that it quickly spread and bloomed out of control over all submerged portions of the reefs. Because of the storm season and their own unpreparedness, the settlers were unable to harvest it fast enough to save the underlying coral.

The algae masses grew denser and denser until, finally, sunlight could no longer pass through. Without oxygen, the underlying coral and its own symbiotic coralline algae died. Without the nutritive base the living reef provided, the Earth algae died as well. Within a single storm season, three entire atolls were turned into useless hulks. It would be a hundred years or more before a fully functioning coral ecology could re-form, if it ever could at all.

''You know that ocean next to the Hawaii recon center?'' Pua said. ''It tasted kind of like the dead reefs on Lesaat. I don't know why that stupid Company doesn't do something to clean it up.''

Angie shifted the tension bar to her fingertips and squeezed, carefully, smoothly, over and over again. "Because now that they have Lesaat, there's not enough easy profit in it," she said.

"Well, Earther's should stop making so many babies, then," Pua said. "Then there could be enough food for everybody."

Unfortunately, that's not profitable, either, Angie thought. It was widely believed, but had never been proven, that World Life Company still surreptitiously supported the powerful anti-birth-control lobby. Early in the century, the group had gotten strict anti-abortion and anti-birth-control laws enacted in many third-world countries, a situation that had resulted in an immediate and dramatic population boom.

In response, residents of other parts of the world had begun deliberately to increase their own numbers for fear of being overrun by people and cultures different from their own. World Life, with its growing control over the world's food distribution, had reaped enormous benefits.

"Earthers are stupid," Pua said. Angie squeezed the tension bar again.

When she wasn't working with her hands or watching the tape, Angie exercised the rest of her body. The muscle tone and coordination that had been diminished by her lengthy stay in the EM field quickly returned.

"You have strong arms," Pua said once while they were arm wrestling. It was an exercise Angie had suggested to help increase her grip strength. "You'll make a good swimmer if we can ever get your head underwater."

Angie looked up at her sharply—

—and Pua slammed their hands to the countertop.

"Spit!" Angie muttered. The girl had done it again, broken her concentration with the simplest of tricks.

"Pay attention, Mountainlady," Pua said without smiling. "Pay attention to *everything*! All the time. It's the only way—" She paused, brows lifted.

"—To survive on Lesaat," Angie finished. "I remember." She rubbed the sting from her fingers and set her elbow back on the counter. "Come on. Let's try it again."

It wasn't until the last day, while they were waiting to board the groundside shuttle, that Angie finally won an arm-wrestling match. Pua used no mental tricks in the contest, and when it was finished she looked to be almost as satisfied as Angie that they had reached relative parity in purely physical strength. She rubbed her shoulder and smiled at her own defeat while Angie winced over sore fingers.

"Don't challenge anyone on the ride down," Pua advised as the call came for them to board the shuttle. She laughed very softly. "There's no way you could do that twice in one day. Come on, let's go."

Angie kept her expression carefully neutral as she stepped into the shuttle's windowless passenger bay. At Pua's insistence, she had not worn the concealing gloves Crawley had given them. "This is Lesaat," Pua had said. "Real waterworlders aren't ashamed of their hands." Meeting the curious stares of the new recruits who would be descending with them, Angie saw that it had been strategically wise advice.

The best seat, aside from those reserved for herself and Pua, was taken by a woman who openly displayed her new hands with their elongated, webbed fingers. She even wore a red ribbon around her bare neck, a clear statement that she was not embarrassed by her physical changes—that she was, in fact, proud of them. Like the others, the woman stared first at Angie's hands, then at her face. When Pua entered the bay, the woman frowned slightly, but did not join in the sudden, soft buzz of conversation. Her look, as it returned to Angie, was filled with both curiosity and challenge.

So, Angie mused, you want to know the pecking order. She nodded to the woman as if she knew her, waited just long enough to recognize the woman's instant of confusion, then slid her hand across the back of the seat, in plain view, as she ushered Pua into the inside seat. Pua snapped on her safety harness, then stared straight ahead at the scarred metal bulkhead. She did not speak again until the shuttle was on the ground.

Which was just as well, Angie decided. Keeping herself from screaming in the claustrophobic bay was taking all the energy she had. It felt like a coffin, and she echoed Pua's sigh of relief when they finally touched the ground.

As the shuttle taxied to a stop, a man's voice spoke over the comm system. Water transportation was waiting for the farm workers, he said. Their personal baggage would be transferred by the Lesaat ground crew. Without further greeting, he began calling a list of names and numbers, farm assignments for the new recruits. The names, Angie realized after the first several had been called, were the farms; the tankers were referred to only by number. She blew out a tight breath and glanced at Pua.

The girl was still staring at the forward bulkhead, frowning deeply. Her long fingers were wrapped tightly around the safety harness mesh.

"Warden Dinsman?"

Angie looked up. A short, dark-haired woman—a water-worlder, Angie saw by her neck and hands—stood in the aisle beside her. Angie nodded.

"My name is Tulina Sanchez. I'm the Company ground rep. If you'll follow me, I'll show you where you can stow your things before the committee meeting."

Angie frowned. "What committee?"

The woman's brows lifted in surprise. "The World Life Farm Management Committee. They're here to advise you on how to proceed at Pukui. And Doctor Haili will want to examine . . ."

Angie unhooked her harness and stood. She was a full head taller than the ground rep. Sanchez stepped back slightly.

"I prefer going directly to Pukui," Angie said.

"I know you're eager to get to the farm, Ms. Dinsman, but—"

"I don't work through committees, and I have no need to see a Company doctor. If your people have anything important to offer, tell them to bring it to the reef. Let's go, Pua."

Pua released her harness and stood.

"According to the very *personal* greeting these workers just received," Angie said, glancing back at the attentive tankers, "there is immediate transport to Pukui waiting."

"But that's just a hydrobus," Sanchez said. "A flitter will be assigned to you right after—"

"The bus will be just fine," Angie said. The last thing she wanted to do right now was to get into a Company-maintained flitter. She stepped into the aisle, forcing Sanchez back farther, then waved Pua ahead of her to the exit. The ground rep immediately began murmuring into her wrist comm. The ribboned tanker laughed.

The shuttle was parked inside a large, open hangar. Sunlight pouring through the translucent roof cast bright, golden light, eerily shadowless. The air was humid and smelled of machine oil and shuttle exhaust, and rotting tropical foliage. In the distance, the sea glinted gold, more vivid even than in the holos.

Angie walked swiftly across the hangar, following the string of blue floor lights the announcer had said would lead to the Pukui-bound vessel. In the distance she could hear the sounds of heavy machinery.

One side of the hangar led back to the runway where they had just landed. Two others opened onto docks and a dead-calm, golden-tinted harbor. As they neared the dock area, Angie activated her polarizers against the glare of the sun on the golden water. She drew deep breaths of the moist, warm air.

Extended focus showed that the white line on the horizon was foaming waves, breaking against some barrier. Coral reef or a human-built breakwater—it was impossible to tell. A dark line of low islets far off to the left indicated at least a partial barrier reef. The hangar's fourth side was attached by covered walkways to a squat, ugly building—cement block and plastic, smeared here and there with what looked like rust but was probably just accumulations of tropical sludge. It looked little different from other isolated Company headquarters Angie had seen.

Beyond the office building was Lesaat's single town of Landing, spread in typical, port-town squalor. Its appearance was as drab as its name, although Pua had assured her that at the end of each successful harvest, the Company squids brought the dismal place to life. Somehow, Angie had expected something better from a permanent planetary HQ.

There was only the one shuttle in the oversized hangar, but a row of flitters and what looked like a full-sized hydrobus were parked on the side adjoining the building. The grounded bus was in obvious disrepair. A pair of workers in faded green overalls gestured in heated discussion at the bus's side. Others, similarly dressed, bustled between the shuttle and various parts of the hangar, transferring supplies.

A Company security squad lounged at the far end of the main building. Their attitudes were casual, but Angie recognized their careful vigilance as she and Pua walked quickly across the open hangar.

"Ms. Dinsman," Sanchez called. She was having difficulty keeping up. "Ms. Dinsman, please . . ."

Pua remained close at Angie's side. "That one," she said as they neared the waterfront, and she began walking even faster. A hydrofoil, similar to the one inside, bobbed gently near the end of a short secondary loading dock. It was the smallest of four such craft berthed along the waterway.

A crewman aboard the Pukui bus looked up at their approach.

"It's Uncle Fatu!" Pua murmured, and a brief smile touched her lips.

He was a huge man, at least half a head taller than Angie and more than twice her girth. He was dressed only in a waist-wrap of patterned blue cloth and—Angie blinked to extended focus again—*tattoos!* Large, intricately patterned semicircles darkened each side of his torso above his . . .

. . . *lavalava*. The memory of a long-past assignment in the South Pacific slid into place. Angie had seen such attire and similar tattoos on a very old man in Western Samoa. She wondered if this "Uncle Fatu's" tattoos extended all the way to his knees as the elderly high chief had assured her a proper Samoan man's should. Angie had thought the old man was the last of his kind.

Uncle Fatu stood slowly. His dark eyes widened as Pua stepped onto the dock. He called something to the boat pilot, then started forward as if to greet them. As he was about to leave the hydrobus, he frowned and stopped.

Angie caught movement in her peripheral vision. She stopped and turned back. Another man was striding toward them across the hangar. He, too, was tall, although not as tall as the Pukui crewman. His eyes had the same, slightly Asiatic tilt as Pua's, but as he drew close, Angie saw that they were the color of the Hawaiian sky, a visual indication of at least some Caucasian ancestry.

Judging from the shape of his thighs and shoulders, Angie suspected he was a strong swimmer. His clothing was as nondescript as any of the hangar workers', but he walked with the sure step of authority. His expression was stern.

Admin, Angie decided.

"Shark," Pua hissed softly. She stayed close at Angie's back. "Doctor Haili, she—"

The man brushed past the ground rep. He stopped in front of Angie. Hands, not as quite as alien as her own, rolled into fists at his hips.

"What do you think you're doing?" he demanded. He looked beyond Angie, and his expression turned angry.

Pua said nothing, but Angie felt a strong hand grip the back of her shirt.

"Is there something we can do for you, Inspector?" she said, hoping Pua's reference to sharks meant what she thought it did. He was staring at her hands.

The man's start of surprise indicated that she was right, even if that was not his public title. His frown deepened. "You can get over to the committee hall and start doing your job," he said.

He pointed toward Pua. His long finger was remarkably steady. "And *you*, young lady, can get yourself directly to my office. You're not leaving Landing.'' The grip on Angie's shirt grew tighter.

"Pua is coming with me,'' Angie said.

He shook his head. "Children aren't allowed on the reefs unless they're with family,'' he said. "That's the law. They're not even allowed on-planet unless they're born here.''

"I'm her auntie,'' Angie said.

"And I'm her favorite uncle,'' he returned. "Look, Warden, you weren't sent out here to babysit. You have a bigger job to do, and the atolls are dangerous. Pua could get in real trouble out there.''

A small crowd had gathered around them. Three men and two women. Angie recognized them from the shuttle. She was relieved to see that the woman with the red ribbon was not among them. She wasn't sure how much more calm she could manufacture. She needed open air and a direct line of sight to the horizon, even if that horizon was the wrong color. She felt as if she had been transported directly from the fire on the mountain to this burning golden seaworld, with only a slice of hell in between.

How the fireloving hell did this happen? she wondered. And more to the point, How am I going to get out of it? She wondered why this Company man was trying so hard to get his hands on Pua. She recognized from his name that he was the planetary superintendent, the official liaison between Lesaat and Earth, or, more practically, between World Life Admin and the U.N. He was paid by World Life. He's probably been told to put Pua on the next ship back to earth.

The inspector had noticed the others, also. He waved a hand toward the bus. "Get aboard,'' he ordered.

The five tankers shifted their gazes to Angie. One of the women, Angie saw, was still having trouble focusing her new implants. She blinked repeatedly at persistent tears from her left eye.

"You the Pukui boss?'' one of the men asked.

Angie nodded.

"You want us aboard that tub—'' He eyed the inspector for a moment, then turned back to her. *"—boss?''*

Angie smiled slightly, then nodded again. "Now's as good a time as any. Tell the pilot to be ready to cast off as soon as I come aboard. Anything that's not loaded now can be dealt with later.'' She stepped aside so the tankers could pass her on the narrow loading dock. "Pua, go with them.''

"Warden, please. Leave her here at Landing," the inspector said. His voice grew quieter, more intense. "I'll see that she's taken care—"

"I can take care of myself," Pua said.

"Your *folks* couldn't even take care of themselves out there, Pua," he said.

"Don't you talk about my—"

"Pua, get on the bus. Right now," Angie said. To her relief, Pua's hold on her shirt released.

"Look, Inspector," Angie went on. "The girl is part of a deal I struck when I agreed to come out here. Check my contract if that'll make you feel better, but she stays with me."

She straightened. "Now, if you or any of your *committee* members want to help get Pukui back on-line, you're welcome to come out and work shifts in the algae pens along with the rest of the squids. Otherwise, stay the hell out of my hair until I call for a harvest crew."

His mouth tightened. He stared at her for a moment more, then turned to stride back across the hangar. Toward the flitters, Angie noted, not toward the committee hall. The ground rep was headed toward the hall.

Angie blew out a slow breath. That had *not* been a standard, by-the-book Company man. She turned back toward the bus— and nearly tripped over Pua.

"Cold spit on the fire lines, girl!" she snapped. "Don't you *ever* do what you're told?"

Chapter 6

~~~~~~~~~~~~~~~
~~~~~~~~~~~~~~~

Fatu tensed as he watched Pua settle her hands on her hips.
He had faced that unyielding stance enough times himself to
know that she would not easily give up now. Let it be, Little
Fe'e, he urged her silently. Whatever fight you have with her
can be dealt with later. Just let me get you away from Landing
before they change their minds and take you back.

"That's not part of the deal, *Auntie*," he heard Pua say.

The woman, the one who must be the new farm boss, stepped
back, controlling herself visibly. She took another deep breath.
"Pua," she said, much more calmly than Fatu expected, "let's
just get on the bus and get the hell out of here."

Pua held her ground for an instant more, then turned abruptly
and stomped the length of the dock to the hydrobus. She met Fatu's
look as she approached, and he signalled her to release the bow and
stern lines. She did so, stony-faced, and tossed them aboard. Zena
had already activated the engines. Spurning the connecting walk-
way, Pua leapt aboard and strode to the bow without speaking.

Fatu tore his look away from her to watch the woman. She
surprised him by waiting for his nod of approval before stepping
aboard. Had he not been witness to her interchange with Toma,
he would never have picked her to be a Company administrator.
She carried herself with an air of self-assurance rather than self-
importance.

She was not a big woman, although she nearly matched Toma
in height. Fatu suspected the slimness was deceptive; she moved
like an athlete. Her close-cropped, light brown hair and pale
gray eyes proclaimed Euroamerican ancestry.

She wore work clothes, although not standard Company issue: dark green trousers and a paler green shirt carefully tucked
in at the waist, and light but durable-looking leather boots. She

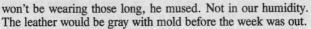

won't be wearing those long, he mused. Not in our humidity. The leather would be gray with mold before the week was out.

Her skin tone was the same as Pua's, and her hands—Fatu found it hard not to stare at her hands. They were larger than Pua's, but otherwise looked identical. Had the Company biochemists found a way to reproduce Pua's hands genetically? It could mean the end to all our plans if they have, he thought. He forced his look away from the long, slender fingers.

The woman acknowledged him with a nod, then crossed the cargo-strewn deck to the stern, where Zena sat on a high stool before the control deck. At Fatu's signal, Zena deactivated the holding fans and eased the bus away from the dock.

Glancing back at Pua, Fatu saw that she had both hands wrapped around the starboard rail. Quickly, he did the same with his own. The slight vibration of Pua's fingernails clicking a message against the plastic rail was just discernable above the tremor of the bus's engines.

"Take me home," Pua sent in Pukui's private language, and then, "Be careful with the woman." Whether she meant for him to beware or protect, Fatu wasn't sure. It didn't matter. He had every intention of doing both.

He tapped a quick acknowledgment, then made his own way to the stern. Zena steered the bus clear of the harbor and through the narrow channel in the surf line. As soon as they reached the open sea, she activated the hydrofoil stilts and increased their speed. The hull lifted clear of the water, and the ride became swift and smooth. Fatu did not relax, but a great weight lifted from his shoulders as the Company-controlled settlement at Landing dropped swiftly behind.

The new squids were silent, as newcomers to Lesaat usually were. They stared around at the empty yellow sea or up at the sky, looking for a glimpse of rings that to their untrained eyes would remain invisible until evening. Fatu could still remember his own first sight of Lesaat. After more than twenty years, he still found the tremendous expanse of golden sea difficult to comprehend.

The woman was also silent. Her glance shifted from Pua to the cluttered deck, to Zena's dark hands on the controls, back again to Pua and again and again, to the horizon. She looks directly at things, Fatu noted. And she watches everything. She would take careful watching herself.

"How's she know which way to go?" one of the new recruits asked. "Those atolls make damn small targets, and the tapes said compasses don't work right here. Something about the planet's magnetic field starting to reverse or something.''

Fatu pointed toward the bow. "See those color changes in the water? That's what Cap'n Zena uses to keep us on course. That and the ever-diminishing stench of Company Admin back at Landing.''

He glanced back at the warden. "He should have paid better attention to the training tapes.'' And if you don't know we're navigating by underwater beacons, you should have paid better attention yourself, he thought. She almost smiled.

"My name is Angie," she said. "Angela Dinsman.'' Her voice was pleasant enough, but she didn't offer her hand.

"I am Fatu o le Motu Poutu o le 'aiga," he replied. At her lifted brow, he said, "Fatu will do.''

"You waterworlders like long names,'' she said with a glance toward Pua.

"Names carry a lot of meaning here," he said. He nodded toward Zena. "Our pilot is Rozena Samuels Apirana. She's the best boat handler on Lesaat. If you need to get anywhere on the surface, Zena's the one to get you there.''

The woman acknowledged Zena's curt greeting, then looked back at Fatu. "You're the acting Pukui farm boss?'' she asked.

He nodded. "You look surprised.''

"Not at you personally, just at your presence here. After the way the tankers were treated on the shuttle, I didn't expect someone of your rank to be here to meet them," she said. "Do you always make the trip in to meet new recruits?''

"I do when I can," he said. "We've been pretty short-handed at Pukui since Zed and Lehua—died, but meeting the recruits is something I generally try to do in person. Gives us a chance to get acquainted before any bad habits get started.''

He straightened. "We weren't told you would be on this shuttle until we got to Landing. I'm afraid Pukui won't be prepared to offer you a formal welcome.'' Why, he wanted to ask, are you riding this reef-loving bus instead of flying directly to Pukui in one of the Company flitters?

"There's no need for formality," she said. "I'm just here to do a job.''

He nodded. "There's one respect in which formality would be useful.''

She lifted a brow. A woman of few words.

"Swimmers, especially those on Company crews, work better when there's a clear differentiation between them and the on-site boss," he said. "The brief notice we got concerning your arrival listed you as Warden Dinsman. Do you object to being called Warden in front of the crews?"

"Warden is fine," she said. Her look never wavered, but he detected a slight hint of resignation in her tone.

She turned to Zena, openly studying the pilot's tattooed lips. "Are you Maori?" she asked.

Zena nodded cautiously.

"I did a job in New Zealand once," the warden said. "There was a problem at one of the geothermal sites near Taupo. One of the locals I worked with was called 'Two Teeth' Apirana. Is he any relation?"

Zena's brows lifted in surprise. "That's my mother's brother's eldest son. He was a pig-headed sonuvabitch back when I knew him. Has he gotten any better tempered over the last twenty years?"

"Without the earlier comparison, I'd have to say I seriously doubt it," the warden replied.

Zena was quiet for a moment, then she said, "You know, I was the one who knocked out those two teeth," and to Fatu's complete surprise, both women laughed. A point to you, Warden, he conceded. There weren't many who could breach Zena's reserve that quickly.

The recruit who had spoken earlier crossed to the starboard rail. He leaned out, looking ahead. "It all looks the same color to me," he said.

"Yeah, puke yellow," one of his companions replied.

"What's the matter, Itoshi?" the first tanker asked. "Water makin' you queasy?" Fatu noted that the man called Itoshi looked considerably paler than he had ashore.

"Kick off, pisshead," Itoshi replied.

Fatu moved quickly to step between them. He guided the ill tanker toward the opposite rail. "Cap'n don't look kindly on squids who chum her deck. If you're gonna vomit, do it over the side."

He turned slowly back to the other man. "And *I* don't look kindly on troublemakers," he said softly. "Any more lip from you, and I'll rip out your gills."

The tanker took a careful step back.

"Si'down, squid!"

The tanker sat.

"Fatu runs a tight crew," he heard Zena say, loud enough so the rest of the squids could hear. It was a lesson the two of them tried to apply early with each load of new recruits.

"How long have you been on Lesaat?" the warden asked when Fatu returned to stand beside her.

"Since they opened the Pukui reef, twenty years ago," he said. "Lehua Pukui's family and mine are related at several places along the ancestral line. I didn't know her personally before coming out here, but when word reached my family compound in Samoa that she was looking for an Island-born algae specialist to help set up the farm, I was the one drafted."

"Drafted?"

He smiled. "Not in any negative way, Warden. I was more than eager to come."

"Are you a phycologist, then?" she asked.

"Of sorts. I know my algae, if that's what you mean."

"Company trained?"

He shook his head. "I grew up in Tokelau, on one of the few Earth atolls capable of supporting an experimental algae farm. Our operations were minor compared to Pukui, of course, but I knew enough to suit Zed and Lehau's needs. The Company was willing to hire me on their recommendation, since I came a lot cheaper than a formally trained algae specialist."

"Do you still work for the Company?" The woman's questions were unoffensive, but very direct. Fatu realized he had already revealed more about himself than he would have preferred, given the chance to think before he answered. He needed to be more careful. He needed to take a more direct role in controlling the conversation's direction.

"I'm a free landholder," he said. "The Pukuis bought my contract from the Company, and I later bought it back from them, along with part of Pukui Reef." Before she could respond, he added, "I'm surprised you didn't know my background already, Warden. Or did you?"

"Are you asking if this is a test of your veracity?" she replied. She laughed, a quick, quiet laugh. "I wish I had enough information to do that."

"Why did you bring Pua back?" he asked.

That response surprised her; a definite touch of anger darkened her eyes. "Why shouldn't I have brought her back?"

And *that* surprised Fatu. He found himself suddenly back on the defensive. "I didn't say she shouldn't be here. I'm just curious as to why you brought her."

The woman matched his stare for a moment. "Because she wanted to come."

A light flashed on the control console.

"Storm sign to starboard, ten o'clock," Zena said. She lifted her gaze toward the eastern horizon. The warden followed her look, blinking rapidly. Telescopics, Fatu thought. Good ones. He blinked his own long-range optics into use and studied the green-gray smudge barely visible in the distance.

"How close?" he asked.

"Still well away from Pukui," Zena said, "but they're moving closer right on schedule. We've got big trouble comin' soon."

We've got big trouble happening right now, Fatu thought. He turned to the warden. "How much experience do you have with waterfarming?"

"None at all," she said unhesitatingly. "I studied some Company tapes on the way out, but Pua tells me they're mostly inaccurate. Aside from that and a few news holos over the years, that's it. My experience has been primarily land-based, forest work mostly."

"Damn," Fatu muttered. Zena's jaw tightened. How in hell were they supposed to save Pukui when the Company kept sending them total incompetents? They don't want us to save Pukui, he reminded himself. At least not right now. That's the whole point.

The warden looked calmly from one to the other. "I'm an environmental anthropologist by profession," she said. "A dryland fire warden during the interims, thus the title, such as it is. My specialty is cultural crisis intervention."

"Are *you* Company trained?" Fatu asked.

"I'm a fully ranked U.N. troubleshooter," she replied. "World Life just holds my current assignment contract." The hair at the back of Fatu's neck lifted. No wonder this woman didn't act like the usual Company reps. This was it then—the Company was making its final move.

"Just how do you plan to solve Pukui's problems," he forced himself to ask, "if you don't know anything about waterfarming?"

She studied him for a moment. "At the limited briefing I got, it was suggested I truth-drug the two of you and let *you* tell *me* the best way to proceed."

Zena's long, dark fingers tensed on the control deck. The warden noticed that, too, before her calm gaze returned to Fatu's face. "I prefer voluntary cooperation," she said.

"I'm sure you'll find that we prefer the same," Fatu replied. She nodded very slightly.

Fatu took a careful breath. Zena had focused her attention on the distant storm.

"I'm open to advice," the new farm boss said.

Fatu blinked. He hadn't expected that. Well, he thought, it's better than following the former line of discussion.

"The Company tried a couple of other bosses after they took Zed and Lehua away," he said, "even though we were ordered to do only maintenance, no harvesting. The first was a tough-assed bitch off one of the penal farms. First thing she did was up the work load, drop the pay, and start shaving the safety margins. The Company sent a full security squad out to back her up."

He leaned back against the rail. Pua was touching it, too, but she sent no further message. "Got herself lost inside a net full of overripe algae, that one did. The shift was shorthanded, on account of so many injuries, and they were already tired from all the overtime hours. Bitch's gills had clogged by the time the crew found her. Took a full day before we could get her body out, and by then she was pretty much algae soup."

He glanced at the woman. "She was the first of three. Company finally stopped sending them. Till now."

"And the security squad?" she asked.

"Still on-site, with orders to do serious damage to anyone who attempts a harvest."

She nodded. "I appreciate your candor. I'll remember to stay out of overripe algae pens."

Fatu couldn't stop a laugh. This was as cool a Company bitch as he had ever encountered.

"Pua's getting itchy," Zena said.

Fatu and the warden turned toward the bow. Pua had removed her shirt and shoes and was standing beside the starboard bow. As they watched, she lifted her long fingers to twist her hair into a topknot. She tied it with a strip of cloth that she must have torn from her shirt, then lowered her hands and stood very still. She stared down at the water.

"What's she doing?" the warden asked.

"Waiting," Fatu replied. Pua's skin flashed gold in the late afternoon sunlight.

The warden turned back to him. "Waiting for what?"

Pua moved again. By the time the warden turned back, Pua had stripped off her shorts. In one smooth movement, she stepped up onto the railing . . .

"No!" the warden shouted.

. . . and dove.

Fatu bit back a smile of relief. "To get home," he said.

Chapter 7

~~~~~~~~~~~~~~~~~~~~
~~~~~~~~~~~~~~~~~~~~

The water closed over Pualei like a blessing. Her lungs sealed tight the instant her nose and mouth were submerged. Her gills fanned, sending a welcome surge of adrenaline through her system. She wriggled her toe webs free and grinned at the sweet-briny taste of the sea.

She dove deep. Down, down, into the crystal gold. Releasing the stored air in her lungs, she laughed aloud at the water's smooth, welcoming caress. Bubbles bounced along her cheeks and through her hair. The pounding vibration of the hydrobus engines slowed, telling her that Zena had retracted the running foils and dropped the bus to low speed. She was circling. Pua laughed again.

The bus's steady mechanical tremor was gradually replaced by the infinitely more varied and exciting touch of the sea. Light and sounds that she had not witnessed for months startled and delighted her. A school of flickerfish flashed into sight, then darted away to her left. She spun and followed, chasing them until, with a flick of her fingers, she shattered the seemingly solid mass into tiny silver shards. The taste of flicker offal made her want to sneeze. Enough excess oxygen had built up in her lungs to allow her to laugh aloud again.

She stopped and held herself still, reveling in the sound and taste and movement.

This is the way it's supposed to be! she thought. Wet and smooth—and fast! She dove again, through a cloud of drifting feather worms. The sucking tension of their tiny dual proboscises tickled as they attempted to attach to her bare skin. She scooped up a mouthful, used her tongue to mash them against the back of her teeth, and swallowed. Their sweet, sharp taste made her grin.

Earth had been so dull and empty. So dark and dry. Not even

the ocean had seemed truly alive. There had been a moon, but it had been all alone in the sky with only cold stars for company. No wonder Earthers are all so sour, she mused. No wonder they never smile with their eyes.

She drifted with the current for a moment, thinking of the woman on the bus above. The mountainlady. The fire warden. The Earther who had taken her hands. Pua didn't understand *her* at all. In her sleep, the woman had talked of mountains and valleys and small creatures that bored holes in trees. She had spoken of a mother who died, and more than once about the man named Nori.

Pua disliked the Nori man immensely. She had tasted his guilt the first time she had seen him; she didn't understand how the warden could ever have cared for him. Still, some of the things they had done together in that tower had sounded interesting.

Once, the warden had told about a great fire and then a storm in some far-off place. She had spoken almost as if she had known someone was there listening and had even answered some of Pua's questions. Pua smiled. Sally Goberlan had been with the mountainlady during the storm, and they had done dangerous and exciting things together. They were obviously the best of friends.

"Well, your Earther friends can't help you here," Pua said into the sea. "The only one you've got to help you is me."

Pua couldn't understand why someone who seemed so smart about some things acted so dumb about others. The warden had challenged Toma right in front of everyone, *with her back to the water!* One push, and her career as a Lesaat farm boss would have ended before it had begun. No farm worker, new recruit or otherwise, would ever accept orders from someone he or she had seen panic in the water.

Pua's grip on the warden's shirt might have helped, although she doubted it would have made a real difference if Toma had decided to fight physically. The first thing any waterworlder did in a fight was get his opponent wet. Pua hated being dependent on someone with such questionable sense.

She blew a slow string of bubbles, a good-luck charm aimed at the sky, then kicked hard and raced the bubbles to the surface.

The hydrobus was still circling. Pua lifted her head from the water about ten meters off the port bow. As she had expected, the mountainlady and the tankers, all but the sick one, stood at the starboard rail, looking toward the spot Zena was circling. Pua activated close focus and grunted in satisfaction when she saw that the mountainlady's long fingers were wrapped neatly around the rail. At least she was a fast learner.

Fatu, also as expected, was looking directly her way when Pua surfaced. He looked older than she remembered. He looked tired. She acknowledged his slow smile with a grin and kicked closer. Fatu casually kicked a line over the side, and Pua grabbed it as the hydrobus passed. She pulled herself close.

"You can't just leave her out here," she heard one of the tankers say. "How will she find her way to land?"

Zena answered, "Don't worry about that one. She couldn't get lost out here if she tried." Not entirely true, Pua thought, but close enough.

"What is she?" the tanker asked. "Some kind of mutant?"

Pua grinned and signed to Fatu that she would meet the bus at the farm pass, inside Pukui's inner lagoon. Fatu's brows twitched in silent acknowledgment. She let the rope go and drifted a few meters back so she could watch as he crossed the deck to speak to Zena. Zena didn't even glance her way before revving the engines to full power and turning back toward the reef.

Pua dove under the bus's frothing wake.

Fatu would admit to the warden that he had seen her, of course—no one lied to a farm boss unless it was absolutely necessary. But, there was nothing the warden could do except be mad at herself. She hadn't told Pua to stay aboard, and she obviously hadn't thought to order Fatu and Zena to report sighting her if she surfaced.

Pua lifted her head above the water again.

"Pay attention to *everything*, Auntie," she called, knowing her voice wouldn't carry over the distance and the bus's humming engines. "Pay attention all the time!" She doubted she would ever get away with that trick again. The mountainlady wasn't *that* dumb.

Pua dove again, leveled at about five meters, and turned toward Pukui. She began to swim—a little fast at first. Then she settled into a steady, strong rhythm that would allow her to reach the reef quickly but with the least possible energy loss. It felt wonderful to stretch again, to cup her hands in the water and pull them back hard and fast. Her hands worked fine. With each double-armed stroke she surged ahead.

She swam with her knees close together, a technique she had learned as a youngster while swimming with the reef rays and false dolphins. Her arms and hands provided power, while her webbed feet and streamlined form allowed for maximum, long-distance speed.

As she swam, her skin began to exude a thin layer of clear

mucus, a protective coating against extended immersion. Its slick feel and the slight increase in speed it provided made her smile. Dr. Waight had never allowed her to stay in the water long enough for the coating response to be activated, so she had never discovered its existence. She had never let Pua swim naked either. Earthers were so strange.

"You never learned a lot of things, Dr. Waight," she murmured, hoping that was true. She worried sometimes about what the Earthers might have asked her while she was still sick.

But it didn't matter now what the old woman had learned. Not at this moment, not in this sea. Here, Pua was free, and fast and strong. A distant pigfish squealed, high and shrill—a mating call. Pua tightened her throat and squealed back.

She could feel the stretch of long-unused muscles; she was out of shape after so long away. I should have waited till the bus was closer, she thought, but she knew she couldn't have. She had stayed out of the water as long as she had been able.

She needed this swim. She needed the ocean's silken touch, the echoing songs of Le Fe'e. She needed the sweet taste of the reef and her family. "I'm sorry," she whispered, and the rhythm of her strokes faltered. "I'm sorry I couldn't bring them back."

"We'll cremate your parents' bodies when our research is finished," Dr. Waight had said when Pua asked for them to be returned to Lesaat, or at least to be taken to her mother's family at South Point. "Then the ashes will be scattered at sea."

"But my mother is a land person," Pua had replied. "Her bones should be blessed and hidden in the burial cave, not left to sink in some strange sea."

"Your mother was no stranger to this sea," Waight said. "She grew up here, remember?"

"But—"

"They're dead, Pua. It doesn't matter where their remains end up."

It does! Pua's tears salted the sea. It does matter! She was acutely conscious of her mother's hair, braided around her ankle. It was the only piece of her parents she had been able to bring home.

She pushed away the memory of the hated doctor's face and swam hard again for the reef. She thought about making a short detour to visit the old man and the others. She wanted more than anything to tell Le Fe'e all that had happened and to hug Pili and Kiki and Keha tight. But Sa le Fe'e was on the other side of the reef. It would take too long. She didn't want to give the mountainlady any excuse to ask dangerous questions.

She crossed the deep-water drop-off and then followed the gradual upward slope of coral toward the surface. Above her, the breaking waves churned the water to phosphorescent foam.

The face of the reef teemed with life. It was not as rich as some other parts of Pukui, those better protected from the pounding eastern swell, but it was alive and growing, and the sealife it supported created constant movement among the colorful corals.

Pua dipped down to drag her hand across the pebbled surface of a candy coral. At her touch, the microscopic algae covering the coral shifted, sending a swirl of fluorescent pink and orange across the seemingly bare coral head. A school of kid fish darted from the cover of a nearby hole and fed madly until the colors faded. "Like kids in a candy store," a visiting scientist had once called it, and that's how both the fish and the coral had gotten their names. Pua still wasn't certain what a store was, but the frenetic activity of the algae and the fish always made her laugh.

She snagged a drifting coiler with a quick twist of one wrist. It wrapped itself neatly around her arm, contracting with smooth, even force, not strong enough at this hair-thin size to cause more than the pleasant sensation of friendly snugness. She admired her shimmering, crimson bracelet for a moment before moving on.

As she swam upward, the current caused by the swells building up against the reef became stronger. She turned parallel to the reef, staying just below the turbulence of the breaking waves. She needed to find a surge channel large enough to take her past the lip of the algal ridge that covered the reef's outer edge. The tide was low, so she made her choice carefully. She didn't want to face the mountainlady missing a layer of skin.

A giant reef grazer moved into view. The sunlight, refracting through the waves, turned the fish shimmering violet. It was only half Pua's length, but it matched her easily in girth. It nosed nearer to the reef, and she followed. She braced herself against the surge, strong now. It lifted her, pressing her closer to the coral, then dropped and tried to suck her away. With quick, fluttering movements of its tail and fins, the grazer held itself almost motionless in the strong ebb and flow.

Suddenly, the grazer disappeared, sweeping inward with the surge and up through a narrow channel in the coral. Pua counted, marked the point at which she felt the wave break, then watched for the fish to return. It did not.

"Ha!" she said, and giggled as a pair of fanning tuba worms turned toward the sound. She slipped into the surge channel, and when the next surge swelled, she relaxed into its grip. It

lifted her and thrust her up and inward. The channel was nar-
rower than she had hoped, but she managed to squeeze through
without scraping her knees on the surrounding coral.

She rode the surge to its foaming end.

As soon as she felt the water begin to ebb, she grabbed the
nearest coral outcrop with both hands. She braced her feet
against rough coral edges and held tight. As soon as she was
freed from the pull of the ebbing wave, she scrambled up the
remaining incline of the surge channel onto the reef flat. Behind
her, the following wave broke and sent foaming effervescence
swirling past her knees. She had reached shallow enough water
to brace herself against its force.

The grazer was feeding placidly nearby. "I'll return the favor
next time I find you in trouble," she called. It was the kind of
promise she always kept, because Fatu insisted the fish would
remember, and she knew for herself that it was never wise to
anger the reef's inhabitants without good cause.

Many months of wearing shoes and walking on smooth, level
floors had softened the calluses on the soles of Pua's feet. Even
with her webs fully folded, she found it necessary to pick her
way carefully across the treacherous reef flat. She leapt as best
she could from one flat, sandy stretch to another, so as not to
damage either her feet or the fragile coral.

She stopped for a moment, staring out across the great Pukui
Lagoon. The barrier reef on which she stood curved around the
inner reef and the central islands of her home like a protective
stone hand. Much of the barrier reef was underwater, even at
low tide, but it still broke the force of the deep ocean swells.
There were many open, sandy beaches along its great expanse,
and a few islets large enough to support palm trees and
thick, tough ground vines.

At the center of the lagoon, Home Island rose in snow-clad
splendor. It wasn't real snow. Pua understood that now. Her
mother had just planted snow-white trees at the summit and
named it Mauna Kea Iki to remind her of her ancestral home.
Now that Pua had seen the real Mauna Kea, she understood why
Earthers always smiled when they heard this one's name. Pukui's single mountain rose to only five hundred meters. Still, it
had been her mother's pride.

Pua's vision blurred. All that she saw and felt and tasted reminded her that she had come back alone. She blinked angrily
and swiped away tears.

A flicker of yellow caught her attention, the fluorescent floats that lined the edges of the algae holding nets on the inner reef. The deep orange of the enclosed algae showed that much of it was fully mature. She was surprised that there were no Company harvesters on-site. Perhaps they were out of sight behind Home or Second islands.

She extended focus and searched the horizon for the hydrobus. After a moment, she spotted it nearing the leeward pass on the far side of the lagoon. Once inside, it would have to double back along the inner reef to reach the farm passage through the algae pens. She had plenty of time.

She crossed a last stretch of smooth sand leading into the lagoon and returned once more to the water. The ocean sounded and tasted different here. Sharper, clearer, except that one had to be more careful of ricocheted sound. Pua clicked a rapid sequence with her fingernails to announce her presence. The sound pattern would identify her to the reef rays and other friendly denizens of the lagoon.

It would also bring her to the attention of the suckersharks, but she doubted they would be hungry enough at this hour to come and investigate. She hoped they would stay away, because without a knife to scrape them off, she didn't care to bother with the stupid creatures.

Unlike the hydrobus, Pua could cross the inner reef wherever she chose, as long as she remained far enough away from the perimeter alarms. She kept an eye on the yellow markers as she approached the nearest of the mature algae pens, and detoured carefully around them. She was even more careful near the seemingly empty stretches between the markers.

Many an inexperienced poacher had been caught when they swam too close to one of the unmarked alarms that were scattered randomly around Pukui's perimeter. Pua had set off a few herself, until Fatu and her father finally showed her how to identify the small transparent cylinders that kept the sensor alarms dry.

When she was sure the area was clear, she dove. The heavily laden net extended deeper than she had expected. Too deep, she thought. She followed it farther and farther down. Why hadn't this pen been cleared? The sludge-filled net reached almost to the coral shelf that formed the sunken inner reef. The net should never have been allowed to get so full. She could taste the rot clearly. It reminded her of Earth.

She ducked beneath the net, then quickly retreated. It was as black as a burial cave under there. The algae had grown so thick that no light at all filtered through from above, and no light showed under from the opposite side. Could the net actually be touching the coral? Pua swam farther along the net. Finally, she reached a place where the darkness was not so intense. She slid under the net again. Yes. There. She could see an opening to the other side. A very shallow opening over razor-sharp coral. She swam carefully into the opening.

The coral's usually riotous colors looked gray. The only light came from ahead of her, and from thin growths of barely luminescent coralline algae. The sea grew more and more silent as she moved forward under the net. The great mass of algae sludge hung like a living thing above her, sighing and bubbling, oozing its foul taste of decay into the darkness. She could see where the net had been stretched well beyond any normal or safe limits.

When she reached the first of the uninsulated deep-water pipes, she stopped, puzzled because there was no discernible change in the surrounding temperature. If anything, the water seemed warmer. They should have been running the coldest water possible through the pen, to slow the growth until the net could be cleared.

She eased herself over the pipe and swam on, a little faster now, because there was so little light, and the horror above her seemed to be sinking lower even as she watched. In her haste, she scraped the top of one knee across a jutting branch of fire coral. It stung, but her viscous skin coating sealed the cut quickly.

It's dying! she thought as she crossed the central, fully insulated pipe. She could see no color at all in the coral she was passing over. My reef is dying! She was the only thing that moved in the gloomy darkness.

After Pua had passed the larger, central pipe she began to feel the distant drumming throb of the hydrobus. It must have already reached the inner-reef farm pass. Well, there was no way she could meet it there now. She dared not swim any faster through this treacherous passage. The mountainlady would just have to wait.

Zena would take the bus directly to the main dock, Pua knew. She supposed the pilot and Fatu would find some way to keep the new farm boss occupied until Pua caught up. She crossed a patch of sand and stopped. She brushed her hand lightly across the sand's smooth surface. Nothing moved. She relaxed her finger into a narrow crack and not even a reef mite shifted at the disturbance. She moved on. Why hadn't they harvested this pen? Why were they letting the reef die?

Finally, she crossed the last of the deep-water pipes and swam from beneath the net into the bright, sunlit inner lagoon.

Instantly, she was attacked.

Flashing silver, the reef rays slid under and around her, buffeting her clear of the net and into deep water. "It's me!" she called, laughing, through it was obvious they knew who she was. None was displaying its teeth or its spines. And all were jockeying for positions where they could brush their forward wingtips against her skin. She reached out to grab the pack leader. Sliding her arms around the narrow place between its front and back wing sets, she pulled it into a tight hug.

The others bumped them upside down. They tumbled over and over in the clear gold water until finally Pua was forced to let go. The pack leader slid out of her grasp, but moved only far enough away to slide both sets of its long, silken wings along her arms. Then it shot to the surface.

Pua followed, laughing again at the sleek, sudden movement of the ray pack. The smaller, single-winged rays, the ones who had not yet coupled into adulthood, darted among their giant double-winged elders. One pair, not yet attached but obviously close to doing so, swam nose to tail along with the rest.

One by one, as the rays reached the surface—and then in pairs—they leapt in long, shallow curves over the water. The shock of their spread wings crashing back onto the surface ricocheted like drumbeats off the reef.

"It's so *good* to be back!" Pua cried as she joined them at the surface. "It's so good!"

Suddenly, she stopped and turned back toward the algae pen. She had expected their wild play to set off at least a dozen alarms. She had certainly been buffeted close enough to the sensors that her presence should have registered.

"What's wrong around here?" she asked the rays. "What's happening?" She swam deliberately close to one of the yellow markers. Nothing happened. There was no wailing siren, no spray of dye along the line to stain the water and her skin. She took the floater in her hands and shook it. Nothing. The alarm was dead. Angrily, she thew the sensor back and swam along the net's upper edge until she reached the next one. It, too, remained quiescent.

Pua followed the markers the length of the pen, becoming more and more concerned when none of them reacted to her presence. The entire security system was apparently shut down. Near the far end, she dropped below the surface to inspect the net.

As she suspected, the net had been opened in several places, but not by any Pukui crew. The openings were jagged rips in the fine mesh, made carelessly, and sloppily repaired. The sludgelike algae was growing through several small holes the poachers had missed. Quickly she pulled the holes closed and tied them with loose strands of the net's filament. Then she scooped up the loose algae and carried it to the surface. The holes must have been freshly made, because she was able to cup all of the orange sludge in her two hands.

"Bugger-boned poachers!" she shouted as she threw the algae back inside the net. It must have been they who had turned off the alarms.

But why hadn't it been noticed, and why had the pen been left to grow so dangerously full? Her mother would be—would have been—furious if she had seen this.

"Well, I'm furious, too," Pua called out.

The rays had followed her along the reef but had stayed in deeper water, well away from the bulging net. "I don't blame you," she said as she rejoined them. "It's a big, slimy mess, and I don't like being near it either. Come on, let's go home."

She clicked her nails in the signal for the main boat dock and spun along with the rays to swim in that direction. After a moment, the pack leader lifted close beneath her. Pua grasped the front edge of the ray's forward wings. Its skin was like silken velvet against Pua's cheek and chest as she pressed close to the creature's back. Abruptly, the ray's wings lifted, and they surged ahead. Pua was caught once more in the joy of being home.

Too soon, the ride ended. The ray slowed as they reached the shallow fringing reef of Home Island, and Pua quickly let go. She slid off into shoulder-deep water. A few quick strokes brought her to the docked bus. Fatu had left the side rope down, so she used it to climb aboard.

"What the hell is going on around here?" she demanded as she slipped through the rail. The others turned and stared. Zena lifted one dark brow, more at her language than at her question, Pua suspected. Well, she didn't care. Her dad wasn't here to scold her, and her mother would certainly have said worse if she had been the one to discover the damaged reef.

"The number-twelve growing pen is about to burst!" she said. "It's actually touching bottom in some places! And the sensors have all been turned off!"

No one moved. The tankers stared at her with open mouths. Pua stomped her foot. "We have to *do* something!"

The silence continued, but Zena and Fatu exchanged a guarded glance. "My reef is dying!" Pua cried, and to her chagrin she felt tears on her cheeks.

Finally, one of the tankers reacted. He laughed.

"Pua, " the mountainlady said.

A look from Fatu silenced the tanker.

Pua stepped closer to the mountainlady. "Do something!" she said. "Order in a harvest crew. That's what you're here for!"

"Pua," the woman replied. Her voice was very, very calm. "Put your clothes on."

Pua stared at her, then down at her own wet, glistening skin. She was wearing only the coiler and the braid of her mother's hair. "Oh, reef rot!" she shouted, and stalked to the bow to reclaim her clothes. She had forgotten all about the stupid Earthers' ways. Furious, she yanked on her shorts and shirt. More carefully, she peeled the coiler from her wrist and tossed it back into the water. "Grow up and crush a Company bus," she called after it.

"Fatu," the mountainlady said behind her, still in that smooth, calm voice, "when you're finished here, get the new workers settled. Then set up the submersible. I want to tour the farm first thing tomorrow. Zena, see that arrangements are made to get the rest of Pukui's supplies from Landing. Order them delivered, at Company cost. You don't need to go back there yourself."

"Aye," both Zena and Fatu replied, and from their tone, Pua knew the mountainlady had gained at least their temporary support. That made her even angrier. She snapped the water from her hair and twisted it back atop her head as she turned back. The mountainlady nodded toward Pua's shoes, then stepped ashore, obviously expecting her to follow. Pua glared after her. She picked up the shoes and threw them after the coiler.

Fatu chuckled.

"I hope your penis grows reef hair, Fatu," Pua muttered as she stepped past him. His grin widened, and he brushed a quick hand across her back. Pua almost broke then, at that touch from her uncle, from her very best friend. She hesitated, wanting desperately to turn back into Fatu's warm, strong hug, to share her pain, her grief at losing her parents, her horror at possibly losing the reef and all of their plans, as well.

"Go on, Little Fe'e," Fatu said softly. All of the laughter was gone from his voice. Pua shivered. She blinked away tears, lifted her chin, and followed the mountainlady ashore.

Chapter 8

A broad expanse of eversmooth grass led upslope to the main house and the nearby farm control center. Both were wooden buildings, raised off the ground so the air could move freely underneath. The house had two stories, the lower wrapped all the way around by a broad lanai. Pua's mother had said the design was once a common one on many of Earth's Pacific Islands, but Pua hadn't seen anything like it while she was there.

Pua bent to snip off a tough blade of grass, and chewed it as she walked slowly uphill. She saw that her favorite mountain apple tree, off to the right in the jungle, was loaded with ripe fruit. They had given her something at the recon center that they said was an apple, but it wasn't the same. The thing they called a lichee had been closer, but even that had been the wrong color.

"It doesn't matter what they call their stupid food," she muttered. "I'm not going back there. Not ever!" She brushed her palm over the top of a carefully trimmed fireflower bush. Its afternoon blossoms were tipped toward the west.

Pua slowed further as she neared the house. This was her mother's place, even though it had been the whole family's home. It was made all of wood, polished and carved, and it glistened in the sunlight, as welcoming as if her mama were still waiting inside. Pua wondered if, when evening came, Auntie Kate sat all alone on the lanai now. She deliberately did not look up toward her parents' bedroom windows.

The warden was waiting for her at the bottom of the lanai steps. She had been looking under the house. "What are the coral markers for?" she asked as Pua approached. "Is there something buried under the house?"

Surprised that the woman's first comment was not a complaint about her going into the water, Pua glanced, startled, down at the neat rows of coral markers.

"Just my shells."

She said it too quickly; the mountainlady tilted her head and lifted her brows.

Well, it wasn't entirely a lie. "I bury them so the animals inside will rot and the gunk will run out into the ground. Sand mites clean out what's left." She hoped the woman wouldn't ask her to dig one up. She wasn't sure she remembered which of the marked spots actually held shells—and the rest of her treasures were none of the Earther's business.

To her relief, the mountainlady merely shook her head slightly and started up the stairs. "Good idea to have the buildings up off the ground like this," she said. "It must help to keep them cool." Sweat stained the back of the woman's shirt. As she spoke, she untucked it from her trousers and tied it at the front, baring her midriff.

Before following, Pua brushed her right hand across the almost invisible layer of crystals on her opposite arm and blew the glittering dust onto the ground. It's me, Pua, she announced silently, to be sure the house would recognize her and not take offense that she had come still tasting of the sea. Her mother's house was a land person's place.

"Mostly it's to keep the nightcrawlers out," she said aloud. "They don't like to climb the stairs."

"Nightcrawlers?" The woman looked back.

"Don't you have those on Earth?" Pua asked.

"Lots of them," the woman said. "I use them to go fishing all the time. But I never had any trouble with them crawling into the house!"

Pua nodded. "They make good bait if you know how to hook them without hitting the dye sack."

The woman frowned and shook herself slightly, then continued on to the top of the stairs.

"This is lovely," she said when she reached the lanai. She looked all around. "After what I saw at Landing, I wasn't expecting anything so . . . hospitable." She walked across the lanai to where the ornately carved main doors were spread wide and welcoming. The carvings told an ancient story about New Zealand; they had been a gift from Zena to Pua's mother. The warden slid her fingers across the carved pictures before pulling open the screened door.

"Aren't you going to take off your shoes?" Pua asked when

the woman started to step inside. Again the warden responded with that quick backward glance, brows lifted.

Pua pointed to the shelf beside the door. Her own well-worn sandals were there, straps still taped and heels worn thin, just as she had last seen them. Her parents' sandals were gone, but Katie's battered reef boots were there, and several spare pairs of thongs. Pua scuffed her bare feet clean on the door mat. Matt burped and shifted comfortably, tickling her softened soles.

The woman turned slightly pale and swallowed hard. Finally she bent to pull off her boots. She carefully placed them on the shelf at the end nearest the door. She did not step on Matt.

The house had been kept open and aired. Pua could tell by the smell. There was only that faint mustiness in the foyer that Katie, for all her scrubbing and disinfecting, had never been able to eliminate. "Let it be," her mother always said. "That last bit of mildew might be the only thing holding this place together." Pua blinked and forced her attention back.

The mountainlady was turning in a slow circle. She paused to stare at the black and white masks bordering the wide entry to the library and office. "Devils' masks," she said. "Now, that's an interesting form of protection for a house so far from Truk." She crossed to the library and glanced inside. Pua was surprised. She had never met anyone but her father who knew anything about Micronesian traditions. She would have to remember to tell Fatu what the woman had said.

The warden lifted her hand toward the painted spear that hung next to one of the masks.

"That's a reef ray's spine on the top," Pua said. "Its poison can kill you."

The warden snatched her hand back. The move was awkward, but efficient.

Pua laughed. "I'm just kidding. Reef rays' spines aren't poisonous. Fatu just used to tell me that so I'd be careful when I played with them."

The warden scowled the way she did each time she lost an arm-wrestling match, but Pua could tell she wasn't really mad. When she turned back to study the other artifacts lining the walls, the Earther kept her hands clasped behind her back. Pua giggled.

"What's in here?" the Earther asked when she reached the Dutch door on the rear wall. Pua wondered why she didn't push it open. Maybe she had seen Katie's furtive movement behind the pantry louvers.

"The dining room and kitchen," Pua said.

The woman nodded and then crossed to where she could look up the open stairway. Finally, she returned to the center of the room. She squatted and ran her hands over the inlaid floor. She stiffened slightly when she saw her long, thin fingers spreading across the polished wood, but recovered quickly. "I see why you leave your footwear outside," she said.

She pointed to a small red octagon at the floor's center, then to several other similarly colored pieces. "What kind of wood is this?"

"Koa," Pua replied. "My mom brought it from Hawaii. The rest are from Lesaat trees. You can tell by the wide grain and the way they've grown together along the edges. Earth woods don't grow anymore after they're cut, at least that's what my dad said."

The mountainlady looked up. "The last koa stand on Earth died of bark blight fifty years ago. This must be very old."

"It was part of a trunk my great-grandmother gave Mama. It got smashed on the way here, so my dad cut it up to make the floor. Mama used to come in here sometimes when she got lonely for her Earther family."

The woman spread her hand again across the patterned floor. "Yes," she said. "It does have the feel of home."

Pua frowned. "What do you mean?"

"Never mind." The warden stood. "Where are the bedrooms?"

Pua motioned her up the stairs.

As she climbed, the woman touched the banister, the wall panels, the base of the stone tiki set into the alcove at the turn of the stairs. All the wooden things. Her fingers traced the varied grains more naturally than Pua had seen them move before. "A land person," she could almost hear her mother whisper. It had always been Lehua Pukui's first assessment of a new person entering her home.

"Which room is yours?" the woman asked from the top of the stairs.

Pua hesitated. "The first on the left."

The woman turned right. She stopped before a set of opened doors. "Your parents' room?" she asked.

"Yes," Pua whispered. From the top of the stairs, she could just see the edge of her mother's day quilt draped across the sleeping candleberry bush. Tapa cloth, pounded from Lesaat paper-tree bark and pattered with nightcrawlers' dye, lined the wall behind it. There was a small tear in the woven floor mat, just where it had always been.

Get away! Pua wanted to shout. You can't use that room! You can't sleep in Mama's bed! She wanted to hit the woman, slide her fingers under her gill flaps and rip them away. Get away from that door! Get out of my house!

She pressed her fingers tightly against her thighs and remained silent.

The woman ran her palms down the face of the smooth wooden door panels, studied the room for a moment more, then moved away to inspect the others.

"I'll stay here," she said when she reached the smallest room, the one next to Pua's. She stepped inside, pressed one hand down on the narrow bed, then crossed to the open window. It was only a few steps. "I can't see Little Mauna Kea from here, but it'll do," she said. Pua couldn't tell from her tone if she was joking or serious. Zena or Fatu must have told her the mountain's name.

By the time they returned to the entry hall, there was a tray of fruit and candied gemfish waiting by the front door. Pua noted with an abrupt return to good humor that there was a small pile of thinly sliced rock bread stacked among the fish and fruit.

"Where did this come from?" the warden asked.

"Auntie Kate put it here for us," Pua said.

"The housekeeper?"

Pua nodded. "She doesn't like talking to people, but she always offers food to visitors. Everyone does on Lesaat. It's bad manners not to." She caught a slight movement behind the slatted window to the pantry. The louvers opened just enough for her to see Katie's wide round eyes peering through. Pua grinned and waggled a finger at her, and the louvers snapped shut. The warden turned at the sound, but Katie could no longer be seen.

"Come on," Pua said, loud enough for Katie to hear. "She won't make sugar soup for dinner if we eat this in here." She picked up the tray—not trusting the warden to carry it in front of Katie—and backed her way through the screen door.

Katie's mind worked slowly, and she didn't understand a lot, but she was fiercely protective of the house and anything she perceived of as belonging to Lehua Pukui. There was no telling what she might do if a stranger dropped food on Lehua's koa floor.

The warden followed her onto the wide porch. "Did you say

your Auntie Kate was one of those who never fully recovered from the deprivation drugs?''

Again, Pua nodded. ''She's a drone.'' She set the food on the sideboard beside a freshly filled pitcher of iced water.

''Does she always stay hidden?''

''Usually. She's extra shy around people she doesn't know. My mom was the only one she talked to, and then only about the house and stuff my mom wanted done. Sometimes she talks to me, too, but I usually don't know what she's talking about.''

The warden lifted a piece of fruit and sniffed it cautiously.

''It's a mountain apple,'' Pua said. ''It has to be peeled.'' She took the apple and slit the green rind neatly around the middle with her fingernail. Squeezing top and bottom, she popped the rubbery rind free and tossed it back onto the tray. She handed the juicy crimson interior to the warden. ''The pit comes out with the skin, so you can eat the whole thing.''

Pua licked her fingers. She scooped a handful of gemfish into her shirt front and then hopped up onto the porch rail. She sat on the wide, flat surface and crunched the sweet-salty treats as she watched the Earthwoman eat.

When the apple was gone, the woman wiped juice from her chin, then carefully peeled and ate a second apple. She ate several of the tiny gemfish before finally reaching for the rock bread. Pua tried to keep her expression carefully neutral as the warden lifted a thin slice of the pasty bread.

''No pits?'' the woman asked, meeting Pua's look.

Pua shook her head.

The Earther bit into the rock bread. She chewed thoughtfully, then swallowed. ''What's this made from?'' she asked as she finished the rest of the slice. To Pua's amazement, she took anther piece.

''Suckersharks' dung,'' Pua replied. ''Preserved, then baked.'' She grinned as she waited for the woman's reaction. Most Earthers grew pale when told the bread's source. Some even vomited it back, although Pua didn't expect the warden to do that. The bread's presence on the tray was Katie's way of testing the newcomer. True waterworlders considered rock bread a delicacy.

The warden examined the bread carefully. ''Tastes a bit like toasted termite larvae,'' she said, ''although the texture's quite different.'' And she ate the second slice, too.

Katie, Pua thought in amazement, is going to be seriously impressed. Pua couldn't help herself. She was impressed, too.

"What's buried under the house besides your shells?" the woman asked softly.

Pua blinked and leaned back against the roof post. "Nothing," she said.

The dark brows lifted.

How does she do that? "It's none of your business," she snapped. How does she always know when I'm lying? And just how to say things so I'll give myself away?

"Does it have anything to do with the operation of the farm?"

"No!"

The warden poured a glass of water. She watched Pua over the rim as she drank it. "Okay," she said finally.

"What are you going to do about the number-twelve pen?" Pua demanded. "You can't leave it like that."

"Fatu's taking me out in the submersible first thing tomorrow," the warden replied. "I'll decide after I've seen it and the rest of the farm."

"All you have to do is call for a harvest crew," Pua said. "Or better yet, just blow it up and kill it. It's not any good anymore anyway. There's too much rot. I could taste it. Fatu and I could go right now and—"

"We can't kill it until we find out for sure what's in it," the warden said.

"There's nothing *in it*! It's just stupid Earth algae, and it's killing my reef! My mother would order it burned if she was here! She'd send *Katie* out there to burn it before she'd let it go on hurting Pukui!"

"I'm not your mother," the mountainlady said.

Pua pressed her lips closed. She blinked and followed the warden's look out over the lagoon. The sun was just disappearing, and the water and the submerged reef were beginning to shine. The rings, too, had begun to glow. The Earther stared and stared at the ever more brilliantly lit sky. Shadow would rise soon and begin moving across the rings, but now at early evening, the rings were full and high, stretching from horizon to horizon across the southern sky. Pua couldn't understand how anyone could ever want to leave this for the dark skies of Earth.

She pulled her look back to the sea. The dark rectangle of the number-twelve pen contrasted sharply with the light surrounding it. And it wasn't the only pen dark enough to be concerned about. Something had to be done, and quickly.

"At least order the cold water back through the outer pipes to lower the temperature," she said.

"The uninsulated pipes are closed?" The warden's surprise showed in her eyes if not her voice.

"It's like an oven under there," Pua said. "The whole center of the pen is completely dead. That's why it's so dark. Only the stuff around the edges is still alive. It needs to be destroyed before it breaks out."

The warden frowned as she continued staring out at the black pool of number twelve. Then her gaze lifted to follow the silver curve of the rings again.

Pua stuffed the last of the gemfish into her mouth and slid off the porch rail. "Well, if you won't do something about it, I will."

"No," the warden said. Her voice had turned that dead calm again. "You won't." It made Pua shiver.

"There are storms coming," she said. "Didn't you see that one today on the bus?" She pointed toward the northwest. "We have to get rid of that algae before they come closer."

"The algae stays as it is until I say otherwise," the woman said. Pua crossed her arms and met her look defiantly.

"How much do you know about your parents' research?" the woman asked.

That made Pua want to laugh. "Enough to know that what Mr. Crawley is looking for isn't in number twelve."

"Do you know where it is?"

"No!"

The warden never moved. To Pua's chagrin, she was once again forced to be the first to look away.

"The total-conversion enzyme is important, Pua," the woman said when Pua finally dropped her gaze. "Not because it's something that can make the Company richer and more powerful than it already is, but because millions, billions of people are in desperate need of proper nutrition. This enzyme, if it does what you say it does, will make it possible to feed them. It will make it possible to move those who want to go to other planets where there'll be room for them to take care of themselves."

"They'll just keep having babies and fill up all the other planets, too," Pua said. "Anyway, I don't care. My daddy cared and my mama cared, and what good did it do them? All I want is to save my reef."

"The two things are tied together," the warden said. "If we're going to accomplish either one, we're going to have to work together."

"Why should I help you?" Pua demanded. "You don't care

about me or Pukui. You're just planning to use us and then leave—and take me with you when you go.''

"I never lied to you,'' the warden said. "You knew all along I didn't want to come to Lesaat. I'm sorry if my needs don't match your personal desires, but I contracted to do a job, and now I have to do it—as best and as fast as I can.''

"Well, I'm not going back with you!'' Pua cried. She turned quickly away, although she was sure the Earthwoman had seen her tears. She could hear them in her own voice. "I can't.'' She wrapped her arms around the porch post and hugged it tight. She pressed her cheek against the cool, polished wood. "I would die if I had to go back there.''

The woman laid a hand on her shoulder. It was the first time she had touched Pua, aside from the arm wrestling and other exercises for her hands. Why were Earthers all so cold?

"They killed my mama and dad,'' Pua whispered.

"They didn't kill your folks, Pua,'' the woman said. "They tried to save them. That poison—''

Pua spun to face her. The hand pulled away. "That's a lie! I harvested the loli we ate that night myself. There was nothing wrong with it! Somebody else poisoned us.''

The warden started to speak, but Pua rushed on. "I got sick, too, Mountainlady, with the same symptoms. Only, if it was really loli fever, I shouldn't have, 'cause I'm immune to it. Mama built it in when she made me. Besides, there isn't any bad loli at Pukui anymore. I guess Uncle Toma forgot about that.''

"Toma?''

"Yes, Toma. The guy at Landing that you almost talked into fighting with you right there on the wharf. He'd have killed you, too, if he'd wanted to.'' Oh, you look worried now, Mountainlady. Now that you know your own life is in danger. "He's planetary supervisor, top Company man on Lesaat. And he was here at Pukui the night we ate the loli.''

"I don't understand. Are you saying that you think Dr. Haili tried to *kill* you?''

"He *did* kill my parents! The Company must have told him to, so he did.''

"But why? The Company had no reason to want your folks dead,'' the warden said. "According to Crawley and Fatu both, this was the most profitable farm on the planet while they were alive. Both their harvests and their research brought the Company tremendous profits. And the TC enzyme was much too valuable to take the chance of losing it.''

Pua turned toward the stairs. "Well, they killed them anyway." The woman caught her arm. Her long fingers snaked around Pua's wrist with a strength Pua knew she would have difficulty breaking. "Let me go," she said.

"Wait . . ."

"I don't care if you think I'm lying!"

"I don't think you're lying. You might be wrong, but I can see you're not lying."

Pua tried to pull away. "I have to go away from here," she said. "I have to go back in the water."

"Take me to the farm control center," the woman said.

"Please," Pua pleaded, no longer able to control her tears. "I won't do anything to the algae. I promise. I just have to go now." She needed Fatu. She needed the rays and the touch of the sea. Le Fe'e, she cried silently. Please, I want to be home! The air, even the rich, moist Pukui air, was smothering her.

"Just show me where the main comm console is, and how to open the cold-water lines to the growing pens," the Earther said. "Then you can go wherever you need to go." Her fingers loosened around Pua's arm. "We have to work together, Pua."

Even in her desperate need to escape the Earther's presence, Pua knew it was true. She hated that they were bound together. She jerked her arm free and led the way to the farm control shed in silence. She watched as the warden deactivated the lock, then followed her inside and pointed out the deep-water controls.

The woman examined them briefly, then nodded. "Okay," she said. "Go now. I can handle it from here."

Many hours later, the crack and splash of a reef ray's wings woke Pua. "What?" She blinked, shivered at the quick rush of her heartbeat, and panicked for an instant before she recognized the whisper of clicker-palm fronds and the distant rumble of the surf. She was home!

"Fatu?"

"Aye. I'm here." She remembered now. Fatu had promised to stay so she could rest freely without going back to the house and chancing another confrontation with the Earthwoman. They had swum together for hours, until Fatu had grown tired. Then they had talked—about Pukui and her parents, about the Company's ban on harvesting and the futile search for the missing research records.

"Stay away from the barrier reef," Fatu warned. "I know

you want to go there, but it's much too dangerous now. Company security is everywhere.''

Pua sighed and agreed, and wished things could go back to the way they had been before. Despite Fatu's urging, she refused to speak of her time on Earth. He told her that Crawley had sent word that she was living with her mother's family at South Point. All those months he had thought she was safe. He pulled a necklace of tiny lemon shells from the folds of his lavalava and slipped it over her head. Then he held her close.

"Tell me a story," Pua had said then. "Tell me a happy story about how it used to be." Her sleep, when it finally came, was deep and dream-laden.

Awake now, Pua pushed herself upright, staying close to Fatu's warm side. She glanced up at the sky. Shadow was already disappearing into the western horizon. It wouldn't be long before morning. Fatu had draped his shirt over her while she slept, but his skin was still as warm as if he had been wearing the soft fabric himself. He gave her a quick hug.

"What's wrong with the rays?" she asked, rubbing her eyes.

"Dunno. They just came now. Something's got them stirred, that's for sure."

"Suckersharks?"

Fatu glanced up at the sky. "Too late for the suckers. It'll be dawn in another hour. Looks like the whole pack's coming in close."

"Must be somebody in the lagoon that doesn't belong, then," Pua said. "Poachers, probably."

Fatu shifted and stretched. "Phaa. Been so many poachers in here the last few months, rays don't even notice anymore. Let's go check the dock." He rose and lifted Pua lightly to her feet. She kicked the sand free of her toe webs and folded them closed before handing him his shirt.

She grinned. "The mountainlady's kind of fussy about bare skin." She scuffed through the circle of moat grass they had scattered around them to keep the nightcrawlers off while they slept.

Fatu slung the shirt over one shoulder. "So I saw." He paused, frowning slightly. "You—" His look dropped to her waist. "You grew while you were away." He paused again, and Pua was startled to see that he was embarrassed. His blush showed even in the ringlight.

"What's wrong?" she asked.

"Nothing's wrong." His laugh was almost shy. "It's just that you've started turning into a woman, Pualei. You need to be more careful around the others, especially the new Earthers.''

"Why should they be more offended by a woman's body than by a girl's?'' she asked. Pua knew she was changing, she knew what it meant biologically and was pleased by that—but she saw no reason why it should change her way of life. Her mother had swum naked, at least with Pua and her dad. Pua remembered the cool, comforting touch of her mother's skin after a long swim in the warm sea.

"I'm not worried about them being offended,'' Fatu said. "You just cover yourself when they're around, okay?''

The ray pack swam close to shore again and slammed their wings against the water's surface, thrashing it into a phosphorescent froth. Pua glanced back at them. "We'd better go,'' she said. "They're going to get hurt if they keep flailing around in such shallow water, and they won't go away as long as they can see me here.''

"Let's take the trail,'' Fatu said. "Better stay out of the water till we know what's going on.'' Pua would have chosen otherwise, but deferred to Fatu's greater knowledge of the present state of Pukui's lagoon. She sprinted ahead along the narrow trail back to the house.

The main house was dark, but the farm control shed was still fully lit. "She must still be going through the records,'' Pua said, then jumped as the shrill whistle of the air-intrusion alarm shattered the night's calm. At the same moment, she heard the approaching whine of a flitter, closer than it should have been to have just then set off the alarm. Lights flashed on along the dock and throughout the house and grounds.

Fatu gave Pua a push toward the control shed. "Get the boss lady. It's probably Toma—he likes to drop in at odd hours. I'll go keep him company till you come.'' He moved swiftly away.

The control-room door slid open easily at Pua's touch—a surprise, because the auto-lock had been engaged when she left the mountainlady inside earlier. The woman had either unlocked it or set it for Pua's touch. She blinked to filter her eyes against the bright light and entered. She covered her ears with her hands.

The warden was kneeling on the floor in front of an opened console panel. She was soldering something to the back of a computer control board. A portable keyboard sat on the floor beside her.

"What are you doing?'' Pua shouted above the din of the alarm.

"Rigging a makeshift security system," the warden called over her shoulder. "Sounds like I caught something. What's going on?"

Pua stepped closer. "There's a flitter about to land. Fatu said to come. He thinks it's Toma."

"One second," the warden said. She snapped off the soldering needle and tapped a command into the keyboard. "I just need to—"

A second alarm blared, loud and low, a ululating waver that lifted chill bumps along Pua's bare arms. The pens! she thought. Security's back on at the pens, and somebody's out there!

"Come on," she said. "Something's wrong out at the growing pens. That's the number-twelve signal."

The warden gave her a quick glance before hitting another sequence on the board. Both alarms faded to silence. She stood. "The whole security system is a mess," she said. "It was probably the flitter that triggered the pen alarms."

"There's somebody out there," Pua insisted. "The rays tried to warn me earlier."

The warden ordered off the lights and ushered her outside. The doorlock hissed into place behind them. "Tell me about the rays," she said, starting downhill toward the dockside landing pad. A flitter was just touching down.

"I was sleeping on the beach," Pua said, running a bit to catch up. "The ray pack came up near shore to wake me. They wouldn't have done that if something wasn't wrong. They don't like shallow—" She stopped. "It *is* Toma! What is *he* doing here?"

The woman slowed her stride until Pua caught up. She looked out toward the growing pens. Too many of them were yawning black pits marring the luminous sea. "Is there any chance it was just the flitter, riding low, that scared your rays?" she asked. She glanced up at the sky.

"Not unless it touched the surface," Pua replied, "or dropped something into the water."

The warden's look turned back toward the flitter. "Okay," she said softly. "Let's go talk to the Company man." It was hard to be sure, but it looked as if the mountainlady smiled. They stepped into the brilliance of the spotlighted landing pad.

"Warden, tell these two idiots to put away their weapons," Toma demanded instantly. Pua was astonished to see that Fatu had a flare gun leveled against Toma's side. A shadow moved, and she saw that Zena, too, had a weapon trained on Toma.

Zena was wearing only a loincloth, and her tight tangle of hair was pressed flat on one side as if she had just come from her bed.

"Damn it, woman, I said—"

"My people are under orders to detain all strangers entering Pukui territory," the warden said without looking at him. She ran a hand down the side of the flitter and squatted to look underneath. Then she straightened and turned.

"I am not a stranger to Pukui," he said. He met her look with a hard stare.

"You are to me," she replied. "Zena, get a crew on the bus stat. I may need you out at number twelve. Set your comm for local pickup only."

"What the hell do you—"

"Aye," Zena said, and was gone.

"—think you're doing?" Toma finished.

"Inspector," she said, turning back to him. "Up at the main house, you'll find a requisition list logged onto the public net. I'd appreciate it if you would relay that list to your people at Landing along with your personal order to expedite. Use your charm or your authority, whichever carries the most weight. I want immediate shipment of the things available locally. Today if possible." Toma's mouth had dropped open.

"Also, I want you to arrange immediate transport for the Company security squads. I want them out of here stat. If World Life wants to play military games, they can do it outside my jurisdiction."

"Those squads were sent to Pukui to protect Company interests," he said. "I expect that includes you, Warden."

"*I* expect both Pukui *and* I will be safer in their absence," she said. "Fatu will escort you up to the house and see that you're made comfortable there. I *expect* Auntie Kate will even feed you, if I judge her right. In the meantime, I need to use your flitter. Fatu?"

"Aye," Fatu said, and nudged Toma away from his craft.

"Hey, you can't take—"

"Read my contract again while you're up there, Inspector," the warden said. "Pay special attention to the section on trouble-shooter's privileges. In the field, I am to receive unimpeded access to all Company resources. They set it up like that so expensive squids like me don't have to sit around on our asses while a bunch of desk jockeys shuffle paperwork and hem-haw over meaningless decisions. Come on, Pua. Let's go take a look at that pen.''

And as suddenly as that, the mountainlady disappeared through the flitter's open hatch.

The engine whirred back to life, and Pua hurriedly climbed inside.

"Wait," the warden said when Pua reached back to close the hatch. "Let me do that."

She reached across Pua and very carefully, very smoothly, *very* slowly, pulled the hatch closed. Then she closed her eyes and sat very still. Her long fingers trembled on the bare metal handles. Her breathing was shallow and ragged.

"I never saw anyone talk to a Company man like that," Pua said quietly. Except for my mom, of course—but she didn't think the warden needed to hear that.

The woman laughed very softly. She took a long, steadying breath, opened her eyes, and finally leaned back. "Okay, Waterbaby," she said as she strapped herself into the passenger's seat. It took two tries. "Let's see how good a pilot you are. Take us up.''

"You want *me* to pilot?"

"You know how, don't you?"

"Yes, but . . ." No one but her father had ever let her pilot, and he had done it only when her mother was away from the reef.

"Pua, I just did one of the hardest things I hope I'll ever have to do," the warden said. Pua glanced back at the hatch. The warden nodded.

"Not only that," she said. "It took me five hours tonight to do a job I should have been able to do in one. I dropped everything at least three times. I broke things when I tried too hard, and then when I finally relaxed, my fingers started sliding into the cracks like warm putty." She lifted her hands. "Do you want *me* to fly this thing?"

Pua stared again at the long, trembling fingers, then slid eagerly into the pilot's seat. Grinning, she snapped on her safety harness. She released the landing brake and lifted the flitter from the pad as smoothly as a suckershark pack rising from the back of a dead ray.

Chapter 9

~~~~~~~~~~~~~~~~~~~~~~
~~~~~~~~~~~~~~~~~~~~~~

Angie held her breath as the flitter lifted. Asking Pua to pilot the light hovercraft had been a calculated risk. Fatu had mentioned the girl's skill during their approach to the atoll the afternoon before. Pua flew cautiously, slower than Angie would have, but Angie was relieved by that. An air race with a hot-rodding teenager was definitely not what she needed right now. She flexed her fingers rhythmically and forced her breathing to slow.

"How'd you know I could fly?" Pua asked.

Angie blinked a focus change as they approached the nearest of the algae pens. It lay like a dark hole in the phosphorescent sea. "Fatu told me," she said. "He said your dad taught you."

Pua sent her one quick glance before returning her full attention to the viewport.

"Looks like he did a good job," Angie said, and that made the girl smile again. Angie relaxed into her seat. She glanced back at Mauna Kea Iki, the summit of which glowed almost as brightly as the water. She had no idea whether the light was bioluminescent from the trees themselves, or if it was simply reflected ringlight. The rest of the jungle shimmered and flickered with self-generated light.

The sky was a true wonder, dominated by the sharp-edged rings of reflected sunlight. They were not far north of the equator, so the band of light lifted high overhead, slightly wider than if it were being viewed edge on. It lit the night with soft white light and, coupled with the bioluminescence on the planet's surface, threw shadows of great complexity.

Several times through the night, she had stepped outside to study the progress of the wide shadow the planet cast across the band. It moved from east to west, like a giant sundial in the night sky. It was disappearing now as dawn approached. Angie blinked and returned her attention to Pua.

Pua's fingers snaked over the flitter's operating deck with a casualness Angie envied after her hours of frustration in the farm control center. The advantages of her newly shaped hands for precision work were obvious, but she had not yet achieved enough dexterity to make such work easy.

Abruptly, Pua's seriousness returned. "There," she said, pointing with one long finger. "On the outer edge of number twelve." She slid the flitter into a sharp curve.

"Careful," Angie said.

"I knew somebody was out here." Pua leveled and skimmed near the surface. She pointed again. "See the dye?"

"I see it. Keep your hands on the controls!"

Pua pursed her lips, but returned both hands to the control deck. The flitter's spotlights highlighted a fluorescent yellow stain spreading along the outer edge of the pen. "They must have triggered more than one canister," Pua said. "There's enough dye there for at least two. Look. That's another release farther down. Whoever it was sure didn't know what they were doing."

Angie leaned forward against the viewport. "I don't see anyone."

"They'd have gone deep and then headed out the pass as soon as the alarm went off," Pua said. "They probably left a big hole in the net, though. You should tell Zena to bring a containment crew right away."

"You hear that, Zena?" Angie asked.

"We're right behind you, Boss," came Zena's instant reply. Pua gave the cabin speaker a startled glance.

Angie slid a finger over the open comm-line control, blocking transmission while she said, "Troubleshooter's rule number one, Waterbaby. Never make an emergency run alone without a real good reason. Remember? I told Zena to monitor the local comm channel. One of the first things I did when I got in the flitter was set the call signal. I opened the transmission after we were in the air." That wasn't all she had done during those first few seconds, but it was all Pua needed to know about at the moment.

Angie opened the comm again. "Zena," she said.

"Aye."

"Dye was released at the seven, eight, and eleven points along the outer edge of number twelve. It's drifting north-northwest, close to the net but very slowly." She turned to Pua. "Why is that? I thought the current was stronger than that in the outer lagoon.''

"It's slow 'cause the tide's about to turn," Pua said. "Zena, you'd better secure the net before the tide changes, or the escaped algae's going to move toward the outer reef."

"Net-repair and containment crews are ready to swim," Zena said.

"It's all yours, then," Angie replied. To Pua, she said, "Let's take a run around the perimeter. I'd like to see the place where you found the net cut before."

Pua pulled the flitter into a long, slow curve around the edge of the holding net. Her flying was as smooth as any Angie had experienced.

"Why would anyone be going after this algae load?" Pua asked. "It's almost all rotten already. There's a lot fresher stuff in other parts of the lagoon." She glanced across at Angie. "Most of that needs harvesting, too."

"Why would anyone be poaching algae at all?" Angie asked.

Pua shrugged. "This is a research farm. People are always trying to get seed algae from our pens. They want to be sure they get samples of anything that turns out to be important."

Angie leaned forward. "What's that rough place near the end, inside the pen?"

Pua dipped the flitter low again and flew directly over the algae. "I don't see—oh, that. I don't know. Unless . . . Is Zena still listening?"

"Aye," the pilot said before Angie could reply.

Pua frowned and slowed to a near hover. The rippling surface of the dark orange mass seemed to be bubbling softly. The seething action was spreading slowly across the pen. "Did someone inject antigrowth in this pen?" Pua asked. "It looks like it's covered with oil, and it's starting to bubble like it does before—"

"Shit!" Zena said. "Get out of there, Pua. Someone must have accelerated the methane release."

"Hold your hover," Angie said quickly. She reached forward, ready to take the controls herself, but stopped when Pua did as she said.

"Warden, you're sitting over a methane bomb!" It was Toma's voice. "One spark, and—"

Angie elbowed off the comm. "Pua, we have to go slow or our own exhaust could set it off. Understand?"

Pua had gone pale. Her hands were tense and trembling on the controls. She swallowed hard and nodded.

"I didn't come all this way to get turned into algae stew," Angie said. Get us out of here! her mind screamed.

The side of Pua's mouth twitched. Her fingers loosened, relaxed, and very cautiously she slid her hands forward across the control deck. The flitter rose.

"Port turn, very easy," Angie said. "Don't worry about height. It's more important to reach the outer edge."

"Straight forward is closer," Pua said.

"It's also upwind, and that's where the bubbling started. Take us to port."

"I wish I was in the water," Pua whispered as she maneuvered the careful turn. Me, too, Angie thought, and for the first time in a year actually meant it. She opened the comm. "Bus out of the way?" she asked.

"We're clear," Zena said.

"We're approaching the net . . . ."

A slick of red-orange slid across the upper end of the pen.

"Go!" Angie shouted. She was thrown back in her seat as Pua hit full throttle. A flaring sheet of flame flashed beneath them. Then, abruptly, they were over open water. The flitter bucked and almost stalled in the sudden rush and drop of air.

"Steady the plates," Angie called. "We're going to get hit . . . ."

The methane exploded behind them. As the shock wave slammed into the back of the flitter, Pua and Angie were thrown against their restraints. The jolt shifted Pua's hands on the controls. The flitter nosed down.

Angie took the board without conscious thought. She fought the grav plates back under control and leveled the flitter. She counted a full, slow ten, then swung back in a low curve to face the burning algae pen. Smoke, blacker than pitch, roiled above a sheet of orange flames. A rough series of explosions rocked the far end of the pen, and streamers of spattered algae smacked against the flitter's ports.

"Cold spit on the fire lines," Angie muttered. She set the flitter to hover and watched as the flames leveled, flared again, then flickered and quickly died. When the last of them had disappeared, she took a deep breath. She blew it out very slowly.

"Wow," Pua said.

Abruptly, Angie turned the flitter away from the pen. She dropped low and skimmed the surface of the water, causing a fan of spray to each side of the light craft. A creature that looked like a cross between a dolphin and a toad leapt raggedly across the bow. She held the flit on a steady course, snapping off the tops of the waves.

"What are you doing?" Pua yelled. Her fingers were wrapped tightly around her safety harness.

Angie glanced at her. She dipped the nose again, enough to drive the spray high up the flitter's sides. "Cleaning the algae crud off the windows," she said.

At Pua's look of disbelief, she laughed. "I'm getting rid of my excess adrenaline, Pua. What's the matter, don't you water-people get a rush out of nearly getting fried?" The adrenaline, and her sudden relief, this one instant of feeling free, made her feel better than she had in a long time. I must be getting back to normal, she thought, and the absurdity of it made her laugh again.

Pua stared at her, then out at the flashing sea. Her mouth twitched. "You're crazy," she said, but the twitch turned into a tentative grin.

"So I've been told, Waterbaby. Here . . ." Angie lifted her hands from the deck. "Take over before I sink this crate." Her fingers had started to shake again.

Pua quickly reached for the controls. Despite her surprised giggle, the flitter's course remained steady. She really was very good.

"We'd better turn the comm back on," Pua said after a moment. "Zena can see we're okay, but Toma's probably still click-ing his nails, and Fatu will be worried."

Angie looked at the comm control in surprise. She had not been aware of touching it off.

"I did it," Pua said. "While we were watching the fire go out."

"Why?"

"I wanted to keep Toma waiting. That Company man's gonna swear dirty when he finds out we're still alive."

"Won't Zena have told him?"

Pua shook her head. "Zena *hates* sharks."

That made Angie laugh again. "Girl, you're crazier than I am." She tapped open the transmission.

"How's the containment coming, Zena?" she asked without a hint of humor. Pua grinned.

"Shit on a bloody reef!" came Toma's soft reply. In relief or in disappointment, Angie couldn't tell. Only his underlying release of tension was clear. The flitter wobbled slightly as Pua shook with silent laughter. It was clear what *she* believed.

"Crew's in the water, Boss," Zena said. Her voice, too, was entirely neutral. "We'll close the net and dredge the overflow, then run a perimeter sweep to catch anything the explosion threw over the top. That was a messy blow."

As they approached the bus, Angie could see a dozen or more swimmers in the water beside and beneath it. Half wore brilliant yellow bodysuits. The rest were equally visible in bright green. Blinking to close focus, Angie saw that they all wore transparent flippers.

"Yellow for the net-repair crew and green for cleanup," Pua replied when Angie asked the colors' significance. "That makes it easier for the on-site boss to keep everybody organized. The suits protect the swimmers' skin if they have to stay in the water a long time."

Angie glanced at the girl, remembering her glistening, flawless body when she had arrived at the landing dock the day before. How do you protect your skin? she wanted to ask. She wasn't entirely sure she wanted to know.

"Warden, you're going to have to issue a disposal order for this pen as soon as the overflow cleanup is finished," Zena said. "Company says I can't touch it otherwise, and this trash has got to be removed right away, before it fouls the entire area."

Angie gave Toma time to react, but the Company man remained silent. "Consider the order issued," she said. "Is there anything else we can do for you from up here?"

"Negative," Zena said. "Squids are swimming smooth. Good training exercise for the new recruits. Itoshi! Get your ass in the water. You barf on my deck and I'll—"

Angie touched off the comm.

"Any reason why I shouldn't have issued that disposal order?" she asked.

Pua glanced at her. "What do you mean?"

"The Company has refused all harvesting, growth stoppage, and disposal of Pukui algae for the last six months," Angie replied. "Now, on *your* first night home, the precise algae load you were most concerned about is totally destroyed. You know exactly what I mean."

"The only thing I saw or tasted in that pen was rotten blue-green Earth algae," Pua snapped. "Type 410 Standard, common food-additive mix. It's grown all over Lesaat. That batch should have been destroyed a long time ago, before it started messing up my reef.''

Angie met her look in silence.

''I didn't put the methane-release triggers in it, if that's what you think. I didn't set it up to burn.''

Angie believed the girl, or thought she did. It was fireloving odd, though. The Company had managed to prevent the destruction of any Pukui algae for almost six months, then a full pen had been lost the first night Pua was back. Like so many other things that had happened recently, the coincidence seemed too obvious to be natural.

''Do you know who did?'' she asked.

''No.''

Angie leaned back against the seat.

''But I'm glad it's done,'' Pua said, ''because now you *have* to get it out of there, and the sunlight will be able to get back to the reef. Not all of the coral is dead. It might be able to grow back someday, a long time from now.'' There were tears in her eyes.

Angie sighed. This job didn't need an environmental anthropologist, it needed a social worker and a private detective—and quite possibly a homicide squad, she thought with another glance at the girl.

''Let's go talk to the inspector,'' she said.

Pua's frown remained fixed as she piloted the flitter upwind around the smoking algae pen and back toward the dock. As they approached the island, Angie said, ''Set us down on the lawn in front of the house.'' Pua gave her that same dark look she had earlier, when Angie had almost worn shoes into the house, but she landed where she was told in silence.

''You don't have to meet with Toma if you don't want to,'' Angie said when Pua stopped at the base of the front steps.

Pua rubbed her left arm. ''Are you giving me a choice?'' she asked. ''Or telling me you don't want me there?''

Angie took a slow breath. Why was it so hard to say the right thing to this youngster? ''I'm telling you to do whatever you want,'' she said, and saw that was the wrong thing, too.

Pua muttered something, then puffed a fine shimmer of dust from her arm. She stepped past Angie. ''I *want* to go to bed.'' She scuffed her bare feet across the door mat and disappeared inside. By the time Angie had removed her boots and carefully stepped over the still-wriggling mat, Pua's bedroom door had slammed.

Fatu stood at the library door. He nodded Angie a greeting, then glanced after Pua.

"She's okay," Angie said. "Just mad at something I said."

One thick eyebrow rose. "What'd you say?"

"Damned if I know," Angie replied. "Thanks for handling this end of things, Fatu. Sorry if we gave you a scare."

"Warden," he replied. "That little fe'e gives me a scare every time she turns around. I'm pretty much used to it." He nodded over his shoulder. "You want me to stay?"

Angie glanced beyond him to where Toma was stretched out in a wicker chair, holding a glass of wine in one long-fingered hand.

"I'll take it from here," she replied. She stifled a yawn.

Fatu offered only the slightest of hesitations before nodding and leaving the house. With Pua upstairs, she doubted he would go far. It was clear he was intensely protective of the girl. She wondered what the two of them had been up to before the alarms had gone off.

Inside the library, the comm screen flickered with incoming messages. Angie ignored them and glanced around the spacious room. She felt as startled now as she had the evening before as her look took in the three shelves of paper books that lined one inside wall. Old-style books were a rare enough sight on Earth; the presence of so many here seemed all but impossible.

Like in the foyer, the walls were hung with Island-style artifacts, most of which, Angie suspected, had never been anywhere near Earth. Someone had certainly put a lot of work into making this place feel as if it had a human past.

She dropped into a chair facing Toma and eyed the glass in his hand.

He lifted it, not quite in toast.

"Candleberry wine," he said, turning the glass to catch the light. "The finest on Lesaat. Making it was one of Zed Pukui's specialities." Early morning sunlight, filtering in through the louvered shades, turned the clear liquid scarlet.

Angie leaned back. "Do you always make yourself at home like this?" She lifted her feet to the low table between them.

He glanced pointedly at her own relaxed posture. His look was not quite as disapproving as Pua's when Angie told her to park the flitter on the lawn, but close. "It's accepted practice for me to serve myself at Pukui," he said. "I've been a guest in this house many times."

"Before or after the senior Pukuis' deaths?"

Toma's eyes narrowed. He rested the glass on the arm of his chair. "Zed and Lehua were my friends. We were family."

"Ah yes, Pua's favorite uncle," she said. According to the farm records, he actually *was* Pua's uncle. He had married Zed's sister seven years before, and buried her two years later. The woman had died in childbirth, of all things, along with what would have been twin sons.

Toma remained expressionless.

"Pua says you killed her parents."

"I did not." He took a sip of wine.

"She doesn't strike me as someone who would accuse a family friend, an *uncle*, of murder, without a pretty solid reason," Angie said.

"I was here when they ate the boiled sea cucumber that was supposed to have killed them, but I refused to eat any of it myself," he said. "I was also here the following morning when they all got sick. She thinks I did something to cause it."

Coincidences? Angie mused.

"Supposed to have?" she asked.

"Pua would never have deliberately given her parents infected loli," he said. "You can't tell if it's carrying the lethal bacteria after it's cooked, not by just looking, but you can while it's still on the reef. Pua knows the reef better than any of us. She just wouldn't have made a mistake like that."

"What killed them, then?"

He hesitated and took another sip of wine. "I thought the Company had closed this case."

I'm reopening it, she told him silently. "Indulge me, Inspector. I'm curious. What do you think killed them if it wasn't the—loli, is it called?"

He nodded. His look became calculating. "The Pukuis were taken off-planet immediately after they were stricken. I was later sent records showing they all carried high levels of the lethal bacteria that causes loli fever, so they must have gotten it somewhere."

"But not from Pua."

"No, Warden. Not from Pua. She adored her parents. And they her. Pualeiokekai, they called her—Precious Child of the Sea. They were as close a family as I've ever known. Even if Pua had been planning to hurt me with the loli, she would never have taken the chance of harming her parents at the same time."

Angie felt as if she were in quicksand. She couldn't find anything in this conversation to hold on to. "Why would she have been trying to hurt you?"

"She wasn't, really," he said. "She was just trying to shame me. She was angry because I'd been arguing with her father earlier. Serving the loli was her way of paying me back." He smiled slightly. "It's considered highly insulting to refuse a food offering here on Lesaat. Pua knows I never eat boiled loli—I have an allergic reaction to it that has nothing to do with the loli fever bacteria. She served it so I'd be embarrassed by turning it down in front of Katie and her parents."

So that's what the business with the rock bread was about, Angie thought. Well, I've been tested with worse.

"Why were the Pukuis taken off-planet? If they were critically ill, why weren't they treated right here?" she asked.

"There is no treatment," he said. "Loli fever strikes about twelve hours after ingestion of the bacteria. There are no early symptoms. Victims simply collapse, with rarely more than a few seconds, a few minutes at the most, before they lose consciousness. Pua is the only one to have ever survived."

Angie was surprised by the softness that came into Toma's tone. He actually seemed to care for the girl.

"I was in the control shed with a group of visiting Earthers when I heard Katie scream," he said. He sat unmoving, his wineglass still in his hand. "By the time I got to the house, Zed was sprawled unconscious on the stairs. A doctor from the Earth team was trying to revive him. I found Katie upstairs, huddled over Lehua's body.

"Pua was already in a state of collapse when she burst in. Dr. Waight came in right behind her and held her back. Pua remained conscious just long enough to hear me say it was loli fever—and to accuse me of trying to murder them."

"I still don't understand why they were taken to Earth," Angie said. Dr. Waight? she thought.

"The Company has been trying to get its hands on Pua ever since they discovered her existence a year ago," he said. "Lehua and Zed refused to allow the Company doctors near her or to release any information about her physical makeup. Waight couldn't take Pua alone, though—that would have raised too many questions. So, she claimed it was a humanitarian gesture and took them all."

He drained his glass, then leaned forward to refill it from a decanter on the table between them. He filled a second glass and offered it to Angie. She watched him for a moment, then sighed and accepted it. He smiled.

The wine was rich, fruity. Like . . . She met his look over the rim of the glass. "I'm surprised Katie hasn't brought you something to eat by now," she said. "What with you being such a good friend of the family and all." She could think of no Earthly comparison for the wine.

"Frankly, so am I. She's usually in here with a tray the minute I arrive, but she's nowhere around tonight." He laughed softly. "She's probably out in the jungle somewhere, watching the spiderwebs glow." He sat back.

"What were you and Mr. Pukui arguing about?"

The smile disappeared. "The TC enzyme. The Company wanted the data on it, and Zed refused to give it to them. I had come out to try to change his mind before bringing the World Life heavyweights to meet with him the next day." He drank, a long, deep gulp. He stared at the wine shimmering scarlet through the clear glass.

"Zed didn't want to sell the TC rights to anyone. He said that when the time came, he'd give the process to anyone with a farm to grow the proper algae base, and he'd sell the finished product to anyone who could demonstrate need. In the meantime, he was retaining all rights for himself and his family."

"Why?" Angie asked. "The farm records show he'd willingly sold the production rights to other advances in algae production and quality."

"The Pukuis maintained a very traditional attitude about communal sharing of natural resources," he said. "They didn't like the idea of World Life controlling the entire production and distribution of so valuable a commodity. They were afraid it would be used as a political tool instead of the life-giving gift it was meant to be."

He's either exceptionally straightforward or an extraordinary liar, Angie thought. He was alluding to the same serious Company illegalities that Pua had spoken of. Spit, but she was tired. She took another sip of wine, wishing its sweet freshness could wash away the sour taste at the back of her mouth.

Toma watched her silently. He was sitting well back in his seat, legs spread, arms relaxed except for where he held the glass. He was an arrogant bastard, confident of his power and position, and—she had to admit it—attractive in his open challenge to her interrogation. Too bad he was a Company man. She wasn't about to take *that* chance again.

"If you believe there might be some irregularities in the Pukuis' deaths," she said, dragging her mind back to the subject at hand, "why haven't you done anything about it? Surely, investigating the deaths of Lesaat's two most prominent scientists fits somewhere within your duties as planetary supervisor—not to mention the fact that you claim them as friends. I should think the Company itself would have insisted on such an investigation."

"The Company declared the deaths accidental and, because of the missing TC records, put an absolute lid of secrecy over the entire affair," he said.

She watched him again, wondering how much of what she was reading from his body language and verbal tone was true. She held no faith at all in his words. It was time to change tactics. She finished her wine and pulled her feet off the table.

"Tell me something, Inspector," she said, yawning. "Were you, by any chance, having a little illicit sex on the side with Mrs. Pukui?"

He sat up so abruptly that his drink spilled into his lap. "That's out of line, Warden!"

"Is that your answer?"

He recovered quickly. She had caught him off-guard, but he was good at this. "I loved Lehua Pukui," he said evenly, firmly—*truthfully*, Angie decided. "I was not *in love* with her. Is that a clear enough answer?"

She nodded.

He stood and brushed the wine from his shorts and his bare thighs. He pulled one of the window shades aside. It was a move meant to distract. She would have done it herself had she been in his place. The sun had risen high enough so that the broad lanai roof prevented it from shining directly into the room, but its diffused light tinged the humid air gold.

"How did you and Zena know so fast what was happening out at number twelve?" she asked, obliging him by changing the subject.

"We set planned methane blows a dozen times a month around here, Warden," he said. "I'd recognize the signs in my sleep."

He turned. "From the description Pua relayed, and the timing of the explosions, I'd say that release was set up by a total amateur. No experienced squid would have set it up so sloppily. A proper methane kill carries most of the algae inward, so it stays inside the net."

"Is that your way of saying you didn't do it?" she asked.

Suddenly, he laughed. "You sound just like my one-on-one instructor at Cody, Warden. Where did you get your interrogation training?"

That came as a complete surprise. "You spent time at a troubleshooter's school?"

"Took the full course," he said. "Four years in Wyoming, another in Denver, then three in the field before I succumbed to World Life's offer of a permanent post here on Lesaat. I've taken refreshers at Denver twice."

Spit on the bloody lines, she thought. No wonder I'm having such a hard time reading him. He probably knows more about one-on-one interrogation than I do. Denver was the training site for the Company's top investigators. She would have to debrief this encounter very, very carefully. She was also going to have to dig a *lot* deeper into Dr. Toma Haili's records. A troubleshooter, for god's sake!

Why the hell hadn't the Company used *him* to do their damned truth-drugging? she wondered. Then she remembered that as planetary super, Toma was in the direct employ of World Life. He could no longer claim fully sanctioned U.N. privileges.

"They must have made you a generous offer," she said. "I don't know of many shooters who've voluntarily gone off-planet."

"They promised me land, Warden, just like they did you. Although I must say, it's quite a coup to have negotiated title to *Earth* property."

Angie conceded him a smile. His answer let her know he had been able to bypass the full privacy code on her contract.

"You didn't do too shabbily yourself," she said. "Talking the Company out of a perpetual-rights lease just as if you'd been an original settler."

He laughed. "Touché, Warden. That point goes to you. It's been a while since I played one-on-one with another troubleshooter. I'm out of practice."

And it hasn't slowed you down a bit, she thought. It was time to end this thing. The wine had relaxed her almost to the point of enjoying herself. She stood and stretched. "I'm sorry to break this up, Inspector, but it feels like at least a month has passed since I got off that shuttle yesterday."

He stepped away from the window and crossed to her side—close to her side. He was a shooter, all right. She could smell it on him. A flood of adrenaline followed by a couple of hours of tight emotional control had done the same thing to his libido as it had to hers. He would be offering her the usual shooter's solution next.

"Is there anything else I can do for you this morning, Warden?" he asked.

She laughed. "An honest offer from a Company man. Wonders never cease. It's a shame to pass it up, Inspector, but unfortunately right now I'm more in need of sleep." And time to figure out just who, and what, the hell you are.

He shrugged good-naturedly and stepped back. She waved him ahead of her from the room. "Did you get my requisition list into the pipeline?"

"There'll be a full net crew here before noon to help with twelve's disposal," he said. "The available materials will be here shortly after, and the rest has been ordered from Earth."

"What about that security squad? I want them out of here today. You should know shooters don't use Company police, not in this kind of situation."

He surprised her by agreeing without a protest. "They'll be shipped out on the vessels that bring the work crews. You do understand the need for immediate action here at Pukui, don't you? The storms . . ."

"I understand about the storms," she said. It was about the only thing she *did* understand.

He nodded and stepped outside onto the lanai. "By the way, how does a case of Maldarian caramels fit into your plans to save Pukui?" he asked.

Angie had been wondering when he would get around to asking about that. The caramels were the only way she had been able to think of to send a private message back to Earth. "They're one of my vices," she said. "I frequently take them into the field with me, but this time I didn't have time to pick up my order before I left Earth. I find chocolate-covered caramels rival even early morning sex for helping me think straight."

He lifted a brow. "An expensive alternative, considering the shipping costs to Lesaat."

She laughed. "When I'm ready for the alternative, I'll let you know, Inspector. Anyway, I'm sure you noticed that I credited the order to my personal account, although technically it is a legitimate field expense."

He offered her a skeptical look before scuffing across the wriggling door mat.

"Don't take the flitter," she said as he slipped into a pair of plastic thongs.

"What?"

"The flitter. Don't take it."

"Now look, Warden, this has been fun, but I've got to get back to Landing. That happens to be my personal—"

"There are only two things on this farm that I trust right now," Angie said. "One is the air-security system I rigged myself last night. The other is your flitter. You can return to Landing with the first supply run, or order yourself some other transportation. You're welcome to take one of Pukui's flits if you want, but I don't recommend it. They look to be in serious need of some good maintenance. Repair parts and personnel are on the req list."

"You—"

"The dock comm is open for your use. Just stay out of Zena's way." She flipped the latch on the door. "It *has* been fun, Inspector. Let's do it again sometime."

She grinned as she turned back toward the stairs, thinking how much Pua would have enjoyed hearing *that* Company man's curse.

Chapter 10

It was past midday when Angie woke. She lay still for a moment, listening to the chatter of fronded trees and distant surf. She remembered waking to the sound of rain sometime during the morning, then being lulled back to sleep by its steady drumming on the lanai roof just outside her window. She felt blessedly rested.

Downstairs, she found another food tray by the front door. She groaned inwardly when she saw that rock bread had been included again. Judging from the number of slices on the plate, Auntie Kate must have decided that Angie actually liked the stuff.

"Thank you, Katie," she said to the empty room. There was a slight movement behind the louvers to the pantry. "The house looks beautiful. You've done a good job taking care of it. Mrs. Pukui would be pleased." The movement stopped, but the louvers did not snap closed as they had when she had looked that way the previous day.

After establishing that the cleanup and disposal of the destroyed algae was under way, and that there was nothing she could do to assist, Angie carried the food outside. Sure that Katie would be watching, she forced down a slice of rock bread, then stuffed mountain apples into her pockets to eat while she explored the grounds around the house.

It was amazingly comfortable, this home compound of the Pukui family. Pua's parents had obviously cared a great deal about it, for it was designed for beauty and comfort as well as for convenience. Even the farm control shed, which was not a shed at all, but a modern, fully equipped laboratory and office, was aesthetically pleasing. It sat adjacent to the main house overlooking the lagoon and was constructed from the same multicolored local woods.

The lawn surrounding the house and its various outbuildings was a perfect two-inch-deep mat. She could see no signs of recent mowing, but it couldn't have been done too long before her arrival. Pua had told her that things regenerated fast on Lasaat, and after examining the fine tips of the neatly cut grass, she believed it.

A garden at the back of the house held both flowers and food plants—in some cases, Angie wasn't sure which was which—and fruit and flower trees were scattered across the back lawn. A waist-high hedge of brilliant scarlet leaves separated the compound from the surrounding jungle.

After a time, Angie turned her look toward Mauna Kea Iki's distant summit. She peeled and ate a pair of mountain apples, then pushed through the hedge and began to climb.

It was much more difficult than she expected. The slope was gradual enough, but the terrain was tortuous. Deep cracks and abrupt outcroppings of stone appeared as if from nowhere. The ground and trees and bushes were thickly tangled with vines. One kind, in particular, seemed to cling to Angie's boots whenever she paused.

Slick, wet leaves, some of them as large as she was, slid along her arms and legs as she pushed through the thick foliage. She ducked under ferns as high as trees. She had been in jungles before, but none quite so voracious as this. She kicked a clinging vine from her boot and doggedly climbed on.

"Like being in a bloody time machine," she muttered as she tripped over the rotting corpse of some long-dead tree. At least, it appeared to have been a tree. She shuddered at the twisting, hairlike growth that undulated slowly across the fallen log. It reminded her of Pua's door mat. A featherlike plant, which for the want of better classification she labeled a fern, stiffened and turned away as she spoke.

"A broken time machine," Angie added, and was astonished when the fern turned quickly back. She bent down to examine it.

"Do you speak as well as you hear?" she asked. The plant shivered and exuded a fine spray of orange pollen. Angie jumped back quickly. An orange stain spread over the toes of her boots.

"Well, spit on you, too," she said and moved cautiously away. The plant reminded her of Crawley.

Near the top of a steep rise—which must, she assured herself, be near the top of this fireloving hill—she stopped to wipe her arm across her forehead. "Perspiration," Nori had always called it. "Sweat," she said decisively as she caught a whiff of her shirt. Her sleeve was already soaked and did little to dry her face. She wished she had Yoshida here now. She'd show him a thing or two about perspiration.

The climb directly ahead was almost vertical, one of the few almost-bare rocky spots she had encountered. The stone was wet, as everything in the jungle was, and it was patched with glistening gray splotches that Angie did not trust at all. She reached for a low-hanging branch and pulled herself into a nearby tree.

Her fingers wrapped easily around the broad, smooth branches. Their slight suction created a surprisingly firm grip, and Angie pulled herself up quickly—faster than she ever could have with her old hands. She pushed the thought away angrily. She was using these hands because she had to, but she'd be damned if she was going to start liking them.

The tree's wide leaves hid her view of the upper slope, but when she had climbed as high as the ridge, she spied a level open ledge covered in what looked like gray-green grass. She climbed slightly higher, then crawled as far as she could onto a thick branch, and jumped. The ground covering lay over firm ground, and she landed with only a slight stumble.

"What're you doing, anyway?"

Angie jumped. She spun around to see Pua near the edge of the ledge, sitting cross-legged on a velvety black lump that might or might not have been a stone. She had a woven band around her forehead, and fringes of moss around her wrists and ankles. A strand of golden yellow shells glinted at her neck.

"Where did *you* come from?" Angie gasped.

"I was on the path. I heard somebody crashing around over here and came to see what was happening. What are you doing?"

Angie stared. She wiped her uselessly wet sleeve over her face again. "There's a *path* up this jungle-eaten hill?"

Pua's expression changed from curious to incredulous. She giggled.

Angie groaned. Every muscle in her body ached. She couldn't remember a time when she had felt stickier. She dropped to the ground and lay on her back, spread-eagled on the spongelike ground covering. "Why didn't you tell me there was a path?"

"You never asked," Pua said, laughing even harder. "There are paths all over the island. How did you think we got around?"

Angie had been away from the land too long. She had needed to touch the earth, even if it was an alien earth. She had needed a physical and emotional time-out from the chaos of her recent human interactions. I didn't think at all, she thought. The mountain was here, so I climbed it. The moss, or whatever it was beneath her, was so soft it felt as if it were massaging her back. She sighed, and relaxed into its cool caress.

"Your hands were working pretty good there in the tree," Pua said. Her voice was still filled with laughter. Angie was amazed at the difference in the girl since her arrival back at Pukui. It was as if the place itself was slowly filling that terrible emptiness she had tried so hard to hide back at the recon station.

Angie took a deep breath and blew it out slowly. "This is one of the damnedest mountains I've ever climbed," she said. "Are we anywhere near the top?"

"I hope so," Pua said very softly.

Angie rolled over. Pua's expression had grown serious, but at Angie's questioning look, her good humor returned.

"Oh, you mean *this* mountain! We're already *at* the top of Mauna Kea Iki. See the snow?" She pointed over Angie's shoulder, and Angie noticed for the first time that she was no longer completely surrounded by jungle. The ledge they were on ran in both directions around the curve of the hill, providing a break between the tops of the jungle foliage and a stand of brilliant white trees.

She sat up, staring. The shimmering, translucent foliage, reflecting the bright sunlight, had a startling resemblance to snow. "It's amazing," she said. "If it wasn't so hot, it would almost seem real."

"It gets cold up here at night," Pua said.

Angie laughed. "You don't know cold, girl." She pushed herself to her feet, twisted her neck to relieve a kink in her shoulder, and walked toward the white trees. Small circular leaves—like aspen, she thought, only not really—shifted and whispered as they turned in the steady breeze. The trunks, thick and smooth, entirely unlike aspen, stretched well over twenty meters.

Angie ducked under a wide branch. The temperature dropped by at least ten degrees. Strangely, the shade was bright and welcoming, totally unlike the ebony shadows of the jungle below. There was no brush, only the smooth, glassy tree trunks rising from the gray-green grass. In places, the soft ground covering had grown up half a meter or more around the broad bases of the trees.

Angie stared around in wonder. "Your mother did this?" she asked.

Pua nodded. "The trees were smaller before. Fatu told me they were scattered all around the island. They got big like this after Mama moved them up here. They like the sun."

"How do you keep the rest of the jungle from taking them over?"

Pua ran her palms over one of the tree trunks. After a moment, she paused and began picking at the shining wood. Angie laid her own hands on the tree. The bark was warm and moist. She could almost feel the sap moving beneath the smooth bark. A meter above her, the trunk split into three wide branches.

If I were alone, she told the tree silently, I would climb right up there into your heart and stay for about three years. The bark was smooth and welcoming under her hands.

"I don't know how Mama did it in the beginning, when the trees were small," Pua said. She had dug deep into the tree. "But now, all we have to do is keep the moat happy. That's what we call the open area around the summit."

Angie looked back to the place where she had first found Pua. "What kind of plant is this ground covering, anyway? A grass of some sort?" She could still feel its spongy warmth caressing her tired back.

Pua leaned forward to peer at the tree trunk closely. She was digging deep into the wood with her sharp nails. "I think it's more of an animal."

"What?"

"Well, Matt's always seemed more like an animal than a plant to me. He might be both, though. Dad said that was possible."

"Who, or what, is Matt?"

Pua looked up at her. "The door mat. You know, the one you've been so careful not to step on? He's a piece of moat grass."

A soft, splitting sound drew both their looks back to the tree. To Angie's astonishment, a deep crack had opened in the shining wood. Pua laughed, and poked one long finger into the upper end of the crack. A small white bead rolled into her waiting palm. She grinned and held it up to catch the light.

"What is that?" Angie asked. It looked like a natural pearl, irregularly round and iridescent.

"Dad said they were just gobs of hardened tree sap, but Mama called them snowballs," Pua said. "They melt if they get too warm, just like the Earth kind."

Angie held her hand very still as Pua placed the marble-sized gem in her palm. It felt like jade against her hot skin. It wasn't really cold enough to be mistaken for snow.

Pua began carefully rubbing the edges of the hole. The wood responded visibly, creaking slightly as it began to press closed. After a few moments, there was only a slight indentation at the place where the hole had been. Pua ran her fingers over the small roughness her digging had caused. It smoothed as easily as if it had been wet clay.

"The trees only open for people they like," Pua said.

"How did you know where to start digging?" Angie asked. She had seen nothing unusual about the place where Pua had first started picking at the wood.

"I felt for it," Pua said. "With my hands. My mama showed me how." She glanced down at the snowball in Angie's hand. Angie handed it back to her.

"I used to have lots," Pua said, "but Katie hid them while I was gone." She smiled slightly. "She doesn't like snowballs in the house, 'cause when they melt, they make a mess. If you don't find them in time, the sap eats right through whatever it's lying on, especially if it's plastic. Once I left a bunch of softened ones on Fatu's best fishing nets." She giggled. "He made me tie him a whole new set."

She motioned Angie back out from under the trees. Angie tried to walk lightly. She glanced behind at where their footsteps had disturbed the shivering grass. "It looks like water," she said.

"That's why it's called moat grass," Pua replied. She ran ahead, scuffing her feet across the ground to set the grass moving. "It likes to be tickled," she called. The grass burped softly in several places. Angie was glad she was wearing boots.

"Do you ever climb the snow trees?" she asked when Pua rejoined her.

"No," Pua said quickly.

Angie decided to let the lie pass. Lehua Pukui might not be on the mountain in person anymore, but she certainly was in spirit, most strongly here at the summit. If the girl didn't want her mother to know she climbed her special trees, Angie wasn't going to be the one to reveal her secret.

I'm thinking like a mountain woman again, she realized sud-

denly, talking to the trees and actually listening for answers. She
laughed silently. It was good to feel strong and healthy again,
not just in her altered body, but in her spirit.

"Why are you smiling?" Pua asked.

Angie blinked. "Sorry. This place makes me feel . . ." She
shrugged. "I guess I just went back home there for a minute."

Pua glanced toward the snow trees. "I used to do that sometimes, back at the recon station."

They circled the hillock of snow trees until they reached a
narrow but easily recognizable trail leading downhill. Angie
shook her head in disbelief, took one last look at the magical
summit, and started down.

The trip took a quarter of the time it had taken her to climb
up. Even so, she was drenched again by the time they reached
the edge of a freshwater pool not far from the main house. Angie
could see the roofline through the trees.

"There's a soap bush over there by the side." Pua pointed to
a low bush hanging over the water. Coal-black berries grew in
small clusters at the ends of leafless boughs. She pulled off her
shirt, grabbed a handful of berries, and walked into the water.
"It's kind of cold."

"Where does the water come from?" Angie asked. This was
not exactly the carefree bathtub she'd had in mind. She crossed
her arms.

"Underground," Pua said. "It seeps up through the sandy
bottom. There's lots of fresh water trapped in caves and tunnels
under the island. The rain up on the mountain keeps them full,
and the pressure pushes the water up here."

She turned back. Angie saw awareness touch her eyes. "It's
not deep. You can stand up everyplace but in the middle, and
the overflow stream stays on the surface from here down to the
lagoon."

I have to do it sometime, Angie thought. She pulled off her
boots and trousers, but left her shirt on as she followed Pua into
the pool. The water was not nearly as cold as the glacier-spawned
waters of the last such pool she had been in. Still, it was not
warm. Goose bumps lifted along her arms.

"It feels wonderful," she said. She sank to her shoulders,
shivering the whole way. She pulled off her shirt, scrubbed it
for a moment in the clear water, then let it drift beside her.

Pua handed her the berries.

At Angie's puzzled look, she took them back, pierced each
one with a nail, then rubbed the released juice into a bloody-

red froth. A pungent, fruity smell stung Angie's nostrils. The underlying fragrance was familiar.

Pua handed the froth to Angie. "Just rub it on," she said. "It should be enough. But you can use more if you need it."

Angie considered Pua's offering dubiously, but decided nothing could be worse than the current slimy feel of her skin. She rubbed the soap along her arms. It acted more like a sponge than a handful of bubbles. It held roughly together even under the water.

"There's a bush like this in your folks' bedroom," Angie said. "Is it the same thing?"

Pua tensed, but recovered quickly. She obviously did not want Angie snooping around in her parents' room. She shook her head. "That's a candleberry bush."

"They look alike. What's the difference?" Angie asked. She scrubbed what was left of the slowly disintegrating soap over her face and hair.

"This one tastes like soap," Pua said. The moss around her wrists had coiled tightly against her skin.

"Ugh," Angie agreed. She quickly rinsed her face clean. As she leaned back to dunk her hair, her fingers brushed across feathery protuberances on each side of her neck. She caught her breath and jerked her hands away.

"It's just your gills," Pua said. "They were starting to open."

Angie closed her eyes and counted. For an instant she found it impossible to breathe. Then she reached up again to run her fingers down the slick edges of the gills. They had closed again, sealed tight to her skin. That touch, she could tolerate. She had practiced it over and over again on the ship. This was the first time she'd had more than a shower to get the gills wet.

"They only flare fully when they're completely submerged," Pua went on. "Your lungs won't close until your face is in the water."

Angie took a deep breath.

"What happened to you, anyway? What made you afraid of the water?" Pua asked.

"I'm not afraid," Angie said. "I'm just—" Pua's lifted brows stopped her. "Oh, all right. I'm terrified. Not of the water itself, but of being caught underneath it."

Again Pua said nothing. She remained motionless in the gently moving water. By training or by nature? Angie wondered. How does she know so well how to broadcast calm? A small yellow insect landed on Pua's cheek. She lifted it off with her fingertips, inspected it casually, then put it into her mouth. Angie shivered.

"I was leading a white-water rafting tour," she said. "About a year ago. One of my passengers went overboard and panicked. I went in after him. I got him out, but I got caught in a deep-water current and was sucked into an underground channel."

Pua remained still, entirely noncommittal.

"I didn't have gills then, Pua."

Abruptly, Pua's eyes widened. Her lips parted, and her hands lifted to her neck. "What happened?" Her voice mirrored Angie's own inner horror at remembering the dark suffocation. "How did you get out?"

"The channel surfaced about a quarter of a mile downriver. The search crew found me there. They managed to get my heart going and get me breathing again."

"You were *dead*?"

"Technically. For a while."

Pua stared at her. "Wow!"

Angie smiled. Telling the story had somehow made it easier to accept. She had told it to others, of course, but never to one who had known what the experience had done to her. Trouble-shooters made a point of never admitting to true terror.

"Maybe we should go down to the ocean," Pua said cautiously.

"It's now or never," Angie said. "I only have so much in the way of guts, and I'm pushing my limit right now. Sink, so I can watch." Her hands had become alien again, twisting into rigid fists at her sides. Or did that mean they had become more a part of her? She was sure her own hands would not have been relaxed at this moment.

Pua cocked her head. Slowly, the awe left her eyes. "Why should this be any harder for you to do than closing the hatch on the flitter?" she asked.

Angie closed her eyes. *I don't know who taught you to deal with panic, Waterbaby, but they were good. I thank them most sincerely.* She met Pua's carefully neutral look again.

"Sink," she said.

Pua grinned, blinked nictitating membranes into place, and slid beneath the clear, cold water. Her hair spread in a dark cloud around her. Just as Angie wondered how she would keep the long strands from tangling in her fanning gills, Pua scooped her hair over her shoulders and knotted it at the back of her neck.

She looked upward through the water and offered Angie an openmouthed grin. Bubbles bounced upward along her cheeks. The golden necklace floated for a moment, then sank and settled. Her gills bulged slowly open and began a rhythmic pulsing.

When she surfaced a moment later, the gill flaps sealed shut smoothly and instantly.

"You didn't do anything," Angie said.

"You don't have to *do* anything," Pua replied. "You don't even have to open your mouth if you don't want to, but I like to taste what's around me."

Angie reached out to touch Pua's neck. Pua jerked back. "Don't do that!" she said. "Don't ever do that!"

"I just wanted to feel . . ."

"Here on Lesaat, your gills are your *life*, Mountainlady. *Never* let anyone touch your neck. If you try to touch someone else's, they'll think you're trying to kill them."

"Kill them?"

"If you get in a fight," Pua said, "and the other guy reaches for your gills, move fast. Rip his out first."

Angie stared at her.

"When somebody's gills get touched without permission," Pua said, "somebody dies. That's the way it is."

Angie could see that Pua was speaking the truth. A sudden thought struck her. "Have *you* ever killed anyone, Pua?"

Pua's face closed so tight and so fast that Angie couldn't even guess what she was hiding.

"I promised I'd help you go under the water," Pua said a moment later. She was still frowning. "So, let's do it. You come down with me this time."

Slowly, Angie followed her underwater. At first she felt nothing, only the cold water caressing her face. She held her breath, lips pressed tightly closed, and lifted a hand to a tickling at the sides of her neck. Abruptly, an unexpected surge of adrenaline sent her bursting back to the surface. She fought for breath, heart racing.

Pua popped up and spat a mouthful of water. "What happened? You were doing fine."

Angie forced her breathing to slow. "I don't know. I wasn't down there long enough to get this scared."

Pua instantly looked contrite. "Oh, the adrenaline. I forgot to tell you about that part. You get a rush whenever your gills come fully open. It triggers the oxygen absorption."

Spit! Angie thought. Then she thought again. She had been

accused more than once of being an adrenaline junkie, of taking on high-percentage risks just for the natural biochemical kicks they provided. Angie had never been one to disavow the claims. Her adrenaline highs were much more exciting than any artificial stimulants she had ever tried.

"Maybe I can learn to live with this after all," she muttered. She crossed her legs and sank to the sandy bottom of the pool. She had to blow out all the air in her lungs to sink fully.

Pua squatted in front of her. Angie watched, fascinated, as the girl's gills fanned, fluttered, and settled into their steady rhythm. They seemed as much a natural part of her as her long, slender hands, which rested calmly now on her upraised knees.

Angie's second adrenaline rush was not as pronounced as the first, since her system was already well stimulated, but she recognized it when it came. She smiled slightly, and Pua cautiously smiled back. A trickle of bubbles escaped from one corner of Angie's mouth. She blew out lightly, and more bubbles floated up.

Water seeped into her mouth. I should be able to just swallow it, she thought. She tried it, and the cold water slid into her stomach like ice. She needed to take a breath.

Angie closed her eyes and forced herself to picture oxygen filtering through her gills, sliding effortlessly into her bloodstream, slowly refilling her lungs. She needed to *breathe*!

Pua took her hands. Angie met her distorted look through the water, snapped her nictitating membranes into place, and met it again. Pua lifted the thumb of one hand in the signal for all's well. I'm suffocating! Angie tried to tell her, but Pua did not release her hands. Water filled her opened mouth. She tried to pull away, but was stopped by Pua's superior strength.

Angie panicked, and gasped for air . . .

Her nose and mouth had filled with water. Frigid liquid sang in her ears. *I'm drowning!* She remembered the experience very clearly. The darkness would come next. Then the suffocating tightness of her body closing down from the inside out.

But nothing more happened.

Pua still held her hands tight. Trembling, Angie forced herself to remain sitting at the bottom of the pool.

Pua nodded, very somberly, and gave her the thumbs-up signal once more. Oh, mother of mountains, they work! Angie thought. The damned gills work! The realization brought her more horror than the touch of the water had.

I am so afraid, Angie admitted to herself suddenly. I am so afraid of this place, this water, this body that is no longer entirely mine. She met Pua's look again. I am so afraid of you, Pualeiokekai Pukui.

It was the first time since Angie had awakened from the fire that she had admitted fully to her terror. It was the first time in her life that she could remember allowing anyone to share so intimate a glimpse of her personal vulnerability.

How can I cry without air? Angie wondered.

Abruptly, Pua let go of her hands. She stood like some fearless water sprite and walked from the pool, gathering Angie's clothing along the way. Very carefully, Angie followed. Her gills sealed instantly shut as she took a deep, deep breath of Pukui's golden air.

She bent to retrieve her shirt from atop the bush where Pua had tossed it, and tied it sideways around her waist. The rest of her clothes were too dirty to put back on now. She noticed an orange stain spread over the toe of one her boots.

Pua was standing a few meters downhill of the pool, with her arms crossed and her back turned. Angie doubted it was because of modesty. What's wrong now? she wondered. The sweet scent of candleberry surrounded her. The aftersmell of the soap.

There was a long silence. Then Pua said, "Why did you say that about my mother?" The anger, the suspicion, the deep, deep sadness—were all back in her voice.

"What are you talking about?" Angie asked.

Pua turned. Her eyes were much angrier than her voice. Angie was suddenly glad they were no longer in the water.

"To Toma. Why did you say that about him and my mom?"

Angie thought quickly. When had she . . .

"I was under the house this morning," Pua said. "I heard everything you said to him."

"Oh, dear god," Angie breathed. She heard me ask him if he'd been having sex with her mother!

"Pua, I was only—"

"My mother was *good*! She was better than you'll ever be, even if you do climb mountains and save people from fires and—!"

"I was interrogating him, Pua. I was trying to startle him into saying something he might not otherwise say."

"But it wasn't true!"

"Of course it wasn't true." Angie took a step toward her. "Pua, every single thing I've heard or seen or learned since I've been here tells me that your parents were devoted to each other—

and to this place, and to you. I did not mean to question your mother's integrity.''

Pua's eyes narrowed. ''You wanted to have sex with Toma yourself, didn't you?''

Angie sighed. This had gone far enough. ''Troubleshooters often share sex, Pua,'' she said, ''and Toma had just told me he was one. His offer, and my response, had nothing to do with anything else that was going on.'' She lifted a hand. ''Look, Pua—''

''If you touch me, I'll kill you, Mountainlady!''

Angie stopped.

Far enough, indeed. ''You won't kill me, and you know it. Not while you're still under my protection.''

''I don't need you to protect me!''

''You need me if you want to stay on this planet,'' Angie said. She pointed toward the lagoon. ''You need me if you want to save that damned reef!''

Pua's chin trembled.

''Our reasons for being here differ,'' Angie said, trying to control her own frustration. It wasn't the girl she was angry with. This whole situation was impossible. ''But we're working toward the same goal. If we're going to work together, or at least not against each other, you've got to stop judging my motives by every separate thing I do or say.''

''You're just—''

''She's right, Pua. Listen to her.''

Angie and Pua both spun around at the man's voice. It was Toma. He was standing at the head of the path leading back to the house.

''Get off my property!'' Pua shouted.

''Pua, listen—''

''Go away!''

''Why are you still here?'' Angie demanded. ''You said you were going back to Landing.''

Toma gave her a long, dark look. The wet shirt clung to her legs, clammy now in the on-shore breeze.

''I changed my mind,'' he said. ''My office staff has taken care of your requisitions; the first load of extra swimmers is already in the water at number twelve. I decided to stay and keep an eye on things.''

He turned to Pua. ''We need to talk.''

''I don't want to talk to you,'' Pua cried. ''You murdered

Mama and Daddy, and now you're trying to take Pukui away from me, too.''

"I didn't—"

"You were our *friend*, Uncle Toma! You were our family!"

Toma grabbed her by the shoulders. "Pualei, I did not kill them!'' There was a movement near the path. Angie saw Fatu there, ready as always to protect the girl. Before either of them could intervene, Pua twisted in Toma's hands. She slipped away from his hold and snaked her long fingers toward his neck.

"No, Pua!" Fatu called, but Toma jerked back and turned quickly away. Pua's nails caught his shoulder instead of his gills. They ripped through cloth and skin. He quickly moved farther back.

"Pukui is mine!" Pua screamed. "Go away!"

Toma pressed a hand over his bleeding shoulder and glanced at Angie.

"You heard her," Angie said.

"You've got a job out here that you haven't even begun to understand, Warden," he said. "You're going to need all the help you can get." He glared at her for a moment more, then turned back toward the house and docks. Like a massive shadow, Fatu followed.

When Angie turned back to the pool, Pua was gone.

Chapter 11

Pua splashed across the overflow stream and headed straight downhill. She thrashed through the thick undergrowth, cursing at the stinging tugs of the nettle-bush seeds and stomping aside clinging friendly vines. Because of the tide, she had to run, then wade a long way across the shallow fringing reef, before she could swim. When she finally did submerge, she welcomed the rush of adrenaline. She used it to refuel her anger.

She swam toward the farm pass, so as not to meet any of the work crews traveling back and forth to number twelve. She would go outside the barrier reef, she decided, swim naked in the deep ocean, all the way to Landing, and be damned with them all.

Then she changed her mind. "It's my lagoon!" she shouted. "I can swim in it if I want!" She turned back. A pigfish blundered blindly into her, squealed, and bumbled away. It was the only living thing that came near.

This swim was far different from the one she had taken the night before. Then, even with Fatu beside her, the rays had swum close, sliding their wings along her body and sharing their warmth and their speed. The reef and its multitude of occupants had sung to her of home, and the glowing nighttime sea had brought her comfort.

Now she swam alone. The sea around her was empty, and she could feel nothing but her own rage. She knew it was her own broadcasting of her anger that kept the reef dwellers away. How are you going to feel, she asked them silently, when you find out I brought a once-dead woman back to swim in our lagoon? She wondered if she would ever get the tide-pissing woman *into* the lagoon. Why had everything gone so wrong?

The rumbling vibration of the disposal barge entered her consciousness. She surfaced to watch from a distance as it lumbered slowly along the upper end of the number-twelve pen. Its surface pipes sucked in steady streams of dead and dying algae to feed its grumbling furnaces, while its screeching winches periodically lifted sections of the net up and through the compression rollers. Acrid green-black smoke billowed from the barge's tall stacks.

"Fire," Pua muttered. "That's *her* element." She thought of the snow trees and the woman's obvious emotional response to them. "And the land," she added grudgingly.

Still, it had been the water that had made the woman cry. Pua felt her own eyes sting as she recalled that terrifying, exhilarating moment in the bathing pool when the Earther had admitted openly to her fear. It had been that one moment of complete honesty that had given Pua the strength to leave her there unharmed.

Pua had held her anger in all morning just waiting for that moment, and then . . . She sank until only her eyes were above water, so she wouldn't have to smell the burning algae.

"I don't know what to do," she said into the sea. "I don't know who to trust." Le Fe'e offered no answer.

She dove deep again.

She wasn't sure anymore if Toma had murdered her parents. Fatu said he couldn't have, and from the woman's voice through the library floor, Pua suspected she didn't believe Toma guilty either. Pua had seen true sorrow on Toma's face, heard it in his voice, and felt it in his hands.

But if he hadn't done it, or hadn't at least condoned it, then who had? And why had he fought so hard with her father, trying to get him to give up the enzyme research after all they had been through to develop and protect it? Toma had always helped Pukui before, imposing Company policy only as strictly as necessary to get the Company to leave the farm alone. He had been her uncle. He had been her friend.

Well, he wasn't her uncle now. And she had no friends, except for Fatu and Pukui itself. She wished the rays would come closer. She pulled the tiny snowball from her pocket and rolled it between her fingers. It glistened pale green in the refracted sunlight. It was cool, even in the water.

Pua had found her other snowballs that morning, while she was under the house listening to Toma and the warden. Katie had buried the shiny balls, one each, under Pua's coral markers. Without light, they had remained solid and bright, undamaged, unmelted. According to Katie's mumbled explanation, she had put them there for safekeeping until Pua's return. Pua drifted for a moment with the smooth gem pressed against her cheek.

She could think of nothing, *nothing* she could do but follow the—

She kicked suddenly for the surface. A ray jumped and splashed far ahead.

"I have to do what she says!" she called to it. "I don't have any choice. I *have* to do what she says."

For now, she amended silently. She slipped just beneath the surface and swam hard after the ray. As if sensing her changed mood, the ray pack turned and sped back to meet her. In the frenzied collision of their greeting, they tumbled and turned until Pua was choking on her own laughter.

"Come on," she said finally, clicking her nails to give them the message in a language they understood. "Let's go look at that stupid algae."

She grabbed the nearest ray's forewings and swung onto its back. When she bumped it with her knees, it surged forward so quickly that she almost lost her hold.

As they approached the barge, the ray slowed and she dropped off. She shooed the pack away and swam closer to the human work crews. The swimmers were idling under the barge, holding onto handbars or just drifting in the warm, smelly water. They were taking a break while another load of algae was sucked from the net.

Only a few of the swimmers noticed Pua's approach; fewer yet acknowledged it with more than a frown or a curious glance at her hands and feet. Pua was glad she had left her clothes on. Fatu had been right about that—and about the small number of old-time Pukui crew left on-site. She saw only three that she knew well—they were the ones who had smiled or nodded when she came near. She recognized some of the others—they were regulars on Company harvest crews. Two of the new Pukui recruits, as well as two others she had seen on the shuttle, were also among the workers. The rest were all strangers.

She wondered why so many old-timers had left. She doubted it was because of larger bonuses offered elsewhere, as the Company had claimed. More likely it had to do with the five Pukui squid who had died since the Company had taken over the farm operations—in accidents or of loli fever, Fatu had said.

"Nobody got bad loli from *my* reef," she muttered.

The staccato beat of a *Ready the net!* order, a harsh metallic pounding transmitted through underwater speakers, sent the swimmers scrambling into quick formation. The yellow-clad net crew divided—two swimmers to the surface at each side to release the net from the float lines, the rest to the base of the net to disentangle it from the coral and repair any resulting tears as the net was lifted. The cleaners, carrying hand vacuums and pickup nets as green as their coveralls, followed the base-net crew down.

"Roll net!" The order was accompanied by a shrill keening wail. Not even a totally untrained squid could hear that sound and not understand that it meant danger in the waters ahead. Pua swam closer to watch as the screeching winches began hauling the net.

The barge traveled lengthwise along the pen, drawing the net toward the center as it pulled up the slack caused by removing the sludgelike algae from inside. The net was squeezed between two giant compression rollers to press the excess algae back into the pen. Had this been an ordinary harvest, the net would have been set on a continuous slow lift. Instead of being piled on deck, it would have been automatically reset off the back of the barge.

This time, because the algae was rotten and the net had been allowed to grow so full that it touched bottom in many places, it was being hauled in sections and kept on board for a later full inspection and repair. The furnaces burned slowly and steadily.

Some of the net crew worked to quickly disentangle the fine mesh as it lifted slowly away from the rough, jagged coral. Others tied up or patched resulting tears and holes. The cleaners moved among them scooping small bits of escaped algae into their nets, then transferring the slime to the portable vacuums. When the main net caught on higher-than-usual outcroppings of coral, netters and cleaners worked together to maneuver it free.

Pua stayed back, knowing from experience that the Company crew, at least, would consider her help an intrusion—despite the fact that she could tie net faster and tighter than the best of them. Or maybe because of it. She patrolled the middle depths instead, the area where the net began drawing together as it was being pulled toward the compression rollers above.

When she spotted holes that the base crew had missed, she flagged them with yellow markers so the deck inspection crew would have an easier job finding them later. She paid little attention to the others and was startled when a strong hand wrapped around her left thigh. It pulled her down and away from the net.

She kicked and turned, fingers spread ready to defend herself, but the swimmer let her go without a struggle. It was the Company crew boss. She recognized him from previous harvests. Klooney was a man whom she had never liked much, but he was in great demand on the harvest circuit because his crews were fast and efficient.

Fatu had told her that Klooney had been one of the most persistent Company searchers at Pukui, even after losing the tip of his finger in the burial cave and suffering from severe overexposure to prickly dust. Pua thought it was particularly clever of Fatu to have sprinkled the burial baskets with the highly irritating powder. Klooney's hands and face were still red lined from scratching, and the rumors about a Company curse at Pukui were stronger than ever.

Klooney pointed with his stubby finger up toward the place where the lifting net began folding in on itself, just below the compression rollers. He pointed at Pua, and then he twisted his fingers together into a tight tangle.

Pua spat a quick stream of bubbles. She signed to him that she wasn't about to get herself caught in the net and pulled up through the rollers. He jerked a thumb toward open water, ordering her off the site.

"Kiss coral," she started to sign, but was interrupted by a shrill whistle from the base crew. Klooney ordered Pua away again, then dove toward the group of swimmers who had called. Pua followed close behind.

One of the new recruits—not one of Pukui's, but Pua recognized him from the shuttle—had gotten his hand caught in the net as it scraped across a branch of knife coral. The tips of two fingers were torn and bleeding. One of the swimmers quickly sealed a medical sack around the injured fingers, and Klooney signaled for the nearest cleaner to vacuum up the blood. This was not a good time of day to attract the suckersharks.

He ordered a swimmer to lead the injured worker topside before turning back to the net. It was still being dragged slowly upward and to the side across the razor-sharp coral. One of the women attempted to cut the knife coral with a rocksaw, but Klooney waved her away. It would take hours to cut through even a few of the iron-hard branches.

Cut and patch, he signaled instead.

Pua moved back. Cutting the net enough to free it was going to cause a large release of algae. Most of the net's slack had already been taken up, and the pressure against the inside was strong. Already, the water was marbled with strings of orange-gray sludge escaping through the coral tears.

Pua glanced up, wondering why Klooney didn't just stop the haul. Profit, she thought. Time is money, so haul it in as fast as you can and never mind the consequences. She moved back farther. A ray slid along her side, then flashed away.

The swimmers arranged themselves around the coral outgrowth, hands reaching toward the opening that would soon be cut. They attached a stretch of patching net above and to the open side of the tangled net. Then Klooney reached underneath with his rocksaw and sliced as far as he could reach around the top and sides of the coral.

"Tie!" came the immediate order, and as the winch continued to haul the net up and away, the crew began attaching the patch around the hole as fast as they could tie. The pressure of the shifting algae ripped the main net upward but the double-strength patching held and kept it from tearing higher.

Maybe he's not so dumb after all, Pua thought as the net began to lift clear of the coral. The tying crew worked furiously to maneuver the patch through the thick algae sludge so they could seal the hole before too much more had escaped. The cleaners drifted at the ready, waiting to move in as soon as the way was clear.

Suddenly Pua became conscious of a new vibration in the water, a shiver of movement that sent chills along her spine. She whistled an immediate warning. *Puhi 'ai pōhaku!* she flashed when the swimmers turned her way. *Rock eel! Get away from the net.* The rays swept close, drawn by her whistle, then spun away again.

Klooney frowned, then dropped his own hold on the patch as the puhi poked its pink snout from a hole halfway between him and Pua. It was within meters of the tangled net.

"Stop roll!" he shouted into his shoulder mike. "Stop roll!" He signaled the crew to back off and then cursed as a portion of the net fell back across the knife coral. Rocksaw in hand, he joined the swimmers as they clustered near the cold-water pipe about thirty meters away.

"Idiots," Pua muttered. They should have gone straight to the surface before the puhi came out of his hole. At least they had stayed together. Rock eels were cautious creatures, not likely to attack a large group of human swimmers if easier prey was at hand. She clicked a signal to the rays to stay away, and slowly, carefully moved to join the others around the pipe.

The eel emerged sinuously from its hole. It wasn't large by Pukui standards, but it was big enough to be dangerous. It wavered for a moment with its tail still hidden inside its home in the coral. It turned toward the net, then swung back toward the swimmers. Pua and the others held very still. She saw that one of the Pukui men was holding a new recruit's arm tightly. The new squid's face was tight with terror.

The eel watched them for a time, first with one glassy green eye, then the other. Then, abruptly, it turned back toward the partially repaired net. Sliding the rest of its two-meter-long body from the hole, it undulated slowly toward the branching knife coral. The blood, Pua thought. He must be awful hungry for such a little bit to draw him into the open with all this activity going on.

The eel nosed the net and the coral, then abruptly opened its wide jaws and snapped them closed around the piece of coral where the new recruit had cut his hand. The coral cracked off as easily as if it had been paperwood.

There was a flurry of movement to Pua's right. The new recruit pulled away from the Pukui swimmer's hold and kicked away from the group, toward the surface. Instantly, the puhi twisted back. It hesitated only long enough to finish crushing its mouthful of coral. Then it spit out gravelly residue and snaked toward the lone swimmer.

Quickly, Pua and the Pukui old-timers rose as a group to intercept the eel. To Pua's astonishment, she saw Klooney signal the Company swimmers not to join them. His swimmers stared, first at their boss, then back up at the eel. Many looked angered by the order, but they did not disobey it.

Pua spun back to grab the rocksaw one of them held out to her, then raced upward toward the others. At first the eel veered away at the sight of them. They stayed close together, trying to reach the thrashing recruit before the eel turned back. One of them grabbed the man's flipper, then his foot, and tried to pull him into the protection of their group.

Had there been more of them, had the entire group come up together, it could have worked. A larger group would have been able to control the panicked swimmer's thrashing and perhaps scare the eel away long enough for them all to reach the surface safely. But there were only four of them, not enough to physically restrain the panicked man. He had completely lost control, his fear broadcast so strongly Pua could taste it. The puhi ʻai pōhaku turned back.

It attacked. The recruit thrust his arms out to protect himself, and one entire hand disappeared between the rock eel's jaws. The eel twisted and jerked away. Blood sprayed through the water. One of the Pukui men struck the eel with his hand vacuum. Pua thrust at its face with the rocksaw, while the others tried again to restrain the injured swimmer. The eel jerked away, slapping Pua hard across the chest with its blunt tail. A strong hold from one of the others kept her from being knocked away from their tight group.

Where are the other swimmers? she had time to think before the eel struck again.

Again, it attacked the new recruit, ripping away a section of the man's shoulder and neck before the others could beat it away. The blood was flowing so thickly that they could hardly see. Pua could feel the distant, dark approach of a suckershark pack and, like the others, kicked hard for the surface. The injured crewman had stopped fighting. He hung limp in their arms.

Once more the eel attacked. Pua jammed the whirring rocksaw against its side at the same time one of the others shoved the end of a vacuum tube into the creature's mouth. The suction was on full, and the eel thrashed away and twisted into knots of agony as it attempted to fight its way free of the machine. The tubing crunched under the force of the eel's powerful grinding plates as the swimmers raced the last few meters to the surface.

Pua's head wasn't even out of the water before strong hands pulled her onto the stern ramp and then up onto the deck of the barge. She lay still for a moment, shaking, listening to her heart pound against the cold deck. Her chest ached where the eel had hit her.

". . . kid was the one who saw it coming," she heard someone say. She looked up to see that the speaker was one of the Company net crew who had been with them below. They must have surfaced while the Pukui swimmers were fighting the eel. How could they have done that?

"You sure she wasn't the one who called it up?" another replied. "You saw how she ordered those rays around."

"Who is she, anyway?" a third asked. "She looks—" They grew silent when they noticed Pua listening. She sat up, wrung the excess water from the bottom of her shirt, and then sat defiantly on a stack of patching net where the reef-pissing Company squids would have to look at her. She watched and listened in silence as Klooney and the Pukui workers argued over what had happened below. Someone had laid a green plastic cover over the Pukui recruit's mutilated body.

She was not surprised that he was dead. There had been too much blood for the man to have survived. She shuddered and ran her fingertips over the braid of her mother's hair. You'd better go back to your hole, brother puhi, she urged the eel silently, or you'll end this night as a suckershark sponge.

It was the sharks that Zena and the Company crew boss were arguing about. Klooney stated emphatically that his swimmers did not stay in bloodied waters. Not at Pukui. Not at late evening. And he didn't even attempt to defend the order that had forced the Pukui crew to fight the eel alone.

"I protect my own people," was all he said. "If yours choose to separate from the group, they're on their own."

That brought a murmur of dissatisfaction from even his own crew. Swimmers worked together, or swimmers died. That was the way it was in the Lesaat sea. Pua glanced back at the dead crewman. Despite a hastily applied sealant spray, blood was still running from under the plastic. The hum of an approaching flitter caught her attention. Toma's bird landed on the starboard deck, and Fatu and the mountainlady stepped out.

Fatu met Pua's look immediately, and she signaled that she was safe. He said something to the woman, who nodded. Then they walked aft together. The warden lifted the bloody plastic and stared down at the dead crewman. Pua glanced at the place where the man's arm and hand should have been, then looked away. She tried not to listen as the argument started all over again.

After a moment the warden stopped it. "Fighting about this won't change anything now," she said. "The man's dead and is going to stay that way. We'll deal with the reasons why later. Zena, what's the status of the net?"

"Not good," Zena replied. "It's still hung up on the knife coral. We can't try to drag it off without a containment crew in the water because it's too close to the outlet valves on the deepwater pipe. If it snags, we could break the whole thing open."

"You're gonna have a reef-lovin' mess if that happens," Klooney said. He pulled his bodysuit open and rubbed his chest. It, too, was lined with overlapping scratch marks. Even without the residual prickly itch, Pua wondered how he could stand being suited up with all that body hair. She hoped none of the babies she hoped to have someday would ever look like that.

She would have to remember to be careful when she started choosing mates.

"We'd have to shut down the pumps all the way along the line if we break the main feeder line open," Zena agreed.

"And keep 'em shut till that rock chomper is cleared out of the area," Klooney added. "It ain't gonna abandon that hole now, not as long as it thinks there might still be food nearby. Best thing to do is wait for the suckersharks to clear, won't take more'n an hour, then send a marksman down there in the sub. He can drop a minicharge down that bastard's hole, and when it comes out, blow its head off." Pua frowned and looked up from carving designs in the crystals drying on her arm.

"Zena?" the warden said.

Zena shrugged. "We can't wait around for the eel to decide to move on its own. It could take weeks. The pen's still two-third's full, and the algae's decaying fast. We've got to get it out before the entire area is fouled."

The warden watched her for a moment, then turned to Pua. "What about you? Any other ideas?"

Pua blinked. She had not expected to be included in this public meeting. She wasn't sure she wanted to be included. The encounter with the rock eel had left her shaken. She should have been aware of its presence much sooner; she should have noticed the well-chewed coral around its hole. With the usual bright colors gone from the dying reef, she had forgotten to watch for the eel's obvious signs. Stupid, she thought. She had even gone into the water without her knife again. I've got to stop acting like an Earther.

"Pua?"

"You could try clearing the net from the other side," she said.

The warden's look remained noncommittal, but both Zena and Klooney shook their heads.

"Moving the whole operation to the other end of the pen's a hell of a lot more trouble than that rock chomper's worth, little girl," Klooney said. "We'd have to call in another disposal barge from Landing, 'cause this one can't be moved with the net like it is."

I'd like to feed you to that rock chomper, Pua told him silently. She crossed her arms against the pain in her chest and focused her attention on the warden.

"There's an opening under the algae just a little way beyond where the net is caught. At least there was yesterday. I swam completely under, from one side to the other. If you could get enough tension on the net, somebody might be able to follow the pipe far enough under to put a cap on the outlet valves. Then you could haul the net off without harming the pipe.''

"With the eel still down there, we'd have to haul all the way to the surface without being able to patch,'' Zena said. ''It would leave a hell of a spill directly on the reef, and the net might just keep tearing.''

"Use the sub to lure him away from his hole while the pipe valves are being capped,'' Pua said. ''If you feed him chunks of sponge coral, one after the other, he'll probably follow you all the way to the barrier reef. Once he finds himself surrounded by live coral again, he'll settle into another hole over there, and we won't have to worry about him anymore.''

Zena looked thoughtful.

The Company boss stood. ''We're wastin' our time here, Warden. I say we just kill the bastard and get on with it. Kobayashi, get your gear.''

"Hai,'' came the quick reply.

"Sit down, Mr. Klooney,'' the warden said, still with that same neutral expression.

The Company man glared at her. He remained standing at the side of the folded net. The rest of the crew grew silent.

"I have a few more questions, Mr. Klooney.''

Finally, he sat. Pua was not the only one to release a long, slow breath.

"These eels,'' the warden said. ''Can they be eaten?''

Zena gave a short laugh. ''Only if you want to die of a hundred different kinds of coral poisons. Puhi eat anything, especially if it's got calcium inside.''

"In general, are they a problem on the reefs?''

"Hardly ever see 'em.''

"And when you do?''

Zena shrugged. ''Ordinarily we just shift operations till they move on. They never stay in one place more than a few weeks. This one probably fell asleep and got caught under the sinking net. Otherwise it would have moved to a better feeding ground long ago.'' She paused. ''We've never had a situation quite like this.''

"What about the toxic effect of a large algae spill directly on the reef?'' the warden asked. ''I understand there's no way it can be fully removed once it's actually in the coral.''

"Algae's going to foul that section regardless of how we lift the net," Zena said. "Already has."

"The reef's almost dead there anyway. That's why the eel is so hungry," Pua added. "It was the blood smell that drew it out. Rock eels don't usually chew knife coral. It's kinda sharp, even for them."

"Kind of sharp," one of the Company men muttered. He was the one nursing a bandaged hand.

"At least the algae is dead," Zena said. "What we can't clean out will kill what it's sitting on, but it can't reproduce and spread."

The warden nodded. "Okay. We'll give it a try. I don't want anyone else hurt, so we'll move the eel before any swimmers go back in the water. It'll be dark soon. Suspend operations for now, and we'll do the job at first light."

"We got plenty of light from the water," Klooney said. "And floodlights from the barge. The suckersharks will clear the area soon."

"Pua," the warden asked. "Could we implement your plan tonight? How would the eel react?"

Pua glanced at Klooney. "I wouldn't even send *him* back down there tonight. That puhi's going to have bad enough indigestion as it is."

That brought a bark of laughter from the crew. Even the Company man's own people joined in. He glared, first at Pua, then at the others. The laughter died quickly, but many were still grinning.

"All right," the warden said. "Zena, we'll need volunteers to go under the net in the morning."

"I'll go," all three Pukui old-timers said at once. Pua restrained a smile. She had known they would support her plan, even after fighting with the eel. At Pukui, it was kapu to harm a reef dweller unless you were going to eat it, or it was going to eat you.

The warden looked somewhat surprised at their quick response, but nodded. "We're set, then. Fatu . . ." She paused, looking back toward the green plastic. "Will you do what needs to be done for that crewman?"

"Aye," Fatu said softly.

The warden nodded her thanks. "Zena, set a night crew to keep the net steady as she is with the tide changes. Then go home and get some sleep."

"Not necessary, Boss," Zena said.

"Yes," the warden replied. "It is. I need you fresh."

"This is going to cost you, lady," Klooney said. "You can't let a whole Company crew sit idle for an entire night. Pukui'll go broke on this one operation."

The warden picked up a data sheet from the wheelhouse windowsill. "Don't you worry about Pukui's finances, Mr. Klooney. I'll be charging this entire delay to the Company." There was an immediate cry of outrage from the Company crew. Mistake, Pua thought.

"Special-operations fund," the warden went on without a pause. "Not to be subtracted from the crews' bonus credits."

"Ho!" one of the crewman said softly.

"Hallelujah," said another, and across the deck, anger changed quickly to surprise and pleasure.

"Reefers!" one woman sighed. "A night off with pay! At Pukui, no less!"

"Good call, Boss Lady," an old-time Company man called out.

How does she know how to do that? Pua thought. A second ago they were ready to gill her, and now she's got them kissing her fingertips. Pua glanced at Klooney. Except for him.

The warden stopped in front of her on her way back to the flitter.

"Are you hurt?" she asked.

Pua straightened. "No," she lied.

The woman watched her for a moment. "Do you want a ride back?"

"Do you have a knife I can use?" Pua asked in return. The woman lifted her brows, but pulled a pocketknife from her shorts and held it out. Pua opened it, examined the blade—it was very sharp—closed it, and stuffed it into her own pocket.

"I'll swim," she said, and waited just long enough to witness the horrified looks of the Company crew before tumbling sideways into the water. Then she swam like a bloody ray with a pack of suckersharks on its tail to clear the area before the eel *or* the sharks realized she was there.

Chapter 12

~~~~~~~~~~~~~~~~~~~~
~~~~~~~~~~~~~~~~~~~~

Fatu met the warden on the barge the following morning. She
had asked him to pilot the sub for the removal of the rock eel
and then give her the tour of the farm they had missed the day
before.

Zena stood by the starboard winch directing the position of
the pump hoses. She glanced frequently toward the northeast,
following the progress of the storm clouds across the horizon.
The distant flicker of lightning attested to this latest storm's vi-
olence; it was one of the true storms of winter, and while it
would not strike Pukui directly, the swells it generated were
already pounding the eastern barrier reef. The wind was brisk,
but fortunately the lagoon waters remained calm.

"Net's about as tight as we can get it without ripping the
whole thing open," Zena called.

Beside Fatu, the warden nodded and motioned for Klooney to
join them. "Zena says your man Kobayashi is the best marksman
on-site," she said to him. "I'd like him with us, just in case."

"Good call, Warden," he replied. "We'll meet you at the
sub."

"You stay on deck," she said before he could turn away.
"Have your repair and cleanup crews ready for immediate de-
ployment as soon as the eel's neutralized and the net cleared."

"They're set to go now," he said. "They don't need me looking after them."

"I want you on deck during the clearing operation, and then in
the water for the cleanup," she said. "There's a big hole in that
net, and we can't afford to make any more mistakes with it."

"Look, lady, I'm crew boss here, and nobody tells—"

She laid a hand on his shoulder. Klooney tensed, as did Fatu
and everyone else who witnessed the move. The woman's long

135

fingers were within easy reach of Klooney's gills. Her touch was one of extraordinary challenge. Fatu wondered if she knew what she was doing. She nodded toward the wheelhouse. Wisely, Klooney did not resist. Fatu moved to where he could watch them through the open door.

"I am *farm boss* here," the woman said as she lowered her hand from Klooney's shoulder. "I'm also a fully privileged trouble-shooter on special assignment. I'm sure Dr. Toma explained to you what that means in terms of your full cooperation."

"I never—"

"I want you to remind your crew that Fatu is the on-site boss when I'm not here, and in his absence, Zena." She lifted a hand to stop his angry response. "One more thing. From now on, we operate with *one crew*. No Company versus Pukui. No old-timer versus recruit. I want no more dead squid. Do you under-stand me, Mr. Klooney?"

He smiled, hard and tight. "Sure, *Boss*, I understand you fine. As of now, I and my crew don't do nothin' you don't tell us to do first."

"Don't play games with me," she said. "You do your job, and you do it right. You wouldn't be here at Pukui right now if you weren't good at your job, because I asked for the best." His chin lifted. "So show me how good you can be."

His brows rose, and he slid a slow look down to her waist, and below. "I'd be real happy to do that, Warden. Any time you feel ready."

Slimy bastard, Fatu thought. He saw the same assessment in the warden's eyes, and a weariness that said she was sorry she had offered Klooney the courtesy of a private discussion.

"Go boss your crew," she said, still in that flat, calm voice.

"What's your hurry?" Klooney asked. He glanced toward the door, caught Fatu's eye, and winked. "Nobody's going to bother us in here. You bein' the boss an' all. Maybe if we was to get to know each other a little better, it might . . . relax the tension some."

The warden didn't move. "Get Kobayashi on the sub," she said.

Klooney grinned and stepped outside the wheelhouse. He crossed the deck, which was full of curious squids, and spoke quietly to the Company marksman. "Hey, Warden," Klooney called as she crossed to the berthed sub. "Let's do it in the water next time. Guaranteed, that'll relax you just fine."

The warden turned slowly to face him. The furnaces continued to grumble; the net groaned as it rubbed against the side of the closed rollers. The humans aboard the barge grew absolutely still.

"If you want to solve that problem you're having with tension, Mr. Klooney," the warden said, "I suggest you take a ride through that compression roller." She glanced around at the gaping others. "Get ready to dive. I want crew on that net thirty seconds after the eel is cleared."

"Netters to the starboard fore," Zena snapped. "On the double. Cleaners ready at port. Ready the dive." Company and Pukui crew alike scrambled to the order. Only Klooney crossed to his assigned place at a walk. His face was red under his heavily pigmented skin.

"Klooney's got a tide-pissin' personality," Fatu said as the warden lowered herself through the submersible's hatch, "but he's a top-rate net man."

"He'd better be," she said.

Despite his bulk, Fatu slid easily into the sub behind her. They took their places in the upper observation bubble, and Fatu activated the engines. Kobayashi came aboard and paused to seal the hatch. As usual, he was chewing on a sliver of betel coral. His teeth were stained brown from the mildly narcotic dye the coral exuded. He was carrying a disassembled pneumatic speargun.

"Stand by in the lockout chamber," Fatu told him. From there, the marksman could fire on the rock eel from a position of relative safety, if that should become necessary.

"I want the crew safe," the warden said, "but I don't want the animal harmed unless there's no other choice."

"Hai," Kobayashi replied.

"If you do have to shoot it, kill it clean."

"What I shoot, I kill, Warden," Kobayashi said. He shifted the coral sliver to the opposite side of his mouth. "And what I kill, I kill clean."

"Fire only on my order, marksman," she warned.

"Hai," he replied softly, and slipped below.

The warden rubbed a hand across her face.

"Don't worry about Kobe," Fatu said. "He won't shoot 'less he has to. His daddy and his grandaddy were both Buddhists. Besides, he's an old Pukui hand."

She surprised him with a questioning glance.

"Didn't Pua tell you? Unless you're going to eat *it*, or *it's* gonna eat *you*, it's kapu to harm a Pukui reef dweller. Plenty fiticoco gonna find you if you break that kapu."

"I understand kapu," she said. "What's fiticoco?"

"Trouble," he replied. "Of any kind and all varieties."

"Is that a Samoan word?"

He shook his head. "Trukese. We use words and phrases from a lot of the old Pacific languages."

He activated the comm link to the barge and the hydrobus, where Pua and the three Pukui volunteers were waiting for their signal to enter the water.

"Ready on the barge?" he asked into the deck mike.

"Aye." Zena's reply was clipped.

"Pua?"

"What's taking you guys so long over there?"

Fatu laughed again. He slid the sub from its berth in the side of the barge so smoothly that it hardly seemed to be moving. Then it began to sink, and the sense of motionlessness disappeared. Water splashed and foamed upward over the observation bubble until, abruptly, the illusion of stillness returned. The water glowed deep gold in the shadow of the barge.

"Do you ever get used to it?" the warden asked. "The color, I mean. It's so . . ."

"Un-Earthly?" Fatu suggested. He turned the nose of the sub away from the barge, then began a wide descending circle around the area of the tangled net. "I never get tired of looking at it, but even after twenty years, I can't say I'm really used to it."

"Pua told me the ocean off Hawaii was the wrong color," she said, "but I didn't understand what she meant at the time. She said it didn't taste or sound right, either."

Fatu smiled. "I'm sure it doesn't, to her. There's our friend. See 'im?" He slowed the sub and pointed.

The woman sucked in her breath as she caught sight of the brilliant green puhi nosing the tangle of net and broken coral. Only its sinuous snakelike body was reminiscent of an Earth-sea eel. The multicolored beaked snout, predominantly bright pink, was more like the face of a parrot fish. A thin, almost transparent dorsal fin wavered like a fan the full length of its body. The warden leaned forward and activated her close-up focus.

"We don't get many chances to see rock eels completely out of their holes," Fatu said. "They're pretty solitary creatures under normal circumstances."

"The color is incredible," she said. "How can that be adaptive in an environment like this?"

"When the reef is alive, he blends right in," Fatu said. "At least, his snout does—the rest of him is usually hidden inside his hole. Only way you can find one of 'em is by watching for the chewed coral circle that marks their territory.''

The puhi stretched open its jaws, then snapped them shut over a broken branch of coral that had caught in the net. Coral and netting both ripped away. Thick algae sludge oozed from the hole.

"I understand now why the thing is so deadly," the warden said.

Fatu laughed. "Hell, Warden, that thing's just a baby. We've got things out here that would make even *you* back off.''

"I don't doubt it for a minute," she replied, and she sounded serious.

Fatu tapped his cheek against his face mike. "Kobe, what do you think?''

"That's one reef-huggin' hungry puhi," the marksman replied. "He musta been stuck under that net for a long time.''

Fatu maneuvered the sub closer. "I'll run past his starboard side. Swish a chunk of sponge in the water to get his attention.''

"Hai.'' The word was hardly spoken before the eel tensed. It swung its head around toward the passing sub, away, then quickly back again. Fatu powered slowly past. The puhi's brilliant snout turned slowly in unison.

"He's interested," Fatu said. "Better drop the shoot and feed him something before he decides to eat the sub.''

"Hai.'' A tube constructed of algae netting uncoiled behind the sub. A small chunk of gray sponge drifted from the tube's mouth. Instantly, the eel was on it. His move away from the main net was so fast it startled even Fatu.

"Nice catch," the warden murmured.

The eel snatched up the drifting sponge, paused for just an instant while the pharyngeal dental plates inside its mouth crushed the nutrients from it, then nosed the end of the tube for more.

"Keep him happy, Kobe," Fatu said. "I'm heading for open water. Let me know if he starts getting nervous about being so far from his hole.''

Another piece of spongy substance dropped through the shoot. After mashing it thoroughly and spitting out the stony residue, the eel nuzzled the tube for more. In its eagerness, it ripped a chunk of netting off the end of the tube. Kobe kept an intermittent supply of sponge coral sliding down the tube as they lured the puhi away from its territory.

As they approached the barrier reef, the warden turned her attention forward again. She was obviously startled by the live reef's riotous colors and myriad marine life. Fatu couldn't blame her. The contrast between this vibrant, thriving place and the bare stone under number twelve was extreme.

"This ocean is like a visual, tactile symphony," she said after a moment. Fatu glanced at her. She was leaning forward, transfixed by the colorful, fluid scene. "So much movement and color and texture. It sings, just like Mauna Kea Iki."

He must have made some small sound. She turned to him. "Is there something wrong?"

Fatu realized he was staring. "No," he said quickly.

She turned back to the reef. "I keep expecting this place to feel alien, or to at least make *me* feel alien," she said. "Individually, things like the rock eel, or Pua's door Matt, or this ungodly color, do. But overall, there's such a sense of balance . . . ." She paused. "There aren't many places left on Earth that sing so joyously of their own existence."

Fatu was more than startled. "I've never heard a Company rep talk like that," he said.

She watched him for a moment. "The Company holds my contract, Fatu, not my soul." She turned her look back to the golden sea.

The puhi didn't seem to notice the reef at first, but then something long and silver flashed with refracted sunlight, and the puhi's snout turned away from the feeding tube. It turned back, but Kobe withheld the next chunk of sponge coral. The puhi swung back toward movement on the reef.

Abruptly, it realized that it was no longer dependent on the elusive sponge coral. It snaked away from the sub and began nosing the varied coral outcroppings. It tested a number of holes, snapped the tips off a pair of feathery coral branches, then slid tailfirst into a small dark opening.

"At least someone's problems have been solved," the warden said.

Fatu touched on the open comm channel again. "Pua," he said. "You can come down now, but stay on the inner lagoon side of the net. Don't come all the way through. Not for any reason. Friend puhi has found a new home, but you'd just about make dessert for him, if he decides to go back and check on the old one."

"Is there any chance of that?" the warden asked quickly.

He laughed. "That baby ain't gonna budge from here for another three months, Boss. I just said that to remind her to be careful in case any of its cousins are still under there."

There was no response from Pua, but a moment later a woman's voice reported, "Four swimmers in the water."

"Transmit locator signals," Fatu said. Three lights blinked on the deck locator grid. "Damn," he muttered.

"What's the problem?" the warden asked.

"None yet," he replied. "But I'm gonna breeze Pua's ass when this is over. She's out there without a locator again."

The warden frowned. She had given specific orders that all members of the net-clearing crew were to wear signal clips and shoulder mikes during this dangerous dive. "Tell the others to send her topside to put one on," she said into the mike.

The message was relayed to the swimmers, but it was too late. Pua was already well ahead, guiding them through the narrow opening under the net.

Fatu turned the sub back toward the inner reef. As they powered forward, Kobe joined them on the observation deck. He nodded to the warden, shifted his pick from one side of his mouth to the other, and began dismantling his speargun. He looked genuinely pleased that he hadn't had to use it.

"Give me a line to the swimmers," Fatu ordered.

"Line open," came the voice from the bus.

"How's it going, Ehu?" he asked.

There was a pause while Ehu sucked in a mouthful of air. "It's spookier than a damn burial cave under here," she said finally. Her water-transmitted voice echoed eerily inside the sub.

"Stow it, Ehu," a man's voice replied. It, too, came from underwater. "It's bad enough down here without waking up the ghosts, too."

Ehu laughed.

"Okay," she said some time later. "We're on the main pipe. It's reef-pissin' hot, Fatu, even with the side lines open. Friggin' Company oughta be sued for turning 'em off in the first—" She ran out of air.

"Any problem reaching the release valves?" Fatu asked.

Another bubbling pause. "Hold a minute. We're checking under the pipe. Can't get through on top. The net's too heavy, even with the tension." There was another pause, broken by occasional echoing curses from the distant swimmers.

"None of us fits under there," Ehu said finally. "Pua's going to try."

"Damn," Fatu said softly, then blinked when one of the three lights on the locator grid began separating from the others along the straight line of the deep-water pipe.

"Relax, waterman," Ehu said. "I clipped my locator to her pants as she slid under."

"Hey, I owe you for that one, lady love," Fatu said.

"I'll take it in flesh," came the quick reply. "Tonight, behind the freshwater pool. Be there when Maram Iki kisses zenith, and we'll work out a payment schedule."

Fatu grinned. Kobe punched him in the side.

"Nothing I like better'n a hot woman under a cold moon," Fatu said into the mike. "I'll be there." Even the warden laughed at the creative suggestions that followed from the other two swimmers.

"Pua's coming out now," Ehu said awhile later. "Looks like she's widened the hole enough for Lui to get under with the capper. She's got a few coral scrapes but doesn't look too much the worse for wear."

They listened while Ehu reported the crew's continued progress under the net. "How much longer before you can clear the area?" Fatu asked finally.

"Cap's in place now and looks solid. We're just untangling and tying holes now," Ehu reported. "You want us to go home?" She sounded eager. Fatu didn't doubt they were all ready to get out from under the load of rotting algae. As a courtesy, he glanced at the warden. She nodded without hesitation.

"Okay, get your tails topside," he said. "We've got a whole bargeful of netters real anxious to get back on the job. Save a little work for them."

"Aye," came the quick reply, and two of the lights on the locator grid began moving back toward the inner lagoon. The third lingered until one of the others returned, paused, and then followed the errant light into the open. Abruptly, that light went out.

"She must have just noticed the locator," Fatu said.

Kobe laughed. "I wouldn't want to be Ehu right now. Pua'll probably sic the rays on her."

"Job's all yours, Zena," Fatu said.

"Net crews in the water," Zena ordered instantly. "Roll net. Let's get this mess cleaned up."

"How long will it take for the reef under twelve to grow back?" the warden asked after they had dropped off Kobayashi and begun the farm tour.

"Twenty, thirty years, maybe," Fatu said. "We can speed it up some by transferring sections of live coral and coralline algae from other parts of the reef, but it's going to be slow."

He pointed. "Here comes trouble."

The warden tensed, then relaxed again when she saw that it was only Pua swimming toward them through a narrow coral passage. She was wearing clothes, Fatu was pleased to see, shorts and a shirt with sleeves ripped into fringes. The shirt was tucked in at the waist, which meant she was probably hiding a bruise from her fight with the puhi the night before.

She had one of her father's diving knives strapped to her thigh, and a crimson coiler as big around as one of her fingers wrapped snugly around one ankle. The little fool. Her mucus-coated skin glistened and flashed in the refracted sunlight.

Pua grinned as she swam toward them. She spread her hands on the outside of the observation bubble. Another coiler, this one only hair-thin, circled her right wrist. Fatu reached up and matched her touch with his own. His fingers were shorter, and except for the tips, much broader. He motioned her inside the sub. She shook her head and signed for them to follow her instead. Fatu smiled and gave her a quick thumbs-up sign.

"She's gonna show off now." He laughed as Pua jackknifed off the observation bubble and kicked cleanly away. Her movement made only the lightest vibration in the sub's stable ride. Fatu followed above and behind as Pua slipped effortlessly through the narrow, jagged openings between coral outcrops.

"Is that safe?" the warden asked.

Again Fatu laughed. "Pua claims it is, and I admit I've never seen her get caught up on anything down there. But . . ." He shook his head. "Sometimes I think she's got seawater for brains. Like last night, for instance, when she went back in the water after the suckers were there. See that small circular scab on her calf? That's where one of them managed to attach."

The woman glanced at him, then looked back at Pua.

"That's why she took your knife," he said. "She wanted to make an impression on the crews, but knew she wasn't likely to get away completely untouched. She needed the knife to scrape the sharks off before they could insert their primary sucking prosbosces and start using their teeth. That's one she didn't get to in time."

The warden frowned.

"It wasn't really as dangerous as it seems," Fatu went on. "Not for Pua. Her skin exudes a protective mucus coating when she's in the water. It acts as a sealant for her own body fluids, and at the same time makes it a lot harder for things like suckers to get a grip on her. It protects her from some of the coral poisons, too. Watch her now—she's found something."

Pua had paused beside a small hole and was wriggling one fingertip inside the dark opening. Suddenly a flash of pink appeared, much the same color as the rock eel. As the coral fish darted from its hole in an attempt to catch her finger, Pua snagged it in her palm. She lifted it quickly to her mouth and bit it behind its bulging eyes. Instantly, it was still.

Pua lifted the fish like a trophy, then swam from sight beneath the sub. She reappeared through the hatch to the lockout chamber.

She grinned and shook the water from her face. "Where're you going?" she asked. If her trip under the algae net had caused her any damage, it didn't show. Her dark eyes sparked with merriment, and her skin shone with the same color as the sea. It was like having life itself back, having Pua back on the reef. Fatu restrained an urge to run a hand across her cheek, to pull her into a hug.

"Farm tour," he said instead.

Pua grinned at the warden, then held the fish out to Fatu. He took it, inspected it, and handed it back. "Want to come along?"

"In this?" She laughed, and shook her head. "I'll take my own tour."

"Stay away from the Company crew," he said. "Especially Klooney. He's not on his best behavior today."

"I'm not afraid of him," Pua said.

"You should be," Fatu said. Her eyes widened. "Do this one for me, okay?"

She sighed, then grinned again. "I don't want to be around him, anyway. He tastes like rock bread." She glanced at the warden and giggled.

"One more thing," Fatu said. "Get that coiler off your leg. It's too big."

"It's pretty," she said. "I like it there."

"It's cutting off your circulation. Take it off."

Pua gave an exaggerated sigh, rolled her eyes dramatically, and dropped back into the lockout chamber.

When she reappeared outside the observation bubble, she was carrying the fish between her teeth, and the half-meter-long coiler stretched between her hands. It was clear that it took her full strength to keep it pulled straight. She tossed the coiler away from her, and it snapped in on itself like a spring. Pua grinned and waved and disappeared back into the coral.

Chapter 13

"What was that business with the fish?" the warden asked as Fatu piloted the sub along the outer edges of the primary growing pens. "It had the look of ritual."

"That particular section of reef belongs to me," he explained. "Pua has unrestricted use rights, but since I was there, she paid me the courtesy of offering me her catch. If I'd been hungry, I would have kept it and sent her after another for herself."

"Is that a Hawaiian custom?"

"More Micronesian," he said. He turned them toward one of the deep-water pump stations.

"You follow a rather mixed bag of Island traditions here," she said.

"We use whatever works," he replied. "Historically, Pacific Islanders were noted for their ability to adapt to new physical and social conditions. Traditional Island ways have all but disappeared on Earth, but we're reviving some of the more useful ones here."

She glanced down at his tattoos.

He shrugged. "And some of the purely artistic ones."

"Women have children, men get tattooed," she quoted, surprising Fatu. Then he remembered her profession and that she said she had visited the South Pacific at least once. She had no doubt studied the same historical tapes that he and the other Lesaat settlers had.

"As I understand it," she said, "the tatau ritual involves a lot more than the purely artistic; at least it did originally. Isn't it supposed to be one of the steps into Samoan adulthood?"

"It's hard to say what the original meanings were," he said. "There are as many interpretations as there are Westerners who've written about it over the centuries, and I suspect most of their ideas were distorted to start with. The Samoans themselves no longer remember, and only a few of the very oldest care.''

''Why did you do it?''

''Respect,'' he said, ''for ancestors long gone, and for whatever spirits inhabit this new place. For me, it represents a bridge between ancient Earth and the Lesaat of tomorrow. The concept of the tatau is old and alien to Pukui, but the designs in the tattoo itself are all taken from land and sea life here. Maybe someday it'll help my grandkids understand the similarities as well as the vast differences between Earth and Lesaat.'' He laughed. ''Or maybe, it'll just confuse them.''

The warden sat back in her seat. She looked thoughtful, as if she had just learned something of considerable interest.

''Syncretism,'' she said after a moment. ''Diverse cultures blending to create something entirely new. I've seen it before, but never on such a large scale, and never where it's been so consciously and deliberately directed.'' She glanced up at him. ''It's encouraging that you're selecting your new 'traditions' with some regard for your new environment.''

''Ah, yes,'' Fatu said. ''The environmental anthropologist's perspective. I'd almost forgotten.''

She looked directly at him. ''You don't impress me as a man who forgets much of anything, Fatu. Least of all who I am and why I'm here.''

Fatu stopped the sub's forward motion and set the rear thrust to hold them steady against the current. They were about twelve meters deep, halfway between the inner and barrier reefs. Above them, the surface flashed white and gold. He turned to face her.

''Is that why you asked to come out here alone, Warden?'' he asked. ''So you can question me privately about the TC enzyme?''

''I asked to come out here because I wanted to see the farm,'' she said. ''But if you'd like to talk about the enzyme, I'm willing to listen.''

Fatu remained silent.

''Do you know where the missing records are?'' she asked. ''No.''

''Walter Crawley, the admin liaison who briefed me, ranked you right at the top of the list of people to question,'' she said. ''Right next to someone named Sa le Fe'e. I haven't been able to find any reference to the latter in the farm records.''

Fatu tried not to react visibly but saw by her expression that he had. He said, as carefully as he could, "I am . . . honored to be placed in such esteemed company."

The warden lifted a brow.

"Le Fe'e is a creature out of Samoan myth," Fatu said. "A kind of demigod that was believed in the old days to live deep in the Pacific Ocean."

"Crawley referred to him as an old man who lived somewhere here at Pukui," she replied. "He said that if I could find Sa le Fe'e, I was almost certain to also find access to the hidden TC records." She paused. "Why is this making you so angry?"

Fatu took a deep breath.

"Le Fe'e is Pua's special friend," he said finally. "She would never have told Crawley about him without coercion, and there is no one else Crawley could have learned about him from. After all Pua had already been through, you people could have at least left her the privacy of her own imagination."

"You called Pua a 'little fe'e' yesterday," she said.

You don't forget anything either, do you, lady? he thought. "It's a term of endearment. A private variation, if you will, on the more common 'squid.' Pua fancies herself to be more like an octopus than a squid. 'Le Fe'e translates as 'the octopus.' "

He glanced at the woman's hands. Those hands made him angry, too, but he understood from Pua that the warden did not have them by choice. She followed his look, then met his gaze again.

"If Pua would speak of this Le Fe'e under controlled questioning," she said, "it must be something she cares deeply about. Something she believes very strongly."

"It's hard to tell what Pua actually believes," he said, deciding truth might well be the best deception with this woman. "We've been sharing Le Fe'e stories, some made up, some traditional, for years. I don't doubt that she's come to believe in him as some kind of physical entity. Especially since she moved him formally to Pukui."

Fatu smiled as he remembered. "At her tenth birthday feast, Pua dressed up like a Samoan talking chief and announced that she had something important to tell us. It seems Le Fe'e had become bored with Earth's oceans. He had experienced all the adventures that were to be had there, and he had decided to find and explore the fabled golden seas of Lesaat.

"First, he swam to Hawaii. There, he wrapped his tentacles around a rising shuttle and let it pull him into high orbit. Then he crawled through the wormhole nexus, having adventures all along the way, exploring places no human has ever seen. When he reached Lesaat at last, he searched the great, golden sea until he found the richest and most exquisitely beautiful site on the planet.''

"Pukui," the warden said with a slight smile.

He nodded. "He made the reef his home."

"She used to tell me stories while I was in the dep tank," the warden said thoughtfully. "I don't remember the words, but I can recall hearing her voice."

"She told me she thought you were dead at first," Fatu said. "She said she picked leaves from potted plants around the recon station and put them in the gel with you, so you'd have some connection to the living world."

The warden sighed, and turned her look back to the sea. She started when she saw the oxyworm that had attached itself to the observation bubble behind her. It was as big around as one of her arms and lay neatly coiled against the smooth glass. She recovered quickly and leaned forward to inspect the worm's tiny suckers and its rhythmically irising mouth.

"We call them oxyworms." He laughed. "It's just a tubular stomach. It feeds by filtering microscopic plankton through from its mouth to its tail. The bubbles lifting off the skin are pure O_2."

The warden looked skeptical.

"The digestive process releases photosynthetic pigments," Fatu explained. "When they're secreted through the skin they interact with the water to produce oxygen."

"Is this a large or a small one?" she asked, glancing up to follow the worm's effervescence toward the surface.

"Pretty good sized for inside the lagoon," he said. "They're fairly fragile and light enough to drift with the currents. Unless they find something smooth to attach to, they usually get carried into the coral before they get much bigger than this. The coral slices them to shreds."

"What about in the open ocean?"

He shrugged. "Well, Pua claims she and Le Fe'e once found one big enough to swim through without touching the inside walls."

"What!"

He laughed. "I know. I don't believe it either. At least I don't think I do. I can only imagine what would happen if a human got caught inside one of those things. It's sometimes hard to tell which of Pua's stories are true.''

He glanced toward the surface and then the chronometer. "We'd better get moving or we'll never make the whole trip in one day." He activated the engines again. The oxyworm peeled away from the smooth glass as they moved slowly forward. The warden watched it closely as it drifted away.

She remained silent as they inspected the deep-water pipes and the underwater pumping station, then followed the main updraw pipe all the way down to the underwater tunnel that carried it through the barrier reef to the open ocean. "Can't get any closer right now," Fatu said as he held off some distance from the actual tunnel entrance. The sub's engines strained against the pull of the current.

"How do you do repairs and maintenance?"

"On the turning tide, when the current slows. Luckily, this pipe doesn't need much attention. It was a tide-pisser of a job to lay it—it all had to be done by hand. But that tunnel's solid basalt all the way through, an old lava tube from the days when this whole place was above water. Best protection in the world for a solid length of pipe. Nothing falling on it, nothing growing up around it. It just lies there real quiet feeding deep-ocean water through as we need it.''

"I presume the tunnel has been searched," she said. Something about the way she held herself led him to believe she didn't particularly want to do so herself.

"It was one of the first places we all thought of," he said. "Pukui crews knew enough to time their searches to the tide changes, but the stupid Earther bosses lost three swimmers to the currents before deciding it wasn't a very practical place for daily work records to be hidden in the first place.''

He took them back toward the surface and showed her each of the primary growing pens. Of the thirteen currently in use, ten showed the deep orange of mature algae, and at least seven of those were in serious need of immediate harvesting. It was obvious that the nets were straining under increasingly heavy loads of rapidly growing algae. Two had already stretched to the point of touching the cold-water pipes at low tide, and would soon be touching coral.

"Has *anything* been harvested since the Pukuis died?" the warden asked.

"Only the three pens that were fully mature at the time," Fatu replied. "Zed had already given the harvest order, so when the Company started stalling on sending out the harvester, we decided to do it on our own. Good thing we did, too. Those reef flats would be entirely destroyed by now. Be fifty years before we could bring them back.''

"How'd you harvest without a Company crew and barge?'' she asked.

"The old way,'' he said. "Sucked it into the disposal-barge hold and hauled it to the old land-based processing plant.'' He paused. "Company was real upset—sent an official inspector all the way out from Earth to complain—but they paid top credit for the finished product.''

"Which was?''

"Not what you're looking for, Warden,'' he replied. "Just plain old 410 Standard.''

"You're certain of that?'' she asked.

"Hell, Zed's the one who gave the original harvest order, and he wasn't sick at the time—nor plannin' to be, I don't expect. Why would he order us to destroy a full batch of what was potentially the most valuable crop in the known universe? Why, for that matter, would he be growing the TC in open pens where any poacher worth his gills could steal seed stock?''

He gestured toward to the bulging orange pens. "No offense to you, Warden—you're the first reasonable body they've sent out here—but the Company's got its nose up its ass letting this stuff grow out of control like this. Either that, or they're deliberately taking the chance of ruining the reef so they can reclaim the lease. Any real waterworlder knows what's in those pens out there. We can taste it. 410 Standard, every one of 'em.''

"What do you mean, 'reclaim the lease'?'' she asked. "I thought Pukui belonged to Pua now that her parents are gone.''

"Technically it belongs to the U.N., like every other reef on Lesaat,'' he said, "but Pua will inherit her parents' perpetual use-rights when she turns eighteen. That's if the Company hasn't taken them over by then. By law, World Life can reclaim any lease in the U.N.'s name if a reef is in actual danger of being physically destroyed. Theoretically, they would then step in to save it.''

He paused. "I expect your presence here is the prelude to their attempt to take over Pukui. The U.N. requires a qualified, non-Company witness to attest to the severity of the situation. I'm sure one of their own ranking troubleshooters will suffice.''

She frowned. Fatu turned the sub back in the direction of the barge.

"I noticed in the farm records," the warden said after a time, "that some of the original perpetual leases have been returned to Company control. Were all of those properties in danger of being destroyed?"

He shook his head. "Most were taken as payment for overdue debts. Some because the leaseholders died."

"Why didn't their children inherit? The census sheet shows most of the first settlers started having kids as soon as they got out here."

"Unfortunately, the Company noticed that, too, years ago." Fatu said. "They recognized it as the threat it was to their own perpetual control over the planet, so they got laws passed saying that only physically altered waterworlders can hold property leases on Lesaat. It probably sounded reasonable enough back on Earth, since most people know you need the alterations to operate the farms properly. But what it really did was disinherit all of the original leaseholders' children. They don't give out long-term leases anymore. Three years is the upper limit before Company review and right to reclaim."

"Why don't the waterworlders send their kids back for the changes?" she said. "Some must be old enough by now."

Fatu adjusted the sub's position slightly to make best use of the current. "Two families tried it. They had to mortgage their holdings to do it, because the Company insisted on advance payment for the entire cost of shipping and recon. Neither of the kids made it through the tanks. One's gills didn't form properly—he drowned. The other never came out of the paralysis."

The warden's shock was obvious. It was clear she understood what he was implying. Whether it would make a difference in how she did her job on Lesaat was doubtful. Toma had told him that troubleshooters, this one in particular, were reputed to always fulfill their contracts.

"So Pua is the only inheritable waterworlder," she said.

And her inheritance is the most valuable piece of real estate on the planet, Fatu added silently. Think about it, Warden. And if you have any honesty in you at all, do something about it.

He nodded. "I never expected to see her back. I thought they would kill her. Or at least keep her. If I'd been at Pukui when she was taken away, I would have killed *them* before I'd have let her go."

"Where were you?"

"On my way back from Landing with a load of new recruits."

She blew out a long, slow breath. "Is it possible this TC thing is a myth, like Pua's Le Fe'e?"

"I've seen the results myself," he said. "Ate nothing but waterwheat for a month and never felt better in my life. According to Lehua's tests, every essential amino acid my body needed for protein synthesis was converted from just that one food source. The only other things I needed were water, salt, and a few vitamin supplements."

"What form was the enzyme in when you took it?"

"Powder," he said. "Compressed into caplets, just like they do the 410. I only took it once. Lehua said it would be active for six months, but I decided a month of gnawing raw grain was enough."

"Do the Company doctors know you were one of the test subjects?" she asked.

He watched her for a moment. "As a matter of fact, I never did bother to tell them. They took blood and tissue samples from everybody on the atoll when they first took over—more'n some of us cared to give, and without offering any choice in the matter. They claimed it was for health reasons, so they could do it legally. I figured if there was anything they wanted to know about me, they could figure it out by looking through their pissholdin' microscopes."

"Why are you telling me?"

He met her look directly. "Because I owed you one, Warden."

She frowned again. "For bringing Pua home," she said.

Fatu slowed their speed and began the wide turn that would bring them parallel to the number-twelve pen. "She said you're going to take her back."

The warden sighed. "I have no choice." She did not speak again until they had reboarded the barge.

Once there, she called Zena and Fatu into the wheelhouse.

"As soon as twelve is cleaned up, I want you to burn and dispose of eleven and thirteen. They're too far gone to salvage," she said. All the introspectiveness was gone from her voice. She spoke with clipped, precise efficiency—as she had with Toma the night of the fire. "Then start harvesting ten and move right down the line as fast as you can get the stuff out.

"We'll use the local processing plant, like you did before, until I can get a Company harvest barge. Use every available vessel for transport of the algae; carry it in buckets if you have to. There's no point in letting any more of this place die.''

Fatu and Zena glanced at each other. Zena looked as startled, and as suddenly excited, as Fatu felt.

"We'll need a lot more crew," Fatu said. "Klooney and his gang are scheduled for storm leave as soon as twelve's empty.''

"Nobody's taking leave until we get this reef under control," she said. "Make up an order for double, round-the-clock shifts and patch it through the house net. I'll see that it's filled.''

A grin crept over Zena's dark features. "Aye!" she said. "The order'll be there before you are, Boss.''

"Let me know if there are any problems.''

Zena nodded and stepped back so that the warden could pass them on her way to her flitter.

"Angela," Fatu said quietly as she crossed in front of him. He held his breath waiting for her reaction.

She turned back. Surprise, and deep, deep curiosity lit her clear gray eyes. It was the first honest familiarity either of them had allowed.

"You *do* have a choice," he said.

Chapter 14

~~~~~~~~~~~~~~~~~~~~
~~~~~~~~~~~~~~~~~~~~

The harvesting went slowly. Too slowly for Pua. She hated the taste of the overripe algae that was choking her reef. She chafed at the endless delays in its removal.

Toma released two Company harvesters for work at Pukui, but both developed mechanical difficulties before reaching the reef. Three additional Company crews joined those already on-site, and while most of the swimmers worked willingly to clear the reef flats before more damage was done, some refused to go into the water. They cited the Company's six-month ban on harvesting at Pukui and their fear of losing personal work credits when Earth admin learned the ban was being ignored. The warden ordered the objectors back to Landing.

There was a surge in progress upon the arrival of two private crews, made up partly of original settlers from nearby smaller reefs. They had finished their own prestorm harvests and volunteered their services to assist at Pukui. Still, the job went slowly. Projects thought to be complete turned out needing to be done all over again; equipment malfunctioned or disappeared. Once, a stone fish got caught in the compression rollers and jammed the gears. Pua didn't think it had gotten there by accident.

"Le Fe'e says the storms will be bigger this year," she told Zena one morning. They were sitting in the wheelhouse together studying satellite weather reports. Zena was charting an updated forecast. "The tides are getting higher, too."

"That's because the moons are coming into alignment," Zena said. "The highest tides will be when they cross right overhead. That'll be the most dangerous time."

"Can we get the algae out before then?" Pua asked.

"Maybe, if we can keep the harvest moving," Zena said, "and if we don't get a storm out of sequence. So far, the storm paths are staying pretty stable. See how they all start to turn north just above our latitude. They'll keep getting closer, but unless one decides not to turn away in time, we should be all right.''

"It's a good thing they finally got the satellite tracking station working again," Pua said.

"Mmmm," Zena replied. "We wouldn't dare keep live algae in the pens if we didn't know exactly how much time we have left." A buzzing *Net clear* signal made her look up. "Well, it's about time.

"Kobe!" she called. "As soon as the swimmers are clear, get that—"

The blare of the *Roll net* order cut her off.

"What—" Zena jumped to her feet as the compression gears engaged with a booming, metallic clang.

"Damn it! Who ordered that roll? We never got a *Swimmers clear*—shit!" The emergency klaxon brayed, and the compression gears clattered to a sudden halt. Zena raced to the deck.

". . . Lacey's caught! Oh, damn . . ." A water-distorted voice, relayed through deck control, told the story. The net had begun lifting too soon, and one of the swimmers had been caught in the coral beneath its heavy folds. Pua ran beside Zena toward the side of the barge.

"Lock it down, Kobe," she heard Zena call. "Nothing— *nothing*—moves without my order. Is that clear?"

"Aye," Kobe's sharp voice responded. Pua could not remember ever hearing Uncle Kobe sound truly angry before. He had been at the barge controls, but she knew he would never have started the early roll. It had to have been done from the emergency controls underwater. That Zena had left Kobe in charge of the lockdown proved how serious the situation was. He was one of the few both she and Pua knew could be trusted totally.

Pua unsnapped the safety clasp on her father's knife and dove. Zena entered the water right behind her.

A flurry of green and yellow showed where the accident had taken place. Swimmers were frantically cutting net and vacuuming the resultant spilled algae as they tried to reach their trapped colleague. By the time Pua and Zena reached them, they were pulling the netter free. Her yellow bodysuit barely showed through a layer of algae sludge.

One of the swimmers, dressed in the blue of a medic, immediately pressed an oxygen canister over the injured swimmer's face. Her gills! Pua thought. She must have hurt her gills! She saw then that what she had thought was algae smearing the netter's chest and shoulders was actually the woman's own skin. It was shredded and torn where she had been dragged across the coral by the lifting net. Blood swirled all around her limp form.

Pua stayed well back from the injured swimmer, knowing that Zena would call her if she thought Pua could help. She watched the others, instead. The Company and private crews had separated into two angry, gesturing groups. There was surely more trouble coming. She saw Zena take note of the same thing.

"All swimmers, out of the water," Zena signed and said into her shoulder mike at the same time. Kobe responded by giving the *Exit water* signal through the underwater speakers. The Pukui swimmers hesitated, but Zena angrily gestured them topside. She motioned to Pua to join them.

A short-hop flitter was already running when they brought the injured netter on deck. She was lifted into it and, along with the medic, was sent immediately to the infirmary. Zena ordered all the swimmers onto the buses and back to the main dock.

"But what about the harvest?" Pua cried. "You can't just stop—"

"Nobody goes in the water until this thing is settled," Zena said. "Stay out of it, Pua. Ehu, where's Klooney?"

Pua knew there was real trouble then, because it had to have been Klooney who had activated the net controls. As Company boss, he was the only one who had access.

"He's on the Company bus," Ehu said, and they turned to see the overloaded bus already making its way back to the dock.

"This time, I'm gonna kill that bastard," Zena said. "Come on, get the rest of the squids on the bus. Let's go."

"You want me to call the warden?" Ehu asked.

"No! And leave Fatu out of it, too. This one's between Klooney and me."

Pua didn't wait for more. She dove back into the water, clicked a call to the rays, and an instant later was racing toward the dock herself.

She reached it well before either of the buses. The flitter had landed, and the injured netter was just being carried into the infirmary. Pua ran to the dock comm. She called Fatu first. He was at the processing plant on the other side of the island.

"Call the warden," he said after her hurried explanation. "I'll get there as fast as I can."

Pua got no answering signal from either the main house or the farm shed. She cursed, and began running uphill.

"Come on," she yelled when she saw the warden on the

house lanai. She waved her arms and motioned for the woman to join her. "There's trouble down at the docks."

"What's wrong?" the warden called. She was already sliding into her boots.

"Another Pukui swimmer got hurt," Pua said. She stopped, panting, at the bottom of the stairs. "Zena made everybody get out of the water. She said she's going to kill Klooney, but he's a lot bigger than she is. He'll—"

"Where's Fatu?" The warden came down the stairs in three long steps.

"At the processing plant. He's coming. Zena said not to, but I called him anyway, from the dock comm."

"Why didn't you use it to call me?"

"It didn't work. I think somebody cut the lines."

The mountainlady's curse was one worth remembering. Pua followed her across the lawn at a run.

Klooney had already come ashore. He stood surrounded by Company swimmers. The bus with Zena aboard was just approaching the dock. As soon as it was close enough, Zena leapt ashore.

"You sonuvabitch," she yelled as she ran toward Klooney. "I'll rip your gills—"

"Hold it!" the warden called. When Zena didn't stop, the warden stepped between her and Klooney. Zena tried to get around her, but was stopped by two of the Pukui crew.

"Stay out of this, Warden! This is my fight!"

"Let 'er come!" Klooney called. The Company swimmers had formed a loose group behind Klooney. Most looked as if they would rather not be there, but Pua knew they would all take part if a fight started. Watercrews never broke ranks in arguments with outsiders. They had to depend too closely on one another when they went back to the nets. The Pukui crew stood in a solid block around Zena.

Zena tried, but was unable to break away from those restraining her.

"What's going on here?" the mountainlady asked. Stall them, Pua urged silently. At least until Fatu gets here.

"I'll tell you what's going on," Zena called. "He just lost Pukui another swimmer. A recruit, on-line only three days. This reef-sucker sent her under the net without a backup, and then called a roll before she was out."

"Standard procedure," Klooney snapped. "The roll is ordered as soon as a *Net clear* signal is received."

"She signaled that the net was clear, not that *she* was!"

"If you can't train your squids right, you shouldn't be dropping them in the water," Klooney shouted back.

Again the warden lifted an arm to stop Zena's surge forward.

"Warden, that swimmer was dragged right across a strand of knife coral," Zena said. "She lost four fingers off her right hand. Full fingers, back of the bone—they're not going to grow back. Her skin is shredded, and her right gill was ripped halfway off."

"Where is she now?" the warden asked. Her expression remained calm.

"Infirmary," Zena said. "But she'd have been better off if he'd killed her outright. What kind of life can she have on Lesaat if she can't swim?"

The warden turned slowly. She settled her fists on her hips. "Mr. Klooney, I recall giving you a direct order that no new recruit was to be used under the nets without a fully trained swimmer as backup."

His eyes narrowed. "That so?" A smirk lifted one corner of his mouth. "Well, I don't rightly remember hearin' that, *Boss*."

The mountainlady didn't even blink. "I also gave you a direct order concerning the division of Company and non-Company crews."

The smirk twitched. "It's your Pukui crew that's refusin' to work. I been mixin' 'em up just like you said."

"And giving us all the shit work," one of the Pukui crew called.

"Yeah, an' you can't even do that right," a Company man close to Klooney returned.

"Shut up. All of you," the warden said. "Klooney, you're off the job. Confine yourself to quarters until transport back to Landing arranged. The rest of you get back to work."

"You an order me off the job," Klooney said. The smirk had disappeared. Now comes the trouble, Pua thought. Hurry, Fatu! One of the Pukui men stopped her from getting closer.

"Ain't nobody here can prove I did anything wrong out there," Klooney said. He smiled. "Besides, there's no way you can clear those pens before the storms without Company crews."

"I'm not firing your swimmers, Mr. Klooney. Just you."

"Company squids don't swim without a Company boss onsite," he snarled. "That's the law."

"Right now, I'm the law," the warden said. "Shooter's privileges, remember? I can truth-probe you, too, if I decide it suits me."

That caused a murmur among both the Company and the Pukui swimmers. Klooney glanced to one side, making eye contact with several of his own people. Most of them had backed off, not enough to break ranks with one another, but enough to distance themselves from him. Klooney met Pua's stare and glared, before returning his look to the warden.

"You're already breaking the law out here, lady," he growled. "That algae's not supposed to be touched, and you know it. If the security squads were still—"

"Take your complaints to whoever hired you to sabotage this harvest," the warden said.

He reached for her. A swift upward thrust of his hands, fingers outstretched.

"Watch out!" Pua cried, but the mountainlady had already moved. She snagged Klooney's wrists in her own long, strong fingers and yanked them to the side. He struggled, but could not break her grip.

"Ordinarily, I dislike killing people, Mr. Klooney," she said. "But if you force me into it today, it won't even make me blink. Ehu?"

"Aye?"

"Get some people you trust and take this—*squid*—to his quarters. See that he stays there until a flit is sent out from Landing."

"Aye!"

Ehu, Kobe, and Dave Chan immediately relieved the warden of the cursing, struggling Klooney. "You won't get away with this!" he shouted as they dragged him away. "You won't . . ."

The warden turned back to the startled swimmers. They looked as surprised as Pua felt at the ease with which the Earth woman had disarmed Klooney. "We need crews in the water," she said. "We need them there now. What's it going to take?"

The question made Zena stand straighter. "Pukui's crews and the independents will swim with Klooney gone, but"—she glanced at the Company swimmers—"they can't. That slime mold was right about them not being allowed to work without a Company boss on-site." The Company swimmers shifted and muttered, many of them obviously uncomfortable, but none of them disputed Zena's words.

"I'll boss 'em," a soft voice said. Pua looked up in surprise to see Lili Kanahele step forward from the Company ranks. "For a fee."

"Who are you?" the warden asked. She looked Lili up and down slowly.

"Liliuokalani Yee Kwan Kanahele," Lili said. "I've bossed

enough Pukui harvests to know how to do this one better'n it's been done so far."

The warden caught Zena's eye, and Zena nodded. Lili was one of the best of the Company bosses. She had been one of Pua's favorites in the days before her parents had died. Pua was surprised that Lili had been working ordinary net shifts with the rest of the Company swimmers. She was known for her carefree spending habits, though. Maybe she needed the bonuses the warden had offered.

"You were on the shuttle, weren't you?" the warden asked suddenly. "You're the one with the ribbon."

Lili grinned. "You impressed the hell out of me, too, Warden."

"What were you doing on Earth?"

"Tech training course at Saipan," Lili replied. "Company paid for the trip, but I still owe big for the fun I had on a little side trip to Guam. What do you say? You want me to do the job?"

"How much?" the warden asked.

"Double what Klooney was getting; double again for over-time," Lili said without a pause.

Pua wasn't the only one to suck in her breath. She had never heard of a Company boss being paid so much.

"Greedy bitch," one of the Pukui swimmers muttered.

The warden watched Lili for a long moment. Finally, she said, "Zena, will you work with her?"

"Aye, but Pukui shouldn't have to pay—"

The warden lifted a hand. She glanced around, matching looks with the Company squids. "What about the rest of you?"

They shrugged and murmured their general assent.

"It's done, then. Lili, see that you're worth the price. Now, get these people back on those nets."

"Aye, Boss," Lili chuckled before snapping a list of orders to the startled Company crew. They scrambled for the waiting buses.

"Zena," the warden said, turning back. "Is it settled? Can you work with it now?" Her voice was quiet but firm.

Zena's sigh was barely noticeable. "I sure as hell hope so," she said.

The warden nodded. "Make sure the injured swimmer is taken care of, then get things back on-line as quick as you can. Fatu's on his way."

Zena turned her slow, frowning gaze toward Pua. Pua shrugged and tried to look innocent.

"Tell him the comm lines to the house and shed are out," the warden said. "I want him to see to the repairs personally."

"Aye, Zena said. She gave Pua one last look before turning away to board the Pukui bus.

As the warden started back toward the house, she motioned for Pua to join her. "Let's go take a look at those comm towers on Second."

"Now?" Pua asked.

"Now's as good a time as any. We can use the flit comm to call Landing."

Despite both Katie's and Pua's objections, the warden still kept Toma's flitter parked just outside the house. "Do you want to pilot?" she asked as they reached it.

"Don't you have any excess adrenaline to get rid of?" Pua returned. The warden laughed, and slid into the passenger's seat. While Pua lifted the flitter and set a course for Second, she opened the comm and transmitted a terse order for Toma's immediate presence at Pukui.

"Tell him I want him personally to escort Mr. Klooney from this reef," she said. She flipped the comm off without waiting for a reply.

As they approached Second Island, Pua turned the flitter into the deep cleft that separated it from Home. It wasn't a necessary part of the tour, but she had always wanted to fly through the narrow passage. Her father had let her fly only over the low reef islets. She was surprised, but pleased, when the warden's hands remained relaxed on her knees.

"It looks like the whole side of the mountain split off," the warden said.

Pua nodded. "Mauna Kea Iki was a lot higher once, back when the volcano was still going. Then it started to sink, and coral grew up around the outer edge. That's what made the barrier reef. Then the volcano erupted some more and the mountain got high again, only not as high as the first time. Then it sank partway down again. The edges of that second mountain are where the inner reef is growing today. That's what my dad said. I think the mountain cracked while it was sinking."

"Must have been a rough quake to crack it wide open like this," the warden said.

"It happened a long time ago," Pua assured her. "About a million years or so, I think. You don't have to worry about it happening again now."

The warden's mouth twitched into a small smile.

Pua lifted the flitter from the canyon between the mountains and flew toward the summit of Second Island. "There's the burial cave," she said.

"Where?"

Pua dipped and slowed, then hovered over a small clearing. "That narrow crack back in the bushes. See? It looks like somebody's cleared a lot of brush away. It used to be harder to see."

"I don't—oh." The warden leaned forward and blinked. "It's awfully small, isn't it?"

"It's great big inside. It goes way back into the mountain. It's scary in there."

"Set us down. I'd like to see it."

"You want to go in there *now*?"

The warden turned to her. "Is there some reason why I shouldn't?"

"Yes! Fatu just took that crewman's bones in there a couple of days ago! His ghost is probably still walking around looking for somebody to eat!" Pua remembered suddenly that the woman had been dead once herself. Maybe ghosts didn't matter to her anymore.

The woman blinked again, but this time it wasn't to adjust her focus. "His ghost?"

Pua shivered. "I'll drop you off if you want, but I'm not going in with you. Not this soon after."

The warden watched her for a moment, then turned back to look at the cave entrance. "When will it be safe?" she asked.

Never! Pua thought. "You'd have to ask Fatu," she said. "He's the one who knows about ghosts and things." She glanced at the woman. "I thought you knew that."

The warden looked honestly surprised. "How would I know that?"

"You asked him to take care of the crewman's body," Pua said. "He's the one who always takes dead people into the cave."

The woman said nothing for a moment. When she shook her head in that way that meant she had come across some new and confusing piece of information. "Let's go up to the towers," she said; and willingly, Pua lifted the flitter away from the clearing. The warden twisted around in her seat to stare back at the cave.

They spent only a short time at the towers. The warden inspected each of them quickly, frowning when she found exposed wires on the weather tower. "This isn't a good time to take chances with incoming weather transmissions," she said. Pua frowned, too. She had never seen the weather and comm towers in anything but perfect condition.

* * *

That evening, as they sat together on the lanai, Pua asked, "Have you ever killed anybody? Anybody human, I mean?"

The warden rested her glass of candleberry wine on the arm of her chair. "Why do you ask?"

"You told Klooney you didn't like killing people. I just wondered if you'd ever really done it, or if you were just trying to scare him."

The mountainlady picked up her glass again. She frowned. "I've killed three," she said. "One was a man already half-dead of pain and with no hope of recovery. One was caught in a rock slide with no way out. And the third was someone who deserved to die. I would have preferred not having to kill any of them. I don't like deliberately destroying life."

Pua thought about that for a while.

"I killed a man once," she said. "Back at the recon station."

The mountainlady stopped in mid-drink.

"It was before you got there. I snuck into the morgue to see my mom and dad, and there was a man there. He was—doing things. My mama's body was all in pieces. He was cutting on her gills." She looked down at her hands. "I wrapped my fingers around his neck, and I choked him. After he stopped breathing, I broke his neck. I would have ripped his gills out if he'd had any. I wanted to cut him up like he was doing to Mama, but Mr. Crawley came in and stopped me."

The warden sat silent for a long time. "Is that how Crawley got the scar on his face?" she asked finally.

Pua nodded. "I like the ones you did better, though."

The mountainlady closed her eyes and took the drink she had started earlier. She drained the glass.

"You should have killed Klooney today," Pua said. "You shouldn't have let him go."

"You can't kill everyone who does something you don't like, Pua."

"Klooney is bad," Pua said. "He's like that bacteria that gets into the loli and makes people sick, only he does it on purpose. He *likes* hurting people. I can taste it when I'm in the water with him."

The warden put her glass on the floor and leaned forward. "Pua," she said, "if Klooney ever comes back here, you stay away from him. You take your rays and all your other water friends, and stay as far away from him as you can get. Do you understand?"

"If Klooney ever comes back to Pukui," Pua said very carefully, "I'm going to kill him."

Chapter 15

~~~~~~~~~~~~~~~~~~~~~~~~~~~~~~~~~~~~~~~
~~~~~~~~~~~~~~~~~~~~~~~~~~~~~~~~~~~~~~~

The next morning, the warden returned to the burial cave. Pua followed, as she always did when the warden roamed the island, but when she realized where the woman was leading her, she quickly let the distance between them grow.

Nothing, she decided, is going to make me go inside that cave. If the Earthwoman gets herself eaten in there, it's her own damn fault.

She waited until the warden crawled into the cave, then chose a hiding place on the far side of the clearing. She stayed near the path, but not directly between it and the cave mouth. She didn't want to be in the way if some angry spirit came rushing out. She settled down to wait.

And wait. The sun kissed zenith and traveled on. Pua moved farther back into the shade. She braided clinger vines and wrapped them in patterns around her arms and legs. She wove herself a headband of paperflowers and counted the spore spots on the undersides of fern leaves. She was unbearably bored.

By late afternoon she was also hungry. When a sugarbug landed on her arm, she caught it in her fingertips, pulled off its leathery wings, and ate it quickly. Then she was sorry, because its sweet crunchiness made her even hungrier. She wished she had thought to carry mountain apples in her pockets like the warden always did. She wished she was in the water where there was always food nearby, and where boredom didn't exist.

Finally, when the sunlight was beginning to fade and Pua was sure the Earthwoman must be dead, she heard scuffing sounds from inside the cave. Hurriedly, she pressed deeper into the shadows. She held her breath as a light flashed out through the cave mouth, then sighed in relief as it was followed by the warden on her hands and knees—dirty, but unharmed.

The woman flicked off her light, glanced around the clearing, then strode back down the path. Pua followed as closely as she dared, not sure which was the most frightening, the ghosts of the dead behind her or their near kin on the path ahead.

During the following days, the warden explored the islands and the reef, sometimes on foot, sometimes from the air or by sub. On a few occasions, Pua swam with her to inspect the coral. The woman swam strongly, and well, but she never stayed beneath the surface long. The rays were disappointed by that, even though Pua explained to them that the woman wasn't always as entertaining as she appeared on those few short trips under the water. When Pua showed the warden the rock eel's former territory on number twelve's barren reef flat, she studied it closely, even pausing to run her fingers carefully over the flat edges of the broken knife coral.

Aside from occasional on-site inspections and frequent reports from Zena and Fatu, the warden took little part in the algae harvest. She expelled three more Company swimmers after they were caught deliberately tearing the nets so that the algae spills were larger and took more time to clean up. But otherwise she left the crew operations to Fatu, Zena, and Lili. The last proved to be surprisingly efficient—even the Pukui crew commented on her speed and fairness of job allocation.

The warden spent most of her time in the control shed, poring over the farm records, or studying the house computer library. She inspected the research labs and the infirmary, the algae-processing plant, even the underwater pump stations. She questioned everyone—including Katie, although those conversations never lasted long, and she always walked away looking confused. That made Pua laugh. Only her mother had been able to make any real sense of the slow-minded drone. She was surprised that Katie talked to the warden at all.

Toma came and went. He always arrived during the day, and the warden always talked to him on the dock or at the flitter landing pad. She did not invite him back into the house. Their conversations were short and sharp, with many more questions being asked than answers given—by either of them.

Whenever the discussion over crew or supplies became heated, the woman would say, "Shooter's privileges, Inspector. Read my contract," and Toma would smile a brief, tight smile and grow silent. He relayed official Company protests against the continuing harvest, but did not suggest returning the security squads to Pukui. He removed Klooney and the other trouble-makers without comment.

"That special order of yours is on the manifest for tomorrow's shuttle," he said one afternoon about three weeks after the harvest had begun. The woman had asked him about it more than once.

"It's about time," she replied.

"What's the matter?" Toma asked. "Having trouble thinking?"

The warden smiled, an open, bright smile the like of which Pua had not seen in recent days. And Toma matched it. Pua wished he would offer to do sex with her again, as he had that first morning at the house. After what the woman had talked about in her sleep, and knowing what she knew of Toma, Pua suspected that a match between them would be an event well worth watching.

But Toma only said, "I'll see that it's sent out directly. They doubled your order, by the way. The extra transport charge has been deducted from your account." The warden's brows lifted at that, but she did not otherwise respond.

The Earther always remained on the landing pad until Toma's flitter lifted and disappeared entirely from sight. More and more often as the days passed, she was frowning when she turned back toward the farm control shed.

Of all the woman's activities, it was her trips to the mountain-top that intrigued Pua most. At the most unexpected moments, she would stop what she was doing, push back from the computer, or step, frowning, from the control shed. She would stare up at the mountain for a moment, then cross the compound to climb the summit path.

All she did up there was sit cross-legged under the snow trees. Her eyes would close; her breathing would slow. Her long fingers would relax until they lay loose and flaccid across her knees. After a time, she would breathe deeply, then stand and stretch, staring out across the lagoons.

Before striding back downhill, she always ran her palms along at least one of the snow trees. When Pua later checked the places where the Earther's hands paused on the smooth bark, she almost always found a snowball hidden underneath. It surprised her at first, because only she and her mother had been able to find the hardened sap deposits so easily. Maybe it's because she's such a strong land person, Pua thought. Or maybe the trees

just like her because of her hands. Pua found it interesting that
the warden never removed the snowballs from the trees.

Then, at the end of the third week, the pattern changed.

The woman had spent many hours in the shed that day, studying some new Earth history and language tapes that Toma had
brought. Pua had watched for a time, trying to understand the
woman's intense interest in things that had no connection to
Pukui, but had finally given up in boredom and retreated to her
usual watching spot under the main house.

As evening approached, Katie delivered food to the control
shed, something Pua had never seen her do before. Katie had
always been afraid of the shed, or, more likely, the machines in
it. Pua waved to Katie from under the house and was soon
brought her own dinner there. She and Katie shared the food,
and while they ate, they talked, mostly of things incomprehen-
sible to Pua. She got the impression, though, that Katie had
decided that the warden was an acceptable addition to the household.

When they were finished, Katie dug up a small snowball that
Pua had missed, and handed it to her with a grin.

"Good job, Katie," Pua told her. "You did just what Mama
wanted." Katie beamed with pride.

Sometime later, the warden emerged from the control shed
and strode directly to the mountain. At the summit, she paced
for a time, staring up at the rings and the rising moons. Then
she took something from her pocket and put it into her mouth.
She chewed slowly. Finally, she called, "Come on up here, Pua.
I need to talk to you."

Pua frowned. She had been certain the woman hadn't seen
her following this time. She pushed aside a fanner fern and
crawled into the open.

"How'd you know I was here?"

"You watched me from that same spot last night," the warden said. "If you're going to follow people around in the woods,
you need to learn to hide yourself better."

Pua scuffed across the moat and ducked under the trees. She
squatted at the woman's side. The warden moved so they were
facing each other and pulled two small brown oblongs from her
pocket. She handed one to Pua and put the other into her mouth.
"No need to unwrap it," she said. "The paper's edible."

Pua eyed the thing dubiously, but knew better than to refuse
a food offering from the mountainlady who, after all, spent more
time studying the local customs than she did looking for the

missing research records. Pua slid the strange brown thing between her teeth. It was tasteless and as hard as a stone.

"How's the harvest going?" the warden asked.

"Why are you asking me?" The thing in Pua's mouth grew
suddenly soft and sweet. Candy! Pua thought. This must be
what was in the big box that had come with the last supply run,
the caramel things the mountainlady had been talking to Toma
about. No wonder she had been so happy to get them.

"You know the reef better than anyone. Does it look like
we've opened those three sections to the sun in time to prevent
any long-term damage?" The warden wiped the corner of her
mouth with her finger.

Pua looked out toward the water. The sun had almost set, and
the reef had begun to glow. She chewed for a while, then swallowed. "Eleven and thirteen are okay. It's too soon to know for
sure about ten, but the silverfish and skudders are coming back.
That means there's still food there. That squall yesterday spattered some live algae from the lifting net at nine, but the crews
cleaned it up without any problem." She nodded toward the
east. "We're going to have rain tonight, and high swell, but
Zena said the storm that's causing it is starting to veer north."

"Yes," the warden said. "I've been watching the satellite
reports. We're cutting it close, but I think we're going to make
it. Fatu has prepared the charges for setting up last-minute methane blows, though, just in case." It was a poor substitute for
clearing the algae altogether, but if the pens were going to be
torn open, blowing them in advance would at least leave only
dead algae to be scattered over the reef.

"Alignment is tomorrow night," Pua said. "After that, the
tides will start to go down. It will be easier to get the last of
the harvest done before the next storm comes close."

"I'm told you're still spending time with the net crews," the
warden said.

Pua unwrapped a string of friendly vine from her ankle and
stretched it out between her fingers. "It's my reef," she said
without looking up.

"That won't mean much if you get yourself killed."

Pua met her look then. She snapped the vine in half.

Suddenly, she laughed. "Do you know what the swimmers
call you, Mountainlady? Puhi 'ai Pōhaku. They say—" She lowered her voice to imitate the swimmers, especially the men, as
they described the warden's likeness to a rock eel. "They say,

'She's nice to look at. She moves real smooth. But watch out! 'Cause if you get in her way, she'll bite your head off.' ''

Pua clutched her sides in her delight at the warden's expression. ''Sometimes you're so funny.'' She giggled. ''Even the rays think so.''

The warden stared at her. ''Sometimes I think Fatu is right about you having seawater for brains.''

Pua straightened. She wiped her eyes. ''Fatu said that?''

The woman nodded.

Pua considered the idea for a moment. It sounded like a fine compliment coming from Fatu. She grinned.

The warden reached into her shirt pocket and pulled out a red string. She stretched it between her two hands just as Pua had the friendly vine, then laid it across Pua's left knee. Pua rolled it over with her finger.

''What is it?''

''A locator signaling device,'' the warden said. ''It's been programmed to respond to one of my implants. I want you to wear it. Tie it in your hair or something. With all the other decorations you wear, no one will ever notice it.''

Pua knocked the string off her leg. The woman caught it easily before it touched the ground. She moved almost as effortlessly as a real waterworlder now.

''It's for your own safety, Pua. It operates on a private channel. I'm the only one who can trace you through it, and if you're ever in trouble, all you have to do to alert me is break the string.''

''*No!* I don't want you following me around. I don't want *anybody* following me around.''

''Somebody else already is,'' the warden said.

''What?''

''They're monitoring me, too.'' The warden's voice had taken on that quiet tone again, that dead-calm tone that Pua had come to dread. Things always went wrong when she used that tone. ''Remember when I first woke up and Doctor Waight turned off the electromagnetic field? My shoulder itched, and she told me one of my locator implants had been triggered accidentally. It never occurred to me then that she would have reason to lie.'' She rubbed a hand over her right shoulder.

Pua wrapped her arms around her upraised knees, feeling suddenly cold. She stared at the string in the warden's hand.

''They replaced one of my implants while I was in dep,'' the woman said. ''That itch must have been a test to be sure it worked. I discovered it about an hour ago when I tried to program this to my private code." She lifted the string.

"I don't have any implants," Pua said, wishing she could keep her voice as steady as the woman's.

The warden glanced at Pua's hands. "You were at the bathing pool this afternoon, then you followed the overflow stream about halfway down. You moved into the woods on the opposite side from the house, stopped for a while about where the mountain apple tree is, then went straight downhill to—"

"Stop it!" Pua cried.

"They've got you on a very restricted channel," the warden said. "But it's long-range and extremely precise. Whoever bugged you knows exactly where you've been every minute since you left the recon center."

"Why?"

"I presume it's because they want you to lead them to what they're trying to find," the warden said.

Pua stared at her, hard. "I *don't know* where the TC records are! If I knew, I'd just give them to the stupid Company so they'd leave Pukui alone." She was afraid to look down at her hands. She had never thought about anyone using them to hide something. Since returning to Pukui, she had tried not to think about her hands at all.

The warden watched her for a moment. "They gave me yours, didn't they?" she asked.

Pua turned to stare out at the sea. She didn't want to think about the woman's hands, either.

"It was a direct transplant," the warden said. She rubbed the tips of her long fingers together. "There was no cloning involved. No dramatic new technique. They just did a direct human-to-human transplant."

Pua hadn't even told Fatu about her hands.

"They knew from my medical records that I would make a compatible recipient," the warden went on. "Hell, the drugs they used to prevent rejection of my new eye implants were still fully active. They didn't even have to prep my system."

Fatu had held Pua's hands so very long that first night she had been home. He had wrapped his wide, strong fingers around hers and held them tight for a long, long time. Was that why he had warned her so strongly to stay away from the barrier reef? Had he known, or at least guessed, about the locator, too?

The woman touched her knee. Pua dragged her attention back.

"Doctor Waight told me these hands would regenerate if they

were damaged,'' the mountainlady said, "right in the very beginning, but I never made the connection. Not even when I noticed that yours were small for your size. I was so horrified by what they had done to me that I never even considered what they might have done to you.''

Pua glanced down at the hand on her knee. It was larger than it had been before, an adult hand, grown to match the warden's full size. Its fingers moved smoothly, gracefully, in patterns she didn't remember as being her own. Still, even on the Earthwoman, it moved like a waterworlder's hand.

"Pualei," the warden said softly. "If I had known. If I had even guessed they were your hands and not just cloned parts, I would never have agreed to use them. Not for any reason. Not even to get my own back.''

Pua met her look. "What good would that have done? If you hadn't made Mr. Crawley let me come here with you, they would have taken my new hands by now, too." She wondered if it was the rising moonlight that made the woman's skin so pale. "Doctor Waight said they'd already found someone else with a close enough genotype match. They were just waiting for my hands to regenerate all the way. That's why they want me back. So they can keep making new waterworlders with my hands. They're trying to clone them, too, because that would be a lot faster than waiting for mine to grow back each time, but they don't know how. Only my mama—''

She paused, and looked down at the warden's hand again. "Mr. Crawley told me they cut my hands off because of what I did to that man in the morgue.''

"Mother of mountains," the woman breathed.

Pua shrugged. "After I saw you, I knew it wasn't true. I knew they just needed somebody to come to Pukui.''

"Pua," the warden said quietly. "Tell me what's going on here. Tell me what's *really* going on.''

Pua blinked. "What do you mean?''

Only the woman's mouth smiled. "You're getting really good at that, Waterbaby. With a little more practice, you might just be able to fool me with that look of innocent confusion.''

Pua dropped her gaze back to her hands. She wished she was in the water. She wished Fatu would come so the woman would talk about something else. She wished the woman had gone into the burial cave and all the Company people had followed, and the ghosts had eaten them all.

"I didn't *make* Crawley do anything, Pua. He intended all along for us to come here together."

Pua glanced up.

"When I told him what I wanted, he didn't even argue," the warden said. "Not about the research. Not about the timing. Not about you. The only things he didn't like were giving me the title to the forest preserve and posting my contract on the public net. But he did both without a fight."

She lifted her hand from Pua's knee. "What is it at Pukui that they're so desperate to find? There's more to it than just the missing TC enzyme research. There are too many other things going on that don't make sense. Too many people with blank faces and tight tongues."

Pua wished at that moment that she dared trust the woman— she was that tired of hiding the truth. But then she thought of Mr. Crawley and Doctor Waight and her parents' bodies lying in that cold, cold room. She said nothing.

The woman sighed. "If I ever have a secret I need to share, Pua, you'll be the one I share it with. You might be wrong in your silence, but no one will ever be able to fault you for the quality of it." She stared out at the water for a moment. When she turned back, the hardness had returned to her eyes. "I've asked Toma and Fatu to meet with us tonight. They're probably waiting down at the landing pad by now."

That surprised Pua. "Why?"

The warden uncrossed her legs. "I asked Fatu, because anything you're involved in, he's involved in. And I asked the inspector, because, despite his Company title, I'm certain he's in this thing up to his neck."

She stood in one smooth motion. She offered her hand, and after some hesitation, Pua used it to pull herself up. The hand no longer felt like her own.

"You still want your other hands back, don't you?" she asked, not understanding how anyone could possibly want stiff, stubby Earther's hands after having had these. She stared at the long, beautiful fingers.

"Yes," the mountainlady said, and Pua let them go.

But the warden did not release her hold. "That's not the right question anymore, Pua. I still want my hands back, but getting them is no longer my prime motivation for completing this job."

Something had changed. What happened? Pua wanted to ask. What did you find out today that you didn't know before?

"I won't go back to Earth," she said. "I don't care what happens, I won't let you take me back there."

"I won't take you back, Waterbaby. I don't know what I'm going to do with you, but I promise I won't take you back to Waight or Crawley or anyone else connected with the Company."

They stared at each other for a moment. Then the woman said, "Come on. Let's go talk to Fatu and Toma."

Pua followed her out from under the trees and down the mountain path. When they reached a place where they could see Toma's flitter resting on the landing pad, Pua paused. In the water, where nothing was ever static, you had to take chances. Sometimes it got you killed, but sometimes . . .

"Gills," she said softly.

"What?" The warden turned back.

"Gills." Pua said it firmly this time—and felt a chill go down her back. It's up to us, Le Fe'e, she sang silently. Fatu and Uncle Toma can't do anything more to help us, so we have to do it ourselves.

"If you're going to save Pukui," Pua told the mountainlady, "you've got to start thinking like a waterworlder. Uncle Toma is in this thing up to his *gills*!"

Chapter 16

~~~~~~~~~~~~~~~~
~~~~~~~~~~~~~~~~

Pua's comment surprised Angie and relieved her greatly. It meant that the girl, while still not willing to reveal Pukui's secret herself, was at least acknowledging that the secret existed. At least, that's what Angie hoped it meant.

She paused as they approached the landing pad and offered Pua the locator string again. Pua didn't look pleased, but she took it. She coiled it around her left thumb before stuffing it into her shirt pocket.

Toma and Fatu were waiting beside the flitter. "Is there something wrong at the house?" Toma asked when Angie indicated that they should sit on the open lawn to talk.

"If you're concerned about being overheard," Fatu said with a sidelong look at Pua, "the library is equipped with a privacy blanket."

"I trust that blanket just slightly less than I trust the two of you," Angie said. She motioned for Pua to sit at her left. Toma sat facing Angie, and Fatu closed the square. Pua didn't look comfortable with the arrangement. The light of the moons and the rings and the surrounding phosphorescent grass made it almost as light as day.

"Pua and I are both carrying high-precision, long-range locator implants," she said as soon as they were settled.

Toma frowned and blinked, but said nothing. Fatu met Pua's look. The girl shook her head slightly, then cursed when she saw that Angie was looking directly at her. Angie lifted a questioning brow, and very deliberately, Pua molded her expression into her very best innocent-confusion look.

Angie smiled. "Very, very good, Waterbaby."

She turned to Fatu. "Would *you* care to explain what that little interchange was all about?"

174

Fatu's face went blank.

"Toma?"

He, too, remained silent. They weren't going to make it easy.

"My bug is in my shoulder, Pua's is in one of her hands," she said. "Can you remove them for us, *Doctor*?"

Toma shifted his look to Pua. "Let me see." Pua put both her hands behind her back.

"You don't need to examine her now," Angie said. "I'll tell you what you want to know. Her hands are full regenerations. Mine are the originals. The switch was done by direct transplant; there was no genetic duplication involved."

She paused. "Now. Tell me, Doctor Haili. Why does that verification bring you such well-disguised relief?" She touched Pua's knee and pointed. "See that, Pua? *That's* how you do innocent confusion."

The look slid very abruptly from Toma's face.

"What's this about, Warden?" Fatu asked.

She turned to him. "What's inside the burial cave?"

Fatu didn't even blink. Angie wished she had a way to read him better, but Fatu's inner feelings remained as much a mystery as the rest of Pukui. Toma, while his training made him highly dangerous, was at least to some degree predictable.

"As you saw," Fatu said in that gentle voice that was so at odds with his enormous body. "Only the dead, and a ransacked storage cache." His dark skin glistened. He smelled faintly of candleberry.

"There's a supply cache in the *burial cave*?" Pua said.

"What happened in there?" Angie asked.

"Not everyone who searched Pukui in recent months used as much restraint as you did," Fatu said. "I offered to disinter the bones for Mr. Yoshida . . ."

Angie frowned—Nori was *here*, too?

". . . but he insisted his own people do it. They tore the place apart every time they went in."

"No wonder so many things are going wrong at Pukui," Pua said. "The ghosts are probably—"

"There's nothing to fear from the ghosts," Fatu said. "I've cleaned and rehidden the bones. The spirits of the dead are at rest. Pukui's problems are being caused by the living." He returned his look to Angie. "Inspector Yoshida is the Earth rep in charge of the TC records search. I assume from your expression that you know him."

Angie glanced at Pua, who was still wide-eyed with concern.

"I do now," she said. Nori, you son of a bitch. I will repay you for this if it takes the rest of my life. A gust of wind blew her hair into her eyes. She pushed it back and returned her attention to Fatu.

"You hold a perpetual lease on about twenty percent of Pukui's land and waters. Is that right?" she asked.

"Aye," he replied.

"Do you consider this to be your permanent home?"

"Of course, but what—"

"Zena and the other Pukui old-timers hold Pukui leases, also."

He nodded. "Zena holds an original perpetual lease, and the others have long-term use rights granted by Zed and Lehua. This is all in the public records, Warden."

"You hold title to a rather sizable piece of Pukui, too, don't you, Inspector?" Angie said. That was something *not* in the public records.

"What?" Pua cried.

Toma sat up. "How did you—"

"I got it the night of the methane fire," Angie said. "The intruder screens were back on-line for some time before I activated the audio alert signal, so I knew someone was out there. I had time to set up the farm comm to accept a data-burst transfer, which I activated as soon as I had access to your flitter's comm. It was almost three minutes before you got up to the house and sent a precautionary wipe order."

Toma went as pale as she had seen him yet. He knew exactly how much a trained troubleshooter could bleed from an open computer bank in three minutes. And his flitter comm had been tied into his private home banks. Her gamble had paid off well.

"What do you mean, he owns part of Pukui?" Pua demanded.

"Five sections of barrier reef, two growing pens, and a vertical slice of Second Island, plus pre-approved options on the rest should anything happen to you," Angie said. "I presume that's to strengthen some future Company claim—"

Pua jumped up. "You *are* trying to steal—"

Fatu started up as well, but Angie waved him back. She grabbed Pua's hand. "Or, it's an attempt to *protect* Pukui from the Company in case something happens to you. Sit down. Please." She pulled Pua down, closer beside her than before. Pua's hand trembled under hers, but she didn't pull it away.

"Either way, Inspector," Angie said, "it could be argued that you have a strong motive for not wanting Pua to inherit."

"Your implication is wrong," Toma said. "I did not try to kill Pua. Not with loli fever, and not with that methane fire."

"But you did fly low over number twelve shortly before the alarm went off," Angie said.

"I make it a point to overfly the pens every time I come out here," he said. "If your screens were up that night, you know damn well I didn't do anything *but* fly over them."

"Is that true?" Pua asked. Angie nodded.

"Then why are you . . ."

"Because it's important that you know these things, Pua," Angie said. "If there's ever a public investigation of your parents' deaths, Uncle Toma here is going to be the prime suspect. He had motive; he had opportunity. He's been in a position to cover up the evidence ever since it happened."

"But you said before, you didn't think he did it," Pua said.

"I don't," Angie said. "But the event was definitely set up so that he would be the one blamed if the murders were ever made public. I can clear him, though."

Pua sat up very straight. "How?"

"By disproving his motive."

"But he—"

"Let the warden talk," Fatu said. Angie nodded her thanks, although she was certain he hadn't meant it as a courtesy to her. He was trying to shut Pua up.

"What's this about, Warden?" Toma asked.

"Permanence," she said. "Permanence and Pukui."

She glanced around at the neatly kept compound, at the beautiful house and grounds, at the clean, orderly docks and farm buildings. "This farm was designed, and continues to be maintained, as a permanent human settlement. A long-term home as well as a working farm."

"Of course, but—"

"That's not true of most of the settlements on Lesaat. It's most certainly not true of Landing. That is as cold and impersonal, and temporary-feeling, a Company town as I've ever seen."

"I can assure you, Warden," Toma said dryly, "World Life considers *all* of its holdings here permanent."

"Politically, economically, I'm sure that's true," Angie said. "But I'm talking about emotionally, aesthetically. Landing is like one of those places anthropologists used to talk about in studies of displaced communities. They claimed that people who didn't *think* of a place as permanent usually didn't do much to *make* it so.''

Pua pulled her hand out from under Angie's and laid it in her lap.

"It confused me at first, too, Pua," Angie said. "But after Fatu told me about the inheritance laws and all the restrictions on long-term leases, it started to make sense. With the exception of Pukui, and maybe even that if we can't resolve things here soon, all productive land and waters on Lesaat will be under Company control by the time the last of the current perpetual leaseholders dies.''

She sat back, leaning on her arms. The grass was warm under her hands. A cool breeze fanned her hair. "If you know your land can easily be taken away from you when your three-year lease is up, there isn't much incentive for investing money and energy on aesthetics. Make what profit you can and take your pleasures on the back streets of Landing. That seems to be the prevailing philosophy on Lesaat.''

"Some people send money home to their families on Earth," Pua said.

"Aye," Angie said. "Even after the debts that forced them into coming here are paid, many of them keep sending their money back. It's because, even though they know they can never return, they continue to think of Earth as their home. The alterations to their hands make them into freaks as far as Earthers are concerned, and the Company would never consent to change them back. Yet they have no real hope for a future here. It's a difficult situation. It explains, at least in part, why this is such a violent place.''

"What are you getting at, Warden?" Toma asked. "We hardly need a lesson in the social problems of Lesaat.''

Angie met his look again. "According to the information in your private files, that sense of impermanence does not hold planetwide. Linina's Reef, which you own in its entirety, and Fatu's cousin's place at Maui Surf, and others—all of them operating under long-term or perpetual leases—continue to be well maintained and improved. Kobayashi's reef north of here appears to be extraordinarily well kept.''

Toma's frown deepened.

"Almost every cent of profit made on those farms is being reinvested," Angie went on, "if not in the same farm, then in one of the others. You've developed an interesting pattern of reciprocal gift-giving here, Inspector.

"You've also established your own set of customs and beliefs. Kobe, for example, still abides by the kapu against harming Pukui reef dwellers, even though he no longer lives here, and Katie, with her limited connection to reality, never fails to serve food to a guest. Pua reintroduces herself to her mother's house whenever she comes there directly from the sea."

That small ritual had surprised Angie as much as anything the girl had done or said since their arrival on Lesaat. It spoke so very clearly about her strong belief in the consciousness of this place. Pua had to have learned that from her parents and Fatu and the others among whom she was raised.

"The Pukui household itself is a museum of manufactured traditions that you all admit to very openly," Angie went on. "Fatu, you've tattooed your body in a very *ancient* tradition for the sake of your *grand*children. That's emotional and psychological permanence. Even your burial customs speak of it. In fact, they speak most eloquently of all. That cave is much more than a graveyard. It's a shrine, a place for future generations to pay their respects to their ancestors."

She glanced around at them all. "Yet, just like everyone else on Lesaat, you know that your children and your grandchildren will never truly benefit from all this. The customs, the traditions—they're nothing without the land. Not here, where they're all made up to start with."

"Some of us still have personal pride," Fatu said. "We choose not to live in squalor."

She shook her head. "If that's all it is, why is there all this fuss over the total-conversion enzyme? If all you want to do is live here on your well-maintained reef until you die of old age, then why withhold the processing records? No, Crawley was right. If I'm going to figure this out, I need to find Sa le Fe'e."

Fatu caught his breath, just as he had the first time she had said the phrase to him. Pua sat up straight. Angie laughed softly. "You led me away from that subject very expertly on the sub that afternoon, Fatu. You spoke about Le Fe'e with just enough reluctance that I entirely missed the change in names.

"I only caught it this morning when I was glancing through one of Lehua's reference books on Pacific Island mythology. A reference suggestion took me back to your Samoan language tapes. Le Fe'e is the name of a Samoan demigod just as you said. But *Sa* la Fe'e is the name given to his domain. Its meaning is somewhat ambiguous, but it can be translated as 'the forbidden place of the octopus,' or—and this is what I found most intriguing—'the *clan* of the octopus.' ''

If she hadn't been looking right at him, she would never have seen Fatu's start of understanding, his involuntary admission that what she was about to suggest was true.

''You're hiding a second generation out here, aren't you?'' she said. ''A generation of legal heirs, just like Pua. Zed refused to turn the TC enzyme over to the Company because he intended, you all intended, to use it as a bargaining tool—or blackmail, if that became necessary—for the safe acceptance of your genetically altered offspring.''

Both Fatu and Toma remained absolutely still. A secret held so completely for more than thirteen years was a hard thing to give up.

''Since Pua hasn't been anywhere farther than she can swim, it still reassured you she hadn't given anything away through the locator,'' Angie said, ''I presume you're hiding these children, or something that leads to them, right here at Pukui.''

''I could swim all the way to Landing if I wanted,'' Pua said.

''Pualei,'' Fatu said softly.

''Well, I could.''

''You've never stopped following me long enough to swim all the way to Landing,'' Angie said. ''Or to any other distant place, for that matter. And you say you don't know where the TC enzyme records are, so it can't be that you're protecting. Also, Toma was obviously tremendously relieved to verify that the Company had not found a way to genetically reproduce you or parts of you. I assume that means someone here has?''

''Doctor Waight tried hard enough.''

''Pua, be quiet,'' Fatu said. This time it was an order.

''Say whatever you want to say, Pua,'' Angie said without turning away from him. He hissed softly, and the sound sent a chill up her back. If there were, in fact, mythical spirits roaming Pukui, she had no doubt that this man could call them up.

''I told you, Fatu,'' Pua said. ''She always knows when people are lying.''

Fatu glared at her.

''Why don't we just show her—?''

Fatu slammed his palm onto the ground. Pua jumped and pulled back. Serious anger from Fatu was obviously not something she encountered often. ''That was stupid, Pualei,'' he said.

Toma spoke at last. "You're a credit to your profession, Warden." His voice revealed a much colder fury than Fatu's. "Your tough talk couldn't budge us, so you manipulated the child instead."

"This child," Angie said, "has seen her parents die, and then lived for six months believing that you, her good friend, her *uncle*, had murdered them. She survived being torn away from her home and everything she'd ever known, and being imprisoned in a place so alien it makes your fireloving rock eels look like teddy bears!"

Her adrenaline was rising. She knew she was losing control, and for just an instant she didn't care.

"This child," she said, maintaining just enough calm to keep from raising her voice above the level of privacy, "has had her bloody *hands* cut off and then been forced to watch them grow back on somebody else! Spit in a bucket, Inspector! You wouldn't know tough if you sat in it!"

And then she knew she had to care, so she forced herself to shut up. There was a movement to her left, and she glanced that way. The girl was staring at her again with that damned look of awe, except this time her mouth was twitching in an attempt to suppress a smile.

"Your passion is very moving," Toma said.

Spit!

"Toma," she said. "You know I can't walk away from this. You, especially, know I *won't* walk away."

"A good troubleshooter never leaves a job unfinished," he quoted. It was like a slap across the face.

"That's right, *Inspector*, and despite my personal feelings about the way this entire situation has been handled, I will not leave this job until it *is* finished."

"Why didn't you just truth-drug us in the beginning like Crawley wanted you to?" Fatu asked. "Why go through this charade of acting sympathetic to Pukui's situation?"

She returned his glare. "Because I don't approve of altering people's bodies, chemically or otherwise, against their will," she said. She lifted a hand to stop him from interrupting, and he stared at her long, thin fingers. "I have used the drugs in the past, Fatu—and I'll use them here if I have to. But I am trying to extend to you the courtesy of not doing so."

"Courtesy?" Toma said. "You set this whole thing up so you'd know exactly what questions to ask when you *do* use the damn drugs."

"What difference does it make, anyway?" Pua asked. "You control all the off-planet transportation and communications, Uncle Toma, so there's no way she can sneak back through the wormhole to tell Mr. Crawley. Besides—" She turned her look on Angie and frowned. "She knows what I'll do to her if she tries."

"Well, you'd better get ready to do it, girl," Fatu said, "because Crawley will be here at Pukui tomorrow morning. He's scheduled to be on the downside shuttle three hours from now."

"What?" Pua exclaimed.

Angie leaned forward. "Crawley's here?"

"He and a full U.N. inspection team," Toma said. "The same Company-controlled team he's used before to reclaim leases from original settlers. You haven't been following his orders, Warden. He's come out to oversee the investigation himself."

"Crawley couldn't investigate himself out of an open petri dish," Angie muttered. Which means he'll be bringing more than a hand-picked inspection team with him. Her fingers twitched at the thought of meeting Nori face-to-face again.

"It seems we have a bit of a situation, here, Warden," Toma said. It was a troubleshooter's challenge. Watch your backfires now, Angie girl, she thought.

"Just how much does Crawley know, or suspect, about your kids?" Angie asked. She might as well get this part over with, too. There was no way it was going to be easy, but it had to be done. Pua needed to know it all.

Pua was on her feet in an instant. "What do you mean? How can Crawley know about my babies?"

Before Angie could answer, Pua flung herself at her. She grabbed Angie's shoulders, and her long fingers snaked around her neck. Angie fell back, trying to make use of Pua's momentum to loosen her grip, but the girl's hold never faltered. The tips of her thumbs pricked Angie's gills.

Angie froze.

"Did you tell him?" Pua asked in that cold, cold voice that did not belong to a child. Her face was just inches from Angie's. Her breath smelled of the sea, and her eyes promised a painful, certain death. "Did you tell him, Earthlady?"

Very carefully, Angie wrapped her own hands around Pua's wrists. They had tested their strength together often enough that Angie knew she could not break Pua's hold without both of them being seriously hurt—if she could break it at all. Toma and Fatu were close beside them, but neither interfered. They think they'd be better off with me dead at Pua's hands, she thought, so the Company would be forced to bring another troubleshooter to do this job and thus gain them more time. They might even be right.

"You told him, Pua," she said.

Pua's fingertips slid under Angie's gill flaps and broke the suction seal. Angie caught her breath at the sudden sharp burn of the inner membranes being exposed to dry air.

"I didn't tell him *anything*!" Pua said.

"Pua, they murdered your parents." Angie gasped. "They set up the accident that took my hands; they were—they still are—prepared to use you as a guinea pig for the rest of your life. Do you think they would have hesitated for a minute to truth-drug you? They don't give a damn about the law that says it can't be done to kids. There was no way for anyone outside to know. They never expected to have to send you back here."

Pua's eyes filled suddenly with tears. She didn't want to believe it, but she did. It was obviously something she had questioned herself about before. "I *couldn't* have told them. I would never . . ."

"They probably did it before you ever regained full consciousness from the fever."

"I never *had* the fever. I told you that!"

"I know," Angie whispered. "I know." She squeezed her eyes closed against the pain, then opened them again. "They didn't get it *all* from you, Pua. They only learned enough to confuse them. That's why they sent you back."

"Fatu, is it true?" Pua said. She sounded like a child again. "Did I tell them?"

"Aye, Little Fe'e," he said quietly. "It's the only way they could have known all the things they knew even before you came home. The warden hasn't sent any messages off-planet. We're certain of that."

Pua's strong, smooth fingers trembled along the edges of Angie's gills. At last, abruptly, she let them seal shut. As Pua turned away, Angie rolled quickly to the side, her hands pressed tightly over her burning gills. There's a lesson for you, trouble-shooter, she thought as she forced herself to stand. Her equilibrium was off, and she stumbled. Toma steadied her. You're vulnerable in a way you never even suspected.

"You all knew, didn't you?" Pua cried. "You all knew they did that to me, and none of you told me! Why didn't you tell me, Fatu? Why didn't you warn me? What if I had gone to see my babies and they had followed?'' Fatu reached out to her, but she jerked away.

"How can they have learned about Sa le Fe'e, but not how to find it?'' Angie asked.

"How is it *you* don't know?'' Toma asked. "You're the one they sent out here to follow her.''

"Damn it, Toma! I was sent out here to use the fireloving drugs on anybody and everybody that might know where the TC records are hidden. That's it. That's the only reason. It doesn't do a lot for my ego, but that's the way it is. Any ranking shooter would have done—I just happened to be the one who made herself most available by holing up for months at a time at a remote mountain preserve.''

She shook her head, wincing slightly at the ache that the movement caused in her gills. She glanced at Pua. "It was stupid of me not to have suspected the locators sooner. I'm sorry, Pua.''

"For someone who's supposed to have been forced into this against her will,'' Fatu said, "you seem to have figured it all out rather easily.''

"Distrust me if you will, Fatu. I can't fault you for that with all you have at stake,'' she said. "But working through situations like this is my business. There was no one more surprised than I when I realized what was going on here. I still don't understand why Crawley couldn't learn Sa le Fe'e's location from Pua, when she so obviously knows.''

"Because she travels by landmarks known only to herself,'' Fatu said. "She probably told them exactly how to reach what they're looking for, but they have no way of translating her directions into anything they can follow.''

"I want that thing out of me!'' Pua exclaimed. "I want it out *now*!''

"There's a med kit up at the house,'' Toma said. "We'll do it as soon—'' Pua didn't wait. She stalked away across the softly glowing lawn.

"Why haven't you gone public with the TC enzyme like you'd originally planned?'' Angie asked as the three of them followed. "With it as leverage, you could break the Company's economic hold on Lesaat. You would be free to bring your kids into the open.''

Toma said nothing. He walked close beside her, as did Fatu. Angie knew there was no way to escape them now, nor would there be any point to it. Not as long as she was wearing a locator.

Toma would be able to find its frequency soon enough if he needed to. The only thing she could do was keep talking, and hope she could find a way to convince them she was more friend than enemy. She hoped that was true.

Damn! Why did Crawley have to show up right now? Angie shook her head in disgust. Because nothing's ever easy, she reminded herself. That was another shooters' motto.

"For something this valuable, and for the chance to break World Life's monopoly on Earth's food supply, the U.N. would be willing to step in directly to protect your lands and your children," she said. But Toma already knew that. She was still missing something. Something important.

She paused when they reached the lanai stairs.

"As planetary super, you have access to public communications lines, Toma, and as an ex-shooter, you certainly know how to get the attention of high-ranking U.N. officials. You could have announced the TC production months ago and had it on the open market by now. Why haven't—"

Something in his expression stopped her. Despair, she thought. And suddenly she understood what their stubborn silence meant.

"You don't have it!" she said. "You've been telling the truth. The TC records really are lost!" She submitted to Toma's prod up the steps. "Spit, but this thing's a mess."

Pua had the med kit open in the library. She stood motionless while Toma ran a scan, not only on her hands, but on the rest of her body—Angie was glad she had made the string she had given Pua inactive without her own signal—then numbed a spot on her left hand. He used a laser scalpel to carve a tiny biobug away from the cartilage that extended into her palm. When he finished, he sealed the small incision with a spray of surgical glue. Pua promptly spat on the spot and wiped the sealant bandage away.

"You next," Toma said to Angie. She was surprised, but willingly submitted. She had assumed he would want to keep her under surveillance himself now that he had the means. She refused the anesthetic spray.

"It's only a local nerve deadener," he said. "I don't plan to carry you out of here."

Pua looked up. "What do you mean? Where are you taking her?"

"We're taking you both away from Pukui," Fatu said. "We

can't take the chance of Crawley getting his hands on either of you, especially now.''

"Oh, damn," Angie sighed.

"I don't want to—" Pua began.

"It'll only be until we can get rid of Crawley," Fatu said. "We'd already decided it was best even before the warden told us what she knew. Now it's even more important that neither of you be here when the Earthers arrive.''

"But I don't want to leave Pukui. I want to stay and help. Le Fe'e needs me to—"

"This is real, Pua!" Fatu said sharply. "This is *real*! We're not telling stories now. The only way you can help Pukui is by leaving it."

"It's not going to help Pukui for me to leave," Angie said. "If the U.N. team even suspects you're holding me somewhere against my will, you'll lose your privacy rights on the spot. They won't even need a troubleshooter present to use the truth probes.''

Toma dropped the second celluloid-wrapped locator disk into the med tray and applied the sealant bandage to Angie's shoulder. "We'll use the locators to lead Crawley and his trackers on a wild-goose chase," he said, meeting Angie's look. "From what I understand of your relationship with him, it shouldn't be too hard to convince him you're deliberately trying to aggravate him by staying out of reach of his orders.''

Pua started edging toward the door, but Fatu laid a firm hand on her shoulder. "If they truth-drug us," he said, "they'll at least have to do it in front of the U.N. team. *Some* of them are honest. There would still be the chance that they would be moved enough to protect our kids, if only for humanitarian reasons.''

"Fatu," Angie said, "most standard Earthers don't consider people like *us*"—she lifted her hands—"completely human. How do you think they're going to respond to *genetically* altered kids? Especially when those kids are laying claim to the most productive reefs on this planet.''

"We'll just have to convince them—" Toma began.

"Damn it, Toma! To get the TC enzyme, that team will turn this place over to the World Life faster than a sucker swallows blood," she said. "This situation is already under an official 'most urgent need' classification. The Company is looking for any excuse it can get to revoke your privacy rights. If I'm not here to control the questioning, you're going to lose everything.''

"Aside from validating the Company's truth probes, just how do you propose to help us?" Toma returned.

Angie shook her head. "I don't know. I just know it won't do you any good to force me away right now. As regards, Pua, yes. Get her the hell out of here. Even if you lose everything else, she deserves to remain outside World Life's control. She's suffered enough."

"You speak so genuinely of protecting Pua," Fatu said. "Yet your determination to complete your original contract duties remains unchanged. Do your hands and that slice of mountain back on Earth mean so much to you?"

Angie lifted her hands and stared at her long, thin fingers. They seemed little more alien to her now than the wrists from which they grew.

She met Fatu's look again. "We spoke once before of choices, Fatu. I have *chosen* not to become so involved in Pukui's pain that I can't act from a wider perspective."

The disappointment on Pua's tear-stained face forced Angie to look away.

"Crawley knew you would react this way," Toma said. "He knew all he had to do was get you out here and you'd complete the job based solely on the TC's potential benefit to Earth. He manipulated all of us, because even we know the TC needs to be found and shared, even if it has to be under Company control."

He tapped a message into the comm—a call to bring Ehu in from the barge. To pilot the decoy flitter, Angie thought. Spit. Now, how am I going to get out of this without breaking somebody's bones? A quick glance at Fatu's massive bulk settled even that option.

"Right now, Warden," Toma said, "our first concern has to be the physical preservation of Pukui Reef. We have to stall a Company takeover long enough to clear the algae. Then we'll find a way to deal with the rest. If we can convince Crawley and the U.N. team that you're touring other reefs on the trail of the TC records, they won't be in a hurry to stop the harvest. It's the records they want most, but they're anxious to keep Pukui, as well."

The comm beeped and he touched an acknowledgment. "Fatu tells me you keep a coded seal on my flitter," he said. "I don't suppose you'd be willing to open it voluntarily."

It was common knowledge that Angie had confiscated his flit for her personal use, so they dared not leave it on the front lawn while claiming she was off inspecting other reefs. Angie knew Toma could break the seal; he had probably learned the necessary skills from the same instructors who had taught her to set it. It wouldn't delay them long, but it might give her time to think of an alternative to their fruitless plan.

"Under other circumstances, I would be most willing," she said. "But . . ." She shrugged.

He almost smiled. "I'm sorry we didn't meet under other circumstances, Warden," he said.

So am I, Inspector, Angie replied silently. So am I.

Pua glared at them both.

"Come on, Little Fe'e," Fatu said. "You can wait upstairs, and pack what you want to take with you at the same time. Toma, set the seals on upper windows." He motioned Angie toward the door and followed when she moved that way. His hand remained firmly on Pua's shoulder, and his dark eyes mirrored his niece's pain.

As they crossed the foyer, Angie paused to stare down at the intricately inlaid floor.

I am a piece of koa, she thought. Sharp-edged, alien, surrounded by blurred boundaries. She tried to remember the sound of wind whispering through high, dry pines, but found she could not.

Chapter 17

As they reached the top of the stairs, Pua pulled away from Fatu and ran into her bedroom. She slammed the door hard.

Fatu ushered Angie into her own room, and closed and locked the door behind her. She heard him knock and call out to Pua.

"Go away!" Pua shouted.

A door handle rattled. "Little Fe'e, unlock your door. I want to talk—"

A crash and a curse that Angie recognized as one of her own cut Fatu off. "I'm never going to *speak* to you again, Fatu!" Pua screamed. "Not *ever*!"

Fatu tried several more times to convince Pua to let him in, but she remained stubbornly silent. Finally, Angie heard him lock Pua's door from the outside, and then his footsteps sounded on the stairs. He did not leave the house; Angie could feel his solid presence even through the closed door. She sighed, and crossed to the window.

How many kids are there? she wondered. There had to be dozens, at least, if they were planning to establish a viable population base. The thought of half a hundred Puas made her shake her head in disbelief. Where the hell can they be hiding that many kids and all the adults and facilities needed to care for them?

A quick test showed that the window seals had been activated. She didn't bother to test the plastic panes for breakability. Her new hands were strong, but not that strong. She rubbed a hand over her sore shoulder.

Use what you have, she thought. But what the hell did she have? "Spit," she muttered.

Her hand brushed a lump in her shirt pocket, the last of the Maldarian caramels she had been carrying. The rest were still in their packing crate in a corner of the library. Katie had not approved of that storage site until Angie showed her what the candies were and gave her a boxful for herself. Then the house-keeper had been quite pleased by the idea of their presence. She had, however, draped a cloth over the crate to hide it from sight.

"Sally, my friend," Angie murmured, "I hope that doubled order means what I think it does." Fatu had been wrong when he said she hadn't sent any messages off-planet. Not that it was going to do her any good tonight.

A shadow moved. Angie stepped to the side of the window and peered carefully out. It was Pua, moving like a wraith across the lanai roof. She paused for a moment at the back of the house, then slipped out of sight.

Angie looked down at her hands. If Pua could break the win-dow seal, surely Angie could. She flexed her long, strong fin-gers, tapped her precision-point nails. But how . . . ?

Of course! she thought suddenly. She deliberately relaxed the muscles in her fingers and watched them go limp. She slides through the cracks!

The maneuver proved surprisingly easy, although Angie was glad she hadn't had to try it two weeks before. Her control of her new hands had become more complete with each passing day. She laid the thin end of her right forefinger along the crack where the window's bottom met the notched sill. She remem-bered what Pua had said about her tongue, and let it grow soft behind her teeth and at the back of her throat. The muscles in her finger responded smoothly to her mental command.

With the slightest of sideways pressure, Angie began pushing her finger into the crack. Pua is right, she thought. I have to start thinking like a waterworlder. I'm a squid now—I might as well act like one.

After a slight initial resistance, her boneless fingers began sliding like a viscous liquid between the window and the sill. She stopped, blew out slowly, and relaxed further. By holding her needlelike fingernail parallel to the sill, she was able to slip it, too, into the narrow opening.

Once she could feel the alarm system's pressure pad, it was a simple matter of holding it down while maneuvering her finger-tip into the small cavity containing the locking mechanism. She smiled at the soft *click* of the lock disengaging, and opened the window with her left hand. She climbed outside and carefully lowered the window back onto the pressure plate.

There was a sound at the back of the house. Angie slid into

the shadows on the far side of Pua's open window. It had either not been fully locked, which was doubtful considering Fatu's caution, or Pua had some way of neutralizing the alarm.

Pua reappeared. She crossed the roof in silence and crawled back into her room. Angie edged closer to look inside.

Pua listened at the door for a moment, then carefully folded the quilt off the bed. She took something from her pocket and placed it on the sheets at the foot of the bed. It moved. Pua lifted her hand away quickly, revealing two small sluglike things. Each had a bright yellow bulge at one end of its otherwise gray body, and what looked like a powerful stinger curving up from the other.

Pua reached into another pocket and brought out a handful of grass. She sprinkled it in a circle around the yellow-gray creatures, leaving an open pathway to the side of the bed. She placed another pair of the sluglike things on the bureau and ringed them similarly with grass.

What is she doing? Angie wondered. Pua's careful movements had almost the look of a ritual. Scaring the ghosts away?

Pua placed two more of her creatures on a stool beside the bed, then turned toward the window. Angie hid again. Pua eased back outside, closed the window, and disappeared again over the edge of the roof. Angie glanced into the room as she followed. One of the slug things on the bed had moved just far enough to show a brilliant yellow stain on the pale blue sheet.

As she lowered herself over the roof edge and shimmied down a porch post, Angie was thankful for the strength and suction of her hands, which allowed her to move in complete silence. Like a windblown shadow, Pua darted across the compound. She made one quick dash in the open, across the narrowest area of carefully tended lawn, then slipped into the jungle. Angie followed.

She would have preferred going uphill—if she was going to hide, she would rather to it on land—but she was not surprised when Pua turned toward the sea. "Where are you going, Waterbaby?" she murmured when Pua reached the beach. Pua walked until the water reached her waist, then quickly disappeared below the surface.

Angie glanced back the way they had come. She didn't want to go into the ocean, but she knew there was nothing more she could do on land. She could probably hide out indefinitely in the dense jungle, but that offered no real solution. The sharp coral sand pressed into her bare feet as she walked through the shallows. She was careful to avoid stepping on or brushing against any of the larger coral outcroppings, and was relieved when she finally reached deep enough water in which to swim.

Pua had disappeared. Angie knew that if she swam on the surface, her splash would surely attract Pua's attention, and that of probably every other nocturnal denizen of the lagoon. She shuddered at the thought of what some of them might be. She counted carefully to calm herself, then submerged.

The night was bright despite the scudding cloud cover. The bioluminescent plankton made it as easy to see underwater as it was above. Angie activated her nictitating membranes, and her view cleared even further. She waited for the kick of the adrenaline release, then pressed a search order into the implant she had coded for Pua. To her very great relief, a tingling itch responded. Pua had either decided to carry the locator string, or had forgotten she even had it.

Angie started to swim.

It occurred to her that Pua might know she was following and would deliberately attempt to get her lost in the open sea. But then she remembered she was inside the reef—two reefs, for that matter. All she had to do was surface and take her bearings off the moonlit tip of Mauna Kea Iki. She glanced up at the gently bubbling surface and tried to relax.

The warm water slid like silk across Angie's skin, totally unlike the icy mountain waters of the forest preserve. In those, she always lost feeling shortly after the first shock of entry. Here, the water caressed like . . . Why do I keep looking for Earthly comparisons? she wondered. There is nothing on Earth that compares with Pukui.

It was clear why Pua preferred swimming without clothes. Angie was tempted to slip out of hers, but she pictured herself climbing ashore naked to face Toma and Crawley, and decided to leave them on.

She could hear the distant roll of the surf on the outer reef, and the mechanical thrum of the disposal barge working the number-nine pen. From this far away, it was more a background vibration than a recognizable sound. There was so much other noise, Angie was not entirely sure just *what* she was really hearing. A shrill chittering squeal sounded somewhere off to her right, making her jump.

The water was splendid in its own golden glow, and the flickering light of its many occupants made it more so. Small creatures approached, flashed their presence, then darted back out of sight. Clicks and sighs, the shivering call of some creature Angie was afraid to even imagine, echoed around her.

It *is* like a symphony, she thought. She smiled, releasing a stream of bubbles from between her teeth. It's like a dance! She could hear the reef singing. It called to her, assured her she was safe here in her home . . .

Angie jerked to a stop. She shook her head angrily, then kicked for the surface. "No," she said as soon as her mouth was clear of the water. "This is not my home!"

This insidious sea was just like the damn mountaintop. It sang a siren's song, and for the first time in her life, Angie regretted her ability to sense so clearly the moods of her ecological surroundings. If she hadn't known better, she could almost have believed the reef was alive and sentient, calling out to her in its resonant, symphonic voice. No wonder Pua had difficulty separating myth from reality.

"Save your songs for your children, Le Fe'e," she said aloud. "Save them for those who *wish* to make this their home."

What am I doing? she thought suddenly. Talking to the damned ocean as if it could hear me. Pua isn't the only one around here with seawater for brains.

Angie turned back toward where she thought the island must be, caught a mouthful of water, and choked. Her gills, of course, had sealed as soon as she had started breathing air directly again. She spat and cursed, and noted that Pua was moving in a straight line away from the beach where she had started.

Abruptly, the direction signal veered to the left. Angie turned to follow, but then realized from the itch's rapidly decreasing intensity that the locator was moving away from her much faster than any human, even Pua, could swim. Spit, she thought. She must have hooked it to a damn fish. Now what am I going to do? Pua could be anywhere.

That thought made her tremendously uncomfortable.

Something splashed ahead of her and to the right—something large slapping against the water. Reef rays, Angie thought. She had only seen the great double-winged creatures from a distance, but the swimmers talked of watching Pua play with them.

"Use what you have, Auntie Puhi," she muttered. She took her bearings, submerged, and swam in the direction of the splash. The song of Pukui remained strong.

From time to time, Angie surfaced and listened. The distant splashes continued to lead her in a direct line away from the beach toward the inner reef. As she approached the strongly

bioluminescent coral shelf, she hesitated. Her path led directly
through the center of a dimly glowing algae pen. This was a
recently matured batch. It was not entirely dark, as were the
overripe and rotting crops that were currently under harvest.
Still, it was not a comfortable sight in the otherwise well-lit sea.

Angie dove deep enough to see that there was at least three
meters' clearance between the load of algae and the reef flat.
She saw a large shadowy movement ahead of her, far under the
net. She blinked telescopic and recognized the vague shape of
a ray. "Oh, mother of mountains," she muttered into the water.
"Why do I keep doing this to myself?"

A good troubleshooter never leaves a job unfinished. Toma's
taunting voice slid through her fear.

"Spit."

She surfaced well away from the alarm canisters, counted to
calm herself, then dove again. The predictable release of adrenaline as her gills reestablished oxygenation gave her the courage
to swim under the shadow of the net.

It was not as dark as she had feared. The coral reef and its
myriad inhabitants glimmered like a slightly out-of-focus light
show. If not for the huge mass of Earth algae hanging above,
she might actually have enjoyed the strange, night-lit world. The
cold water was not running through the noninsulated pipes, so
the temperature remained constant, warm, and comfortable. She
was thankful for that at the moment, but made furious once
again that her orders regarding the algae pens were being ignored. She glanced up at the looming net, swallowed her anger
and her terror, and kicked hard for clear water.

When she finally reached the other side, she swam only far
enough to be sure she would not trip any alarms. Then she
headed directly for the surface.

A flash of movement close at her left startled her off course,
then the bump of something hard and smooth across her back
forced her down and farther away from the net. She twisted and
spun, trying to escape a second buffeting attack by the great
gray creature. A reef ray, she realized at once.

The thing turned back and knocked her upside down with the
sweep of one wide, flat wing. A second, then a third ray appeared. They surrounded Angie, tumbling her over and over
until she was completely disoriented and as near panic as her
stunned mind could achieve.

At least I won't have to worry about hiding out anymore, she
thought absurdly. Something thin and strong wrapped around

her arm, and abruptly the buffeting maelstrom subsided. The double-winged creatures swept away. Angie was yanked to one side, then up. Suddenly she was at the surface, gasping clear air and facing an entirely enraged Pua.

"Why are you following me?" Pua shouted.

"Pua—" Angie gulped and choked on a mouthful of splashed water. Pua's grip was still crushing Angie's arm; her second hand was tangled in Angie's hair. She shoved Angie beneath the water, then yanked her back to the surface.

"I thought that reef-pissing string only activated if it was broken!" Pua shouted before Angie could catch enough breath to speak.

A ray splashed nearby and water cascaded over them both.

Angie reached behind Pua with her free hand, grabbed the girl's knotted hair, and yanked her head back. At the same time, she wrapped both legs around Pua's thighs. She knew Pua's legs were stronger than her own, but if they couldn't reach her, they couldn't hurt her. The immediate strain on her own thighs gave at least partial lie to that idea. The girl's skin was as slippery as if she had been oiled. Angie locked her ankles behind Pua's back.

They rolled underwater, and Pua's grip, like Angie's, tightened with a fresh infusion of adrenaline. They thrashed back to the surface.

"Stop it, Pua!" Angie managed before they went under again. She was sure her hair was being pulled out by the roots. She yanked harder on Pua's, and the girl almost let go. Angie yanked again and squeezed her legs as tight as she could.

Abruptly, Pua did let go, but only to shift the grip of both hands to Angie's thighs. They broke surface again.

"Stop it!" Angie called again.

The strength of Pua's kick kept them upright long enough for her to answer. "You lied to me! You put another tracer into me!"

"No, I followed the—" They went under again. When Angie finally sucked in air again, she yelled, "Rays, damn it!"

Through the splash, she saw Pua's eyes widen. The bone-crushing grip around her thighs loosened, then abruptly let go. Instantly, Angie released her own hold and backed quickly away.

"I followed the rays. Their splashing. I listened, and followed." She groaned suddenly, and rolled forward to hug her aching knees to her chest. *I won't be able to walk straight for a week!* she thought.

A ray swept near and brushed the tips of what she could see now were its forward wings along her arms. She was reminded that she might not be walking at all in a few days, or ever, if she couldn't convince Pua not to kill her. She straightened and lifted her head above water.

Pua was treading water just an arm's reach away. She looked as furious as Angie had ever seen her.

"I didn't lie, Pua," she said. "I saw you go out the window, and I followed. Once you were in the water, I used the locator, but after you got rid of it, I had no idea where you went. I heard the rays splashing and decided to go after them."

"Why? Why did you follow any of us?" Pua demanded.

"Why not?" Angie snapped. "It was better than sitting back there waiting for those two idiots to lock me up someplace where I can't do anything to help anybody. Why did *you* sneak out?"

Pua's lips tightened. She jackknifed and dove. A moment later, she broke surface behind Angie. Angie spun to face her.

"I don't want to be locked up, either," Pua shouted. "I don't *ever* want to be locked up again!"

She dove again. Angie submerged, too. A ray, easily three times Pua's length, lifted beneath the girl. Pua grabbed the forward edges of its front wings and hugged it close. She braced her feet on the forward edges of the back wings. The ray turned in a slow, graceful circle, like a giant double-winged bird doing loop-the-loops in the sea. Pua saw Angie watching, pushed away from the ray, and shot back to the surface.

"I know where Toma wants to hide us," she said. "It's cold and dry. I won't go there, Mountainlady." She looked around, running her hand along the underside of a caressing ray. "I won't let you give me back to Mr. Crawley, either."

"I told you I wouldn't do that," Angie said.

Pua's laugh was hard and humorless. "You told me you would never come to Pukui, too." She scooped up a mouthful of water and spat a high curving stream into the air.

Angie rubbed her hand over her stinging shoulder. The sealant bandage over Toma's incision must have torn loose during the fight. "You'd make a hell of a troubleshooter," she said. The muscles in her thighs and calves felt strained beyond repair.

"I'm not kidding, Mountainlady!"

"Neither am I." Angie pushed her hair from her forehead. "Look, we need to go somewhere where we can talk."

"We're someplace right now," Pua said. She took another mouthful of water.

"Pua, you might be able to tread water all night, but I—"

Pua spat, the entire mouthful at once. "Are you bleeding?"

Angie glanced down at her shoulder. "It's just the cut Toma made. The bandage—"

Pua grabbed Angie's arm, and for a moment Angie thought she was going to drag her under again. "Earthers are so stupid!" the girl said. "Don't you know you should *never* bleed in Pukui waters at this time of night?"

She yanked Angie's blouse off her shoulder and then ripped away the loosened patch.

"What are you doing?" Angie asked as Pua rubbed the back of one hand over the open cut. A thin, slick film was left behind. It stung sharply for an instant, then quickly numbed.

"Stopping the bleeding," Pua said. "This is the suckers' time. We've got to get out of here. The rays will take us—you just hang on."

She shoved Angie's head under the water, clicked her nails in rapid sequence, and pointed. A dark cloud of seething movement was approaching from under the net. Two rays rose directly under Angie and Pua. Pua pressed Angie's hands over the forewings of the smaller ray and shouted, "Hold on!" She clicked her fingers again, and the ray surged forward, nearly yanking itself away from Angie's grip.

It was only Angie's remembered image of the blood-maddened suckers under the disposal barge the night the crewman had died that gave her the courage to stay with the giant winged creature. She lay prone on its back, her face and chest pressed hard against its velvety warm skin. She caught a glimpse of Pua streaking by on the second ray. The girl had wrapped her legs around the ray's narrow center, and Angie carefully did the same to relieve some of the tension on her arms and shoulders.

The water rushed over Angie's body like a high mountain wind, hard and strong. She clung with all her strength to the great gray creature, and after a time, entirely to her own amazement, she found herself grinning against its back. This was by far the most terrifying, the most exhilarating flight of her life. The reef was singing to her again, loud and clear, and because there was no way to avoid it, she listened and enjoyed.

The ride continued for much longer than was necessary to simply escape the suckersharks. Each time Angie thought the rays must surely be slowing to let their passengers off, they veered in a new direction and swam effortlessly on. Do they ever tire? she wondered.

It was difficult to distinguish sounds through the rush of water past her ears, but Angie realized after a time that Pua was directing the rays with quick staccato clicks of her fingertips. Gradually, the feel of the sea changed. Its touch became cooler, stronger. The water began to taste of great distances and depths. Before long, the vibrating roar of nearby heavy surf drowned out all other sound. Mother of mountains, Angie thought, she's taking us outside the barrier reef!

She thought about letting go of the ray and kicking her way to the surface, then swimming back to the island, or at least the reef. She did not want to be lost in the middle of the fireloving Lesaat sea. But then what would you do? she asked herself. Go turn yourself in to Toma? She held on. The rays turned again and swam parallel to the glowing outer reef.

At last, they slowed. Pua and her mount came abreast of Angie. She pointed down. Angie shook her head and pointed up. She needed to take a breath of real air. Pua pointed down again, clicked her nails, and both rays descended so fast Angie was afraid to let go.

Finally, the rays slowed almost to a stop and Pua slid off. Warily, Angie followed. They were in deep water, cold water, along the side of a steep drop-off. There was still light enough to see, but it came from the reef itself, not the floating dinoflagellates that filled the surface waters. The pressure in Angie's ears was strong. We're going to have to ascend a lot slower than we came down, she thought.

And then she remembered that nitrogen narcosis was not a problem for waterworlders. Their gills drew oxygen directly from the water, so the potentially deadly buildup of gas bubbles in the bloodstream was not a problem. Angie had seen no sign of a hyperbaric chamber on Pukui grounds.

Pua waved her toward the reef and pointed to a dark opening.

"Oh no," Angie said. "I'm not swimming into any underwater hole—" The excess oxygen in her lungs ran out.

Pua pointed again. She leaned close and called, "Air inside."

Angie glanced back up at the foaming surface, so far above. "Spit," she said, but there wasn't enough oxygen buildup yet to make it worth much. Pua grabbed her arm and yanked her inside the hole. The traverse was only about a meter and a half, but to Angie the time spent in the near-total darkness felt like an eternity. When light appeared ahead, she kicked rapidly toward it.

They surfaced inside a long, narrow chamber. They were

inside a pocket of only mildly stale air. The walls were covered with pale, viscous splotches. Slime molds, Angie thought, and shuddered, although it was the thought of being trapped inside the stone that disturbed her, not the luminescent slicks that covered it.

"Watch," Pua said. She slapped her hands against the wall nearest her, then pointed to the narrowest end of the cave. Nothing happened for an instant, then the light flickered and dimmed. The colors on the wall began to change. They swept in spiraling designs toward where Pua pointed.

A figure began to form. It was the face of an old man, lined and toothless under a shock of pure white hair. The expression on the face shifted until the dark eyes appeared to be staring directly at Angie. She knew it was just a trick of the light, but still she shivered.

"It's me," Pua said very formally, just the way she did outside the house after having come from the sea. "It's Little Fe'e. I brought someone to meet you. Her name is Puhi 'ai Pōhaku. She's from Earth, but she can hear Le Fe'e sing."

Angie glanced at Pua, then back at the image, which was already beginning to fade. The cave returned gradually to its original muted glow.

"What was that?" Angie asked.

"Fatu calls him the Grand Old Man of Pukui," Pua said. "I pretend sometimes that he's Le Fe'e, so we can watch each other while we talk."

Angie stared at the place where the image had formed. There was nothing there now but slime-covered stone. "Is it a holo?" she asked, although she was sure it was not.

Pua shook her head. "It's just the mold. When it's startled, it moves like that. It only does it once, so you have to look fast or you miss seeing him."

Angie looked around, shivering again. "Why did you bring me here?" she asked.

"You said you wanted to talk, and I wanted to be sure Le Fe'e knows who you are. You never stayed in the water long enough before."

"Pua . . ."

"And I wanted to show you my babies."

Angie caught her breath. She glanced toward the underwater entrance they had just used.

"The rays are still out there," Pua said. "They won't let you out unless I tell them to."

Angie couldn't help but laugh. "You really *are* getting good at this."

"I've been watching you, Auntie Puhi," Pua said. "Come on." She pulled Angie back underwater. They swam through another dark channel, one that in her earlier haste to reach the light Angie hadn't even noticed, then up a slight incline. The light that met them this time was flat and white.

As they surfaced, Angie squinted against its artificial glare. They were inside a half-submerged airlock chamber. Angie had barely recognized it for what it was before Pua flipped open a ceiling hatch and hauled herself up and out of sight. Quickly, Angie pulled up after her. She blinked to adjust her eyes to a dimmer, more natural light.

A woman the size of Gibraltar awaited them. Kin to Fatu, Angie thought, and then some. There was no mistaking the resemblance. She wore a loose, full dress, brightly colored— and carried a golden baby on each hip. The infants clung to her with long, thin fingers.

"Pualeiokekai Pukui," the woman demanded, "what the hell are you doing here?"

"Pualei?" a shrill voice cried before Pua could answer. "You came back!"

A boy, no taller than Angie's waist, darted around the woman. He was followed by a second, identical child. Both were naked except for mossy fringes around their ankles and wrists. Straight, ebony hair bounced across their wide shoulders, and their dark eyes were wide with delight. They raced toward Pua, long-fingered hands stretched forward in welcome.

Chapter 18

～～～～～～～～～～

～～～～～～～～～～

"I told you I'd come back." Pua laughed, and scooped Kiki and Keha into her arms. "I told you I'd always come back!"

"You stay where you are," she heard Auntie Nola say. Pua hoped the mountainlady would have sense enough to do what she was told, just this once. She squeezed the boys tight, and they shrieked and pulled at her hair and arms. She tumbled over backward, then rolled and rolled with them across the moss-lined floor. Oh, she had missed them so much!

"Pua! Stop it!" Nola demanded. "You're going to hurt somebody."

"We can't get hurt," Pua called. "We're too *tough*!" She shouted and laughed and wrestled with the screaming boys until they were all choking for air. Finally, she collapsed under them and lay still, hugging them tight. Kiki and Keha stopped fighting at once and cuddled close. They tangled their fingers tight in her hair.

"I missed you so much," she whispered, and squeezed them both tighter.

"Did you bring us some new snowballs?" Keha whispered back.

"The old ones melted," Kiki added.

"On Auntie's catch nets," Keha said.

Pua laughed. "I have a whole bagful. Wait'll you see."

Suddenly, both boys were yanked up and away. Auntie Nola's strong hand replaced their grips in Pua's hair. Pua yelped when Nola tugged on the place where the mountainlady had yanked before. "I asked you a question, young lady," Nola said.

Pua grinned up at her. "I missed you, too, Auntie Nola, but I couldn't come before because somebody was following me."

Nola glanced pointedly at the warden.

Pua looked over her shoulder at the mountainlady, who was kneeling beside the open hatch. She was staring at the babies Nola had set on the floor, and rubbing her legs. Pua grinned again. That had been a good fight they'd had. The woman's skill and strength had surprised her. Her own legs were sore from the strain of trying to break the woman's clever hold.

"Come on, get up," Nola said.

Pua stood. The boys clung, one to each leg. Pua rested her hands on their backs and faced their auntie. She could feel Nola's pleasure at seeing her, even through her anger and concern.

"The Company man is coming back tomorrow," Pua said. "Toma wants me to go away from Pukui again."

"Auwe," Auntie Nola said softly. She reached out then and pulled Pua into a hug. It was a real hug, hard and full, and not in any way reticent, as Fatu's had been. Nola was not afraid to touch her just because she had grown.

"I missed you, Auntie," Pua said, squeezing her tight as far around as her arms could reach. "I missed you all so much." Nola's loose dress was damp across the front; it smelled of sweet babies' milk.

She pulled back slightly and reached up to transfer the string of lemon shells from her own neck to Nola's. "Where's Pili? And Misako? And—"

"They're with Hana taking lessons," Nola said. She hugged Pua again, then straightened. "You'd better close the hatch, lady, unless you feel like swimming after those two," she said.

Pua peeked around Nola's wide side to see the babies crawling toward the open hatch. The warden slid it shut quickly, then pulled back when the youngsters converged on her instead. Without hesitation, they reached up and pulled themselves into her lap. One tugged boldly at her wet shirt-front. Pua laughed, because the mountainlady appeared totally helpless under the onslaught. She could feel Nola's parallel chuckle.

"Boys," Nola said. "Go help." She turned so that they could both watch the mountainlady, but did not release Pua from her hug. Willingly, Pua remained leaning against her side. Kiki and Keha each lifted a baby away from the warden.

Keha settled his charge on one hip. "Who're you?" he asked.

"Keha," Nola warned.

"She's the farm boss," Pua said.

Keha's eyes opened wide. "The puhi 'ai pōhaku?"

The warden sent Pua a cool look. Pua giggled.

The warden returned her look to Keha. "My real name is Angela Roberta Dinsman. What's yours?"

"Kehakehaokalani noun Toma me Kilisou." Keha's shoulders straightened. He was exceedingly proud of his name, especially now that he could say it all in one breath.

The warden's brows lifted. "That's a very big name for such a small boy. You must be someone important." Pua was not sure if the warden's surprise was feigned or real, but it was clear that Keha was pleased by her reaction.

"I'm going to get bigger pretty soon," he said.

The warden smiled. "I'm sure you are." She reached out for the baby, and Keha passed it back to her without question.

That was too much for Nola. She moved Pua to one side and stepped forward. "I'll take her," she said.

The warden looked up from the baby's hands. "I wasn't planning to hurt her." The two women stared at each other for a moment. Then Nola reached out for the baby, and to Pua's surprise, the warden handed the child up to her willingly. The baby promptly peed down the side of Nola's dress.

Nola scowled at Pua's snigger of laughter as she shook the trickle of moisture from her skirt. "I see you're not as unfamiliar with children as it first appeared," she said to the warden.

"I've handled a few that size," the warden said. "Enough to know how many times you can pass one back and forth before it starts to leak."

"Pua, what's this all about?" Nola said, growing serious again. "Why did you bring her here?"

Pua glanced from her to the warden. "We needed a place to talk—and maybe hide. Toma really does want to send me away. Her, too."

"Don't go," both Kiki and Keha said.

"I won't," Pua replied.

"Toma is going to know exactly where you are, Pua," Nola said.

"Maybe. But he won't take the chance of coming here now. Not with so many Company swimmers around. And not when he doesn't know for sure she's with me."

They all looked at the mountainlady. The warden was watching Pua. "You knew I was following you all along, didn't you?" she asked.

"Only after you started swimming. How come you're so quiet on the land but so noisy in the water?"

"Did you deliberately slow the rays so I wouldn't get left behind?"

"How did you know not to follow the one I put the locator on?"

"How come nobody ever answers?" Kiki asked.

"Why did you try to kill me, Pua?"

"Pua!" That was Auntie Nola.

"Did you?" Kiki and Keha shouted.

"If I'd wanted you dead, Mountainlady, you'd never have gotten past the inner lagoon." That stopped them all, and Pua was almost sorry she had said it. She didn't want to make an enemy of the warden now. It was obvious Toma and Fatu didn't know what to do. They were only buying time. The mountainlady was Pukui's only hope, if Pua could just figure out how to use her.

"You know, Pualei," the warden said quietly, "sometime soon, you and I are going to have to stop testing each other and find a way to work this thing out."

Kiki pulled at Nola's skirt. "Did Pua really try to kill the puhi?" he asked. Auntie Nola shushed him.

"Now?" Pua offered.

The warden nodded, slowly. "Do you want to start? Or shall I?"

"I already started," Pua said. "I brought you here."

"So you did." The woman was silent for a moment. "Do you remember my friend Sally? The one I talked about in my sleep?"

Pua nodded.

"Her cousin runs the company that makes the candies we ate today. He always tells her when I order more than a single box of that particular kind. It's a way we have of passing messages back and forth. Troubleshooters sometimes do things like that so they can communicate privately. By ordering a full case of caramels all the way from Earth, I let Sally know there's something very important, and very dangerous, going on here—and that I need her help."

"What can *she* do?"

"I don't know," the woman admitted. "But I got back twice as many as I ordered, which means she's doing something. We're not entirely alone in this, Pua. And there's something else. I don't know if it means anything, but when I asked Lili how much pay she wanted to boss the Company crews, she asked for 'double' Klooney's."

"And double again for overtime," Pua said.

The warden nodded. "I checked Lili's hire record later, and discovered she hadn't come to Pukui with any of the regular crews. She was working the nets as an unpaid volunteer. Have you ever known a Company boss to do that?"

Pua shook her head. She had been surprised, herself, at Lili's presence among the swimmers; that she had been working without pay was almost unbelievable. "I've never known *any* Company squid to do that," she said.

The baby in Nola's arms cooed.

"How many of these kids are there, anyway?" the warden asked.

"Nine," Pua replied. "Counting me."

"Now, just a minute . . ." Nola said.

"Nine!" The warden's eyes widened. She leaned back against the wall. The light shivered, then steadied. "Nine? That's all?"

Pua nodded.

The mountainlady turned to Nola. "You're planning to take over an entire planet's economy with *nine* kids?"

"There are some more that haven't been born yet," Pua said, "at least—"

Nola grabbed her arm. "This has gone far enough. Don't you say another word." She shoved Pua behind her.

"But, Auntie Nola . . ."

"Kiki. Keha. Take the babies to the nursery pool. Stay there with them until I come."

"But, we want to watch the puhi—"

"Go!"

"Auntie Nola . . ."

"Shut up, Pua. Warden, you may have fooled these children into thinking they can trust you, but you haven't, and you won't, fool me."

"I told you before," the warden said. "I'm not planning to hurt your children." Oh, rot! Pua thought. The warden's voice had gone all calm again. Pua yanked her arm away from Nola. Why were adult humans always so hard to control?

"I know all about you, troubleshooter," Nola said. "I know what the Company promised you to get you out here, and I know your reputation for never leaving a job undone. Well, lady, if the Company ever gets *this* job done, it won't be because you helped them. I guarantee you that."

She brushed her fingers across her wrist comm, and Pua heard the distant thud of the outer airlock doors closing. The hatch shifted slightly and clicked into locked position.

"Oh, rot." Pua said it aloud this time.

"Pua, go in with the boys," Nola said. "Stay there until I say otherwise. Warden, you come with me."

Neither Pua nor the warden moved. Pua was acutely conscious of Nola's shock at being disobeyed. It was not something Pua had ever done openly before, and she found it curious that Nola's obvious irritation caused her so little concern. Something has changed, she thought, and realized it must be herself. The mountainlady's look never strayed from her own.

"Is this complex below the basalt level?" the warden asked.

Pua nodded. "Most of it. Part extends up into the coral. Why?"

"Damn it, Pua!" Nola exclaimed. "What did they do to you back there at that place? This woman works for the Company! Don't you have any sense left?"

"All I have left is Pukui and my babies—and her." Pua returned her look to the mountainlady. "Why did you ask how deep we were?"

Nola activated the intruder alarm.

"Have you ever heard of a place called Mururoa?" the warden replied over the low buzz of the alarm.

Pua shook her head. She clicked a quick sequence with her fingertips to let Kiki and Keha know there was no danger but to remain alert for her orders. Nola frowned at that, because she didn't understand the click-talk when it was done rapidly and didn't like Pua using it here.

"Mururoa is an atoll on Earth," the warden said. "In French Polynesia. Actually, it's what's left of an atoll. It was used for many years as a nuclear testing site." She glanced at Nola. "I see you know of it."

Nola had gone pale. "You wouldn't . . ."

"I'm sure the Company won't nuke Pukui," the warden said. "They want to preserve the reef for their own use if they can. But the data provided by decades of blasting at Mururoa show just how much explosive power is needed to do anything from causing a small coral slide to cracking open the entire understructure of a reef. How long do you think you and your *nine* kids can survive down here if somebody decides to just shake you out? I can't believe you only have nine kids. Surely you have more hidden somewhere else."

She straightened suddenly and shifted her attention to the doorway. Pua caught her breath as Jaime Sorens and Mariko Saito entered. An angry, red scar ran the length of Mariko's right thigh. She was limping heavily. A chill slid down Pua's back. Zena had told her that Mariko had been killed in a netting accident three months earlier.

Nola turned off the alarm. "Jaime, Mariko," she said, "the warden here will be staying with us for a while. Seems there's more Company admin on the way, and at the least, Toma wants her out of contact."

"Auntie Nola, if you would just lis—"

"It's all right, Pua," the warden said. "How many people live down here, anyway, Nola?"

"None of your damn—"

"There were four adults before I left," Pua said. "Plus the kids."

"Jaime, get her out of here before she tells this bitch everything down to our shoe size," Nola said. "Take her into the nursery with the rest of the kids. Now, Warden, I asked you before to come with me."

The warden finally stood. She did it slowly. She rubbed her thighs, then wiped her hands on her shorts. "I'd like to go with Pua," she said.

"You're not going anywhere with Pua," Nola said. She motioned to Jaime, and he took Pua's arm in a grip Pua knew she could break only by hurting him. His look told her that he understood that, too, so she shrugged and submitted.

It occurred to her that bringing the mountainlady here so openly might not have been such a good idea. Now she was going to have to figure out a way to get them both out. She tapped the fingernails of her free hand against the wall behind her.

"Stop that, Pua," Nola said. "If you want to talk to the boys, do it out loud. They're not fish. They need to learn to speak properly."

Pua stopped in midmessage, but kept her palm pressed against the wall. A faint vibration told her that Kiki was just outside and had caught her meaning. *Pili's coming,* he sent.

"Toma took a locator biobug out of Pua's left hand earlier tonight," the warden said, surprising even Pua. "But she still has a homing device in her right wrist. If you separate us, I'll activate it and broadcast this location to every Company receiver from here to Landing."

Pua caught her breath. She jerked her hand away from the wall. Then she rolled it into a fist. "You puhi bitch!" she breathed. "You *did* lie to me!" She reached up to yank away the locator string which she had tied back into her hair. How could she ever have trusted . . .

And then she saw the lie in the mountainlady's quiet stare. She would never have recognized it if she hadn't once seen full truth in those eyes, that first day back in the freshwater pool. She's lying to make them keep us together, she thought. To cover her surprise, she pulled the comb from her hair and hurled it at the woman. The warden ducked away easily, and the comb bounced off the wall.

"Come to the surgery," Mariko said. "I'll take—"

"No!" Pua pulled away from Jaime, and to her relief, he let her go. "I'm not letting anybody cut me open ever again."

"Pua . . ."

"I'll rip my gills out before I let anybody cut me open again." Pua slid her fingertips beneath the edges of her gill flaps and lifted them far enough to show their color. The dry air burned against the sensitive membranes, and it made her think of what she had done to the mountainlady earlier that night. She wished she could be certain whether the woman was a friend or an enemy.

"Pua, don't," Nola said quickly.

"She can't get out," Pua said. "Even if she gets the airlock open, I left the rays outside. She won't hurt anything here. I won't let her. Please, Auntie Nola." She squeezed out a tear and carefully avoided the mountainlady's eye.

Nola took her wrists and gently pulled her hands away from her gills. The flaps sealed instantly, but the burning ache continued.

Nola turned back to the mountainlady. "If you even *look* like you're going to harm her or any of these children, you'll be dead before you know what hit you. Don't test me on this!"

The warden winced and rubbed her thighs again. "I doubt I could even *attempt* an escape right now. I don't know about you, Pua, but that little wrestling match we had just about wrecked my legs."

Nola turned quickly to Pua. "What's she talking about? Are you hurt?"

"I'm just sore," Pua said quickly. "We—we were playing with the rays. It would feel good to sit in the thermal pool, though." She rubbed her own legs. Nola looked skeptical, but finally motioned them from the room.

"Come look, Pua," Keha called as they passed the nursery entrance. "We got a new one!"

Despite Nola's order to the contrary, Pua darted inside. Kiki was standing shoulder deep in the nursery pool. He grinned and lifted a tiny, wriggling baby.

"Kiki!" Nola and Jaime called at the same instant. "Put her down!"

"Ha!" Pua raced to the pool. Sliding over the side, she took the new baby from Kiki's sure hands. It was a girl, and she was beautiful! Her dark eyes were wide and wise, and her golden brown skin was as slippery as a freshly peeled mountain apple.

The baby wrapped her tiny fingers around Pua's thumbs and opened her mouth wide. Pua mimicked her and laughed. "Like a scooperfish!"

"Put that baby down and get out of there," Nola ordered. She and Mariko were still at the door, preventing the warden from entering.

Pua hugged the baby, then dunked her to see how her gills flared. Perfect! The baby didn't even blink, just spread her webs and started pulling at the water.

"Pua, please!"

Pua lifted the baby high overhead and turned to the mountain-lady in triumph. "Look!" she cried. "Now, we have *ten*!"

Chapter 19

~~~~~~~~~~~~~~~~~~~~~~
~~~~~~~~~~~~~~~~~~~~~~

"Pua," Jamie said from beside the pool. "You're giving your auntie a stroke. Put the baby down."

"Ten!" Pua laughed again. She gave the squirming baby another hug, then tossed her back into the water.

Jamie caught his breath. "She's only three weeks old," he said. "You have to be more careful with her." Pua climbed out of the pool and shook herself. As Jaime turned away from the spray, she signed a quick order to Kiki. He flicked his brows in acknowledgment.

"She's gotta learn how to splash," she said, "or she'll be scared when she goes outside with the rays."

"She won't be going outside with the rays for a long time," Nola said. "Come on. Get out of here. Mariko, you stay with the kids." Mariko stepped into the pool and scooped the baby into her arms.

"Is she yours, Jaime?" Pua asked. He nodded and grinned.

Pua held her hands close to her face and breathed deeply of the baby's sweet, salty smell. "Where's the other one?" She knew this baby's mama had been carrying twins. The altered embryos had been implanted just a few days before Pua and her parents had been taken away from Pukui.

She looked up and around at the sudden silence.

"They were born early," Jaime said. "The other one's lungs weren't strong enough for her to survive, and her gills never functioned properly."

"Auwe," Pua said softly. The mountainlady sighed.

"She needs a Pukui name," Keha said. He had followed them from the nursery and was tugging at Pua's wet shirt. Pua wished she could just take the shirt off, but knew that with Jaime and the warden here, it would just cause more trouble. Someday, she thought, Pukui is going to be a place where only real waterworlders can come. Born waterworlders. Then we can do anything we want.

"What do you call her now?" she asked.

"Nellie."

Pua wrinkled her nose. "That's an Earther's name." She thought for a moment. "Her Pukui name is 'Umi Iki. Little Number Ten, because that's what she is."

"Oh, Pua, don't call her a number," Nola said. "You know the other kids will do anything you say, and she'll end up being stuck with it for the rest of her life."

"It's not good for a waterworlder to have an Earther's name, Auntie Nola," Pua said. "Le Fe'e might not recognize her when she's swimming in the ocean." She saw the mountainlady's brows lift slightly. *Pay attention*, she wanted to tell her, but said instead, "Come on, Keha. *Auntie Puhi* and I have some snowballs to show you."

"I'm going to breeze Fatu's ass for filling you with all this nonsense," Nola muttered.

When they reached the thermal pool, the mountainlady didn't even hesitate. She tested the bubbling water with her hand, then stepped into the pool, clothes and all. Without another word, she lay back and sank to just below the surface.

Keha stared down at her. "She's funny, Pua. Where'd you get her?"

"Earth," Pua replied. "She used to live on a mountain."

"Like Mauna Kea Iki?"

Pua peered down at the woman. She had relaxed completely in the water. Her eyes were closed, and she looked like she did under the snow trees sometimes—as if only her body were present, and her spirit had gone somewhere else. Her gills pulsed with the rhythm of a very slow oxygen intake.

"I don't think so," Pua said.

"What's she doing?"

Pua shrugged. "I don't know. She just does that sometimes, usually up on the mountain. She'll wake up after a while."

"She's meditating," Jamie said. "Calming and centering herself. I never saw anyone go so deep so fast before."

"She's not very deep," Keha said.

Pua stepped into the water. It felt wonderful on her aching hips and thighs. It had been a good idea to come here, in more ways than one. She grinned.

"Here, Keha," she said. She lifted the bag of snowballs from around her neck. "Don't drop them in the hot water, or they'll melt." She clicked a quick message against the side of the pool as Keha took the bag and squatted eagerly beside the pool. He dumped the snowballs into his hand. There were too many to hold, so he poured them into a pile on the moss.

"So many!" he whispered. His eyes were bright with excitement, and his obvious pleasure made Pua feel as warm as the water.

"Where did you get them all?" Jamie asked. He lifted the largest of the balls, one about the size of Little Ten's fist when her fingers were all rolled up. Pua liked that image and decided to add it to her personal list of weights and measures. Of course, the baby's fist would grow, but that didn't matter. Pua and Le Fe'e, and the rays, would remember what the measurement meant.

The warden surfaced beside her. She looked as surprised as the others when she saw the snowballs.

"Katie saved them from before," Pua said. "She buried them under the house with my shells and things."

"Poor Katie. She never did like those things lying around the house," Nola said. She glanced at Keha. "Neither do I."

"Kiki left the ones you brought before on Auntie Mariko's catch nets, and they ate a hole right through," Keha said. He grinned.

Pua nodded. "They dissolve anything with plastic in it really fast. You have to be careful where you put them. Specially when they get warm." Keha had lined the snowballs along the edge of the pool. Pay attention, Mountainlady, Pua thought.

The sudden sound of crying babies came from beyond the gate.

"Jaime, go help Mariko," Nola said. "I'll take care of things here, but lock the gate on your way out. Just so you know, Warden, all the locks down here are designed to thwart fingers like yours. You might be able to trip the locks, themselves, but you won't be able to do it without triggering the alarms. Keha, don't let those fall in the hot water. They'll make an awful mess."

The warden submerged again.

"What's she doing now?" Keha asked.

"Probably thinking up another question," Pua said.

The mountainlady surfaced and pushed her hair back from her forehead. "How many more kids do you have *in utero*?" she asked.

"See what I mean?" Pua said, and Keha laughed. "Three," she told the warden.

Nola cursed softly. "You're bound and determined to tell her everything, aren't you, girl?'' She met the warden's look. "We have two more pregnancies, a single and a set of twins. Both are due very soon."

The warden got that startled look again, like she had before when Pua told her there were nine waterbabies already born. "Why are there so few?" she asked.

To Pua's surprise, Nola answered. "Because Lehua was the only one who could manipulate the embryonic genomes properly. And because, since we had to live and work in absolute secrecy, we were selecting willing parents from a very small pool."

The warden was silent for a long time. "Pua," she said finally, "is she lying to me?"

That startled Pua. The warden had always been able to tell when someone was lying before. She shook her head.

The warden shook her own head, slowly. She stared at Nola. "You have a total, a *total*, of ten kids with only three more on the way, and no way to produce more in this generation. How can you people possibly think you can populate this planet with thirteen kids? Even if you do manage to get them past the Company inheritance laws."

"When the time comes," Nola said, "they'll take mates from among their standard cousins up above, numerous mates—they won't have the luxury of monogamy for the first few generations. At least half of their offspring will be born with the water changes, and twins will be the norm in those cases. It's not as hopeless as you seem to think."

"I don't think it's *totally* hopeless," the warden said. "It's just—I'm just—well, spit! I thought I was going to have a little more to work with here."

"Anyone coming to live down here, child or adult, has to be legally 'dead' topside," Nola said. "Dead in such a way that their bodies are never missed. I came down thirteen years ago, when Pua was born. For the benefit of the census records, I was trapped inside the hold of a hydrobus when it sank in deep water. I birthed a set of twins carrying my own genes later on, and have been surrogate for two more. The rest were carried openly above, but claimed as stillbirths for the record and brought here immediately after being born."

The warden glanced at Keha.

Nola nodded. "His mother had planned to live down here with us, but unfortunately her death was real."

Pua made a handsign, and Keha bumped a snowball into the pool. Nola glared at him. Pua quickly fished the ball out and set it aside, on bare stone. Its short immersion in the hot water had left it sticky. Pua clicked her approval of Keha's "accident" against the side of the pool.

"I'm going to have three babies at a time," Pua said. She tapped her nails on the stone again, under the water so Nola wouldn't see or hear. She felt an immediate answering vibration through the water. It was Pili. Finally. She had been afraid he wasn't going to get there before Nola made them get out of the pool.

"I'm going to teach them all how to find their own snowballs," she said to cover her answering tap, "so they'll have plenty whenever they want them."

"They'll make an awful mess," Keha said in a perfect imitation of Auntie Nola.

Pua laughed. "Oh, Keha, you're so smart." She reached out to tickle him. He collapsed and rolled and fell right into the pool. A handful of snowballs tumbled in with him.

Nola jumped up. "Keha, get out of there. Right now. Warden, don't you go anywhere near him!" The warden backed away.

"Auntie Nola! Let me in!"

It was Kiki, right on schedule.

The gate rattled, and Kiki called again. "Open up. I want to come in. Jaime said there were snowballs. Auntie Nola!"

"Get those damn snowballs out of there, Pua," Nola ordered. "Keha, help her, then get out of the water."

"Open up!" Kiki called.

"I'm coming, Kiki. Stop yelling." Nola turned toward the gate.

"You are *so* smart," Pua whispered into Keha's ear. "You and Kiki both." He giggled, and reached out to sweep the rest of the snowballs into the water. Pua scooped up a handful and motioned to the mountainlady.

"Follow me," she whispered.

"Stop hanging on the gate like that, Kiki," she heard Nola say. "I can't get it open until you let go."

"What—"

"Do you want to get out of here or not?" Pua whispered. The warden's eyes widened.

Pua lifted Keha back out of the pool so he could help delay Nola further, then dove straight down through the warm water. The warden followed, close at her side. At three meters, not quite at the bottom, a plastic safety grill covered the pool's outlet pipe. Pua peered through it and saw by the faint light from above that Pili was waiting on the other side. He grinned and waved.

Pua quickly passed him some of the fast-melting snowballs. They were already soft and pliable. She pressed the remaining snowballs over the plastic hinges of the locked grill. Pili did the same on the opposite side.

The mountainlady looked surprised, but caught on immediately. She scooped together other snowballs as they drifted down from above, and added them to those already covering the hinges. The water surrounding the hinges began hissing softly. The mountainlady spread the melting sap more evenly, glanced up, then tested the grate with a yank. It shifted slightly.

Pua motioned her to one side, so they could both twist their fingers through the grate. They braced their feet and pulled, hard. Pili hit the grill at the same time from the other side, and it snapped open, sending the warden tumbling into the smooth rock wall. Pua saw her grimace.

Pili slid out of the pipe, touched Pua's cheek in greeting, then turned and disappeared headfirst back into the narrow hole.

Pua felt a splash from above. Keha, she judged from the size of its reverberation. He was providing one last distraction.

It occurred to Pua suddenly that the warden might not fit into the small pipe. But it was too late to stop. She urged the woman after Pili. The warden gritted her teeth, shut her eyes, and squeezed herself into the pipe. Her wide shoulders just fit; they brushed along the sides.

A second, much larger shock vibrated through the water, and Pua hurried after the warden. She slid into the pipe feetfirst, ready to fight with her hands if she had to; but Auntie Nola's face appeared at the hole just as Pua wriggled beyond the length of her long arms.

Nola was much too big to follow them through the pipe. She shouted an Earther's curse after them instead.

Turning in the narrow space was impossible, so Pua scooted backward as quickly as she could. At the first bend, she crouched, turned, then sped forward after Pili and the warden. Just beyond the turn, the pipe opened into a larger, natural channel.

The water began to cool, and then to grow cold. Pua felt the tug of strong currents ahead and heard Pili whistle as he exited the channel. She hoped he would remember to hold onto the warden as she followed him into the main cold-water tunnel. She was not sure the woman would be able to handle being swept by the current all the way through the barrier reef. Even with light, and gills to provide oxygen, the warden would be hard put to remain calm through that.

It was strange how a woman so otherwise brave could have such a deep fear of this one thing. It made Pua wonder if she, herself, held such a fear; if there was some great terror hidden inside her that she had never had to face. Or maybe I've already done that, she thought. She shivered as she remembered the barren, miscolored sea outside the Earth recon station.

Pua passed quickly through the protected side channel where she sometimes brought the older kids to play, when Nola and the other adults were too busy to notice. There was a small pocket of air high up in the coral, kept fresh by the gentle oxyworm that Pili had coaxed into attaching itself there. Pua thought about taking the warden there to give her a respite before the trip through the main tunnel, but decided in the end that it was better to just get it done all at once.

When she reached the hanging slime-mold barrier that hid the channel entrance, Pua squeezed through the rubbery layers carefully. No use marring the camouflage if it wasn't necessary. It looked as if Pili and the warden had passed through the mold wall just as carefully as she. They had left no sign of their exit.

Pua saw them as soon as she was through the slick, shimmering barrier. She swam to the mountainlady's side and slipped an arm around her waist. The water was terribly cold. The deep-water pipe was uninsulated at this depth.

Pili was holding the warden from the other side and bracing them both against the strong current with a grip on one of the pipe struts. There was just enough light from the molds and their own effervescence to show that the warden's eyes were wide with only partially controlled terror.

Pili pointed upcurrent toward the nearer exit into the open ocean. Pua shook her head and pointed toward the inner reef. They had to get the woman out, but it was better to get it all done at once than to have to bring her back through later. The surf was too rough to take her over the top, and the pass was a long way away.

Pili nodded, wrapped his arm tighter around the warden's waist, and let go of the strut. They all kicked along with the current and shot like a triplet of rays through the long, straight lava tube. Pua was sorry the woman was too frightened to enjoy the ride.

They surfaced as quickly as they could after reaching the lagoon. Shadow's position showed that a third of the night was gone. Pili and Pua helped the warden across a narrow shelf of coral and onto a sandy beach. It had rained while they had been below, and the air smelled of the distant stormy sea.

As soon as they let her go, the warden sat on the ground, hugging her knees tightly. She was trembling.

"Are you okay?" Pua asked. She spoke softly, as she always did when one of the other kids was with her on the surface. There was clearly no one around, but she never took chances with her babies. Not until tonight.

The woman took a long, shuddering breath.

"Mountainlady?"

"Little Fe'e," the woman said, after yet another of those ragged breaths, "someday I'm going to stuff a *real* snowball right down your shorts."

"Ha!" Pua shouted in a whisper. "You made it!" She jumped up and grabbed Pili. "We made it!" They wrestled each other to the ground, laughing without sound, hugging each other tight. They rolled over and over through the course sand. It stuck to their wet, mucus-slicked skin and felt *good*! It was so *good* to be home!

Finally, they rolled to a stop. Pua brushed the sand from Pili's cheeks, kissed him soundly, and then pulled him back toward the mountainlady.

The warden was still sitting with her arms tight around her knees, but the terror had left her eyes. She was staring open-mouthed at their play.

"This is Pilimanaia noun Fatu o le Motu me Ehukai," Pua said. "He's eleven—the oldest, except for me. We're going to build a house on Second Island someday, and he's going to live there. And we're going to make a bridge between Second and Home, and carve a path right down to the water. And we're going to grow mountain apples and sell them to the Earthers, and when he gets big enough we're going to do sex and make babies and lots of other stuff."

The warden blinked.

"I'm big enough now," Pili said.

Pua looked him up and down. His naked skin glistened where it wasn't covered with sand. He had a coiler wrapped around his left wrist, and a fringe of braided seaweed tied just below his right knee. He was as beautiful as Little Ten, and it was true that he had grown—he was almost as tall as she. Still . . .

"I don't think so," she said. "Not quite yet."

The mountainlady started to choke. Quickly, Pua squatted beside her and slapped her back. "Are you okay? I'm sorry about the pipe, but it was the only way out." She frowned. "I guess it wasn't such a good idea to take you in there like that."

"I'm fine," the warden said, pushing away Pua's hands. Pua realized she was not choking at all. She was laughing.

"What's funny?" she asked.

"Nothing, Waterbaby," the warden said. She laughed again. "Everything. Where the hell are we, anyway?"

"On the barrier reef. This is one of the reef islets. We just came through the cold-water pipe channel."

"That much I'd guessed. How soon can Nola contact Toma about our being down there, and about our escape?" She stopped and peered closely at Pili. "Are you Fatu's son?"

Pili nodded. "And you're Puhi 'ai Pōhaku, the mountainlady, right?"

The warden sighed. "Right."

Pua grinned. "With so many Company crews on-site, Nola won't dare send a swimmer out, and they never use the comm system when there are outsiders in the lagoon. Unless Fatu comes out here tonight, and I don't think he will, he won't find out about us being here until after Crawley leaves."

"That was a good trick you did with the snowballs, Pua," Pili said. "Where'd you get so many?"

"They're my old ones," Pua said. "The ones I kept in my room before I went to Earth. Mama told Katie to bury them."

The warden sat up straighter. "What?"

"They don't melt if you keep them cool and dark," Pua said.

"No," the warden said. "What did you say about your mother?"

Pua hesitated. "I guess Mama wanted Katie to save them for me. Katie knew I used to hide my shells and other important stuff under the house, so that's where she put them. It was a good idea. She might have forgotten where they were, otherwise."

The warden stared at her for a moment, then turned to look across the lagoon. Mauna Kea Iki was barely visible behind scudding rain clouds. "Well, I'll be damned," she said softly.

"It's a good thing you had so many," Pili said.

Pua laughed. "It's a good thing Auntie Puhi fit through that pipe!"

"How far are we from the nearest farm access comm?" the mountainlady asked suddenly.

"Not far. The rays can take us if you want to go. Why?"

"Are you going to help us?" Pili asked.

The warden was still staring at the distant mountain. She nodded. "I'm going to try, Waterboy. I'm sure as hell going to try."

Chapter 20

"Nightcrawlers!" Fatu muttered.

He stared down at the poor dead creatures. Six of them, each coiled tightly at the center of its spilled dye sack. "She fooled me with a handful of nightcrawlers."

Brilliant yellow trails, bordered by lines of scattered moat grass, told the tale of Pua's deception. Since nightcrawlers never crossed moat grass, their steady, slow roaming had eventually led them to the edges of the bed, the bureau, and the stool.

One by one over the last hour and a half, they had fallen, thunked solidly to the floor, and then wandered the shadows for a time before reaching the patch of moonlight shining through the window. Then they had punctured their dye sacks to release their spores. Fatu had heard their small sounds and thought it was Pua moving around in the room.

He had expected silence from the warden. She was, physically, one of the quietest humans he had ever known. She moved only with a purpose, and rarely made a sound even then. Pua, on the other hand, never stopped moving, and the noise made by the nightcrawlers had been just enough to convince him she was still safely inside her room.

"Don't blame yourself," Toma said. "I knew better than to let Dinsman out of my sight. I just didn't want her standing over my shoulder smirking while it took me half the night to unlock the damn flitter. We both should have guessed Pua was up to something when she refused to speak or to open her door for so long." He looked up from his examination of the window seal.

"This isn't the first time she's gotten out this way. She even managed to reactivate the lock after she was outside. The warden's window was closed so the alarm wouldn't trigger, but the lock was jammed. She's good with those hands, but she can't match Pua. My guess is, Pua went out first, and the warden followed.''

''Pua would have headed straight for the lagoon and then Sa le Fe'e,'' Fatu said. ''Once she was in the water, she couldn't have been followed without being aware of it. The rays would have told her the woman was following, if she didn't hear her herself.''

Toma glanced back at him. ''Well, there's no way we can stop either one of them now. If the warden somehow finds the nursery, with or without Pua's help, Nola won't allow her to harm the kids, or to leave until she gets clearance from us. As for Pua, I suppose she's as safe there as anywhere for the moment.''

''Pua has sense enough to stay out of sight while Crawley's here,'' Fatu said, ''but we'd better be prepared for the warden to show up at any time. Looks like we end up having to trust her after all.''

Toma shrugged and stood. ''The hell of it is, I've trusted her all along. It's just that what I trust her to do isn't necessarily what we need done. She'll honor her contract no matter what else happens.'' He glanced out the open window. ''And aside from the satisfaction, it won't do her a damn bit of good. That lady doesn't stand a skudder's chance in a puhi hole of getting back to Earth, not with her connections there and what she now knows about Lesaat.''

''You think Crawley will try to kill her?'' It was as much a statement as a question.

''He might,'' Toma said, ''although it's awfully hard to get away with killing a U.N. troubleshooter. It's more likely he'll just make it impossible for her to return to Earth now, and maybe try to arrange for an accident later. According to her contract, the payment of her medical bills is contingent on her finding the TC records *and* saving Pukui's reef. She may have accomplished the latter, but she's no closer to finding the TC than we are. Judging from what I've seen of her personal financial records, she's going to be stuck here for a *long* time.''

''I sense that wouldn't make *you* entirely unhappy,'' Fatu said with a small smile.

Toma looked embarrassed for just an instant. ''I have to confess, she's the first woman I've been attracted to since Kilisou died.''

Fatu lifted a brow.

''For more than strictly physical reasons,'' Toma amended.

Fatu sighed. ''Well, no matter what else she does here, we

have to thank her for at least giving the reef a chance. We're harvesting the last of the primary pens now. If we can keep it moving for another forty-eight hours, we'll beat this next storm. So far, it's staying right on track, so we'll get the edges of it as it turns north, but it shouldn't be anything we can't handle.

"Once the algae is clear, we can batten down the farm for the direct hit that's bound to come next. We'll be safe for the season then, because after tomorrow night, we'll be past the alignment tides and even the direct storms won't carry as much force."

Toma shook his head. "That's not the report Crawley's going to want to give the inspection team. He wants this place to be in enough danger for the Company to reclaim the lease. My guess is, the minute he's off the shuttle, he'll order the harvest stopped."

"I'll take care of that," Fatu said. "Harvest crews can't follow orders they don't get. You stall Crawley at Landing as long as you can, and we'll keep shoveling algae. Pukui may be flat broke when this is over, but with any luck at all, we'll still have the reef, plus an outdated processing plant full of prime algae to get us started again."

Toma nodded. "Ehu's already on her way with the flit and the locators. The Company snoops are bound to be monitoring our comm channels, so we can't chance calling her back now. I told Ehu to ignore all calls for the warden, so that'll slow things up some, too." Toma squeezed Fatu's arm before starting down the stairs. "We've known all along it wasn't going to be easy, my friend."

"Aye," Fatu said. But I never imagined it could be this hard, he added silently.

He waited until Toma was outside before looking down again at the dead nightcrawlers. Casualties of war, he thought, and wondered how many more Pukui lives would be lost before this was finished. The pain of Lehua's and Zed's deaths was like a scarlet coiler crushing his soul.

Did we do the right thing? he wondered. Did we do the right thing by bringing those babies into a world that might be taken from them before it's ever really theirs? He brushed the remaining moat grass from the bureau top.

Katie was going to be furious about the stains. She was already upset about his opening the warden's crate down in the library. She had actually tried to chase him out of the house. But, "troubleshooters never do anything without a reason," Toma had said, so while Toma unlocked the flitter, Fatu searched the crate. He had found nothing but boxes of candy, and indications that this was not the first time the crate had been searched. Whether it had been done by the warden or by others before her, it was impossible to tell. Probably both, he decided.

There was nothing to be done about the stains now. He scooped the nightcrawlers into a fold of his lavalava, then relocked the room. Hopefully, Katie wouldn't notice the mess until he had thought up an acceptable excuse for it. Admitting that he had locked Lehua's precious daughter in her room was not likely to please the overly protective drone any more than the stains. He wondered, How can I even be thinking of such unimportant things?

"Because it's all part of the same thing," he muttered. "You can't create a future unless you care about the little things right along with the big ones."

After setting a scramble on all incoming transmissions to Pukui and then locking the comm, Fatu left the house. He tossed the dead crawlers into the grass and made a careful circuit of the building. It didn't take long to find the spot where Pua had come down from the roof. He could even see where she had trapped the nightcrawlers under the house.

The moat grass had come from Matt, of course. Fatu stopped to run his hands over the poor, plucked creature and set it back up on the lanai. Matt could make its own way back to the door.

He studied the shadows across the lawn for a moment, then followed the route Pua always took to get her to the sea as fast as possible.

In the jungle, he found signs of her passing—a bent leaf, an overturned seedpod, a freshly snapped bough on the mountain apple tree—and, farther on, the shards of an apple peel. A true Islander. He couldn't help smiling. She never pass up an easily available meal. He bit into one of the apples he had picked for himself.

At the beach, Pua's broad footsteps led in a straight line across the smooth sand. With the locator gone, she would have headed straight for Sa le Fe'e. Fatu didn't doubt it for a minute. It was a testament to her trust in him and his cautiously worded warnings that she had not gone there before. He had not dared to be more specific for fear of what the bastard Earthers might have done to her.

He stared out at the distant reef.

"Be careful, Little Fe'e," he murmured. "Be careful who and how much you trust."

Le Fe'e's song was powerful in the cool night air. Pua claimed that the darkness that eclipsed the rings each night was not really the shadow of Lesaat blocking the sun's rays. It was, she said, the great god Le Fe'e, crawling across the sky to survey his domain.

Fatu looked up at the spreading shadow. He wished he could believe in the demigod in as literal a way as Pua did. He wished he had a way to call some powerful mythical creature to her aid. An image with the face of the Earthwoman was the only one he could conjure and that was not in the least reassuring.

Fatu could find no evidence of the warden's presence on the beach, but that didn't surprise him—nor did it mean she hadn't come this way. The woman traveled as effortlessly on the land as Pua did in the water. Pua had told him some days before that despite the mountainlady's being such an obvious land person, she stayed as deliberately conscious of her surroundings as a reef dweller. It was the highest compliment Fatu had ever heard Pua give to an Earth-born human.

A gust of wind, the harbinger of an approaching squall, lifted the edge of his lavalava. "Another few days," Fatu asked of the wind. "Just give us another few days, and we can offer you a clean reef."

He turned his look back toward the glowing reef. The wind quickened. It was useless to waste time searching for either the warden or Pua, and delaying Crawley was up to Toma for the time being. Fatu couldn't even go out to help on the nets, because he had to be there when Crawley arrived, and there was no telling when that would be.

The approaching squall hissed like an oxyworm out of water as it rushed toward him across the inner lagoon. The first drops of rain struck wet and cool against his skin.

Delay, he thought. But how? Everything that could be done had already been set in motion. Then he thought of the Earthwoman again, the anthropologist, and what she had said about their way of life.

"Syncretism," he said. "New traditions created by combining the old." An idea began to form. He smiled slowly. It would not hold Crawley off forever, but done right, it would provide at least a few extra hours. Right now, every one counted.

He took a quick last look toward the barrier reef, scuffed away Pua's footsteps, then headed for the cookhouse.

Chapter 21

It was Pua's idea to meet and delay the Company bus.

After Pili had returned to Sa le Fe'e, she and Angie had ridden the rays to the nearest, and most private, computer terminal— in one of the underwater pump stations. While Pua patrolled outside, Angie carefully set to work bypassing the various locks and alarms that had been set during her brief absence. She finally gained access to the farm library and began searching the files.

"What are you looking for?" Pua asked once when she slipped inside to check on Angie's progress.

"Precedents," Angie said.

"What's that?"

Angie laughed. "Legal ways to keep you out of trouble, I hope. Go guard the door, Waterchild. I'll explain later." It took her two hours to find what she needed.

When she had it, she called Pua back inside and showed her a carefully shielded incoming transmission from Landing. Just before shuttle touchdown, an unplanned methane blow at Kobayashi's Reef had resulted in an emergency call for all available cleanup crews.

All air transport had been pulled off Landing to ferry swimmers to the damaged reef.

"I'll bet that's a diversion," Pua said. "I heard Fatu and Uncle Toma and Kobe planning it a long time ago. Toma probably ordered it to try to keep Crawley away from Pukui so we'd have more time to clear the algae."

Angie nodded. "That would explain the scramble that's been set up to block all incoming transmissions. Company crews can't follow orders they don't receive, and Crawley would have tried to order them out of the water as soon as he got off the shuttle. Fatu probably did that. It has his touch."

"How come Crawley's still trying to destroy Pukui?" Pua asked. "Fatu told me that he was sure the Company was only using that as a threat to make him tell where the TC records are. Nobody ever really believed the TC enzyme was in the algae pens. It's stupid for them to destroy the reef when they don't have to. Even if the Company doesn't own it, it still makes a lot of money for them."

"He's doing it because of me," Angie replied.

Pua's brows lifted. She looked up from where she was braiding colored seaweed into the edges of her shirt. She had a pencil-thin scarlet coiler wrapped around one wrist and a circle of feather ferns attached to the other. She was as colorful as the reef itself.

"My contract is worded so that I have to find the TC enzyme records *and* save Pukui before I can complete my obligations and return to Earth for payment."

"You mean he wants you to stay here?"

Angie shrugged. "I doubt the Company considers me a good risk for being sent back to Earth right now, Waterbaby. They know damn well I'd do everything I could to expose what's gone on here. Even if I *can't* prove anything legally."

Pua was quiet for a minute. "Well, if you're going to stay," she said finally, "you should probably start being nicer to Uncle Toma."

Angie glanced at her. "Why?"

The corners of Pua's mouth twitched. "Because Toma makes good babies."

"Mother of mountains," Angie muttered, and turned back to the flickering screen. "Damn," she said as soon as she saw it.

"What?"

Angie pointed toward an incoming message. "The diversion didn't work."

Crawley, apparently unwilling to wait the full day or more that the emergency at Kobayashi's would take, had ordered the U.N. team and half his security squad aboard a Company hydrobus. The bus was already on its way to Pukui.

"Spit," Angie said. "If they're running at top speed, which I'm sure they are, they'll be here by dawn." She glanced once more at the satellite weather map and saw that the nearby storm was just beginning to turn north, away from Pukui. At least something was going right. She touched off the comm.

"We have to stop that bus," Pua said. "Come on. I know how to do it."

"We're not going to sink the hydrobus, Pua," Angie replied quickly.

Pua gave her a long-suffering kind of look, as if sinking the bus and every Earther on it wasn't exactly what she would do if she thought she could get away with it. She looked down to inspect her braided fringe, then up again, coolly. "You always try to solve things using legal stuff, like talking and things like that, before you do anything. Sometimes that's backwards. Sometimes you have to just *do* things and talk about them later."

Suddenly she grinned. "Can we go if I promise not to break any laws, Mountainlady?"

And because there was nothing more to be discovered through the comm lines, and it was foolish to take the chance of being caught by Fatu if they joined the work crews, Angie had finally agreed. Now, shoulders numb with fatigue, she clung to the velvety back of another, or perhaps the same, ray and listened to the water sing while racing through the open ocean.

After a long, long ride, Pua signaled them to the surface. Dawn was still at least an hour off, but the moonlight and the rings and the water's phosphorescence made the night almost as bright as day.

"I feel the bus coming," Pua said as soon as they reached the air. "This is where we need to do it." She pushed herself up to sit astride her ray's narrow middle. Angie did the same, and the rays moved slowly across the water, lifting and lowering with the shapes of the swells. It was like riding a double-winged horse.

Pua grinned. "These high seas are going to make it fun."

"Make what fun?" Angie asked. "Pua, what are you going to do? That bus is going to be moving well over a hundred kilometers an hour. How can you slow it without getting killed? You're not planning to show yourself, are you?"

"With swells like these, they're probably only doing about a hundred," Pua said. "Toma's going to be slowing things down as much as he can. And no, I won't show myself. Toma wouldn't stop, anyway, and if somebody else made him, I'd just get the fireloving hell out of here. I don't want to get anywhere near those people."

She rubbed her ray's back, then clicked a signal—first outside the water, then under it. Instantly, the rest of the ray pack surfaced, slammed their wings against the water, and dove.

"Pua, what's going—"

"Come on," Pua shouted, dropping back to her stomach on the ray. "You just watch!" Angie had just time enough to grab her own mount's forward wing edges before being pulled under again. Thank god for the adrenaline rush, she thought as she pressed her cheek against the ray's back. It continually astonished her that the ray's skin was so warm.

They dove deep—deep enough for Angie to feel the pressure change. She's going to kill us both, she decided, before finally, she saw the ray pack rising toward them. Something large and red was rising with them.

As they drew closer, Angie saw that the rays were carrying the red thing in their teeth. She was as shocked at the size of the rays' protruding gray teeth as she was at the sight of the snake-like creature that twisted and writhed in their grasp. It was as big around as her waist, and if it were stretched out straight it would measure at least ten meters. A dozen or more adult rays held it taut, lifting it, fighting it, closer and closer to the surface. The single-winged youthful rays circled, but stayed back from harm's way.

Angie's ray, too, held back from the thrashing, struggling pack, but Pua's took her directly into the maelstrom. Pua reached up as they swept beneath the scarlet creature, and slid her hand along its skin. The circle of red at her wrist matched the giant she caressed.

"Dear god, it's a coiler!" Angie whispered into the waves. It was the great-great-grandmother of coilers, from what she could see, and it was making a tremendous effort to spring inward around the rays—and Pua.

"Get the hell out of there, you idiot!" Angie shouted. Her ray bucked slightly, startled, no doubt, by the alien sound of her voice.

Suddenly Angie became conscious of a new sound, a different feel to the sea. The hydrobus—approaching at high speed. Her ray carried her upward, parallel to the pack, close enough for her to see but not be caught in the turbulence of their passing.

The rays carried the coiler directly into the speeding hydrofoil's path. Just when Angie was sure the entire pack, Pua and coiler included, would be sliced through by the hydrofoil's submerged wings, the rays released the coiler. Instantly, Pua and her mount dropped with the others into a steep dive. The coiler, still stretched open, was struck by the starboard forward foil.

It snapped closed instantly, coiling itself tightly around the outer edge of the foil and one of the struts.

The bus dropped and skewed sharply to starboard, its hydrodynamic lift destroyed. The throttle was chopped immediately, and the bus's hull settled with a heavy thud into the water. The hydrofoil wings quickly retracted. Only the port fore and aft wings pulled fully into their holding bays, however. The tightly wrapped bulk of the coiler prevented the starboard wings from retracting all the way inside. The bus continued to skew slowly to the right, listing sharply in the swell.

"Holy mother of mountains," Angie breathed. "She did it!" Her ray moved—whether at the sound of her voice or at some command of Pua's, she wasn't sure—toward the surface. Pua met her there and motioned her off the ray. Treading water so that only their heads would show, they watched as the crippled hydrobus circled. Because of the heavy seas, they could only catch glimpses of the chaos on the bus's deck before being dropped back into watery troughs.

Pua was beside herself with delight. "Did you see her, Mountainlady? Did you see how long she was. Wasn't she beautiful? I never saw such a beautiful coiler! Her skin felt like snow-tree bark." She laughed and spluttered as a breaking wave tip caught her face-on. "She was as smooth as the sea. Oh, I love that mama coiler! I do."

She unwrapped the tiny coiler from her wrist, stretched it out between her hands, and kissed it. Then she set it free. It snapped into a tiny tangle and tumbled toward the deep.

"Grow!" she called after it. "Grow into the greatest coiler of them all." And then she laughed and stroked the crowding rays, praising their strength and agility and fantastic bravery— and despite the chill the scene aboard the hydrobus had given her, Angie laughed right along with her.

"How long will that thing stay on there?" she asked.

"At least a day," Pua said. "Look, they're going in the water. Come on." She led the way under. She was careful, Angie was pleased to note, to remain well distant from the swimmers who had come to surround the great tangle of scarlet coiler.

Angie recognized Toma's powerful form and, to her disgust although not her surprise, Klooney's blocky body, as well. She blinked extreme focus, watched for a time more, then motioned Pua back to the surface.

"Klooney!" Pua spat as soon as she reached air.

"Worse than that," Angie said. "Did you see the hands on the swimmers in gray?"

Pua shook her head. "What was wrong with them? How can you see that far?"

"Wait," Angie said. They reached the top of a swell, and she blinked long focus again to study the humans aboard the bus. Most had been riding on the open deck, and it was clear that there had been injuries among them. Of the twenty or more she could see from this angle, all but three wore bodysuits of steel gray.

"Spit," she said. "We're in for it now."

"What?" Pua asked. "What do you see?"

"There's a whole troop of Earther waterguards on that bus," Angie replied. "Come on, let's move back. The last thing we want now is to be seen anywhere near here."

"What's a waterguard?"

"An Earther with gills. A swimmer trained as a soldier to patrol Earth seas. They're all straight Company liners. Crawley's not taking any chances with waterworlder loyalties this time." She remembered that he had said he had permits to bring the waterguards here.

"But what—" Pua began as she and Angie rose upward on the back of another swell.

"Sink, Pua. This is serious."

Pua disappeared. They met the rays underwater and swam farther back from the bus. Very carefully, Angie surfaced again, just long enough to see that the swimmers had returned to the deck of the bus. She gave Pua a thumbs-up signal under the water. The bus was well and truly crippled. There was no way they could remove the coiler without lasers, and that would damage the foil.

The bus was wallowing in the rough seas, riding off-angle and deep in the water. They could not achieve hydrofoil lift, so they would have to proceed to Pukui hull down. They would be lucky to make more than fifteen kilometers per hour. Pua and her rays had given Pukui at least a fourteen-hour reprieve.

When Angie submerged, she gave Pua a sound hug—laughing at the girl's look of astonishment—then motioned them back toward Pukui.

They found Fatu in the community cookhouse, pounding boiled taro root with a stone pounder twice the size of his massive fist. His oiled body glistened in the morning sunlight. He swayed to the rhythm of his strokes and the beat of some ancient Island chant.

Pua motioned Angie to silence and squatted just outside the open door to watch and listen. Angie, not sure she would be able to get up again if she sat down now, leaned against the doorjamb. She wasn't aware of making any sound, but Fatu stopped suddenly, in midstroke, and turned toward them. He was on his feet instantly.

"Please don't throw that," Angie said quickly as his grip tightened on the pounder. "I'm not sure I could dodge it right now."

"Where is Pua?" he demanded.

"I'm right here," Pua said.

He turned his startled look toward her, and the tension drained visibly from his stance. "Where were you all night?" he asked.

"We went to meet the bus," Pua said. She stood. "We dumped it right in the water, Fatu!"

"What?"

"Crawley was coming to Pukui on one of the Company buses, so the rays and I snapped a coiler around one of the hydrofoil wings and wrecked it. You should have seen her, Fatu! That coiler was the biggest one I've ever seen, and the rays held her in their teeth. They said after that it was fun, and wanted to do it again, but I wouldn't let 'em, 'cause we only needed to do it once. And anyway, I don't think Le Fe'e would have given us another coiler. This one might get killed if they try to use lasers to get her off."

Fatu knelt in front of Pua and took her shoulders in his hands. *"What* are you talking about?"

"The bus," Pua said. "The Company bus was bringing Crawley and the Earthers, so we wrecked it."

He glanced at Angie, then back at Pua. "You sank a *hydrobus*?" His expression made it clear that he believed her fully capable of doing such a thing.

"With a coiler," Pua said proudly.

"They didn't sink it," Angie said. "The bus is just disabled and slowed way down. The passengers might have a few broken bones and plenty of bruises from the sudden stop, but nothing more serious."

"Holy mother of god," he said.

"They did the methane blow at Uncle Kobe's," Pua said. "That's why Mr. Crawley's on the bus. He didn't want to wait till tomorrow for the air transports to get back to Landing."

Fatu's attention snapped back to Angie. "You opened the incoming comm lines?"

"Just enough to get information. No Company orders got through. I made sure of that. I presume that's why you set up the scramble?"

He nodded slowly.

"What's all the food for?" Pua asked. She peered around him into the cookhouse. "Hi, Katie," she called.

Fatu shook himself slightly. His look remained on Angie. "Was it your idea to go after the hydrofoil?"

Angie shook her head. "I was just an observer. Remember how you said you weren't sure which of Pua's stories were true? After what I saw tonight, I'd be willing to bet most of them are."

Pua tugged at Fatu's lavalava. "What's the food for?" she asked again.

"A welcoming feast," he said.

"For Crawley?" Pua voiced Angie's startlement.

"Just because we don't like him," Fatu said, "doesn't mean he's not an important guest—and he's not coming alone." He looked back at Angie. "You've been studying Island history, Warden, you should understand the importance of a welcoming feast and its attendant ceremony, particularly under the present circumstances. Lesaat custom dictates that we treat our Earth visitors with proper Island protocol."

Angie stared at him for a moment, before suddenly understanding. "Present circumstances meaning the need to gain as much time as possible before Crawley takes control of Pukui?"

He nodded and seemed to relax slightly.

"Do you think he'll stand for it?" she asked. "He's not likely to be interested in formal greetings and food presentations. He'll want to get right down to business."

"Crawley has sat through feasts on Lesaat before," Fatu said. His voice and his body had grown calm again, although he remained obviously and fully alert. "Most of the inspection team he's bringing have, too. Earthers consider 'traditional' Lesaat feasts to be one of the perks of traveling this far. It gives them the chance to yuk it up with—and at—the 'natives.' "

"So even if Crawley objects, the others are likely to want to go through with it," Angie said. "It might just work."

"Crawley accepted food from Lehua the morning she died," Fatu said. "He won't conduct business here again without first facing full and formal Pukui ceremony."

"I'm not sure any of those Earthers are going to feel like eating when they get off that bus," Pua said.

"That's true," Angie said. "Have you checked the weather map recently, Fatu? The swells out there seem awfully strong."

"The storm's moving slowly, but it's still on track to the northwest. It'll parallel Pukui for a while more before moving out of our range," he said. "The only thing showing behind it is a full seven days away. If we can keep the Company crews working for at least one more day, we'll be able to clear the rest of the algae on our own." He paused. "Are we working together on this, Warden?"

"We've been working together all along, Fatu. It's just that neither of us was sure of the other's boundaries."

He waited.

"Pili has your habit of silent patience," she said.

He blinked and tensed. "You met him?"

It was her turn to nod.

"Do not mistake my self-control for patience," he said softly.

There was no danger of that. "We went to Sa le Fe'e," she confessed. "I saw five of the kids. Six, counting Pili. I spoke briefly with Nola. Then we left. Nobody got hurt."

"How did you get out?' he asked. "Nola wouldn't have let you go willingly, not without authorization from here."

Angie nodded toward Pua, who had squatted beside Fatu's pounding board and was scooping up wads of taro paste to suck noisily from her fingers.

Fatu sighed. "With Kiki and Keha's help, no doubt."

"And Pili's," Angie said.

"Of course. There's no way Pili would stand aside if there was trouble to get into. He and Pua are a pair."

"So I saw," she said, smiling. "Are you familiar with the Native Reparations Act, Fatu?"

His eyes darkened. "The sellout of Earth's last few indigenous peoples?" he said. "Of course I'm familiar with it. I grew up on one of the reef reservations, remember?" He motioned toward Pua. "Her mother grew up on that pitiful piece of land at South Point, thanks to that tide-pissing act."

"I spent some time studying it tonight," Angie said. "I think I might be able to use it to help your kids."

He shook his head. "We already tried that, years ago when they first changed the inheritance laws. Earthers on Lesaat are formally classified as immigrants, not indigenous peoples. Native rights don't apply here. Neither the Company nor the U.N. will even listen to your case.''

''They might,'' she told him, ''if the natives in question control access to the TC enzyme.''

He blinked, caught his breath, then became very still. ''You found the records?'' he said very softly.

She nodded. ''Lehua told me where they are.''

He reached for her, but she stepped easily aside.

''What—'' Pua began.

Angie and Fatu faced each other. ''You couldn't beat this out of me any more than I could you, if you were the one who knew, Fatu,'' she said. ''So, for the sake of my aching body, let's not waste time trying, all right?''

''What's going on?'' Pua demanded. ''Why are you fighting?''

''Does Pua know?''

Angie shook her head.

''Know what?'' Pua stopped. She looked from Angie to Fatu, then back again at Angie.

Angie smiled. ''Now, it's *my turn*, Waterbaby.''

Chapter 22

The warden's plan made sense. Fatu recognized that; he even agreed to implement it. But it still left him highly uncomfortable.

He found himself watching the woman with deep suspicion. How, after all that time, had she found the missing records? Pua swore she and the warden had been together the entire night. The only time the woman had been alone was while she was studying the computer files in the underwater pump station—and she only laughed and shook her head when they asked her if the TC records were there.

"They're much closer than that," was all she would say. They finished the food preparations and transferred the entire feast to Second Island. The wind was still rising, and rain squalls were frequent, making an outdoor event impossible. Fatu did not want to use crews' quarters or the main house to stage his ceremony, so he chose the burial cave instead. In addition to offering the best storm shelter at Pukui, the cave seemed the most appropriate place to confront Crawley and his minions.

The warden agreed readily, but Pua balked.

"I don't want to go in there with the ghosts," she said.

"The spirits in that cave belong to Pukui," Fatu assured her. "If they are angered by anyone's presence, it won't be by ours. The ghosts of Pukui's dead would never do anything to hurt you."

"How are they going to tell us apart?" she asked. "Auntie Puhi said some of those Earthers on the hydrobus have gills. What if the ghosts get us mixed up?"

"Nothing bothered me while I was in the cave," the warden said. "And I was entirely new to Pukui then."

Pua glared at her. "Well, of course they wouldn't bother *you*! You're practically one of them!"

The warden started. Pua declined to explain the remark, but the warden obviously found it intriguing. Several times during the morning, Fatu caught glimpses of her standing very still inside the cave, one or both hands spread across the cool, damp stone. She appeared to be listening.

Pua agreed to the site finally, but during their preparations, she rarely moved past the entrance to the cave. She carried food packages and supplies, clicker fronds, and armloads of friendly vines just inside, then hurriedly retreated. At first, Katie was reticent about working in the cave, too, but the warden talked her into it with a handful of Maldarian caramels.

By midday, preparations in the cave were complete. They had been held up only once, when the warden stood to stretch in a low-ceilinged portion of the cave. Her fingers brushed the trailing roots of friendly vine plants and were immediately tangled in the strong, thin fibers. The roots wrapped much faster and tighter than their companion vines growing aboveground. Fatu had laughed and cut her free, but Pua began glancing at dark corners again.

Pua and the warden slept for two hours, while Fatu remained awake to watch. Then they all joined the net crews. The crippled bus would be easy to spot as it approached the reef, so there would be time to return to the Second Island dock well before the bus reached it.

The water was rough in the outer lagoon. Great rolling waves crashed over the exposed western barrier reef, churning the shallows atop the reef flat into a froth. The tide was still low enough that most of the turbulence remained in the outer lagoon, but even the inner lagoon waters were increasingly dangerous to the swimmers.

Zena kept a constant check on the satellite reports of the passing storm, and at the warden's orders was prepared to pull the swimmers from the water at any point she felt it was too dangerous for them to continue.

"I don't remember ever getting this much surge from a storm so far off," Zena said as evening approached. "Feels more like it's coming right at us."

Fatu frowned toward the horizon. The ominous mass of clouds felt too close. "We can be glad this one *isn't* coming at us. It's a great-grandmother of a storm even if the cameras don't show it."

"Swimmers are getting edgy," Zena said.

Fatu nodded. "Keep 'em in the water as long as you can. Remind them there's clear sky due tomorrow and the warden set a double bonus for anyone working tonight. You know it's supposed to mean good luck if you pass the night of alignment before the first big storm hits."

Zena nodded, but her dark expression didn't change. She continued to watch the horizon. They both ignored the *Pull crew* order that flickered on the incoming-message screen. Lili was underwater with her crews and had not seen the order. She had, in fact, not come near the comm for the past several hours.

"The Company guards will probably take to the water as soon as they're inside the pass," Fatu said. "They won't be carrying lasers—the Company won't take a chance on breaking the law now. But they'll have spearguns and knives, and they know how to use them." He tapped the message screen as he was about to leave. "Be sure this gets busted before they get here."

"Aye," Zena replied. Her steady gaze never left the sky.

Fatu ordered two swimmers to meet the bus at the farm pass and lead it to the Second Island dock. Then he went there himself with the aid of one of Pua's rays. He was amazed at how calm the giant creatures were in the turbulent waters. They seemed entirely under Pua's control. She rode with him and the warden as far as the dock, then disappeared back under the water. She had promised to return in time for the feast.

The dock was located inside the channel between the two islands, where it was protected somewhat from the wind. The wind still gusted with force from time to time, however, and the sound of it whistling through the trees on the upper slopes echoed eerily. Fatu checked the satellite map again before joining the warden in a nearby freshwater overflow stream. They rinsed away the taste of the sea, then checked the cave one last time.

When everything was prepared to his satisfaction, Fatu carefully wrapped his finest formal lavalava around his waist and fastened it with a wide, woven belt.

"Is that candleberry?" the warden asked as he rubbed sweet-smelling oil onto his arms and chest.

He nodded. "From the bush in Lehua's room. I want her to be here for this."

She was standing with one hand on the wall, completely at ease in the cave. She had donned a clean shirt and trousers of the same color she always wore, green on green. She wore no insignia of rank.

"Lehua is here now," she said.

"How is it that a mainlander like you feels the spirits of this place so clearly?" he asked.

She smiled. "Islanders aren't the only humans who maintain conscious connections with their environment, Fatu. I was brought up close to the land. I was taught to pay attention to it. Not many who grow up in the industrialized world have that opportunity anymore. Most are insulated from the land from the moment they're born, and they grow up believing that's the way it's supposed to be. Technomythology, I call it—the mistaken belief that technology is the prime factor, and the natural world just its adjunct."

He glanced toward the med kit she had brought into the cave. "You still make use of technology," he said.

"Does a Samoan refuse a fish because it was caught in a plastic net?" she replied.

He lifted a brow. "You're very skilled at using other people's cultural values to rationalize your own."

She shrugged.

Fatu glanced up at the trailing friendly vines. "I envy you," he said. "I envy you your role as a warrior here at Pukui." He lifted his hands and stared at his calloused palms. "I am a strong man. I am not afraid to fight or to die. I was one of those who made the original decision to take this course, and I have been a part of it ever since. Yet it is you, a stranger, and Toma and—and sweet Pua who must continually face the enemy directly."

He stared around at the cave, which was almost festive in its ceremonial splendor. "Always, I must remain at the side. Watching, controlling our enemies' actions by my own inaction. Even now, on this day of final confrontation, all I can do is offer welcome to the very people who are trying to steal our land and our children."

"No honest cause succeeds without a strong heart," the warden said. "You once told me that names carry great meaning here. Your own name translates as the 'rock' or 'heart' of the island, the strength of the families. Your role of silent patience is, by far, the most difficult one.

"But it was your strength that allowed Pua to survive the Earth recon station, Fatu. I realized that as soon as I saw you together. It was you who kept Pukui from being destroyed all those months

Pua was away. And it is you who have provided us with the means to set the battle in motion tonight."

"I would rather be the one who cracks the bastards' skulls," he said. He left her there in the cave and descended to meet the bus.

Toma looked exhausted when he came ashore. It was clear that the long, slow trip had been difficult, even for those fortunate few who had not become sick along the way. The deck of the crippled bus was strewn with the wreckage of its abrupt encounter with the coiler. Injured and exhausted Earthers lay amid tangles of broken line and scattered cargo.

"What the hell happened?" Fatu asked, feigning surprise.

"You're never going to believe it," Toma said. He reached out to assist one of the Earthers onto the dock. She was an elderly woman, whom Fatu recognized as a member of the U.N. team. He pointed her toward several Pukui swimmers at the end of the dock. They would guide the visitors to the stream and then the cave. They and their less obvious companions would also serve to keep an eye on the Earther waterguards still in Crawley's party.

"We were two and a half hours out, running smooth," Toma said, "when a reef-loving coilar hit one of the hydro struts. Damn thing's almost as big around as you are, and it's wrapped so tight around that wing, it'll take lasers to get it off." He wiped an arm across his forehead. "We couldn't get hydrofoil lift, and the wing couldn't retract all the way, so we had to come in hull down at full slow. I couldn't even call Landing for a rescue bus—the comm got smashed in the crash. It was not a comfortable trip."

Nori Yoshida stepped onto the dock as Toma was speaking. He looked as primly clean as the last time Fatu had seen him, although considerably more tired. Somehow it did not surprise Fatu that the inspector was not prone to seasickness. He did, however, smell. The entire bus stank—of overstrained engines, spilled fuel, and human sweat and vomit.

"A coiler?" Fatu had no trouble expressing his shock. Even after all these hours and seeing the damaged bus itself, he still had trouble believing it.

"That's what's causing the starboard list," Toma said. "I'll take you down later for a look. Maybe you can figure a way to get it off. Right now, we've got a lot of sick Earthers on our hands."

Fatu expressed what he hoped was an appropriate amount of

sympathy for the bus's passengers and crew. He directed another stumbling Earther past Yoshida, who did nothing to help, then asked, "What were you doing on a bus in the first place? Crawley and the inspector, here, were never interested in the scenic tour before."

Crawley appeared at the door of the bus's cabin. He was being supported by the elderly Dr. Waight, who looked as cold and hard and healthy as she had the morning Zed and Lehua had been taken away. Fatu gained a moment of satisfaction from the fact that Crawley had obviously not fared as well. The admin man looked positively green.

Toma explained about the methane fire at Kobayashi's Reef. "The rest of Crawley's security guards will be out when air transport is available. Probably sometime tomorrow morning."

Fatu frowned. "Just what Pukui needs. More tide-pissin' Company swimmers who don't know what they're doing." Yoshida shifted but said nothing.

"Were there injuries at Kobe's?" Fatu asked as Crawley and Waight approached the side of the bus. He would be expected to show concern.

"A few burns," Toma said. "One swimmer got tangled in a hunk of torn netting, but they got her out with just bruises and a couple of gashes on her legs. She'll carry scars, but she'll swim again. They figure a week or more on the cleanup. A lot of good reef is going to be lost." A small price to pay, his eyes said, if it has helped to save Pukui.

As Crawley stepped onto the dock, he pushed away from the old woman. He stank worse than Yoshida, and the makeup he always wore was smeared and streaked. It highlighted the scars on his cheek.

Good for you, Pua, Fatu thought. There was no mistaking the shape of scars left by a waterworlder's nails, and at least one of those crisscrossing Crawley's right cheek was old enough that it could only have been made by Pua. Either she or the warden had gotten him again more recently.

"I want you to send as many Company swimmers as you have transportation for to Kobayashi's Reef," Crawley said. He coughed and spat into the water. His breath reeked. He swayed, but pushed Dr. Waight's arm away.

"I told you," Toma said wearily, "it won't do any good to disrupt things here at Pukui now. There's nothing more that needs doing out at Kobe's that can't be done by the crews already there."

"I'm not talking to you, Doctor Haili." Crawley's sharp glance snapped back to Fatu. "You heard my order," he said. "Get on it."

"It's a long swim to Kobe's," Fatu said calmly.

Crawley frowned. He glanced at Toma, then at Yoshida, who was still standing close by, then back at Fatu.

"We *have* no transport here at Pukui," Fatu went on. "Company orders have stripped us of all but the slowest of inner-lagoon vessels. The only thing that could even make it there is the disposal barge, and that would take at least a week."

"You have flitters," Yoshida said. "You can ferry—"

"We *had* flitters," Fatu said, turning to him. "One is down for routine maintenance, two have been sabotaged by only the reef knows who, and the rest were conscripted for Company use months ago. The only properly working long-distance flit we have is the warden's, and that's not here right now."

"You had no business allowing that woman to leave Pukui," Yoshida snapped. It was a small slip, enough to let Fatu know that they had, indeed, been tracing the locators.

"She's *your woman*, Inspector. *You* keep track of her."

Something deep in Yoshida's dark eyes confirmed what Fatu had suspected but had not been able to determine from the warden's few cryptic comments: Yoshida had been the warden's lover—and he had used that relationship to deceive her. Not for anything along the wormhole would I want to be in your shoes right now, Inspector, he thought. He glanced down. The Company inspector was actually wearing shoes. Fatu bit back a smile.

"Why did you bring us here to this godforsaken place?" Crawley demanded. "I won't allow any more stalling, Fatu. I want—" He collapsed in on himself, clutching his stomach. He dropped to his knees and heaved. After hours of seasickness on the bus, there was nothing left to come up but a thin string of yellow mucus. Yoshida stepped back.

Fatu steadied Crawley, then lifted him again to his feet. "Come on," he said. "You'll feel better after a bath and something to eat." Crawley almost heaved again, but controlled the reflex.

"The wind and tide are too high to use the main dock," Fatu explained as he led Crawley and the others toward the makeshift bathing area. "We've set up a shelter in the burial cave. It'll be safer there if the storm gets worse. It shouldn't, but it never hurts to be careful."

"I want all the Company crews out of the water," Crawley said. "Do it now!"

"Seas aren't all that rough yet," Fatu said.

"Do it!" Crawley shouted. "Send an order out to those barges *now*."

"You already sent the order through your waterguards," Toma said.

"Barge comm's been out for the last two hours," Fatu added. "Something got dropped on it, I think."

"This is just another one of your—"

"You should take better care of yourself, Crawley. You look terrible."

They all stopped at the warden's unexpected voice. She was leaning, arms folded, against the bole of a clicker-palm tree. Her green on green, and her absolute stillness, had kept her invisible even to Fatu.

"What are you doing here?" Crawley said. His shock at her presence was gratifyingly clear.

She lifted one brow. "Where else would I be?"

"But your—" He caught himself. "He—Fatu said you left in the flitter."

"I'm back," she said. She nodded at Dr. Waight, who was staring at her casually displayed hands, then turned her slow look toward Yoshida. "Hello, Nori," she said. Her voice was so pleasant it sent chills up Fatu's back.

"Warden," Yoshida replied softly. He, too, was staring at her hands.

"Fatu has prepared a welcoming feast," the warden said without turning away from Yoshida. "You'll probably want to clean up and rest a bit first. Then we can start the ceremonies."

"We're not going through any phony ceremonies," Crawley said. "You order those crews out of the water right now." He glanced around at the watching, listening U.N. inspection team. "It's—too dangerous to keep them working in this storm."

The warden eyed him for a moment, then motioned one of the Pukui swimmers nearer. "Take word out to Zena that Lili can pull her crews till the weather clears," she told him. "Then tell Lili and the other crew bosses to come up and join us. The non-Company crews don't need them on-site, and they're probably ready for a little merry-making about now. They've all put in a heavy day's work."

"You've exceeded your authority, Dinsman," Crawley said.

"You weren't supposed to destroy any of that algae until the TC records were found. I want an explanation, and I want it—"

"Get yourself cleaned up, then we'll talk about it," she replied. She stood away from the tree and started along the path to the stream.

From close behind him, Fatu heard the soft click of Toma's fingernails. *Is she with us?* Toma asked.

Fatu clicked a quick affirmative. Then he thought for a moment and offered Toma a second reply, a visual one this time. He moved his hand to where Toma could see it, and crossed his fingers.

Chapter 23

Angie paused outside the cave entrance.

". . . don't give a damn what she said." Crawley's voice came from just inside. "You never should have allowed the harvesting to begin."

"You're the one who sent her out here," Fatu replied.

"She claimed troubleshooter's privileges," Toma said smoothly, "and according to her contract . . ."

Angie glanced at Nori, who had climbed the path just behind her. He was dressed in a fresh uniform, ordered ashore from the bus through one of the waterguards. The inspector's insignia flashed on his sleeve as he lifted his hand to run it through his wet hair. The wind whipped the hair back onto his forehead. He met her look and lowered his hand.

"You still look surprised to see me here, Nori," she said. "You know, you really shouldn't have put all that much faith in a hidden locator. Things like that tend to get misplaced in situations like this."

"When did you realize you were carrying it?" he asked.

"Right after I got here," she lied. "We've had rather a bit of fun with those things, Pua and I. Especially Pua. You'd be amazed at the variety of creatures she's managed to attach them to, and the places they've gone."

He didn't want to believe that. He didn't want to believe that all the tracking he and his people had been doing over the past weeks had been for nothing. There were probably waterguards out there at this very moment following Pua's weeks-old trail.

"If that's true, why did you wait until last night to send them away from Pukui?" His voice only hinted at his irritation. He had obviously been tracking the locators closely ever since his arrival. The unavailability of a flitter must have aggravated him dearly.

She shrugged. "Turnabout's fair play, *Inspector*. You've surprised me a few times recently."

"You had no way of knowing I was coming . . ."

"Nori love, Crawley would never come out here alone, and—" She touched her fingertips to his cheek, and he flinched. "—I knew you'd never give up the opportunity to pay me a visit."

She laughed at his horrified yet fascinated look at her long, webbed fingers. "You're not afraid of me, are you, Nori?"

His look snapped back to her face. "Of course not."

She touched him again, and although he tensed, he did not pull away. Oh, Nori, she thought. You're so afraid of me right now, you're about to pee your pants. "I'd hate to think things had changed between us."

Startled curiosity flickered in his dark eyes. His short hair blew forward. He pushed it back.

"It's been a long dry spell here in this wet, wet place," she said. And hearing that, he actually smiled. How, she thought, was I ever taken in by this tide-pissing liar? Because she always relaxed her normal troubleshooter's vigilance when she went to the mountain preserve. She *went* there to relax, and the Company and Nori had taken advantage of that. I won't relax here, she promised.

Crawley's colorless voice called them into the cave.

"Have you seen Pua?" Fatu murmured as Angie passed him on her way in.

She shook her head. Both Crawley and Dr. Waight had already asked about Pua on the way uphill. Angie hoped the girl would come. Her case would be difficult to plead without her physical presence.

The U.N. reps were eager to relax. Bathing and getting solid land under their feet had abated most of the nausea they had experienced on the bus, and Crawley's objections to the welcoming ceremony were easily overcome. They sat on stacks of friendly vine and clicker leaves, looking drained but tremendously relieved to be safe and dry and out of the wind.

Three of the nine had elected to remain wrapped in the colorful lavalavas they had been given at the freshwater stream. The others had changed into clothing brought off the bus. None, Angie was pleased to see, had been seriously injured in the hydrobus incident. They seemed to consider it more an adventure than an accident, now that it was over. Crawley sat slightly apart from the rest, scowling and rubbing at his scarred cheek.

The Earther waterguards had not fared as well. Most had been on deck when the coiler caused the abrupt stop and skew of the bus. They had been thrown hard against cargo and deck gear. The worst of the injured, five with broken bones and four more with deep gashes, had already been attended to, but Dr. Waight and another woman, obviously a medic, moved among them applying clean bandages and administering anesthetics. The guards' gray uniforms stood out clearly in the bright light of fluorescent lamps.

Seven healthy guards had accompanied Crawley and their injured comrades to Second Island. Two of those stayed with the bus, while the rest climbed the hill to the cave. The others had gone into the water as soon as they were inside the pass—to see to the orderly withdrawal of Company swimmers from the harvesting operations, Crawley had claimed.

Fatu seated the guests in a floor plan that vaguely fit Angie's impression of the formal seating arrangements described in the Samoan history tapes she had studied. She, not surprisingly, found herself sandwiched between Fatu and Toma near the entrance to the cave. Crawley sat opposite, flanked on one side by Waight and on the other by the leader of the inspection team. The rest of the team, and the Lesaat crew leaders, sat along the sides, creating an open oval center. Nori was placed in the second row behind the crew leaders and among the injured waterguards. He did not look pleased.

The welcoming feast would be based on no single Earth island cultural tradition, Fatu had explained to Angie earlier, but rather on as many as he could remember. "We'll do it the Lesaat way," he said. "Whatever works best and takes up the most time."

When everyone was settled, he began. First, he had one of the Pukui swimmers pass sticks of betel coral and Maldarian caramels among them, apologizing all the while for the lack of a proper kava-drinking ceremony. Then he greeted all of the visitors very formally, listing them by rank and title, and welcoming them to Pukui. He continued with a long speech describing the reef and its history, its current troubles, and Pukui's appreciation for the honesty and generosity of its distinguished visitors.

He spoke with great emotion, almost whispering at times, then lifting his voice in laughter or shouting with great power.

He gestured freely with his hands and occasionally flicked the large and bulky sennit whisk he carried for emphasis. Angie recognized the fly whisk as a true relic of Earth, one of the symbols of office of a Samoan high chief. There had been several smaller imitations on display in the main house.

There was a stunned pause when Fatu finished. He had left them all breathless. Into the silence, Fatu invited Crawley to speak.

"Don't be absurd," Crawley replied. "Get this thing over with. We have business to do."

Fatu gave him such a polite nod that even Yoshida looked embarrassed. Many of the U.N. team members frowned. "Who, then, will speak for our Company visitors?" Fatu asked.

Toma rose. He spoke eloquently for the Company, addressing World Life's sincere desire to aid the peoples of the Earth, as well as the inhabitants of Lesaat and Pukui. The decisions they would make at this meeting of friends, he said, might certainly prove to be difficult, but they would be made with fairness to all and with careful attention to the law. Fatu and the waterworlders, and even some of the U.N. team, nodded their approval. Crawley scowled throughout.

The U.N. team leader spoke then. He had obviously done this before and, although somewhat embarrassed, seemed to enjoy his role. His speech was eloquent enough, but it sounded as if it had been memorized and, most probably, used before.

Others spoke. Waterworlders, mostly. Leaders of the crews that had come to assist in the emergency harvest. Angie glanced toward the cave entrance. She saw Fatu do the same. There was still no sign of Pua. Fatu enticed several more members of the U.N. team to speak, poking gentle fun at them for their reticence. That part was more reminiscent of a resort-town tourist show than proper Island ceremony, but it took up time.

Angie had yet to speak; she had not really planned to, not at this point in the proceedings. But without Pua, she might be forced to. She was debating how to begin when there was unexpected movement at the back of the cave. Pua appeared from the deepest shadows. Crawley spun around at the sound of her approach. She stopped less than a meter behind him and could easily have touched him if she had so chosen. The entire gathering watched her in stunned silence.

Pua stared at Crawley for a moment, then walked slowly around the center oval of seated adults. The only sounds were those she, alone, made. Dozens of tiny shells clipped and clicked together at the edges of her shirt and on the elaborate woven headdress she wore. Her skirt of thick, wide leaves rustled and sighed. She wore layer after layer of strung shells and coral around her neck, and friendly vines and seaweed were woven in colorful patterns around her torso and along her arms and legs.

She carried a whisk just slightly smaller than Fatu's, made of some local material, and a carved pole that Angie assumed was meant to represent an orator's staff. She circled, stared at each of the visitors, at Fatu and Angie and all the rest, before returning to her starting place.

She lifted a hand.

"Greetings to all the chiefs and talking chiefs gathered here at Pukui," she began.

"Hail to the spirits of this dark cave, where the bones of Pukui's heroes are laid.

"Hail to the great spirit of Le Fe'e, who has given his blessing for this important meeting and who stands guard over the children of this lagoon."

Angie glanced at Fatu. If he found Pua's highly distorted imitation of a Samoan high talking chief offensive, he did not show it. His face held only stunned amazement. His fragrant body remained absolutely still.

Only once during Pua's long list of honorific greetings did he react, and then it was with a quickly suppressed smile. Angie reminded herself to look up the Samoan term that Pua had used in reference to Nori.

Fatu was not the only one caught by Pua's performance. Only Nori and Toma were glancing about like Angie. Toma smiled a small, cool smile when their looks met. Nori eyed them both coldly and passed his look on. Everyone else was transfixed by the chanting girl. Angie listened again as Pua completed her list of honorific greetings.

"They call me Pualeiokekai noun Zedediah me Kalehuaokalae Pukui," she said then. "I am the first of my kind. I live in Lesaat's great golden sea with my family and with Le Fe'e, who is my friend."

She flicked her fly whisk precisely as Fatu had earlier. "You probably remember Le Fe'e. He once lived on the planet you call Earth. But he was always restless there. Ask the Hawaiians. They know. He moved from place to place, shifting his colors, never content, because deep in his heart he knew there was another place. A better place. A place with rich golden waters, and peopled only by creatures who know how to smile with their eyes. One day, he decided to seek this sea . . ."

Pua slid smoothly into the colorful tale of Le Fe'e's journey from Earth to Lesaat, the one Fatu had told Angie in the sub weeks before.

Pua chanted her story; she sang it like a song. She moved and swayed with the rhythm of her tale, and the soft click and rustle of shells and leaves provided music to fill the small silences between her words. *This is her creation chant,* Angie realized suddenly. *She is sharing the beginnings of her personal identity with us.* She realized, too, that she had heard the song before. Last night, deep under the sea.

It was Le Fe'e's song.

"I offer you this kumulipo," Pua said finally. "This story of the beginnings of my people. Taste it and know what it is to be of Pukui and the Lesaat Sea."

There was total silence when she finished. She maintained her own silence for a moment, proving that she was as fine an actress as she was a storyteller. Then she flicked her whisk and stepped between Crawley and Waight to the center of the neatly laid clicker fronds.

To Angie's total amazement—and Fatu and Toma's, as well, judging from their quick intakes of breath—Katie followed Pua into the circle. She, too, was decked with shells and twisted vines, although not as regally as Pua. She carried a large, leaf-covered wooden bowl, another artifact from Lehua's collection, which Pua instructed her to set before Crawley. Pua thanked Katie formally. When the drone had disappeared again into the shadows, Pua sat cross-legged in front of the bowl.

"Welcome," she said, staring straight at Crawley. "Please accept this small amount of food which Pukui has provided." She lifted a pair of broad leaves to reveal a huge mass of dark green paste.

"Oh, dear god," Fatu breathed. Others among the waterworlders caught their breaths. Toma was on his feet instantly.

"What is it?" Angie asked.

Fatu had gone pale. "She's offering Crawley boiled loli."

"I'll show you how it's eaten," Pua said in her most innocent, childlike voice. The U.N. team members smiled, oblivious to the tension among the waterworlders. Pua scooped up a fingerful of paste.

"Get the rest of the food in here," Angie said. "Do it now." She quickly joined Toma at Pua's side, having no idea how she was going to stop Pua if poisoning Crawley was what she had in mind. Crawley stared at all three of them suspiciously.

The U.N. leader nudged him in the side. "Go ahead," he whispered. "Take some. It's impolite to refuse food here on Lesaat. You know that."

Pua sucked loli from her fingertips noisily.

"Pua," Toma said. "The first food should be offered to Warden Dinsman. She is, after all, our highest ranking guest."

Angie felt her jaw go slack. You reef-sucker, she said to Toma with her eyes. He smiled in return. She quickly composed herself.

Pua blinked. "She is?"

"Technically, that's true," the U.N. rep said. He was smiling, enjoying himself greatly. Crawley stared at each of them, obviously not sure what was going on but knowing that something was. Angie looked down at the potentially deadly loli, wondering if Pua would really let her die. There was no way to know until the next day if the loli was bad, and by then Angie would have accomplished all that Pua needed done to protect her and her babies.

"Help yourself, Auntie Puhi," Pua said. Her face revealed no expression whatsoever.

Angie gave Toma one glaring glance before scooping up a gob of loli paste. She had to trust that Pua would not let her eat it if it carried the deadly loli fever bacteria. Before it reached her mouth, however, Fatu reached over her shoulder.

"You forgot my rank," he said as he, too, lifted a fingerful of loli. Pua made no move to stop him. She watched them both solemnly as they sucked the paste from their fingers, chewed for a moment, and swallowed.

Then she smiled sweetly. "Where's the rest of the food?" she asked. "These people look like they're starving."

The tension was abruptly broken, at least among those who didn't understand what had been going on. Angie counted to still her heart. Platters of food were quickly circulated, and the Earthers, many of them famished after being emptied so thoroughly on the hydrobus, greeted the meal enthusiastically.

Angie glanced at Fatu, who was only then regaining color in his cheeks, and returned to her former place. She looked up to see Nori standing against the far wall. He gave her a slow grin. *He* had known what the loli was. And he had done nothing to warn Crawley about the food's possibly deadly contents.

The meal proceeded without further incident. Pua entertained the visiting Earthers with stories of life on the atoll, speaking seriously with them at some times, charming them with her wit and laughter at others. She even drew a smile from some of the waterguards. Crawley and Dr. Waight were the only ones not pleased. Several times, Angie saw Waight reach for Pua's hands, but Pua always moved smoothly and seemingly innocently away from her touch.

You'll get your chance at her soon enough, bitch, Angie thought. Late into the meal, a swimmer slipped through the entrance and spoke briefly to Fatu, then left again. A waterguard came in and did the same with Nori. Nori relayed the message to Crawley, and for the first time that evening, Crawley smiled.

Trouble at the nets, Angie thought, not caused solely by the storm. Thank goodness they had a few days of calm weather coming. With luck, any damage done that night could be cleaned up before permanent harm was done. Still, if Crawley was happy, it was time to move things along. She stood.

"I would like to conduct some business," she said. Her voice was soft, but her words brought an immediate hush over the gathering. She motioned for Pua to bring her the med-recorder kit she had brought into the cave earlier. She handed it to one of the U.N. members who examined it silently, nodded, and handed it back. That brought absolute silence.

"I was sent here to do two things," Angie said. "To find the missing total-conversion enzyme records, and to save Pukui Reef. I find that to accomplish at least one of those goals, I must invade the privacy of our host. I have chosen to do it now, before witnesses. Fatu, will you join me?"

Fatu showed just the right amount of reluctance.

"Warden," Toma said quickly. "Is this really necessary?"

"It is," she said. Crawley's thin lips twisted into a tight smile.

"Fatu?" Angie said again, and finally he joined her. They sat facing each other on the cool, smooth clicker-palm leaves. His skin shone in the brilliant light. His candleberry scent teased her across the short distance between them, and his shallow breathing belied his outward appearance of calm. Nori edged forward and pushed his way in between two of the waterworld crew leaders. They frowned but, at Fatu's lifted hand, allowed him to remain.

Angie snapped on the recorder.

"Angela Roberta Dinsman, troubleshooter first rank," she said. "Second Island, Pukui Atoll, Lesaat. I am conducting this interrogation at the request of other interested parties, but ultimately by my own decision. I am under no personal coercion. I have found no other way to accomplish what needs to be done."

"I protest the use of drugs," Fatu said. "I am a free citizen of Lesaat and offer to speak freely without drug intervention."

"Do you know where the total-conversion records are?" she asked.

"I do not."

"This is the only way I have of proving that," she said. "Toma, you're the keeper of the law here. Can you name any reason why I shouldn't question this man, given the seriousness of the situation?" Angie hoped Fatu had had a chance to tell him they were working together. It would be awkward if she had to stop now.

Toma stared at Fatu for a long moment. "The 'interested parties' must be formally recorded before you begin," he said.

Angie nodded, relieved, and turned toward Crawley. "World Life Company," he snapped. "On behalf of the United Nations Earth Preservation Service."

"The United Nations, on behalf of all the peoples of Earth," the U.N. rep said.

And then into the brief silence, "Pualeiokekai noun Zedediah me Kalehuaokalae Pukui, on behalf of the children of Lesaat."

"What—" Crawley began.

"Recorded," Toma said, although it was clear that he had not expected Pua's comment. He watched her—they all did—as she made her way to Fatu's side and sat.

Angie broke the seal on the med kit and lifted out a small adhesive patch. Fatu tensed but did not protest as she applied it to the side of his neck. He blinked, then closed his eyes, fighting the drug despite his agreement to their plan. He blinked his eyes open again. "I still protest," he said.

"Will you answer my questions?" she asked.

He shook his head no. He said, "Yes."

Angie sighed. She hated this, even when it was done voluntarily. She ran a quick list of standard questions given in all such interrogations to determine the depth of veracity the drug had induced.

"Fatu, do you know where the missing TC records are?" she asked finally. Crawley and several of the U.N. reps leaned forward.

"No," Fatu said.

Crawley slapped the ground. "He's lying. He has to know."

Angie asked the question again and again, wording it in every possible way. The response remained the same.

"There's something wrong with the drug," Crawley said.

The U.N. rep who had examined the med kit shook her head. "The seal was unbroken," she said. "He's telling the truth."

"Fatu, who is Sa le Fe‘e?" Nori said sharply.

All eyes turned toward Nori, then Angie, then quickly back to Fatu. Fatu remained silent.

"That was the wrong question," Angie said very softly. She lifted a quick hand to stop Nori from speaking again. "And if you speak to my interrogation subject again, I'll have *you* up here. Do you understand me, *Inspector*?"

His chin lifted. The U.N. team members murmured among themselves. "Warden, we'd like you to pursue Mr. Yoshida's question," one of them said. Nori smiled smugly and sat back.

Thank you very much, Nori love, she said silently—and meant it. She turned back to Fatu. "Fatu, what is Sa le Fe‘e?"

Fatu's huge body seemed to cave in on itself. He had held the secret for so long that, even willingly, he had difficulty giving it up.

"It's where we hide our children," he whispered at last.

"Fatu, what children?" she asked above the startled reactions of his audience. It grew silent again.

"Our waterworld children. The changed ones."

"The other ones like Pua?" Angie pressed.

"Yessss . . ." It was a long, soft sigh.

"Fatu, tell us where they—"

Angie backhanded Nori away from Fatu. He tumbled into the waterworlders, who immediately gagged and restrained him. "Take him out of here," Angie said. "Put him someplace safe but not necessarily comfortable." The inspection team buzzed with questions as Nori was wrestled from the cave.

Crawley started to his feet, but Waight whispered something to him and pulled him back down. The waterguards shifted to create a protective phalanx around Crawley and Waight. Interesting, Angie thought, that they don't seem concerned about Yoshida. He and Crawley were definitely not on good terms.

"Fatu," she said, "are the TC records hidden at Sa le Fe‘e?"

"No," he said. Then he frowned. He looked right at her. "I don't think so."

"What is this about other children?" one of the team members asked. "What's he talking about?"

"*Find out where they are,*" Waight urged.

Pua stood. This was the part they had planned—the part Pua had insisted on doing herself. Her earlier performance, Angie now understood, had been designed as a perfect prelude. Pua lifted her hand for silence.

"I'll tell you what Fatu is talking about," she said. Toma looked as if he were about to choke, but Angie shook her head slightly, and he held back.

"My good friend Fatu speaks of the children of Lesaat." Pua's compelling orator's voice and stance returned. "He speaks of the true children. The waterchildren. *My* children. We have remained in hiding because we are so few and our lives are very precious. We are the children of Le Fe‘e, and we ask for your protection."

"We didn't come here to listen to this little brat's nonsense," Crawley said. "Continue questioning the man, Dinsman."

Pua turned to the leader of the U.N. team. He was one of those most closely aligned with Crawley, but it was the proper protocol. Angie had coached Pua very carefully about that.

"We, the true children of Lesaat, invoke our rights as guaranteed under the Native Rights Act of 2017," Pua said. "We petition for the protection of our lives, our lands and waters, and our way of life."

"What—"

"This is ridiculous," Crawley said. "You can't—"

"Is she *serious*?" one of the U.N. people said.

"Are there more like her?" another asked. "I thought she was the only one."

"You were hired to find the TC records for the Company, Dinsman," Crawley shouted. "Not to find ways around Lesaat's inheritance laws. I'm not going to stand for—"

"We're still recording, Mr. Crawley," Angie said, and that shut him up fast.

She stood. "Pua and the others in her small band meet all the traditional and legal requirements set for establishing indigenous-peoples status. They are a small group, culturally and physically isolated, they have their own unique language, and they most definitely live in intimate proximity with their environment. Most important, they exhibit a measurable biological unity, with genetic characteristics found nowhere else among human populations."

She glanced at Crawley. "That last requirement, I believe, was one World Life Company lobbied hard for back in the days when the legal definition of indigenous peoples was being devised." It had virtually guaranteed that no new Earth-bred peoples could claim that status. "Pua's request has been entered on the public net as well as being made formally to this United Nations team. It cannot be withdrawn without some resolution."

"Warden," the U.N. leader said, "this is all very interesting, even moving. And it certainly warrants further study. But what does it have to do with either saving Pukui Reef or finding the total-conversion enzyme? I assure you, those two things, particularly the latter, remain our primary concern here. That is, after all, why you are questioning this man."

"Pua and the children of Lesaat *are* Pukui," Angie said. "We cannot protect one without protecting the other."

"That's rubbish," Crawley said. "You're just—"

"You cannot gain access to the TC enzyme," the warden went on, "without negotiating through Pua. And since I am Pua's legal guardian, you can't deal with her without first dealing with me. Now, shall we discuss this or not?"

Chapter 24

~~~~~~~~~~~~
~~~~~~~~~~~~

Pua just loved it when the mountainlady did things like that—set everything up so that everyone thought they understood but really were confused, and then dropped a bomb on them. The shells at the edges of her headdress tickled the edges of her gill seals as she attempted to restrain her laughter.

Crawley had jumped up and was nose-to-nose with the warden, shouting and gesturing. The warden just stared at him in her calm, quiet way. The others were up as well and were shouting and demanding attention and explanations. Only Dr. Waight and Fatu remained seated. The old lady was probably too full to get up. She had eaten like a pigfish out of every dish but the one containing the loli.

Thinking of that made Pua grin. She had gotten them all with that one, except for Crawley himself, who was too stupid to know what he was being offered.

A hand touched her shoulder and pulled her around. "Is it true? Do you know where your parents' records are?" the U.N. team leader demanded. His breath still smelled faintly of the hydrobus ride. "You have to tell us. They're very important. You can help."

Toma separated them before Pua could answer. "Address your questions to the warden," he said sharply.

"Do you know?" he breathed into Pua's ear.

She shook her head. *But she does*, she clicked. She nodded toward the warden. Toma's eyes widened.

"Stay close to Fatu," he said. "I'll try to settle things down."

Pua squatted beside Fatu and pursed her lips at Dr. Waight, who had been leaning forward toward him. "Get away," Pua said, and the old woman backed off quickly, glowering. Pua lifted a strand of shells from her neck and placed it around Fatu's.

"Fatu," she asked softly. "Can you talk?"

"Yes," he said.

She glanced up at the warden. Toma was trying to intervene between her and Crawley. Neither was paying Pua any attention. She leaned closer to Fatu.

"Do you really have to tell the truth, even if you don't want to?"

"Yes."

She grinned and leaned closer still. "Fatu," she murmured. "What did you and Ehu do together that night after we cleared the puhi from number twelve?"

The warden slid down beside her. "Fatu, don't answer that." She eyed Pua coolly. "Do you want me to put you out in the rain with the inspector, Waterbaby?" she said. But there was laughter behind the words. Pua could hear it, even if no one else could.

Calm began to reassert itself in the cave. As the noise level dropped, the distant sound of pounding surf and wind whistling through the inter island canyon could be heard again. The weather seemed to be getting worse instead of better. Pua suddenly found herself eager to get back to the reef. She became conscious again of being inside the burial cave. She glanced around, but whatever ghosts were there remained hidden.

"This is the situation," the warden said, loudly enough so that everyone stopped talking and listened. Pua wondered if she, too, felt uneasy about this storm that wouldn't stop. "Pua is the publicly acknowledged heir to her parents' properties. That includes the rights to the TC enzyme production technique. The enzyme was developed completely independently of any World Life work requests or orders, so the rights to it belong entirely to her. Hold on, Crawley, I'm not finished."

She paused while the U.N. team urged Crawley to silence. Then she said, "Zed and Lehua Pukui had planned to keep the basic economic rights to the TC compound, but to widely distribute the formula for its production. They did not wish for it to fall solely into the hands of one monopolistic group."

"The Company—"

"Has no say in this matter, Crawley," the warden said. "The distribution is entirely up to Pua."

"She's a minor," Crawley said. He was so angry that the scars on his cheek stood out clearly. "Her holdings and her care fall under the administration of World Life Company until she reaches her majority. Toma, tell her that's true. Pua can't even legally stay on Lesaat without family. She's going to have to leave.''

''The Company has appointed me as her legal guardian for the duration of my stay on Lesaat,'' the warden said. ''You drew up and legalized that contract yourself. And pulled a few strings to get it done, I believe. You claimed it was a humanitarian gesture at the time. Are you saying that there were other motives for returning the girl here?''

A low buzz shivered through the cave, a mechanical buzz that cut right through the murmured questions and comments that followed the warden's remark. Crawley glared.

''That's the air-intrusion alert,'' Toma said. He touched his right shoulder and glanced at the warden. ''It's my—your flit.''

''If someone's flying, the storm must be letting up,'' one of the Earthers said hopefully.

''Why would Ehu be coming back now?'' the warden asked.

''She wouldn't,'' Toma said. ''Not unless something else has gone wrong.'' He knelt before Fatu. ''Permission to question, Warden?''

''Granted.''

It grew very still inside the cave again, except for the alarm and the continued roar of the storm outside, which continued to shout its mighty song. Pua could hear Le Fe'e's rumbling call and ached to answer. Soon, she promised. I'll come soon.

''Fatu,'' Toma said. ''Do you have a private comm here in the cave?''

''Yes.'' A soft, reluctant reply.

''Where is it?''

''Behind the green mold and beyond the spirit of Le Fe'e's small kin, in the second deep crevice on the mountainside.''

One of Crawley's waterguards moved instantly in that direction. ''Don't let *him* find it!'' Pua cried. Toma waved her back and followed the guard himself, without hurrying. He had not yet passed the first turn when a shrill scream echoed through the cave.

The ghosts! Pua threw herself into Fatu's lap and covered her eyes and ears. Fatu's strong arms closed around her.

She had known they would come. She had *known* they couldn't bring all these people into this cave and not have the ghosts come. ''Come on, Fatu,'' she whispered. ''Let's get out of here. Keep your eyes closed so you don't see them.''

Someone touched her, and she almost screamed herself. But it was just the warden's hand. Pua opened her eyes long enough to be sure. The waterguard who had gone after the comm screamed and screamed.

"Sit tight for a minute," the warden said. She peeled the patch from Fatu's neck and cracked an inhalant vial under his nose. "Deep breaths," she said. She held the vial steady while she watched the back of the cave. Cautiously, Pua followed her look.

The Earther stumbled into view. He was scratching and tearing at his face and hands. The other Earthers backed rapidly away.

"Somebody bring me what's left of the loli," Toma called. When the bowl was passed to him, he thrust it at the squirming, shrieking waterguard. Pua could see now that the Earther's skin was covered with tiny, wriggling grubs.

Mold maggots! She watched, fascinated, horrified, as Toma convinced the man to plunge his hands into the loli and then to smear the thick paste on his face and neck. At the touch of the sea cucumber, the phosphorescent maggots began to fall away. Land and water things didn't always mix. Pua understood that, but she had not known that loli would scare moldies away so easily. Toma and Dave Chan used clicker fronds to brush the still-wriggling maggots into a pile.

When the last of them had released its hold on the Earther's skin, and the man sat moaning and crying against the wet stone wall, Chan scooped the maggots onto a broad leaf and carried them back into the recesses of the cave. When he returned, he was carrying a woven basket containing Fatu's private comm.

"I warned you before we got here," Toma said, staring around at them all. "Don't touch *anything* until a waterworlder has told you it's safe." Several of the Earthers moved farther away from the walls. Toma knelt at the injured guard's side. "This fellow crawled right into a mold maggot's nest. He'll live, but his swimming days are over, from the looks of those gill edges."

Pua pressed her face against Fatu's broad chest.

"That was deliberate!" Crawley said. "That was a deliberately set trap."

"Fatu warned us that the comm was protected," Toma said.

"By a *spirit*!" Crawley shouted. "That's superstitious nonsense!"

"From the looks of your well-chewed guard, Crawley, that protective spirit did its job very well," Toma said. "Let me remind all of you again that we are still on private property. Fatu and whatever physical or spiritual entities he chooses to employ have every right to set as many protective traps as they wish."

"Just who are you working for, Toma?" Crawley demanded.

Fatu stirred. "Are you okay?" Pua asked quickly. The warden was still with them, touching them both, but watching Toma and Crawley.

"I'm doing the job you pay me to do, Mr. Crawley," Toma said calmly. "Trying to keep the Company on the right side of the law."

"You're in on all this, aren't you? I knew—"

Fatu blinked and shook his head. "Is it finished?"

"Yes," the warden said. "How many of me do you see?"

He looked at her. "Too many." She smiled and squeezed his shoulder. "You did fine, Fatu."

"What have you done, Warden?" It was the U.N. team leader, Crawley's man. "Why did you bring him out of it? We hadn't finished questioning him."

"*I* had," the warden said. She lifted a hand. "Fatu agreed before you got here to speak freely of the children of Lesaat and the situation here at Pukui. He doesn't need to be drugged to continue the discussion."

"But—"

"What proof do we have that these—waterchildren—actually exist, Warden?" another of the Earthers asked. It was one who had remained quiet throughout, one whom Fatu had told Pua earlier he had never seen before. Pua wasn't sure whether that meant they should trust him more or less than the others.

"It's one thing to claim special status for an individual," the man said, nodding at Pua, "and quite another to claim it for an entire group. We would have to know exactly what we were dealing with before any decisions could be made."

"When the storm abates, we'll arrange for you to meet the others," the warden said. "Pua has agreed to that with the condition that their physical safety is first assured."

"Of course, but what—"

There was a loud roar outside the cave, then a splintering crash. Pua grabbed Fatu again, and he held her tight. There was the *whumph!* of something soft and wet hitting the ground, then only the hum again and the background roar of the wind.

"That's a flitter!" the warden said. "Who'd be idiot enough to try landing here in this wind?" She started for the entrance, but stopped as a white-shrouded figure crawled inside. Pua screamed.

"Pua, no. It's all right," Fatu said. His voice still sounded rough, scary, as if the ghosts had gotten inside him and were . . .

"It's just Ehu, Pua. It's just Ehu. Open your eyes."

Pua opened her eyes. It was, indeed, Ehu, although she looked as terrifying as any ghost Pua might have expected. She was covered with a froth of white anti-incendiary foam.

"Sorry about the paper tree, Fatu," Ehu said. She shook foam from her hands. "The vegetation's going to be burned all to hell from this stuff, too. But we needed more space and a cushion to set down on. The wind is deadly out there."

Toma had reached her by then. "What are you doing here?" he asked. He glanced back at Crawley, who was receiving a whispered report from one of his guards.

"What are *you* doing in *here*?" Ehu demanded. "They're still hauling live algae out there. Zena flashed us from the barge that you were up here, but we could see that the house and farm buildings haven't even been closed, much less battened down for the storm. What are you waiting for?"

"This is just the tail end of the weather," Toma said. "Satellite report shows the main storm mass will be beyond our range before morning."

A second figure followed Ehu into the cave, a short woman with very dark skin. The warden stood slowly.

"I don't know what satellite you're getting your report from, Toma," Ehu said, "but trust me, it ain't orbiting over *this* ocean. We've got a great-grandmama of a howler headed right at us. Two hours tops before that algae starts sloppin' into open water."

Pua swung her look toward Crawley. He was smiling.

"You made them send us the wrong pictures!" she said. "You're trying to kill my reef!" She scrambled up from Fatu's lap. Fatu tried to rise, too, but sank back before reaching his feet. The warden grabbed Pua and held her arm tight.

"Chan," Toma called. "Get the comm on-line and have Fatu set it for the flitter. He knows the code. Ehu, I'll need your help."

"What are you going to do?" the warden asked.

"Let me go!" Pua shouted.

"We'll try to set up a comm patch between here and the barge," Toma said. "If we can't get them, I'll have to fly out there. We have to get word to Zena to get the swimmers out of the water and blow the pens." He nodded toward three of the waterworld crew leaders who were already pushing their way through the others toward the cave entrance. "They'll swim the message out, just in case."

"I'll pilot," the warden said, and to Pua's surprise, Toma nodded.

"Watch the waterguards," he called to the swimmers. "They

may try to stop you." He dropped to his knees beside Fatu and Chan as once again the U.N. reps murmured and muttered their confusion.

The warden turned to the small black woman who had come into the cave behind Ehu. She had moved away from the entrance and was calmly wiping foam from her legs. She was wearing a skintight scarlet bodysuit, and if she had been taller, she would have looked just like a coiler. She stood up straight at the warden's approach, and rested her hands on her narrow hips.

"Why is it, Dinsman," she said, "that every time I pay you a visit, I end up pulling your ass out of a fire?"

"Shooter's luck, I guess," the warden replied with a grin. The woman glanced down at the warden's hands. Pua yanked on her arm again, but the warden still wouldn't let her go. "What are you doing here, anyway? How'd you get to Lesaat?"

The woman glanced at Crawley, who was surrounded by his guards and several of the U.N. crew. Pua didn't see Dr. Waight. She hoped the old woman would go poke around in the mold maggots' nest.

"I came steerage on the same ship he did," the black woman said. "Brought another inspection team, too, if that's of any interest to you. Unfortunately, they're still stuck at Landing. I managed to crack the locator code that was supposed to be you and got hold of Ehu instead. When she heard who I was, she offered to pick me up and fly me out here."

"But what are you *doing* here?" the warden asked again.

"U.N. Special Service sent me out to check up on a few things," the Earther said. "Seems there were a few irregularities concerning that fire in the forest preserve. You don't mind my looking into that, do you? I assume that's what all that caramel business was about."

"Sally," the warden said. Sally! Pua thought. "If you can pin a few 'irregularities' on these bastards, I'll love you forever."

"Sally?" Pua didn't realize she had spoken aloud until the woman looked at her. Her studied glance slid down Pua's body and back again. She lifted a dark brow.

"And you are?" she asked.

Pua scowled. She turned to the mountainlady. "You never told me she was *short*!" Then she jerked her arm again. "Let me go. Le Fe'e is calling. I need to get in the water."

A quick look flashed between the warden and Sally. "You can

go with us in the flitter if you want,'' the warden said. She let go of Pua's arm.

Pua hesitated, but decided the rays would be faster. And a lot safer. "I'll meet you at the barge,'' she said.

"Need a knife?'' The warden didn't smile, but Pua knew she was trying to make a joke, trying to remind her to remain calm. Pua pulled her father's finest shark knife from beneath her skirt. She flashed it at the warden, eyed the Sally woman over its tip, then hurried back to Fatu's side.

"I'm going out, Fatu,'' she said, pushing between Toma and Dave. "Le Fe'e needs me. But you'll be okay here. That Sally lady, the Earther that came with Ehu, is going to stay. She's—she's the mountainlady's friend or something. Anyway, she's a troubleshooter, and she's going to help.''

Toma and Dave glanced at each other, but Fatu watched only Pua. "I hear Le Fe'e calling, too,'' he said. He tried to push himself up. "I'll come with—''

"You'd better stay here to finish the other thing,'' Pua said, holding him back. It wasn't difficult—he was still limp from the warden's drugs. Then she smiled. "Besides, somebody has to be here to keep the ghosts away.''

She could feel his chuckle as he hugged her one last time. She transferred all but one of her leis to his neck.

"Be careful, Little Fe'e,'' he said.

"You just listen to me sing!'' she said, and darted for the entrance.

"Hey, don't let her—'' Crawley's voice.

The waterworlders stopped Crawley's guards from following her.

"Let's go, Warden,'' Toma said.

"That child shouldn't be going out . . .''

"The storm . . .''

A babble of voices chased Pua from the cave. The melting foam carried in by Ehu and the Earther was cool under Pua's hands and knees. *I'm here, Le Fe'e!* she called as she crawled out into the wind. She looked up. Le Fe'e's long, dark arms were reaching up toward the crossing moons.

Chapter 25

Toma's hands were white where he gripped the deck edge and the side of his seat.

"Am I scaring you, Inspector?" Angie called. The flitter bucked and twisted, dropped in a sudden lull, then slammed hard against an upsurge.

"Hell, yes," he yelled back. "Who taught you to fly, anyway? Watch that—" But Angie had already banked to avoid the wind-borne clicker frond. She steadied the flit and brought it back to the center of the inter-island cleft.

"A guy named Johnnie Kneubuhlman," she said. "Used to be a Hollywood stuntman before he retired to a farm near my dad's. I was shooting canyons like this before I could walk. Hold on." Another frond whipped past the starboard port.

"Do you always deactivate the sound dampers?" he shouted.

She laughed. "Can't fly a good wind without hearing it, Inspector. Besides, it keeps my adrenaline running. How're you doing back there, Ehu?" she called over her shoulder.

"Wishin' I'd gone with Pua," Ehu groaned. "Watch out for this last section. There's a reef-sucking downdraft off the cliff-face. Your friend Sally nearly slid us right into the opposite bank on the way in."

Angie suspected that Sally had ridden the draft just for the fun of it. She, however, gave herself enough altitude, despite the gusting wind, to avoid the downdraft altogether. There was one last lift and stomach-wrenching fall. Then they were out of the canyon and over clear, churning water.

Angie turned the flit into the direct, steady wind of the storm. She activated the sound dampers, and a sudden hush filled the cabin. Toma immediately spoke into the comm mike.

". . . signal's fluxing, but we read you," Dave Chan replied. "There, that's better."

". . . care who you are." Crawley's voice sounded in the background. "No troubleshooting bitch is going to . . ."

Angie winced as Crawley ended his complaint with a screech. "Sally does *not* like being called names," she said.

"She mentioned that to the Company guard we met outside the cave," Ehu said. "The one we stepped over on the way out. Did she have time to tell you there's another whole U.N. team at Landing, one *not* selected by Company admin?"

Angie nodded. "Can you relay the storm-warning loop from the cave, Toma?" He had been murmuring into the mike, fussing with the comm controls.

"The loop is set," he said. "Only the barge can't hear us. Ehu, you ready to swim?"

"Aye. Hands're on the hatch. Just say when."

"We'll drop you on the inner-lagoon side of the barge," he said. "Tell Zena I'll take care of the methane blows. Have her pull the crews stat and clear the area. Stand by for the shock waves. Number seventeen hasn't been worked at all yet, so there won't be anyone around. I'll blow that one first. Then nineteen and twenty."

"Aye. You sure you don't want help?"

"I'm sure I do, but there isn't time. The warden can get me in and out faster than any swimmer can do it, and somebody has to alert the barge. Tell Zena to set the release triggers in the pen she's working. Use distance timers. Here's the code. We'll blow that one last, after we see the all-clear signal."

"I'll set the timers myself," Ehu said.

"Send someone back to Home and the processing plant, just in case the warning loop isn't getting through," Angie said. "Tell them to close things up as best they can in the time we have left."

"No more than an hour," Toma said. "After that, everyone needs to be in one of the caves or deep underwater. From the feel of this thing, I suspect the caves are going to be safest."

"Aye," Ehu said again.

"Barge coming up," Angie said. "Looks like you're going to be landing in white water." Even in the inner lagoon, the surface water was churning with phosphorescent chop. The barge itself, large and lumbering as it was, was lifting and falling awkwardly with the swell.

"No problem. Hey, Warden?"

Angie could not spare a look back.

"Fatu told me what you're trying to do for Pua and the kids. I—we all appreciate it."

"Let's just hope it works," Angie said, "and that they have a home left to live in if it does." Then, "Drop point; go on my call."

Ehu popped the hatch. A rush of wind sucked into the cabin. Angie fought the flitter back under control. "Go!" she shouted.

Ehu dove headfirst through the open hatch. As quickly as her feet cleared the sill, Toma swung it closed. He immediately pointed Angie in the direction of the number-seventeen pen. He pulled an equipment bag from beneath his feet and began assembling methane-release triggers in his lap.

"What's the plan?" she asked. "I watched them set a couple of small blows when they were cleaning the pens, but it was done from the water."

"It's safer that way, and a lot less messy," he said. "But neatness won't make any difference tonight. Fly directly over the pen from the upwind end. I need six drop points equidistant from the sides. I'm setting self-timers on the triggers. We'll have about sixty seconds from the last drop to clear the area before the first one blows."

"Gee, why such a wide margin?" she asked. He laughed.

"Seventeen, coming up," she said. "Why'd you bring me along on this trip, Inspector? I didn't think you trusted me this much."

He unbuckled his safety harness and moved back toward the hatch. "Fatu told me he'd seen you shoot the inter-island canyon a few times. There aren't many who'll try that, even going slow. I figured if anyone could get me out here fast enough to do any good, you could. Besides, where better to keep an eye on you?"

She could hear laughter in his voice and wondered whether she should tell him that it had been Pua whom Fatu had seen racing through the inter-island cleft. Tonight was Angie's first time in the pilot's seat. She decided to leave well enough alone.

"Trigger's ready," he said.

"There's a safety line in back of my seat," she replied. "Use it."

"You scared I'll fall out, Warden?"

Damn fool troubleshooter! she thought. Of course I am! "I'm scared of what Fatu would do to me if you did," she said. "Use it."

He laughed, and slid the safety belt around his waist. "Ready when you are."

"Pop the hatch," she said. "I want to get the feel of flying with it open before we start the drop."

The sudden roar of the wind filled the cabin again. It smelled of the deep, distant sea. The flitter bucked and jerked.

"Starting run," she called aloud. "Drop on my call."

She struggled with the flit, forcing it to remain steady over the effervescent algae pen. The extreme, and still rising, tide had lifted the net high off the reef. The entire structure was swaying noticeably with each of the deep, heavy swells that swept over the barrier reef and across the lagoon. The surface was a churning caldron of breaking waves.

"Drop one!" she called. She fought across the wind to the second drop point, then downwind to the third. Across the pen again, another swift ride downwind, across again, and they were out. She hit full throttle.

"Shit on the bloody reef, woman! What's your hurry?" The words were barely out of Toma's mouth when the upwind end of the pen blew. Angie continued full-speed, straight away from the pen, until she had heard all six methane triggers blow. Then she swung back into the wind.

"You still with me, Inspector?" she called. The seventeen pen roared with flames.

The hatch slammed shut.

"Just barely," Toma said. "You almost threw me right out the door with that last move."

"Better shorten your tether," she said. "It'd be a bumpy ride till I could get you back in." She was grinning. The wind, the waves, the tremendous cacophony of storm and sea, made her feel enormously alive. This was an instant to savor. The world might end before morning. This world, Pukui's world, would most certainly be heavily damaged by then. Perhaps even fatally so, since it was meeting the storm totally unprepared.

But this moment, this instant, this personal touch of the storm, was glorious in both its power and its beauty.

She laughed. "Number nineteen, coming up!"

"You enjoying yourself, Warden?" Toma asked.

"No point letting a good adrenaline rush go to waste," she replied. From his voice, she judged he was enjoying himself as much as she.

"Ready the drop," he called, and popped the hatch again.

"On my call," she shouted.

As they cleared the second pen, Angie was relieved to discover that Toma had lengthened the timing fuses slightly. This time they actually had sixty full seconds to clear the area before the charges blew.

"I think I know who set the methane blows the night Pua and I arrived," she said after he had closed the hatch again.

"Who?"

"Katie."

"What!"

"You said the triggers had been set by an amateur," Angie said, "and there aren't many of those here at Pukui. Remember? Katie wasn't at the house that night when you arrived. We both remarked on it."

"But why . . ."

"Earlier that evening Pua and I were talking on the lanai. Katie was inside listening. I saw her in the pantry. Pua told me very emphatically that her mother would order the number-twelve pen blown immediately if she were there."

"And Katie does whatever she thinks Lehua wants done," he finished. "Damn! You're a lucky woman, Warden. You and Pua both."

"Let's hope it holds," she said as she banked toward the third pen. They made their drops, then fought the wind back to the barge. An automatic all-clear signal flashed from the wave-washed deck. At first they almost didn't see it through the churning water.

"One of the mooring lines has snapped," Toma said. "We're going to lose it for sure. Damn that Crawley. He'd better hope your friend Sally kills him tonight, because if she doesn't, I'm going to do it in the morning. Pull back and stay upwind over the outer lagoon this time. I'll use the remote to blow the triggers Ehu set."

A sharp sting brought Angie's hand to her right shoulder. The flitter bucked. She brought it quickly back under control. She turned toward the barrier reef, then quickly back toward the barge, trying to determine the locator signal's direction.

"What're you doing?" Toma called.

"I've got to go down," she said. "One of my implants just went off. Pua's in trouble."

He was beside her in an instant. "You have her bugged?"

"Yes, Inspector, I have her bugged. Take the deck."

"Where is she?" he demanded.

She pressed the locator again. "Not close enough to get a

clear reading. There's too much turbulence up here. I need to get in the water.''

Toma slid rapidly back into his seat, unhooking the safety tether as he did so. He reached for the deck. "Stand by the hatch and go at my call," he said. "I'll be right behind you."

"Not even I could land on the barge in this wind," she said. "Your best bet is the open lawn in front of the main house."

"I'm not going to land," he said.

"You're going to *ditch* my flit?"

"Easy come, easy go, Warden. Stand by the hatch. We'll blow the pen after we're in the water."

"Spit," Angie said, although she didn't really object to having a strong swimmer at her side in these raging seas. She was astonished at how quickly the storm had grown out of control. She slipped out of her safety harness and her seat. "Ready at the hatch," she called.

Toma swung the flit low over the waves. "Pop it."

A spray of saltwater swept in with the wind. He was a lot lower than Angie would have put them. "Go!" he yelled.

It was not a graceful dive, but she cleared the flit without major damage, and the surface of the water was no harder than she had expected. She blew out all the air in her lungs and let herself sink, fighting the instinctive urge to kick directly back to the surface. Her gills activated, and the quick infusion of adrenaline gave her the courage to continue downward.

The water churned with conflicting currents, and Angie was buffeted and rolled. She kicked as hard as she could to maintain her dive, but it was the strong webbing between her fingers that pulled her through the turmoil. Through it all, she felt the shock of the flitter smacking into the surface. She hoped Toma had made it through the hatch in time.

Not until she reached five meters did Angie have any real control over her movements in the churning water. As soon as she was stable, she pressed the locator implant. She turned in the water until she was facing the direction of the signal. A dark figure dove toward her through the turbulence. Toma.

Immediately, he signaled for Pua's direction. Angie pointed. He stopped her before she could start swimming that way and pointed back the opposite way. He lifted the methane detonator. At the same moment, Angie saw something behind him. She grabbed his shoulder and pointed.

Rays, an entire pack of them, were lifting from the depths. They swept close, circled, and dove, and suddenly Pua was there. She brought her face close to Angie's. "What happened to the flitter?" she called through the water.

"What happened to *you*?" Angie cried. She lifted one of Pua's hands to her shoulder, where the locator was still emitting a weak, intermittent vibration. Pua's eyes opened wide.

"Why?" Angie called.

"Pili!" Pua said. "I gave the string to—" Her air ran out. She clicked her fingers, a signal to the rays, for they swept close again. Panic glowed in her eyes.

Toma touched them both in warning and lifted the detonator again. He activated the release just as one of the rays lifted under him. Angie grabbed hold of her own waiting ray, and with Pua in the lead, they raced from the site. The booming thunder of exploding methane chased them through the water. As soon as the shock wave had passed, Pua turned her ray back toward Angie.

Angie nodded, and pressed the locator for direction. Pua must have given the rays some other command then, because Angie's ray surged ahead. When Angie felt it going off course, she applied a slight pressure to the ray's back with her knees. The creature responded as easily as if it had been a horse she was riding.

It soon became clear where the signal was leading them. The deep-water pipe tunnel, the nearest entrance to Sa le Fe'e. A strong current was sweeping down off the barrier reef face, and an even stronger one began pulling them ever faster toward the tunnel mouth. The rays slowed of their own accord. Toma motioned them up and in, toward the reef.

Pua did not look happy at the delay, but she clicked her fingertips, and the rays took them that way. They carried them under a coral outcropping and slowed. Angie slid from the ray and swam after Toma and Pua. They crawled through a patch of sponge coral, then swam up into a mold-lit cave.

". . . in trouble," Pua was shouting when Angie surfaced. "We have to go help them!"

"Pua, the rays don't want to go through the tunnel," Toma said. "The current is too strong."

"The current is always strong," she said. "We have to go."

Toma shook his head. "The storm is dumping so much water over the reef and into the lagoon that the outflow through the tunnel is three times its usual tidal strength. Even if we could make it through there safely, we'd never be able to cross the outer reef face to Sa le Fe'e's entrance. The surge must be tearing the coral apart by now. Even the fishing exit may be impossible."

"We don't have to go outside. There's a way into Sa le Fe'e from inside the tunnel," Pua said. "We can go in through the hot-tub overflow."

"That pipe is too small," he said.

Pua nodded toward Angie. "*She* got through it."

Toma sent Angie a startled glance.

She shrugged. "It's a tight fit, but I did get through. You'd never make it, though." Toma's shoulders were a good deal wider than her own. Angie cringed inwardly at the thought of squeezing through that dark space again.

"Okay," Toma said. "We have a back way in, at least for the two of you. How are we going to escape the current when we reach the outflow channel? I'm not exaggerating its strength, Pua. I don't know if even the rays can do it."

"They'll try if I tell them," she replied. "What do you think is wrong?"

"Could be storm damage," Toma said, "but that's not likely at the basalt level. The main cave's never been seriously affected by storms before."

"Maybe there was a slide or something in one of the upper chambers," Pua said.

"Pua," Angie asked, "did you see anyone else in the lagoon?"

"Just the work crews leaving the barge," she said. "There were a lot of Company squids still out there working when you came in the flitter. Zena told me they stayed to help even after Crawley ordered them out of the water. They didn't like those Earther swimmers telling them what to do."

"Did you see any of the Earther waterguards?" Angie pressed.

Pua shook her head. "Zena said they all left awhile earlier."

Angie met Toma's look. "There was a lot of cargo aboard that bus. Any idea what it was?"

"Crawley said farm equipment; the guards wouldn't let me near it," he said.

Angie thought for a moment. "It was probably a pair of minisubs. They rarely work without them for backup. That would give them shelter outside the reef, although it'd be a rough ride. They'll also have hand jets, which will give them maneuverability in the rough water."

Pua stared at her. "You think the Earthers are at Sa le Fe'e?"

"I don't know, Pua," Angie said. "Is it possible Pili might have been somewhere outside when he broke the locator string?"

"If he was hurt and in the water, Le Fe'e would be able to tell me what's wrong," Pua replied. Again Angie met Toma's look. Myth or reality? How much of what Pua told them could they believe literally?

"Let's start with the hot-tub outflow," Toma said. "If I can't get through, you two go ahead in. Pua, you open the fishing exit gate, and I'll come in there. We'll play the rest by ear."

"How'll you get through the surge?" Pua asked.

"There's a small hand jet in the last rest station. Maybe the guards missed it on their way through, if that's how they *got* through."

"Some of them probably tried it," Angie said. But how had they found Sa le Fe'e at all? She was sure that they had. She could feel it. She could taste it! "Watch for them at the other end of the tunnel."

"Hell, I've been watching for them ever since we left the cave," he said. "Don't worry about that."

"I'm going," Pua said. "I'll tell the rays what to do."

"Wait." Angie grabbed Pua's arm. It seemed she had been doing that a lot lately. "Do you have to be with the rays for them to do things for you, or can they understand well enough to do something on their own?"

"Like what?"

"Like bring us a few reinforcements."

"The swimmers, you mean?"

Angie nodded. "Would they recognize the Pukui people?"

"Of course. Shall I tell them to go get some?"

"Yes!" Toma said. "Ehu and Kobe will still be in the water, and Zena. You know the others we can trust. Go. Do it."

Pua swam ahead of them out of the cave. She must have sent her message to the rays while she was still passing through the sponge coral, because only the three largest were waiting. They mounted, Pua clicked her nails, and they swung directly into the tremendous outflow current of the barrier reef tunnel. Angie closed her eyes, then quickly opened them again. All she could see was glowing, rushing water.

The ray's great wings lifted and fell. Slowly. Smoothly—with a controlled power Angie could feel through the warm, velvety skin. She had been aware of the creature's great strength before, but this was something she had not expected. She was being *carried* through the maelstrom of the current, not swept. The ray was in complete control.

She wondered, not for the first time, why these great, gray creatures allowed themselves to be ruled by such a tiny, human child. Then she thought of her own association with Pua and acknowledged that she and the rays had something in common. "Pua controls us all," she said against the ray's back. The water sucked her words away, but a ripple of movement under the velvety skin made her wonder if the ray had heard her.

Mother of mountains, Angie thought, as she considered what that might mean. It was not the first time she had wondered if the rays understood more than just Pua's click-talk. I'm not sure I can handle a second indigenous peoples' battle right now, she told the ray silently.

She had expected a return to the terror her first trip through the tunnel had inspired, a return to the horror of her helpless sweep through the icy mountain waters of home. Instead, she found herself pondering the political complexities that would arise if a sentient, or even just a near-sentient, species was found to exist in the precious Lesaat seas.

Spit, she thought, I am truly out of my league.

The ray slowed. They must be approaching the hot-tub out-flow. The water began rushing over Angie from the rear, and she found she had to hook her knees around the ray's narrow middle to keep from being swept forward off its back. Torn leaves and clicker fronds swept past. Something long and bright pink and green flashed by. It looked suspiciously like a rock eel. Angie huddled close to the ray's back.

Pua's ray, which had preceded Angie's through the tunnel, slapped a giant wing against the right side of the tunnel. A large rubbery leaf of slime mold tore and peeled away. The ray's back wing struck the same place, and the whole camouflaging wall of hanging molds collapsed and was swept away with the current.

The ray slid inside, just far enough to deposit Pua, then backed out again. Angie and Toma were taken into the shelter of the side channel in the same way. Angie brushed her hand along the edge of her mount's wing as she slid away. "Many thanks," she whispered after it, then turned to follow Pua back to the hot-tub pipe.

Suddenly, she stopped. She pressed her locator implant for a stronger reading. "Pua!" she called. The girl was already far ahead. Toma heard her, though. He clicked a quick signal with his nails. Instantly Pua rolled into a ball, turned, and kicked back toward them.

Angie tapped her shoulder and pointed up. The signal locator might just be in a part of the nursery that was over their present position, but Angie wanted to make sure. If there was a way she could avoid squeezing back through that pipe, she would definitely like to find it.

Pua's eyes opened wide. She took a mouthful of water, held it for an instant, then spat it out.

"Blood," she said. Abruptly, she shot straight up toward the high, narrow ceiling. Toma and Angie exchanged startled glances and followed.

Pua led them into a crack so narrow they had to pull themselves upward with their hands. There was a turn, and another turn, and suddenly they were back in a space large enough to swim. Pua motioned them away from the perfectly coiled oxyworm that rested on the smooth bottom of the chamber. Then she took them up again.

They surfaced into warm, moist air and the muffled sound of a crying baby.

"Mariko," Toma cried. "What are you doing here? What happened?"

Mariko was kneeling on a slime- and blood-slicked ledge, aiming at them with a raised speargun. Five children huddled behind her. They stared with wide, dark eyes. As she recognized Toma, Mariko dropped the gun and collapsed onto the stone. The side of her face was covered with blood.

Toma lifted himself onto the ledge.

"What happened?" Pua demanded.

Pili dropped into the water from a shadowed ceiling crack. Angie started her attack the instant she saw the shadow of his move, but because Pua was between them, she had time to recognize the boy before she did him serious damage. He gave her a cautious look before turning his attention to Pua.

"Earthers," he said. "They blew the airlock. We had both hatches sealed because of the storm. That's what gave us time to get out. They had to blow both doors. Mariko got hit by a stone that broke loose and fell into the nursery pool while she was trying to get the babies. She was bleeding and could hardly see, so I broke the string like you said and brought her here. . . ."

Pua ordered the oldest girl into the water with the crying baby. As soon as the infant was submerged, the whimpering stopped, and an almost instant grin appeared. The baby was one of those

Nola had been holding when Angie had first entered Sa le Fe'e. It blinked its wide eyes open and clung to its caretaker's hair.

"You did just right, Pili," Angie said. "Tell us what happened. Did you actually see the Earthers?"

Pili nodded. "They were men mostly, all but one. They had gills, but they were Earthers. I know because of their hands."

"Were there any waterworlders?" Angie asked.

Pili's eyes turned very hard. "One. A big hairy one with scratch marks on his skin."

Pua's eyes narrowed. Once again Angie found herself wrapping her long fingers around the girl's arm. "Where are Kiki and Keha?" Pua asked, without trying to pull away.

"They're hiding by the fishing outlet gate. They couldn't get out because of the storm, but they were still okay when I brought the last kids through the hot tub."

How does he know that? Angie wondered, and then remembered the click-talk.

"There was an old lady with them," Pili went on. "She didn't have gills, only an oxymask around her neck. I think she was the boss."

"Doctor Waight," Pua said softly.

How had Waight found the nursery? How had that bitch known where to come?

"She must have asked Fatu where Sa le Fe'e was," Pua said. "I saw her close to him."

Suddenly Angie remembered the confusion that Crawley's outburst had caused. She had left Fatu's side for just one instant to argue with the Company man, and once again she had been played for a fool.

"Where's Nola?" she asked.

"She stayed to fight," Mariko said. "To give us time to get the kids out. Jaime was caught in the blast. I think he's dead. Hana and Manuel stayed with Nola. They're both injured, I don't know how seriously."

Suddenly Pili blinked. "Pualei, I'm sorry." Angie realized the sudden thickness in his voice was tears.

Pua looked startled, as well.

"That old woman," he said. "I couldn't stop her."

"It's not your fault," Pua said.

"She's got Little Ten!"

Angie might as well not have been holding her. Pua escaped her grasp in one slick move and was gone.

Chapter 26

~~~~~~~~~~~~~~~~~~~~~~~~~~~~~~
~~~~~~~~~~~~~~~~~~~~~~~~~~~~~~

The grate leading into the thermal pool was closed but not locked. Pua listened carefully before opening it. She pressed her palms against the warm plastic but felt no vibrations. The water inside the tub was calm, disturbed only by the constant, bubbling inflow from thermal vents. She eased from the pipe.

Before breaking surface, she stopped to listen again, hands spread on the warm stone wall. The mountainlady rose beside her and touched her arm. She was pale, but she had followed just as Pua had expected. Pua lifted high enough from the water to listen again, then climbed carefully from the pool.

She motioned to the warden to follow, pointing for her to stay on the heaviest moss, where their drip would not show. Pua had shed her leaf skirt and her headdress back in the inner lagoon. All she wore now were friendly vines and seaweed—and her father's knife. Seawater ran in cool rivulets along the vines' designs.

They edged around the corner toward the sound of human voices—adults arguing and 'Umi Iki's tiny, terrified cry.

Nursery, Pua mouthed over her shoulder.

Doctor Waight's ugly voice lifted over the others. "Well, they have to be here someplace. Keep looking."

"There's gotta be another exit. There's no sign—"

"Find them!" Waight shouted. "They'd never take those babies out into this storm."

The warden yanked Pua back just as a figure stepped into the corridor ahead of them. They waited until the Earther came close, then the warden reached out and grabbed him. Before he could make a sound, her hand hit his mouth, then the side of his neck. He fell like a lump of basalt.

Pua blinked at the suddenness of it, then helped the warden drag the man back to the thermal pool.

"He's small enough," the warden said. "Take him out through the pipe and secure him outside somewhere."

"I'm not leaving," Pua said.

The warden closed her eyes for a moment. "We have to get rid of him, Pua," she said. "I'm too big to maneuver him through the pipe."

Pua stared at her. "Okay. But I'm just sticking him in the pipe. I'll call Pili to pull him out the other end. You wait for me."

"Go," the warden said.

She helped lift the limp body into the water. Pua dragged it down and stuffed it headfirst into the pipe. The Earther's gills pulsed rhythmically, so he wasn't dead. Pua was sorry about that. She kept his arms at his sides, so if he regained consciousness, he wouldn't be able to move in the narrow opening. She clicked a message against the side of the pipe, repeated it twice, and hurried back to join the mountainlady.

Once again they listened. Pua pressed one hand against the wall and tapped a query to Kiki and Keha. The warden lifted a brow, but Pua shook her head. There was no reply.

"This way," she whispered, and guided the warden through a narrow crack that led past the back of the nursery and on to the distant fishing exit gate. First she would get Kiki and Keha. Then they could go back for Little Ten. The warden followed so quietly that Pua looked back from time to time to be sure she was still there.

Once past the nursery, she tapped for the twins again. This time, she thought she felt a reply. Very short. She couldn't make out the sequence, but it must mean someone was near the boys who might overhear. She signaled to the mountainlady and crept forward.

The fishing gate, like many places inside Sa le Fe'e, was disguised by a hanging mold wall. Pua suspected that the boys were hiding between the wall and the gate. "Look here," she heard an Earther voice say. "There's a shelf behind this damn slime. I thought it grew directly over the rock."

"That must be how they're hiding," another hard voice snapped. "Start tearing it down. We'll strip this whole slimy place. They're in here somewhere."

"Whaddaya think the old bitch's gonna do with 'em?" the first man said. "Weird things, aren't they? You see the hands on that little one? Looked like a damned baby octopus all spread out like that.''

There came the sound of a slime-mold leaf sucking away from stone. ''Why do you think they call them squids?'' They both laughed.

The warden's hand rested lightly on Pua's shoulder. Pua pushed it away. She didn't need to be reminded that caution was needed here. She clicked a fast query and received a single tap in return. Kiki and Keha were at the gate.

''What was that?'' one of the men said.

''What was what? There's so much storm noise the place sounds like it's gonna collapse,'' came the reply.

Pua clicked an order to the twins.

''That clicking . . .''

One of the boys sneezed.

''There!'' Both Earthers came into view as they dashed toward the wall behind which the twins were hiding. As quickly as their backs were turned to tear at the slime mold, Pua and the warden were on them. Pua slid a hand around one man's mouth and the other around his neck. Her nails lifted one of his gills, wide.

''Move and you're a dead swimmer,'' Pua muttered. The man froze.

The warden already had the other man unconscious and on the ground. Without hesitation, she whacked the one Pua was holding, too. As he went limp, Pua let him go.

''Check the boys,'' the warden whispered. Her knife was out and open, and she was slicing the long sleeves off the waterguards' suits. Pua clicked her nails, and Kiki and Keha parted the leaf molds just enough to peer fearfully out. She motioned for them to stay where they were.

The warden gagged the waterguards and tied their hands and feet, stringing them together behind their backs. She nodded toward the boys. ''Is there room back there to hide them?''

Pua nodded.

The boys came out then and helped them maneuver the bound waterguards behind the slime-mold wall. The storm was very loud so near the outer reef face. The constant roar of the surf seemed to vibrate the very walls. Intermittent crashes and thumps told of great chunks of coral being ripped free and tossed across the reef face. Pua wondered how Uncle Toma could ever hope to come in through this gate. The boys clung to her legs.

''Is this a double-doored airlock?'' the warden asked as she examined the gate. Pua nodded. The warden squatted in front of the boys. "We need your help," she said. Both boys glanced up at Pua for approval, then nodded in unison.

"Toma's going to try to reach this gate," the warden said. "Someone has to open it when he gets here. Can you do that?"

"Papa Toma's coming?" they both asked.

"He's going to try," the warden said. "The water is very rough outside. When he presses the signal, you need to open the outer door immediately. I've set the controls so he can close it himself and get the rest of the way on his own."

"What if somebody else comes?" Keha asked.

"You watch for their hands when they lift the hatch," she said. "If you see anything other than a waterworlder finger, you jump right on the hatch and slam it closed and locked. Then you get away from here as fast as you can, because if it's the Earthers, they'll blow it open. Try to get out through the hot tub. If it's Toma, get away from here fast, too, because the Earthers will hear the lock opening and come to check."

"Go to the secret playhouse if you get out," Pua said. "Mariko is there with the others."

"Pualei, that Earthlady has 'Umi Iki," Kiki said.

"And Auntie Nola," Keha added.

Pua hugged them. "I know. Auntie Puhi and I are going to go get them now. Do what she says, okay?"

"Okay," came their dual reply.

The warden lifted a throw net from its wall peg, checked its size, and slung it across her shoulder. She would never be able to throw a proper circle holding it that way, but then she wasn't going after a school of fish. She took a pair of fish spears, too.

There was nothing they could do about the torn slime molds farther along in the corridor. They would just have to take the chance that no other guard would come this way before Uncle Toma arrived. They slipped back into the crack leading to the nursery.

'Umi Iki was still crying, the thin hiccuping wail of an unhappy newborn. "Let me nurse her," Pua heard Nola say. "She's hungry and scared."

There followed a thud and a grunt of pain. Someone had hit Auntie Nola! Pua flexed her fingers.

"Just tell us where the rest of them are hiding," Dr. Waight said. "Then you can have this one back."

"They're gone." Nola was hit again.

"You damn fool," Waight said. "There's no way those kids

could have gotten out of here. Even if they did, they're still nearby. The current through the tunnel and the storm surge are too dangerous for them to survive outside.''

"You don't know *what* they could survive," Nola said.

Waight laughed. "I intend to find out." Little Ten shrieked in sudden pain.

"For the love of god, woman!" Nola cried. "Leave her alone. She's a newborn. You're going to kill her."

"Oh no," Waight said. "I won't kill her. I won't kill this one. The rest are going to die, though, unless you tell me right now where they're hiding. My guards are setting charges all along this section of reef, and as soon as we leave here, they're going to blow this whole place apart. Pukui's little *indigenous* population will disappear right along with it.''

Pua and the warden had reached the nursery. They were behind and somewhat above where Nola sat huddled against the wall of the nursery pool. One leg was twisted all wrong under her. Klooney and two Earthers were guarding her. Watching them, Pua knew who had been doing the hitting.

Other Earthers, all of them in uniform gray, were tearing the room apart. They lifted things to look under them, then threw them down. They yanked out drawers and dumped them onto the moss. Cabinets were ripped from the walls and their contents scattered.

Doctor Waight was holding 'Umi Iki in one arm. She was standing near the main corridor door. An oxymask hung from her neck.

Pua touched the warden's net and pointed toward the group around Nola. One of the searchers had come close, so now there were four, counting Klooney. The warden nodded, and lifted the net from her shoulder. She tapped Pua's arm and pointed toward another of the guards who had just stepped into the shallow pool.

"*Go!*" she shouted so loud that even Pua jumped.

Pua leapt into the room and onto the back of the guard in the pool. She heard the swush of the net being thrown behind her. The guard had been startled by the warden's cry, enough so that Pua was able to get a hold around his neck. But he recovered fast. He twisted and spun, trying to tear Pua's hands away with his own stubby fingers.

"This is for Nola!" Pua cried, and ripped the man's gills wide open. He went slack under her, and Pua jumped clear. She had time to see that the warden's net had caught the waterguards near Nola, but Klooney was rolling away. Then another Earther was on her.

He reached, stupidly, for Pua's hands. She slashed his fingers with her sharp nails, and when he pulled back, she reached up and found another set of vulnerable gills. The guard gasped and went white with pain, but kept fighting feebly. Pua cracked his neck.

The warden had freed Nola. She still had her knife in one hand, a spear in the other. Pua saw that the second spear was resting in the chest of yet another Earther. Klooney and Dr. Waight had disappeared. They had taken Little Ten with them.

A loud thunk and crash came from the back of the cave. The waterlock. Uncle Toma had come! A thud and Toma's powerful shout came just before a waterguard's shriek. Nobody could fight like Uncle Toma. The warden raced ahead of Pua out of the nursery. Well, almost nobody, Pua thought.

They followed Waight's shouting to the main entry. Waight was just disappearing through the blown hatch. She still had Little Ten clutched to her chest. Klooney dropped through the hatch behind her.

The warden dove for him, but she was knocked aside by a waterguard. They wrestled to the side, he reaching for her hands, she for his gills. Pua dove after 'Umi Iki.

The outer door was completely blown away, and she had to pick her way through a narrow opening of stone and metal rubble. She raced through the dark passage to the outer chamber. Ahead of her, a waterguard grabbed Dr. Waight's arm and pulled her down, toward the exit channel to the open sea.

Pua dove after them, but was stopped by a strong blow to her stomach. Someone had kicked her. She doubled up and rolled away, retching. A hand grabbed her arm. A waterworlder's hand. *Klooney!* She straightened and kicked in return, but she could not match his strength. He grinned in the dimly lit water.

They rolled to the surface as Pua fought to reach Klooney's gills. His arms were longer than hers, but her finger length almost made up the difference. They twisted and turned, fighting the fight of waterworlders. He slammed her against the wall, and she cried out in spite of herself. A sharp pain stabbed through her side.

As she surfaced, she saw Klooney glance around in confusion. The light flickered and changed. Her body slapping against the stone had triggered the shifting light show that brought the

Grand Old Man to life. Pua had time to rake the nails of both hands down across Klooney's face and chest.

He screamed in fury, grabbed her, and lifted her high out of the water. He threw her against the wall.

As Pua struck the stone, the world went black, then exploded with brilliant pain.

She opened her eyes to meet the angry stare of the Grand Old Man. As she slid, helpless, down the cold, stone wall, her fingertips caught in the slick folds of the Old Man's hair and tore the flickering image away.

Chapter 27

~~~~~~~~~~
~~~~~~~~~~

Fatu sat bolt upright as Le Fe'e's scream of rage ripped through the burial cave. The ground shifted, and a pair of lanterns fell and shattered into darkness. Wind gusted in under the entrance, spinning storm debris across the abruptly terrified humans. They cried out while shadows spun.

"What was that?" someone called.

"Earthquake!"

"Gotta be the wind . . ."

". . . storm surge hitting the island."

"It's Le Fe'e, you fools!" Fatu was on his feet. His bellow was almost as great as the god's own. He strode toward the entrance.

"Stay where you are!" one of the idiot waterguards shouted. She stepped into his path.

"Get out of my way, Earther," he said.

"My orders are to keep everyone in the cave," she said. She lifted a small pneumatic speargun, little more than a dart gun, and pointed it at his chest. It made Fatu want to laugh, that sorry excuse for a weapon. He could see in the woman's eyes that she wished it were a laser.

"You've had fair warning," she said.

He moved.

She fired. It was a quick, sharp sting over his heart.

Fatu stopped. He held the waterguard's startled gaze as he snapped the molded plastic off with his fingertips. He knew better than to attempt pulling the barbed tip out without assistance. Before she could fire again, he wrenched the gun away, crushed it in his palm, and tossed it to one side. The woman took a fighting stance as he moved again toward the entrance.

"Idiot," he muttered. He slid his wide hands around her thin waist and lifted her toward the ceiling. She threw her hands up to protect her head, and they brushed the trailing roots of the friendly vines. The thin, strong strands coiled around her wrists.

"Hey, let me go! Let me down!"

Fatu released his grip, and she remained hanging there by her entangled hands. She screamed and swore.

Pua's orator's staff was lying on the clicker fronds near Fatu's feet. He picked it up and turned back to the others. He straightened the staff where it had been cracked by someone's careless step. The wind shrieked and howled.

"Listen!" Fatu cried. The Earthers backed away, carefully not touching anything but one another. "Do you hear it? Pua's cry rides that wind. And the tiny, precious wail of 'Umi Iki rides at her side. That is the cry of Le Fe'e. It is the death cry of a god." He wondered if it was possible for a man's soul to break. How can I hear it so clearly? he wondered. How can I know just what it says?

He pointed Pua's staff at Crawley, who was paying him no attention. The Company bastard was still under the influence of the red-clad troubleshooter's truth drug.

"They went there, didn't they?" Fatu said. "Your murderers. They went to Sa le Fe'e, and now they are attempting to destroy our children. How? How did you know where to send them?"

A sudden flash of memory stopped him, shook him so that he almost fell. He now understood Pua's exquisite pain at that moment when she learned she had given Sa le Fe'e away.

"You took it from *me*! The old woman, she spoke to me while the drug was still working. I remember now."

Fatu moved slowly forward; the Earthers backed farther away.

Lehua's sweet candleberry scent lifted around him. "You came to Pukui six months ago, and Kalehuaokalae fed you. You came here to kill her, and she *fed* you!" He was shouting now. "Because that is the Lesaat way, Company man! That is the *Island* way! To offer courtesy and hospitality to visitors in your home. To honor the trust that must exist if peace is ever to happen among humans and their worlds."

He pulled the staff back and cradled it against his bloodied chest. His voice dropped to a whisper. "And you killed her!"

He took another step forward.

"You knew she had eaten loli the night before, so you used a fast-acting mimic of loli fever symptoms so everyone would think that's how she died. A small scratch, a prick to the side of the neck. That's all it needed. Lehua first, upstairs and alone.

Then Zed, as he rushed to her aid. And then Pua. But you used something different with Pua, because you wanted her to live. Then you took them all away before any tests could be made here that would prove your lie."

Fatu pointed the staff again. "Ask him if what I say is true, troubleshooter. Ask him right now if it is true."

"Crawley," the woman's level voice said—she remained as damnably calm as the warden. "Is what Fatu says true? Were Lehua and Zed Pukui killed deliberately?"

"Yes," came the soft, bitter reply.

"Who gave the order for their murders?"

"I gave it."

"Who did the actual killing?"

"Waight."

"Doctor Ruby Rewald Waight? The elderly woman who was here earlier tonight?"

"Yes."

The troubleshooter sat back. The other Earthers, even the waterguards, stared at Crawley in horror.

"I am Pukui, too, Company man," Fatu said. "I will avenge *all* of Pukui's deaths. I claim your miserable, greed-laden soul, in Pua's name and in the name of my family. I don't even care that you won't know what's happening," he said. "Be glad, Earther, that the drug makes you numb."

The last of the uninjured waterguards started for him, but Lili pulled him back. Lili, the Company crew boss who had been with them all along without their even knowing. She had explained that she had been called to Earth months before by the troubleshooter Pua had called Sally. The Earther had been following Crawley's foul trail from the beginning.

Lili had hidden at the Ka'u spaceport for months in order to travel back to Lesaat with the warden and Pua, and then, once there, had formally documented the Company's attempts to destroy Pukui's algae harvest.

"I can't let you kill him, Fatu."

The troubleshooter, the small scarlet-clad woman, stood between him and Crawley. She was little taller than Fatu's waist, and so dark of skin that the pigment could only be natural. He could break her apart with one hand.

"If you kill him," she said very calmly, "then Pukui might still be lost."

He waited. He wanted more than anything to kill this man who had eaten once again on Pukui land.

"He is our witness," the small woman said. "He must be kept alive to speak the Company's crimes. There is more than Pukui at stake here tonight, Fatu. I sympathize with your pain, but I cannot allow you to kill him."

Fatu took a long shuddering breath. Always, it came back to this. The greater good for the greater number. Once again, he must stand at the side and watch while others faced the enemy. He ran his fingers along Pua's staff. Finally, he nodded, hating the movement. The hanging waterguard whimpered.

Outside, the storm raged.

Inside, Fatu began to sing.

"This is the night of alignment," he began. "It is a night to be feared and respected, for on this night, the paths of Lesaat's moons cross. They become as one just as Shadow kisses Zenith. The timing of all Pukui's harvests are based on this night that happens only once in every three years. It is a night that even the Earth, with all its hungry people, must respect."

He lifted the staff, small and broken. He held it as Pua had done. "I will tell you a story that my good friend, Pualeiokekai, once told me." The Earthers shifted and whispered, then stilled. They were wise to fear him just now. The troubleshooter watched them all without apparent emotion.

"The shadow you've seen crossing Lesaat's heavens each night is not a shadow at all," he said, "but Le Fe'e, crawling along the rings to survey his domain. Tonight, when Le Fe'e reaches halfway, he will be close enough to reach up and touch both moons. He is attracted by their light, and they will tempt him, as they do every three years on this special night, to join them in their cold, dark sky.

" 'The tips of your tentacles are warm,' they will call, for they remember how Le Fe'e was pulled from the Earth long ago. They will try to trick him, for they are greedy and would like to have his full warmth, not caring that it would leave the planet below bereft.

" 'Wrap your tentacles around us and share your warmth,' they will say. 'We will light your ocean in return. See how brightly we shine, both of us traveling so close together, sailing hand-in-hand in the sky.'

"And because Le Fe'e is a great and generous god," Fatu said, pulling the staff close again, "he will offer his hospitality to the cold moons."

Fatu's fingers played along the carvings of the orator's pole. What magic do these markings hold? he wondered. And then,

Is this how a belief system begins? Fatu was no longer sure what he believed, only that it was rooted in this time and this place. His fingers reached the crack in Pua's small stick.

He went on. "A great battle will ensue. For the moons have conspired to trap Le Fe'e's tentacles between them just as they cross paths. With their doubled strength, they will try to dislodge him from the rings.

"But Le Fe'e always keeps two of his long tentacles anchored around his Pukui home. He does not wish to leave this joyous, golden place." A tear scalded Fatu's cheek, and he rocked with the cadence of Pua's song. The sound of wind and pounding surf slid through the cracks in his words.

"The moons will pull and pull. They will pull Le Fe'e so hard that his hold on Pukui will stretch the very seas. The water will rise higher and higher as Le Fe'e is stretched away by the moons. The struggle will cause a great whirlpool of wind and rain, which will rip and tear at Le Fe'e—and at Pukui, and at all things nearby. Mountainous waves will be torn from the sea and thrown onto the land. Maram and her small sister, Maram Iki, will pull and pull until Le Fe'e is nearly torn in half.

"But always, the great and gentle Le Fe'e will continue his journey across the rings. Using his four remaining arms, he will pull and crawl his way along the rings' sharp edges. He will be cut and bloodied, beaten and battered, but he knows that if he can reach the western horizon, the moons' strength will fade. Their light will be made useless by the coming dawn. They will be forced to release their hold, and Le Fe'e and Pukui will be free."

Fatu looked slowly around at them all. "If you have a god that you pray to," he said softly, "spend this night praying that Le Fe'e has the strength to reach the western horizon before Pukui is ripped entirely from the sea."

He bent and laid the orator's staff beside Lili. She covered it with a protective hand. Fatu wiped a trickle of blood from the wound in his chest and crossed again to the cave's entrance.

"Do not follow me outside," he said without looking back. "No unprotected Earther will survive Shadow's crossing tonight. Le Fe'e has promised me that. Your only haven is this cave of the dead."

As Fatu crawled from the burial cave, the wind suddenly slowed. He stood, and the howling scream stopped. Fatu o le Motu walked forward into the eye of the storm.

Chapter 28

~~~~~~~~~~~~~~~~~~~~~
~~~~~~~~~~~~~~~~~~~~~

Angie reached the outer cave just as Pua fell. She kicked hard toward her, but was slammed away and into the wall by Klooney as he dove toward the exit channel. A waterguard, the last Angie could see in the bloodied water, fired at her from close range. She tried to turn away from his line of fire, but the water slowed her movements. A short, barbed spear caught her left hand near the base of the last two fingers. She shook her hand, but the spear did not dislodge.

The waterguard fired again, wide to Angie's left, then made the mistake of attacking with his hands. There was no contest then. Even with her left hand disabled, Angie's long, strong fingers reached his gills easily. The guard's eyes opened wide, his mouth wider in a scream, as Angie's nails caught and ripped through the sensitive tissues. She kneed him in the stomach and left him to retch and choke as she turned back to Pua.

Pua had sunk to the bottom of the cave. She was blinking rapidly, hugging her right arm tightly around her chest. Her left hand was not moving. There was no question that she was hurt. She jerked when Angie touched her, but before Angie could move her or even speak, she said, "Get 'Umi! Go, Mountain-lady!"

Angie hesitated. She didn't want to leave Pua like this. There was no telling what internal damage the girl might have suffered. The skin along her chest and thighs was scraped raw where she had slid along the wall. If it had not been for the friendly vines that patterned her body, the wounds would have been much deeper. As it was, they glowed with embedded shards of slime mold.

"Go." Pua pushed her away and struggled upright.

Angie knew she was right. They could not allow Waight to

escape with Little Ten. She brushed her good hand along Pua's arm and dove for the exit. As she swam through the dark, watery tunnel, she faced her suffocating terror of such places once again. It had not diminished, but this time she accepted it as a gift, because it was a good, clean fear, born of simple accident rather than human greed.

As she left the shelter of the channel, she was struck by the underwater fury of the storm. She had almost forgotten that it was still going on. The continuous roar of the swells pounding the reef had become background noise inside Sa le Fe'e. White noise, she thought nonsensically as she kicked away from the reef into the furiously bioluminescent sea.

The noise was no longer background. It pummeled her like a living thing, tugging and pulling at her like the wildly fluctuating currents. Far to the left, she saw the foaming mouth of the tunnel exit. The effervescent, debris-laden current stretched far out to sea. Gray-clad swimmers moved here and there along the reef face between her and the outflow tunnel. Setting charges, Angie thought.

A swirling eddy caught her and thrust her back into the coral. She managed to stop herself before being scraped too far across the jagged surface, but then her left hand brushed against a jutting branch of knife coral. The spear caught in the iron-hard thicket. A plume of sand and shards of broken coral swirled past. Shreds of rubbery orange sludge clung to her skin.

Algae, she thought. It's already being carried outside the reef. Thank god it's dead!

A movement away from the reef face caught Angie's attention. She activated her distance focus. It was a swimmer—no, two swimmers close together, fighting the current toward the dark oblong shape of a minisub. She blinked rapidly again, and saw that it was Waight, still carrying 'Umi Iki. The waterguard with her carried a bright yellow detonator on his belt. He was dragging Waight along with the aid of a hand jet.

Angie twisted and pulled at her hand again, but it was well and truly caught. There was only one way to free herself. She ducked a tumbling chunk of brain coral as she wrapped the two caught fingers around the razor-sharp branch that held them. She yanked. Hard and fast, with all her strength—

—and shuddered with screaming pain as the barbed spear, and her fingers, were sliced away. Quickly, she wrapped a strip of her shirt tightly around her hand. She held a breath she didn't have and blinked back to a clear focus. She kicked away from the reef and into the swirling storm.

"Le Fe'e," she called as she fought against the conflicting currents. "If you exist, this would be a good time . . ." Her air ran out just as she caught the edge of a current that drew her faster in the direction of the sub. She saw a pair of waterguards point and start her way, but their hand jets were not strong enough to carry them through the crosscurrents between them.

Angie wished she had one of Pua's rays. They had moved so effortlessly through the storm-tossed seas. At least Waight and the waterguard seemed to be having as much trouble controlling their movements as she. More, she saw. The minisub suddenly bucked, rolled, and swung away, then began making its slow way back toward them. It would not be an easy pickup.

Another of the free-swimming waterguards saw Angie and turned her way. He stopped abruptly as a small scarlet coiler, riding open on the currents, brushed against one of his legs. The coiler snapped shut, and the waterguard bent hurriedly to try to pry it off. Angie concentrated on the swimmers ahead.

An algae-laden current struck her from behind, and suddenly Angie came face-to-face with Ruby Waight. The same current that threw them together swept Waight's waterguard up and away. The touch of yellow at his belt flickered through the phosphorescent sea.

Waight stared at Angie through wide, pale eyes. She clutched 'Umi Iki to her chest with one hand, while paddling uselessly at the surging water with the other.

Angie reached, not for the baby—'Umi was too small to survive a tug-of-war—but for Waight's oxymask. Waight twisted away. She lifted the baby to shield her face. Little Ten hung limp in her hands, and Angie couldn't tell if the child was alive or dead. Waight resisted with surprising agility. She refused to release the infant even when it was clear she had no hope of reaching the sub, which had been forced far off again by the swirling seas.

Waight bared her teeth behind her transparent airmask, and Angie could taste her hatred right through the storm. They tumbled and rolled at the mercy of the conflicting currents. They were deep enough so that the main fury of the storm was above them, but the currents were still strong—strong enough to sweep yet another pair of waterguards away. Still, no matter how she twisted and turned, Angie could not get a hold on Waight without endangering the infant.

Suddenly, there was a change in Waight's expression, and a tension in her body that had not existed the moment before. Fear. Angie recognized it instantly. Terror flooded Waight's icy blue eyes.

All at once, she stopped fighting. She released Little Ten, and Angie snatched the child into her arms before the current could sweep the tiny thing away.

Instead, it was Waight who was drawn away, away and down. Something dark and thick had wrapped around the old woman's legs. Angie blinked. Waight screamed behind her mask and bent to scrape her hands along her thighs.

There's nothing there, Angie told herself. She's just caught in a current. She blinked again, but could see only inky darkness engulfing Waight's lower body.

Waight stared up at Angie. She cried out and lifted her hands. She screamed and shrieked; Angie heard her clearly through the sea. Angie reached out with her injured hand—an instinctive move, human to human in this tumultuous alien ocean—but an icy current swept her and Little Ten up and out of reach. Only Angie's torn hand did not feel the cold; her missing fingers burned as if they were still back in the fire where the battle had begun.

She twisted and turned, fighting the water's pull, but by the time she could turn back, Waight had disappeared.

The baby moved, and Angie shifted her far enough up her chest to hold her with her injured hand. She was tremendously relieved to see that the child's tiny gills were flared and pulsing. Little Ten twisted her miniature fingers in the tatters of Angie's shirt, clinging instinctively, as Angie tried to turn back toward the reef. The infant's skin was warm and slick.

The current that had separated them from Waight collided with another, and they were tumbled and rolled and tossed back down. Knowing that the deeper water would be calmer, Angie finally stopped fighting the current and let it carry them down.

A shadow crossed their path. Klooney, making for one of the subs. If she had not been holding the baby, Angie would have gone after him. Troubleshooter's ethics be damned. She would have gone after him and killed him right here in this storm-tossed sea.

Then she saw Pua.

The girl was swimming with her left arm limp at her side, her father's knife clenched between her teeth. Torn friendly vines and seaweed still circled her limbs, and a long, thin strand of algae trailed from one ankle. She followed haltingly on Klooney's bloody trail.

Klooney must have sensed her approach, for he turned suddenly and looked back. He tensed, then relaxed. A slow grin spread across his scarred and bloodied face. He pulled a knife from his own leg sheath. Again, waterguards tried to intervene. They aimed their hand jets into Pua's path, but she evaded them without ever straying from her own straight course toward Klooney.

Angie glanced down at the baby. There was no way she could help. If the sea had been calm, she could have left the baby to drift, at least for a short time, but in the battering storm currents, she could not let the child go. And she could not fight with the baby in her arms. She rode the current and watched.

"Take care, Little Fe'e," she whispered into the water.

Would the thing from the deep rise to rescue Pua as it had Little Ten? Angie wondered. She saw no sign of whatever it had been. It was just a tide-pissing current! she told herself forcefully. Still, she watched for its return.

Pua came within reach of Klooney. She still held the knife in her teeth. He thrust at her with his knife, and she bent away from his reach. Angie saw her face twist with pain. Pua slid her sharp nails along Klooney's arm. He yelled silently, and backed away. They circled.

If the currents were affecting them, Angie couldn't see it. It was as if they were fighting in a vacuum, a closed space all their own. No waterguards went near them.

Klooney struck again, nicking Pua's left arm. Again, her nails reached him, this time along his left side. He winced and turned, and she raked him across the back.

He was furious now, wilder in his movements—and at every instant of carelessness, Pua bloodied him further. Little Ten squirmed, and Angie looked down at her. She did not want to watch Pua kill, or be killed by, this man. This was a different battle from those Pua had fought inside Sa le Fe'e. There, she had struck in an instant, killing fast and sure to save her own life and those of the people she protected. Just as Angie had herself.

Now, it was almost as if Pua were toying with Klooney, scratching at him line by line, although Angie was certain that the instant an opening occurred, Pua would rip out not only the man's gills but his blackened heart if she could. She wondered why Pua did not use her knife.

Something velvety smooth slid along Angie's back. She spun
around, not an easy thing to do in the turbulent sea, and almost
wept with relief. It was one of the reef rays. She stroked its
wings as it swept past a second time, and when it returned to
lift under her, she gratefully accepted the ride. She clung to it
with her legs and her one free hand.

She saw the other rays then. Many of them, circling the roiling
currents. Human swimmers, in pairs and sometimes threes, were
clinging to their backs. Even some of the smaller, single-winged
rays carried riders. The Earther waterguards had begun gathering around the minisubs. The rays took their riders near and
slowed for them to dismount.

Angie wondered if the rays themselves would attack the
Earthers, but they did not. They swept in wide circles, defying
all but the strongest currents, and left the humans to fight their
own battles.

The waterguards turned instantly to the defense. It was clear
they fought as a well-trained unit, swift and sure of their movements in the sea, even this turbulent sea. They fired quick vol-
leys with their hand spears. Two of Pukui's defenders were struck
before they could get close.

Then an Earther jerked and sank back. Another quickly followed. And a third. The Earthers broke ranks suddenly and
scrambled to take cover behind the subs. Angie saw Kobayashi
take aim again, and another Earther tumbled away with a bright
yellow dart protruding from his chest.

Another pair of waterworlders were struck by the Earthers'
crossfire, but by then the rest had gotten close enough to fight
the Earthers hand to hand. The Earthers' stubby hands were no
match for the waterworlders' long, needle-tipped fingers. Years
of working the algae nets had left the Lesaat swimmers strong
and agile in ways the Earthers had never faced before.

One of the subs powered forward and rammed three of the
waterworlders. They spun helplessly away. Two others tried to
grab the sub as it passed them, but they could do nothing to stop
it. It started into a wide turn back. But it skimmed too close to
the powerful tunnel current. The clang of metal striking metal
shivered through the water as some shredded remnant of Pukui
farm equipment struck the sub. The vessel tumbled helplessly,
out of control in the storm-fed current, toward the open sea.

A roar and a rumbling crash sounded from the reef face. An
explosion! Angie huddled over Little Ten and clung to the ray
as the shock wave passed.

They were blowing the reef, just as Waight had said. The waterguard with the detonator must have made it into the remaining sub. The ray would not take Angie to Pua, so she urged it back toward the reef. She had to find Toma, or Pili, or someone who knew the click-talk of the rays. They had to evacuate Sa le Fe'e before the rest of the charges were blown.

"Pili!" she called to the ray, thinking that Pili would probably be the most familiar to the rays. Her mount's great wings lifted and lowered. They slid through the battering sea almost as if it weren't there. We'll have to pull everyone from inside the reef, injured or not, Angie thought, and take them deep enough to ride out the storm. She thought of Nola and her twisted leg and wondered if it could even be done.

Suddenly, Pili was beside her, astride the back of one of the largest rays. He stared at her across the distance between them, the width of two rays' wings, then suddenly grinned when he saw Little Ten. The baby was sucking contentedly on Angie's shirt. For just an instant, Angie wondered what seawater would do for the infant's digestion. She motioned Pili close.

When he joined her on the back of her ray, she pointed to where the blast had occurred and then toward the sub, making the motions of activating a detonator. Then she pointed back to Sa le Fe'e. "Get everyone out," she called. "Hurry!"

Pili's eyes darkened as he caught her meaning. He clicked his nails in rapid sequence, and before she could thrust Little Ten into his arms, he kicked back to his own ray. They swept away.

Directly toward the sub.

"No! Pili!" she cried, but she had no air to force the warning out. She watched helplessly as Pili and the ray raced on a collision course toward the unsuspecting minisub. In the last instant before they struck, the ray flicked Pili from its back. The boy tumbled away in the current as the giant ray smashed into the sub's side.

The observation bubble popped free, and a great gout of air burst upward and shattered into bloodstained effervescence. The sub's stabilizing engines ripped away. The ray's force carried its body almost through the sub. Had it been just a little stronger, it might have actually shaken the jagged metal container free of its wings. But a long gash had been opened along the ray's underside. It lost strength quickly as dark fluid poured into the sea. The tangle of dying ray and twisted metal sank together into the cold sea.

Another ray swept close to Angie. Both Toma and Pili were

riding its back. Urgently, she waved them back toward Pua and Klooney. With her extreme focus, she could just see them. The man and the girl were still fighting. The rays took them closer, circled, but still did not interfere. Pua had weakened greatly. Her movements grew slower and slower. She could not find a way to reach fully beyond Klooney's guard.

Klooney recognized that, too, and increased his own faltering efforts to kill her. The water swirled with their blood. Angie released her hold on the ray and would have gone to Pua's aid despite Little Ten, but the ray swam beneath her again and bumped her up and away. A second ray glided close to her side, and Angie shivered at the flash of exposed teeth. Toma, too, tried to reach Pua, but was restrained by both the rays and Pili.

Suddenly, Pua tensed. She glanced around and quickly backed away. She took the knife from between her teeth. Klooney grinned. He had her now—even from a distance, Angie could see triumph light his eyes.

A shrill whistle screamed through the sea, then a series, a multitude, of high-pitched whistles. Even Klooney spun back to face the sound.

"Suckersharks!" Angie breathed.

A dense black cloud was boiling from the mouth of the tunnel. It expanded as it reached the open water. It paused, then condensed again and turned toward the human swimmers. Suckersharks, drawn all the way through the reef by the smell of blood. The waterworlders raced toward Sa le Fe'e's entrance. The rays swept among them, scooping up those too slow and the injured, Earther and waterworlder alike. They deposited them at the channel entrance. Despite Toma's protest, his mount bore him and the boy that way, as well.

"Pua!" Angie screamed.

The girl was almost motionless in the water. She paddled slowly with her wide, webbed feet. She watched without apparent concern as the black cloud swept closer and closer.

At the same time, Klooney was panicking. He was already covered with bleeding scratches, and he knew he had no chance of survival. He flailed at the converging sharks with his knife. He fought them away, one by one, then by the dozens. But for every one that he killed or scraped away, another found some unprotected place on his body. They pulled themselves tight with their suckered mouths, then extended their ragged, hollow teeth through his skin. Klooney screamed airlessly into the sea.

Pua reached down and scraped one of the suckers from her

own slick skin. Her movement was slow and spoke of great pain. Angie could taste Pua's exhaustion riding on the swirling eddies.

At last, Angie's ray moved. It glided down, then rose under Pua so that Angie could reach her with her injured hand. She pulled Pua to her side, keeping the baby between them, and the ray slid swiftly away. A suckershark attached to the ray's forward wing, but Pua reached out with her knife and flicked it away.

Pua shifted so she could see Little Ten, then sighed and closed her eyes.

A tiny flood of warmth pooled against Angie's chest. 'Umi Iki was releasing seawater back into the sea. Pua's mouth opened slightly; her tongue flicked out. She grinned without opening her eyes.

When they reached the reef face, Angie slid from the ray's back. Toma was there to take Pua; Pili took the infant. They disappeared immediately into the dark entrance to Sa le Fe'e.

Angie glanced back once at the raging bioluminescent sea, shadowed now by the roiling cloud of rapacious sharks. Le Fe'e rumbled and roared.

"I don't know what you are," Angie whispered. "I'm not even sure *if* you are. But you sing a fireloving fine song."

She followed the others inside. Midway through the dark channel, she realized that her terror of the closed, wet space had disappeared.

Chapter 29

"You should have seen Papa Toma jump out of the lock, Auntie Puhi," one of the twins said. Angie was not sure which was which. They both sat cross-legged in front of her. One had a patch above his left eye; the other, a bandage wrapped around his knee. Both wore braided moss around their ankles.

"He looked like a skudder jumping out of a puhi hole," the other one said, and they both laughed. They had told her the story half a dozen times already, and each time it became more exciting and dramatic.

"Boys, leave the warden alone. Let her rest."

Nola spoke from across the nursery. It was the area that had sustained the least damage from the fighting and the blasting and was being used now as a makeshift infirmary. Injured Earthers and waterworlders lay side by side on the moss. Nola's splinted leg was stretched in front of her on the floor. 'Umi Iki was at her breast. The infant, at least, seemed none the worse for her adventure into the storm.

"It's all right," Angie said. "I can't sleep anyway."

She glanced down at Pua. The girl had not stirred since she had been brought into the cave. Not even when Toma examined her and then splinted her broken left forearm and taped her ribs. Sa le Fe'e was well equipped with medical and diagnostic equipment, and after running a series of scans, Toma assured Angie that Pua had sustained no serious internal damage.

The friendly vines, tattered and torn though they had been, had saved the girl from the worst of Klooney's knife attack, but her skin was still crisscrossed with bloodied markings. After peeling the vines away, they had immersed her in the nursery pool so her skin would continue excreting its protective and healing mucus coating.

296

Fatu had appeared sometime during the night, at what sounded like the height of the storm. He did not say how he had gotten there. It must have been via the rays, but there was something in his expression that encouraged Angie not to ask. When he arrived, there had been a pneumatic dart–tip imbedded in his chest. Toma had cut it neatly away.

Now Fatu was sitting beside the pool, chanting and stroking Pua's injured arm, rocking to the cadence of the diminishing storm.

Angie's own injury had been bandaged and a pain-control patch applied to her wrist. There was little more that could be done. The fingers would regenerate, both Toma and Nola had assured her, and be just as strong as before.

One of the boys touched her injured hand. "I lost a tip once," he said. It was Keha, she decided, because he was the most talkative of the two. "It hurt."

"He cried," Kiki said.

Keha frowned.

"But not much," Kiki added quickly.

"How come you have hands like ours?" Keha asked. "We thought only kids—"

"Come on, you two." Toma, hollow-eyed and pale with exhaustion, tapped the boys' behinds with his foot. "Go help at the thermal pool. They need somebody small to carry rocks through the pipe." He shooed the boys from the nursery.

"Sleep," he said to Angie.

She nodded, and tried. It was useless.

She could still feel the storm. It roared and rumbled and shivered through the solid stone. It must be deafening where Mariko and the rest of the kids are, she thought. A slide, caused most likely by the Earthers' blast, had blocked the outlet pipe from the hot tub, so they were weathering the storm in the small outer cave where Angie had first seen them.

They were known to be safe, because Pili had led Zena, the smallest of the adults, through a maze of narrow cracks and hidden pools to a place where they could communicate with the stranded group through the children's click-talk. A crew that occasionally included Kiki and Keha worked to clear the blockage. Others searched Sa le Fe'e and the surrounding reef for the remaining explosive charges the Earthers had set.

Pua's eyes opened. She woke in that strange way of hers—all at once, without any prior movement. She blinked and tried to sit up.

"Ooow!"

And dropped back underwater. She blinked again, more rapidly, as she fought away tears. Her eyes widened slightly when she saw Fatu. He and Angie reached into the water to help, and this time Pua made it upright. She winced and grimaced. She grunted a few times, but she didn't cry again.

" 'Umi?'' she asked as soon as she had breath. She stared straight at Angie. Watching to be sure I'm telling her the truth, Angie mused. Spit, but she loved this little waterbrat. Never get too close, her rational side intervened. But it was much too late.

" 'Umi Iki's fine," she said.

"And Pili and—"

"They're all fine. Kiki and Keha each have a bandage, but their injuries are small. They just wanted to look like the rest of us."

Pua's look dropped to Angie's hand, then shifted across the room. "Oh, Auntie Nola," she whispered. A tear sneaked out then.

Nola shifted Little Ten to her other breast. "Don't you worry about me, Pualei," she said. "I could still catch you if I had to."

Pua smiled and turned back to Angie. "Did we do it, Mountainlady?" she asked with that same direct look.

Angie nodded.

"Ha!" Pua said softly.

Then she demanded food and a full recounting of all that had happened during the night. When she heard of the ray that had died along with the minisub, she cried again.

They all listened with rapt attention as Fatu described Crawley's questioning back at the burial cave, and Pua nodded her approval when he admitted to sharing her story of Le Fe'e and the greedy moons. Like Angie, she did not ask Fatu how he had gotten from the burial cave to her side.

Kiki and Keha had raced back to the nursery as soon as they learned Pua was awake, and once again they shared their own adventurous tale. Keha was particularly proud, because his small injury, made larger by the story, had occurred when he slipped while throwing a rock at Klooney.

"Pua," Angie said. "Why didn't you use your knife when you fought that man?"

"Why would I use a knife when I have my hands?" Pua replied.

"Well, then, why did you carry it in your teeth all that time?"

"When they talk, nobody ever answers," Kiki explained to a nearby swimmer.

Pua laughed. "Because I knew I'd need it to scrape the suckers off after the fight, and the sheath strap got cut while we were still with the Old Man."

"But why wouldn't the rays, or even Pili, let Toma and me help you?" Angie asked.

Pua's eyes darkened. She was quiet for a moment. Then she said, "Because Klooney was mine."

Angie did not question her further.

Some hours later, an opening was made through the slide, and Mariko and the rest of the children were brought back inside. They were fed, and Mariko's injury was cared for, then all the stories were told over again.

No one even spoke of leaving Sa le Fe'e until a full day had passed. Then they timed their departure to take advantage of the changing tide. They waited until the racing storm current gave way to the more orderly tidal movements through the barrier reef channel. Pili and Pua called the rays to the fishing exit gate, and all but Nola and the younger children, and four Pukui adults to help her care for them, made their way back into Pukui Lagoon.

Even underwater it was clear that the unprepared farm had been destroyed. Tattered shreds of netting hung from pens that had not been lifted before the storm. The barge was nowhere to be seen. Several full lengths of cold-water pipe had been torn from their mountings and lay bent and broken across the reef flats.

Great boulders of coral had been carried on the storm surge all the way to the inner lagoon. Later, some were found well inland on both Home and Second islands. The smaller, more fragile coral had fared worst. Brilliantly colored shards were scattered everywhere, and skims of dark, dead algae streaked the rubbled surface.

Pua spotted a giant grazer caught in a tangle of netting and insisted they stop to free it. She refused to allow the fish to be taken back to the island for food and had them bring it to her to kiss before they set it free.

Out of the water, the devastation of the farm was even worse. The main dock was gone, along with all the crews' quarters and science and production buildings. They lay in scattered heaps across the perfectly manicured lawn. The grass seemed not to have suffered at all.

Pua cried out in shock when she saw the main house, or what was left of it. Only the first-story floor remained, incongruously surrounded by the undamaged lanai railing. A few upright posts and a portion of the stairs remained, but the rest had been scoured clean. It was wind damage, because the sea had not reached that high. The rain had washed the floor clean.

The cookhouse and Katie's small cottage had disappeared, and the housekeeper had set up temporary residence under the main house floor. She had already gathered a small pile of broken artifacts from Lehua's prized collection. Only the farm control shed remained intact. Some strange quirk of the storm had left it almost unscathed.

Crews were already at work cataloging and sorting the damage, digging through the collapsed buildings for salvage. The deep-water pumps had all been shut down, and the lines were being inspected. There was no division between Company and non-Company crews, just as there had been none among the waterworlders who had fought outside Sa le Fe'e. This was a waterworld tragedy, and on this job they worked as one.

When word spread about Crawley and Waight and how Zed and Lehua had died, Sally had to set extra guards to keep Crawley from being torn apart by his own Company swimmers. The Earther waterguards, those few who were left alive, were locked inside the cave to wait for the first transport off Pukui and the planet.

Pukui's freshwater pools flowed stronger than ever after the downpour of the storm, and the sea still provided its bounty of food. Windfall in the jungle provided enough edibles for a week of feasting. The waterworlders and the much subdued U.N. inspection team settled in for the cleanup.

By the second morning, airborne crews from Landing arrived. They set about cleaning up as much of the dead algae as possible from the inner reef. Later in the day, three hydrobuses loaded with relief supplies and additional crews came through the pass.

It was on that day that Angie found Nori Yoshida, still secured under the dripping, moss-hung ledge where the swimmers had put him the night of the storm. They had fed him since, but otherwise left him alone. Although he had been protected from the worst of the weather, a muddy runoff of jungle sludge still oozed past his feet. His uniform was torn and filthy, and when he saw Angie, he cursed and swore and threatened dire revenge.

Angie watched him for a moment, finding it curious that the

pain of his betrayal and the rage she had used to protect herself from it no longer existed. She felt nothing toward him but disgust.

Later, she suggested to Sally that Nori would make a good companion for Crawley when the disgraced Company man was transferred to his new permanent assignment on Mensat.

"Nori has a strong back," Angie said, "and they say that after the first decade or so, Mensat settlers hardly notice the guano's stench."

When Sally's second U.N. inspection team arrived that same day, Pukui's entire story was told one more time. This time it was formally recorded.

Angie watched the proceedings, but allowed Sally to lead them. She refused to reveal the site of the missing TC enzyme records until Pua and the children's indigenous-rights claim had been settled. Pua roamed in and out of the burial cave while the discussions were taking place, usually with Pili at her side, and the Earthers from both inspection teams paid her very careful respect. She finally decided their deference was funny, and began smiling again.

Late on the fourth day, Sally called Angie and Fatu to one side. "We need to talk," she said. Grayson, the real U.N. team leader, joined them, as did Toma and Pua.

Angie sat at Sally's urging. Something else had gone wrong. She could see it in Sally's eyes. Fatu leaned against the wall. He had grown even quieter since the storm. Calmer, Angie thought. At peace with himself in a way he had not been before. Angie looked forward to a time when they could sit together privately and speak of the things they had done and seen the night of the storm. She wondered if he understood them any better than she.

"World Life has formally filed to reclaim all Pukui leases," Sally said, pulling Angie back to the present with a thud.

Fatu straightened. "What?"

"They can't—" Angie began.

"The reef has been seriously damaged," the U.N. leader said, "and the farm has been completely destroyed."

"It can be rebuilt, Mr. Grayson," Fatu said. "There's no live algae out there to bloom, so—"

"It can't be rebuilt without major financing," Grayson said. "The combined assets of Pukui's current leaseholders aren't nearly enough. If the partial harvest could have been saved, it might have made a difference, but the processing plant and all its contents were destroyed."

"Surely Pukui can get a loan against the expected profits from the TC production," Angie said.

"The only Earth banks approved for off-planet loans are owned by World Life," Sally replied. "None of them will touch Pukui right now."

"The U.N. . . ."

"Can't step in financially without going through Company channels," the U.N. rep said.

"Well, hell, I have enough to keep this place afloat through at least one harvest," Angie said. "You know that, Sally. You've been handling my private accounts for years. *I'll* loan Pukui the credit it needs."

"You?" Toma said.

Angie grinned up at him. "You didn't break the code on *all* my personal records, Inspector."

Sally didn't join in her humor. "It's true you have enough," she said, "but . . ."

"Major investors in Lesaat development have to be directly related to the leaseholders, or else be approved by the Company," the U.N. rep said. "That's why the other Lesaat lease-holders are ineligible to contribute, despite their secret reciprocal investments prior to this. Some of those earlier investments, by the way, sound highly questionable."

"It's these damn Lesaat laws," Sally said. "During the past twenty years, World Life has put a stranglehold on this planet's economy. With the exception of the last perpetual-lease hold-outs, they've established a virtual monopoly on any financial activity here. It's been tolerated because no one outside recognized how far it had gone, and those who might have suspected kept quiet for fear of losing their access to the 410 Standard."

The U.N. rep spoke again. "We can establish indigenous status for the kids. I'm sure we can get that through, although it's going to take some careful maneuvering. They'll end up with free access to all lands and waters on the planet and full inheritance rights to specific reef areas through their biological parents. But there's nothing that can be done about Pukui. The farm has to be rebuilt immediately, and the only one in a legal and financial position to do that is World Life."

Angie glanced up at Pua. Angie wondered if the Earther would be speaking so casually if he had witnessed Pua's defense of her territory three nights before. Fatu laid a hand on Pua's shoulder, but his own lips were tight with rage.

"I've gone at this from every angle I can think of," Sally said. "I can't find a way out. I'm sorry."

"The children, as well as at least a few of the current residents," the U.N. rep said, glancing toward Fatu, "will be allowed to remain living at Pukui. But the leases will have to be returned to the general pool. When Pua turns eighteen, she'll become eligible to apply for lease rights here just like any other adult waterworlder."

"But on a short-term basis," Angie said. "With forced renewal every three years or less so the U.N. and the Company both can keep her under their control."

"The law has to be—"

"I won't let it happen," Fatu said softly.

"Nor will I," Toma said, and that drew a truly startled look from the U.N. man. Toma was the primary keeper of the law on Lesaat. He was the last one the Earther had expected to defend breaking it.

Pua's jaw was clenched so tight that her lips had turned white. The nicks and scratches on her arms had nearly healed, and she stood straighter now, as if the pain of her cracked ribs no longer bothered her, but she still cradled her casted arm in her opposite hand. Her eyes blazed with fury.

"Pukui is *mine!*" she said.

They had gathered an audience. To Angie's dismay, she saw that it had already split along Earther and waterworlder lines. She lifted a hand against the murmur of disquiet. Then she returned her attention to the U.N. rep.

"There must be a way around this," she said.

Grayson shook his head. He was not entirely displeased by the situation, Angie suspected. The U.N. wanted the Company's power broken, but they had already expressed concern about what kind of control Pua and the other Lesaat heirs might choose someday to exert. Better the devil you know, Angie thought. Spit!

"What if there were another heir to the Pukui leases?" she asked. "An heir of legal age and with the financial means to begin rebuilding the farm. Would that make a difference?"

"What?"

"There's no—"

"Warden," the U.N. rep said, "we all know there is no other heir."

"Would it make a difference?" Angie insisted.

"Of course, but what—"

"Your team has been processing genetic identification checks on the Pukui kids all day," Angie said. "Tell them to take a tissue sample from one of my hands and run a comparison check with Pua and her parents."

Sally blinked in surprise. Both Toma and Fatu straightened.

"You'll find that Pua's genetic fingerprint and mine are identical," Angie said. "The way the current law is worded, that defines us as biological twins."

The shells along the fringe of Pua's shirt went silent. It was the first time Angie had seen her stand perfectly still.

"You'll also find, naturally, that my ID bars match those of Lehua and Zed Pukui closely enough to legally define me as their biological daughter."

"Warden, you can't be—"

"In their will, which has already been accepted as binding by both World Life and the U.N., Zed and Lehua left all of their worldly possessions, in particular their perpetual leases to Pukui, to their beloved daughter Pualeiokekai and to any other offspring of their union—assets to be distributed equally. They must have recorded that will before Lehua discovered she couldn't bear any more children," Angie said, "but that's the way it's written."

"You can't claim your genetic identity from those hands," the U.N. rep said. "A sample taken from anywhere else on your body would prove you're no more Pua's sister than I am."

"You took the kids' tissue samples from their hands," Angie said. "Why should I be treated differently?"

"But those aren't your hands!"

Angie lifted her long, strong hands and spread her fingers. Five on the right, three on the left.

Toma spoke before she could. "It *is* common practice on Lesaat to take tissue samples from people's hands. In fact, Lesaat's immigrants are legally defined by their hands."

"That's true," Sally said slowly. "Any Earther with the money can get gills. I know a few who've done it just for sport. But only off-worlders are given waterworlder hands."

"Only off-worlders would want them," one of the Earthers muttered.

"But we have proof now of criminal acts at the Earth recon stations," the U.N. rep said. "We'll be able to step in and make those places safe. You could get your own hands grown back."

The shells on Pua's shirt clicked softly. Fatu's grip on her shoulder loosened.

"You'd never get away with changing your genetic ID more than once, Angie," Sally said quietly. "You can be certain that very dangerous loophole will be closed the instant this case is settled."

Angie nodded.

"If you choose to do this," Sally went on, "it's going to be permanent."

Angie glanced at Fatu. The side of his mouth lifted into a small smile. *Permanence,* she remembered saying to him once, a long time ago. *Permanence and Pukui.* The two things did have a way of going together. Toma lifted his hand in a trouble-shooter's salute.

"Don't you understand, Warden Dinsman?" the U.N. rep insisted. "You can get your *real hands* back."

Angie turned her hands over. One by one, she coiled her fingers into her palms. Then she flicked them open again. The U.N. rep jumped. "These are real enough for me," Angie said.

"Ha!" Pua huffed softly. "I knew if I could ever get her in the water long enough, I could turn her into a real waterworlder."

And then Angie laughed. A good, clean laugh that washed away the last of her indecision. She listened for the sound of whispering evergreens and found it right where it had always been, singing sibilant accompaniment to Le Fe'e's rumbling roar.

Some time later, Toma met her at the top of Mauna Kea Iki. He sat beside her under the leaf-stripped snow trees. Whatever damage the storm had done to the bark had already disappeared. Like Pua's skin, Angie thought. She glanced down at her left hand. There was no sign of new fingers yet, but the gaping wound had nearly closed. She no longer even kept it bandaged.

Toma had the good sense to remain quiet.

Angie stared at the glowing mountainside, at the ocean—brighter now than ever—and up at the gloriously ringed sky. Shadow had just begun its nightly journey. The shimmering night hid most of Pukui's scars.

Finally, she tapped Toma's arm. "Come," she said.

She took him to the base of one of the largest snow trees, the one that split into three thick branches high over their heads.

"Did you ever climb one of these things?" she asked.

"Lehua's snow trees?" he replied. "She'd have had me by the throat."

"You can lie better than *that*, Toma!"

He laughed. "Of course I've climbed them. We all did after Lehua died. This seemed the most obvious place for her to hide the TC records. We looked into every crack and under every leaf. I even ran a scan for foreign material inside the wood itself. The trees are as clean as they look."

"Give me a lift," she said. "I want to show you something."

He gave her a boost up, and when she reached the wide, smooth hollow that divided the three upper branches, she reached down and gave him a hand to follow. There was room for them both, but just barely. Toma stood behind her as she ran her palms slowly along the smooth, shimmering bark.

"What are you doing?" he asked.

"Looking for a snowball," she said. From this height, she could see evidence of new leaves budding. There was a direct line of sight to all points along Pukui's barrier reef.

Angie found what she was looking for near the base of the branch. She squatted and began picking at the glowing bark. She continued scratching until, with a soft, tearing sound, the wood began to split. A crack opened, leading deep inside the tree.

Angie reached a finger into the narrow opening. She rubbed the split edges of the wood with her opposite hand and blew softly into the crack, just as Pua did when she was extracting a larger-than-usual snowball from one of the trees.

Her fingertip clicked against something hard. It shifted. The crack widened a fraction more, and a thin brown tube dropped into her waiting palm.

Toma caught his breath.

"Ha!" Angie said. "I guess this tree likes me."

"The TC records?" Toma asked. She glanced up. He was staring openmouthed at the thing in her hand.

She nodded. "It has to be. Part of them, anyway." She turned the wooden case over in her hand. It was made of koa wood; its red-brown sheen glistened in the sunlight. Its grain was infinitely finer than that of the snow-tree bark. Angie found and released a simple wooden latch at one end of the tube and looked inside. She smiled, then held it up so Toma could see.

"Paper!" Toma said. "Wood and paper. No wonder our scans didn't find it."

"The tree sap would have eaten through a plastic container," Angie said. "Besides, Lehua knew either plastic or metal could be too easily found. She knew from the foyer floor that koa is acceptable to, but not affected by, the living local woods, so. . ."

She handed it up to him. "It's beautiful, isn't it?"

"But how did you know it was here?" he asked. He squatted behind her in the narrow space. His skin was warm where his thighs touched her back. He smelled faintly of candleberry, but more strongly of the sea. He reached around her to touch the crack in the tree.

"When we were in the hot tub at Sa le Fe'e," Angie said, "the first time, I mean, Pua said that after she was taken to Earth, Katie buried all of her snowballs under the house."

"So?"

"She told Pili and me later that *Lehua* had told Katie to do it."

"Lehua!"

Angie nodded. "It had to have been right before she died or Katie would have buried the balls sooner, and Pua would have known about it before she went to Earth. You said Katie was with Lehua when you found her, didn't you?"

"Aye," he said softly.

"Lehua knew how vital the records were, both to Pua and to Earth," she said. "If she realized she had loli fever, then she would have known that both she and Zed were going to die, but that Pua wouldn't—not of the fever, anyway. She had only a few seconds to leave a clue for Pua that the records were hidden here in these trees. The snowballs had no value other than the sentimental one between her and Pua, so Lehua must have reasoned their preservation would mean nothing to anyone who didn't know their source."

Toma sighed. "Those wads of tree sap were dug up a dozen times during the search. Even Fatu and I thought Katie was just being stubborn by putting them and the rest of Pua's shells and coral back each time."

"Lehua probably knew that Katie wouldn't, couldn't, reveal anything under formal questioning," Angie said. According to Crawley's testimony, Katie had been secretly truth-drugged, but the slow-minded drone had not made any more sense under controlled questioning than she did at any other time.

Angie took the case from Toma and slipped it back into the tree. There would be others, and there would be time to find and study them all. This calm, ringlit night was better suited for other, more personal things. She thanked the tree silently for sharing its treasure.

"Lehua also knew how seriously Katie took her direct orders," she said as she pressed the edges of the healing wood together. "She took the one chance she had that someday Pua, or maybe you or Fatu, would discover that it was *she* who had ordered the snowballs saved, and understand what that meant." She smoothed the cool bark beneath her fingers.

"She took a bigger chance than you realize," Toma said. He slid his hand over hers and turned it palm up. "Aside from Lehua and Pua, you're the only one these trees have ever voluntarily opened for." Her long fingers twined around his without conscious direction.

Toma's warmth against Angie's back was like the smooth caress of the Lesaat sea; his breath brushed like a sun-warmed breeze across the sensitive edges of her gill flaps. She wondered, suddenly, if it was true that waterworlders never touched each other's gills unless they were trying to kill one another.

"Katie told me," Toma said after a moment, "at least I think she told me, that the last of your Maldarian caramels got blown away in the storm."

That made Angie laugh.

She pulled her hand from his, stood, turned, and squatted again, this time stepping over Toma's legs so that she sat in his lap. It was not entirely comfortable, but it certainly presented an interesting challenge. Toma's look slid down to the place where their bodies met. His touch was as firm as the snow tree's shimmering bark.

He was grinning when he looked up again. "Warden, is there something else I can do for you this evening?"

Angie laughed. "As a matter of fact there is, Inspector." She proceeded to show him just what she had in mind.

Chapter 30

Pua waited for the mountainlady at the main house—she knew the warden would come there eventually. She sat on the smooth, polished floor, tracing the outlines of the koa-wood inlays. Katie had scrubbed and polished the remaining bits of the house until they shone. She had even, finally, gotten that faint mildew smell out of the foyer.

Pua grinned at the joke she knew her mama would have told if she had been there—about how the mildew really *had* been what held the place together.

The Sally woman—the one Pua still found so astonishing in her smallness; she was not much bigger than Pua herself—had promised to return her parents' bodies to Pukui. It would take some time, Sally had said, but Pua was used to that. Everything the Earthers did took time. Pua still was not entirely comfortable around the mountainlady's friend, but she was beginning to trust her.

Finally, the warden came. She strode across the lawn to the house and lifted herself up onto the raised floor. The steps no longer reached all the way to the ground. She scuffed her bare feet across poor, battered Matt before stepping onto the patterned floor. Matt burped contentedly.

Or was that the woman? Pua grinned.

The warden sat facing her. She smelled of Toma and the freshwater bathing pool. "So, Waterbaby," she said. "Did you and Pili learn anything useful up there on the mountain tonight?"

Pua blinked up at her.

The warden laughed. "Oh, Pua, that's perfect. That's just perfect. You have innocent confusion down pat."

Pua held the look for a moment, then giggled. "How'd you know we were up there?"

"I'm the land person, remember? I always know when you're on the mountain with me."

"You didn't that first time."

Another laugh. "True. I missed you the first time."

"I liked it best when you kicked him out of the tree," Pua said, and they *both* laughed.

"Fatu said the damage at Sa le Fe'e wasn't as bad as we first thought," Pua said. "We'll still be able to use it. And Le Fe'e told me he's going to grow the Grand Old Man back to guard the door just like he did before."

The warden blinked slowly the way she did whenever Pua talked about Le Fe'e. "Did you hear that the coiler disappeared from the hydrofoil wing?" she asked.

Pua nodded. "Some of the Company swimmers are refusing to swim between the islands. They say it's down there, waiting."

"Is it?"

Pua put on her innocent look again. "How would I know?"

Then she grew serious. She ran her hand across the polished, patterned floor. "Pukui is still mine, Mountainlady," she said. "Mine and Le Fe'e's."

"Legally," the warden replied, "almost half of it is now mine."

Pua looked up. "Which half?"

The mountainlady watched her for a moment. "The top half. I'll take the dry part, and you can have the wet part."

Pua pursed her lips. "You can't divide an atoll that way. We'll slice Home and Second like pies, from the top of their mountains. Every slice will have mountain and shoreline, and reef and ocean."

"That sounds reasonable," the warden said. "But how do we decide who gets which slice?"

Pua thought for a moment, then stood and crossed to the library door. There was no door—there wasn't even a wall—but she walked through the place where the door would have been. She picked up the small table that Katie had mended and placed carefully back in its former location, and carried it to the foyer. She set it in front of the mountainlady.

Then Pua sat again, on the table's opposite side. She carefully placed her right elbow on the scratched tabletop and extended her hand.

The warden's brows lifted slightly. "Ha," she said. Her expression grew serious as she set her own right elbow on the table. They clasped hands.

"We'll count the wins till you turn eighteen," the warden said. "Whoever ends up with the most gets first choice."

"By the time I turn eighteen," Pua replied, "you'll be so far behind we won't even need to count."

Their grips tightened and locked. The warden's cool gaze shifted to their interlocked fingers. Pua felt the woman's great strength clearly, a mirror image of her own. Their hands did not move.

"How long are you going to wait before you let Uncle Toma get you pregnant?" Pua asked.

The warden's look jerked back to Pua's face, and in that instant, Pua slammed their hands to the table.

She grinned.

"Spit!" the warden said. "You little waterbrat. You did it to me again!"

Pua laughed. "How many times do I have to tell you, Auntie Puhi? You're a waterworlder now. You have to pay attention to *everything*—all the time."

Glossary

Fatu o le Motu Poutu o le 'aiga—*(Samoan)* lit. stone or heart of the island, strength of the families

fe'e—*(Samoan)* octopus

fiticoco—*(Trukese)* trouble of any and all varieties

kapu—*(Hawaiian)* forbidden, prohibited

kava—*(Tongan and Marquesan)* ceremonial drink made from the roots of the kava plant, used throughout much of the Pacific

Kehakehaokalani noun Toma me Kilisou—*(Hawaiian and Trukese)* lit. pride of the chiefs, offspring of Toma and Kilisou

kumulipo—*(Hawaiian)* creation chant

lanai—*(Hawaiian)* porch, veranda

lavalava—*(Samoan)* a rectangular cloth worn like a kilt or skirt in Polynesia and especially Samoa

Le Fe'e—Samoan demigod; lit. the octopus

Lesaat—*(Trukese, from ''le sat'')* lit. the ocean

loli—*(Hawaiian)* sea cucumber

Maram—*(Trukese)* Lesaat's largest moon; lit. moon

Maram Iki—*(Trukese and Hawaiian)* Lesaat's smaller moon; lit. little moon

Mauna Kea—*(Hawaiian)* mountain on the island of Hawaii; lit. white mountain

Mauna Kea Iki—*(Hawaiian)* little white mountain

Mauna Loa—*(Hawaiian)* mountain on the island of Hawaii; lit. long mountain

Pili—Samoan demigod, mythological hero

Pilimanaia noun Fatu o le Motu me Ehukai—*(Samoan, Trukese and Hawaiian)* lit. Pili the beautiful, offspring of Fatu o le Motu and Ehukai

Pualei—*(Hawaiian)* precious child

Pualeiokekai noun Zedediah me Kalehuaokalae—*(Hawaiian and Trukese)* lit. precious child of the sea, offspring of Zedediah and Lehua of Ka Lae [South Point]

puhi—*(Hawaiian)* eel

puhi 'ai pōhaku—*(Hawaiian)* eel that eats rocks

Pukui—*(Hawaiian, from pīku'i)* lit. to gather or assemble

Sa le Fe'e—*(Samoan)* 1. the domain of Le Fe'e; 2. the forbidden place of the octopus; 3. the octopus clan

tatau—*(Samoan)* tattoo

tiki—*(Maori and Marquesan)* a wood or stone image of a Polynesian supernatural power

'Umi Iki—*(Hawaiian)* lit. little number ten

About the Author

Carol Severance is a Hawaii-based writer with a special interest in Pacific Island peoples and their environments. After growing up in Denver, she served with the Peace Corps and later assisted in anthropological fieldwork in the remote coral atolls of Truk, Micronesia. She currently lives in Hilo, where she has worked as an artist, a journalist, and a playwright. She shares her home with a scholarly fisherman, a surfer, and an undetermined number of geckos.